VINCE

BOOK TWO OF THE PERFECTLY INDEPENDENT SERIES

AMANDA SHELLEY

Visit my website at
www.amandashelley.com

CONNECT WITH AMANDA SHELLEY

Want to be the first to know about upcoming sales and new releases? Make sure you sign up for my newsletter as well as connect with me on social media and your favorite retail store.

Website:
www.amandashelley.com
Newsletter:
https://geni.us/AmandaShelleyNL
Facebook:
https://www.facebook.com/authoramandashelley/
Instagram:
https://www.instagram.com/authoramandashelley/
Twitter:
https://twitter.com/AmandShelley
Reader's Group:
https://www.facebook.com/groups/AmandasArmyofReaders/
Tik Tok:
https://www.tiktok.com/@authoramandashelley
Goodreads:
https://www.goodreads.com/author/show/19713563.Amanda_Shelley

Book Bub:

https://www.bookbub.com/profile/amanda-shelley

facebook.com/authoramandashelley

instagram.com/authoramandashelley

bookbub.com/profile/amanda-shelley

pinterest.com/authoramandashelley

It's funny how one night can change everything.

As a bartender near campus, I'm certain I've heard it all. Rarely a shift passes without some guy taking his best shot, hoping I'll end my self-proclaimed dating diet.

Of course, this is exactly how I meet Vince.

Except, he isn't the one running his mouth.

No, he simply shuts down his idiotic friend, then stops my heart with the simplest of smiles and walks away.

Just when I force myself to forget him, he bumps into me on campus.

Our connection is consuming, and my world is knocked off

kilter. It's far beyond physical attraction. He's smart, sexy, and feels like—*home*?

Wait, that can't be right...

Whatever it is, Vince has me breaking my rules to spend time with him.

My entire life I've prepared for meeting the wrong guys.

What the hell should I do when I find the right one?

VINCE

Normally, I don't watch the clock. Especially in this class since it's my favorite. But today I'm restless. Each minute feels like an hour as I watch the hands slowly move. If I didn't know any better, I'd say that time is standing still.

Will it ever end?

My mind drifts to thoughts I can't afford to think about, and a dull ache in the center of my head forms.

Immediately, I tamp those thoughts down.

This isn't the time or the place.

Today of all days, I deserve to be happy.

I've made a promise to Van, and I fully intend to honor it.

Switching gears, I focus on counting my blessings. I have so many things to be thankful for. Today's not the day to wallow or self-destruct, no matter how much I miss them.

Having no idea how long I've zoned out, somehow through my fog-like state I hear my favorite professor finally announce the words I've been waiting for, "I'll see you Monday."

With my trance lifted, I quickly gather my things, stuffing them into my backpack. Ignoring the classmates I usually talk with at the end of class, I take the stairs two at a time, eager to get some fresh air and shake away my thoughts.

With each step I take, my chest loosens, and my thoughts easily become about the here and now, rather than the past. They aren't bad memories per se, but the past has a way of pulling me into a rabbit hole I'm not prepared to enter today.

By the time I reach the center of campus, I feel more in control of my thoughts. Hearing my name shouted from behind me makes me stop and turn around.

I can't help but smile at Ryan's goofy grin as he towers above the crowded courtyard. I'm just over six feet, and the man has a half of a head over me in height. "Wait up, man. What's the rush?"

Ryan and I met as freshman. He may not know it, but he's helped me through more than he'll ever know. My body instantly falls into a relaxed stance, and the tension from before nearly disappears. "Not much," I say, running my palm along my neck to relieve what's left of the tension built there. "I thought I wouldn't see you until later tonight?"

"Class got out early, and I'm on my way home. Is Vanessa coming out with us?"

"Nah..." I say, shaking my head. "Couldn't find a sitter. She'll go out tomorrow night."

Wait... is that disappointment I see in his eyes? Before I can think twice about it, Ryan's expression returns to carefree. "So... it'll just be us guys tonight?"

Weird. I must've imagined it.

"Looks like it. I'll text you later when I'm ready. I'm doing dinner with the fam, then we'll meet up."

"Sure thing, man. I'll pick you up since I'm DD. There's no way I'm walkin' home tonight."

Before I can respond, my phone buzzes in my pocket. Knowing it could only be a handful of people at this time, I immediately pull it out to find a text notification.

Van: We're slammed at work and short staffed. Can you pick up J? I won't make it there in time.

I notice the time. Shit. I have twenty minutes and of course, I chose to walk to campus today.

I don't even hesitate as my fingers fly across the keys to respond.

Me: Of course. I'll see you when you get home.

Van: I'll make it up to you by bringing home dinner.

Me: You won't hear me complaining.

Van: Haha—like you'd ever complain about not cooking. See you at home. Thanks again.

Looking up to Ryan, I explain, "Sorry, man, gotta pick up Jules. I'll let you know when I'm ready. Thanks again for driving my ass around. I promise not to get too out of control," I tack on just to put a smile on his face.

This earns me a dramatic eye roll. "No one deserves this

more than you. I'm happy to help out." He knows I won't drink much. And he knows why I'd never take the chance behind the wheel. Yet he won't let today pass as just another day either. That's what good friends are for.

With that, I turn and lengthen my strides across campus. It figures with this being farthest class from Jules, today would be a day Van can't pick her up. At this time of day, it's difficult to be on time without making any stops. But there's nothing I won't do for her—or Vanessa for that matter.

In fact, I've done everything I can to make sure their needs come first. Refusing to let them be another statistic based on the stack we've been dealt. Hell, don't get me wrong, I've learned to love Columbia River University, but it wasn't my first choice. No—I'm here because it was Vanessa's first choice. Me attending CRU is the only way she'd be able to reach her dreams, too.

Don't get me wrong—I'm by no means a martyr. I'm getting a great education, but my plans to go away on my own to school went up in smoke right after graduation. Thank goodness, I'd already been accepted to CRU, and my counselor pulled some strings when he explained our situation. CRU's become home to us, and I think it was the best decision I've ever made. Life's way too damn short to live with regrets.

It helps that I love it here.

Walking across campus, I'm reminded of exactly why. Where else can you see St. Helens, Mt. Adams, and Mt. Hood from one location? Not to mention the Columbia River in the far distance, from this particular spot. It's just one of the many perks of living in the Pacific Northwest. I couldn't have picked a better place if I'd tried. This was the perfect decision for our family, and the people we've met along the way have welcomed us like family of their own.

I arrive with minutes to spare. Walking into the daycare center, I'm greeted by Shannon, the girl who usually runs the pick-up station at this time of day.

"Hey, Vince. Julia will be out any minute. I saw you walking up and already told her to gather her things."

"Thanks, Shannon. Vanessa had to work late."

We're interrupted by the sound of feet tapping against the tiled floor. I turn to see Julia's bright smile as she closes the distance between us, practically running. God knows a three-year-old can't walk inside, no matter how many times we remind her. Especially when she's excited.

"I thought Momma was pickin' me up?" she says as I bend, pulling her into a hug. She eagerly embraces me tight. She smells of fun and innocence. This hug is like a breath of fresh air, after being trapped with my thoughts all afternoon.

"Nope." I pop the p purposely, making her giggle. "You get me tonight, squirt." Standing to my full height, I bring her with me as she clings to my neck like the monkey she is.

"Can we make a cake when we get home? Momma said we'd make cake." Her serious tone is just like her mom's when she wants something. Clearly, the apple hasn't fallen far from the tree.

This girl has a one-track mind. "Who do you think you're dealing with? Of course, we'll make a cake. But I get to lick one of the beaters." I bop her on the nose with a grin. "You know the rules."

This earns me an exasperated sigh, just like I'd get from Van if she were here and an intense eye roll from a pair of eyes that mirror my own. "You're silly. I share with you. Always... Or next time, I don't get any."

Yep. She's got the rules down pat. I set her on her feet and pat her head playfully before instinctively reaching for her hand. "You ready to get out of here and let Miss Shannon get on with her night?"

"Night, Miss Shannon." Julia beams. "See you tomorrow. We're makin' a cake."

Shannon chuckles lightly as she waves. "Have fun, you two. Don't get into too much trouble."

As sweet as can be, Julia smiles wide. "Don't worry. Unks is trouble. Not me."

2

VINCE

WITHIN THE HOUR, JULES AND I HAVE THE CHOCOLATE CAKE IN the oven, and we're doing dishes. Well, I'm washing the dishes; she's been scrubbing the same bowl for the last few minutes, using lots of soap and water. It's a good thing I'm standing next to her, or we'd have to mop the floor, too.

She's still got faint lines from the batter on her face as she diligently works at cleaning up our mess. Vanessa should arrive any minute with dinner, and Jules can't wait to celebrate.

We've barely finished when the front door opens, and Vanessa calls out in the singsong voice she uses to get Julia's attention. "I'm home. Anybody here?"

Julia squeals and rushes to greet her mom. "In here, Momma. Unks and I made cake. Do we have candles?"

I turn around the corner just in time to see Jules launch herself into Vanessa's arms. The love they share for one another makes my chest constrict. I don't know what I'd ever do without them.

Of course, I've been with Van since the womb. Thankfully, I've never had to live without her. She managed to beat me into the world by a whole seven minutes, a fact she's never let me forget. I've always been her "little brother," though I've towered over her in height our entire lives. I took after Dad, while she looks more like Mom.

"I've missed you, sweet girl," Vanessa says as she squeezes Jules in a hug that wiggles her whole body, causing infectious laughter to spew from my niece.

When the laughter dies down, Jules squirms, letting it known it's time to let go. The second her feet hit the floor, Jules reaches for Vanessa's hand. "Come on, Momma. Let's go see if the cake's done."

"Just a sec, Jules. I need to grab dinner." I notice she's already dropped bags of food on the entry table. I have no idea what she's brought, but the smell has my stomach grumbling.

Before she can reach for the food, I intervene. "I've got the bags. The cake should be done any second. Let's go pull it out."

Maybe it's a twin thing or the fact that we've lived together our entire lives, but after pulling the cake from the oven, Van and I work seamlessly to put dinner on the table. I love that Van's brought home my favorite. Steak and mushrooms for the two of us and Julia's favorite, homemade mac and cheese. As I help Vanessa plate our food, I notice a large side of steamed broccoli. A huge grin forms, knowing Jules' reaction.

Without a doubt, Jules will eat every last floret she can get her hands on, especially if it has any amount of butter on it. I'm not sure which she likes more, the broccoli or the butter. If Van or I are to stand any chance of getting any, I dish us first. Maybe it's a family trait, as we can't get enough of it.

What's funny is Mom wouldn't be caught dead eating a green vegetable that wasn't salad or green beans. But Vanessa and I devoured whatever vegetable Dad put in front of us. We'd always laugh at the faces she'd make as we wolfed down our veggies. That's probably the only thing I ever saw my parents be so polar opposite about. Dad and his green veggies always got Mom grumbling.

Though it's a happy memory, my chest tightens as I fight to recall exactly how disgruntled Mom used to act. I'm not so sure if she really felt that way, or it just became an expected behavior.

It's funny how grief hits in the strangest of times. One minute, you're reliving a happy memory; the next, it's painful. Fuck... I can't remember the exact sound of her voice.

"Unks, you're gonna dish me more broccoli, right? You know I eat lots," Julia interrupts my thoughts, and I'm thankfully brought to the present.

"Of course, squirt. How can I forget?" I tease as I put another huge helping onto her plate. Then I do the same for both Vanessa and me, making sure we get our share before she devours the rest. I'm certain she'll eat more broccoli than mac and cheese tonight.

Just as we make it to the table and are ready to dig in, Vanessa opens Pandora's box by asking Jules, "So, how was your day?"

Jules beams as she holds the bite of broccoli she's forked close to her mouth. The overexuberance only a three-year-old can possess. "Great... You're never gonna believe what happened at school today..." She takes a huge bite of broccoli, chews it fully, then proceeds to tell us every minute detail of her day. The girl must have a photographic memory or something because she'd put many college students to shame with the amount of detail she can describe about ordinary things.

We learn about Cyrus's shoes being on the wrong foot, how Miss Shannon forgot who was supposed to be line leader, and it caused a fight between Grace and Eli. She also tells us about how she made an art project she couldn't bring home tonight because it wasn't quite dry.

This. Right here is what family's all about.

I wouldn't trade a moment for these experiences. Van and I interject when we can, but for the most part, we simply eat our meal and let her get her chatter out. It's amazing how full of life and optimistic a three-year-old can be. They always tell it like it is, and you never have to doubt what's on their mind.

Of course, with all her talking, Vanessa and I finish eating long before Julia. Eventually, Vanessa gets up and clears her plate while I do the same. Once Julia's finished, she eagerly asks, "Can we have cake now?"

I feign shock, making my eyes go wide and my mouth drop open. "Just where are you going to put this cake, Jules? Do you have a hollow leg I don't know about?"

This earns me another giggle and a dramatic eye roll. Yeah. She's all Van in this moment, especially when she levels me with an expectant stare. "Unks. You know..." She pauses for exaggeration. "There's *always* room for cake."

"If you say so..." I draw out sarcastically. "What do you say we frost the cake now that it's cooled enough?"

Julia hops up from the table to clear her plate. Then rushes to her stool in the corner and drags it to stand at the counter with me. Taking the can of coconut-pecan frosting, I pull off the lid. Julia reaches for the frosting spatula we'd set out on the counter before dinner, loads it up, and plops the frosting in the center of the cake. Since the cake is still a little warm, it doesn't spread as easily as it should, but Julia gives it her best effort. Thank goodness, we've kept the cake in the pan because at the rate she's going, there's no way it would spread all around the edges. But it's not like either Van or I care. This cake is made purely with love from our favorite tiny baker.

Vanessa takes this time to wipe down the table and pull down some plates for cake. She finishes long before we're ready for her. When she can't take it any longer, she swoops her finger into the frosting and nabs a taste for herself. This, of course, earns her a disgruntled, "Momma. You gotta wait for us. No tasting the cake until we sing! It's the rules, you know!"

"Hey, it's my birthday," Vanessa feigns defensiveness. "And I'm the oldest. I get to make the rules around here."

"It's Unks' birthday, too. You gotta share this cake, Momma. Or no presents!"

Vanessa's mouth morphs into the perfect O as her eyebrows nearly shoot off her head. "Presents... You didn't tell me anything about presents." She looks between Julia and me, and it's all I can do to keep a straight face.

"Only for those who wait until *after* we sing *Happy Birthday* to eat the cake," she deadpans.

Once Julia's finished frosting the cake, she reaches for the box of candles I set out and proceeds to put the whole box of twenty-four, but Vanessa stops her.

"Hey now… we're only twenty-one. There's no need to use the whole box. Leave three off."

Julia does as told, then Vanessa grabs the matches and lights the candles.

Holy shit. The cake's a fireball.

Instinctively, I pull Julia away from the cake and take her to the table. "Next year, I say we just get the candles with the numbers on them, or the house might go up in flames."

"No kidding," Vanessa grumbles as she carefully walks the cake to the table.

As soon as the cake's safely on the table, Julia sings, and we eagerly join in. It's tradition that we sing at the same time. Vanessa and I learned at a young age it's never worth waiting for the song to be sung twice, when all that matters is getting our slice of cake.

For the past few years, I make the same wish, in fear of it not coming true otherwise.

Help us be okay without them.

After Vanessa and I each make our secret wish, we blow out the candles with ease as Julia claps excitedly. It doesn't take long before we're devouring the cake and immersed in eating the rich chocolate perfection.

The second Julia's done, she pops up from the table and runs out of the kitchen, leaving Vanessa and me to stare at one another, wondering what Julia's up to now.

We don't have to wonder long because before we can voice our thoughts aloud, Julia storms back into the room, her hands full with two hand-drawn bags in her hands.

"It's time for presents. Mommy, since you ate the cake first, Unks gets to open his first."

I'm surprised to find the bag is much heavier than I expect. I already know what's in Vanessa's bag, as I picked it out. But I'm confused at what she could've picked out for me that's this size.

Julia's eyes are wide with excitement as I reach into the bag and discover a package the shape of a shoebox. She's dying to help me rip into the package as she is for all special occasions. Her cuteness is completely undeniable. "Get over here, squirt, and help me open this."

Julia squeals with delight as she helps me rip into the packaging and shreds it to pieces in a matter of seconds. "What is it, Unks?" She practically pants. There's no way she has a clue because this girl can't keep a secret to save her life, so I glance over to Van to see if she'll give us another clue.

Nope. Just a knowing grin. I should've expected this as she's like a vault when it comes to secrets. It is indeed a shoe box, but I'm still not convinced that's what's in it. It still feels too heavy. But when I pop it open, I find the pair of running shoes I'd been looking at the last time we made a trip to the mall. They're supposed to be light though, so I pull one out and find it's weighted down with something.

"What the…" I wonder as I reach inside, only to find five rolls of quarters in each shoe. "Why on earth would you do this?"

Vanessa's eyes challenge me. "You always guess what you get before opening. I wanted to throw you off. Besides… you know it's tradition to get money to spend how we want. So… what are you spending yours on?"

Rolling my eyes at her antics, I chuckle. "Uh… quarters are

a nice touch, but you don't have to spend money on me. The shoes were more than enough."

Vanessa's head shakes back and forth as her eyebrows narrow in my direction. If I didn't know better, I'd think she was pissed. "I've been saving tip money for weeks to pull off this prank. The least you can do is thank me."

I glance to Julia, who's watching expectantly. I should know better than to refute a gift from my sister. "Thank you, Vanny." I tack on her old nickname to make her crack.

Her lips tip at the end, and her eyes twinkle in mischief. But she remains silent.

Of course, Julia can't stand the silence, so she quickly gushes... "What about your present, Momma?"

Yeah, that makes Vanessa crack. She cannot handle the surprise turned on her. She eagerly picks up her package. I didn't go to the extent of wrapping anything. I'm all about gift bags. She quickly removes the tissue paper and pulls out the small white box I placed inside and sets it aside, as she reaches for the frame I'd placed beside it. Her mouth forms a perfect "o" when she pulls out the framed selfie I'd taken of the three of us at the beach.

"Oh, Vince, this is perfect."

It is. The sun is setting, Julia has the most adorable expression on her face, and Van and I are cheek to cheek with her. Julia had just said something to make us crack up, and all of our smiles are wide. Our matching hazel eyes all dance with amusement.

"There's somethin' else, Momma." Julia points to the box.

Vanessa hugs the frame quickly before setting it down on the table in front of us, then reaches for the small white box.

Most would assume it's jewelry, but the smirk forming on Van's face lets us all know she expects what's inside.

Yeah. I don't disappoint.

Van lifts the lid, and Julia gushes, "Look, Momma, I made that."

Sure enough, she painted the rock covering up the hundred-dollar bill inside.

"See... I also follow tradition." I waggle my eyebrows, bringing lots of memories to mind.

"At least you follow the tradition of putting money *with* the rock, like Mom forced you to all those years ago. Jules, I can't tell you how many years he got away with only wrapping a rock up for me. Grandma finally made him put money inside, or I'm sure Scrooge here would never part with his funds."

This makes us all laugh.

"Unks... that's just... mean. Why would you give Momma rocks for her birthday?"

"It's okay, Jules. Vinnie has been doing this for as long as I can remember. Grandma caught on pretty quick, so I always get money, too."

Nodding in agreement, I add, "I have no idea how it started, tradition is tradition. We've gotta hold onto those." I bop her on the nose to make her squeal with laughter. "Okay... who wants cake?"

Ryan and I make it into the bar a little after nine. Music reverberates through my body from the moment we walk through the door. Wondering what all the hype is about, I take a moment to look around. Sure, people are scattered across the dance floor, and tables line the walls and are scattered off to one side. A rectangular bar sits in the center of the room for people to access from all sides. It's what I'd expect from a place like this, but I can already tell it's not my scene.

I can dance—or at least I used to in high school, but if given the choice, I'd rather just hang out. I'm here to experience this 'rite of passage' my friends claim I can't let slip by. When I spot Derek and Brayden at table near the back of the bar, I beeline it to greet them.

"Hey, man!" Brayden bellows as he stands and reaches out his hand to shake mine. "Happy Birthday!"

Before I can respond, I'm pulled into a bro-hug, and his large palm smacks my back. When he releases me, I manage, "Thanks. Glad you could make it out."

"Man—I wouldn't miss this for the world."

Derek stands to pull me into a bro-hug as well. "Seriously, Vince. We're happy to be here." He looks around for someone I don't see. "I thought your sister and her friends were joining us."

I shrug. "Nah, she's home with Jules. They're going out tomorrow."

He shrugs, like it's to be expected, then he quickly glances to the dance floor. "Maybe I'll have to come out tomorrow night, too. To make sure they behave themselves."

That earns a laugh from all of us. God knows those girls can handle themselves. None of them are heavily into partying, but you can't be in college and not go out from time to time.

Ryan guffaws, "Brayden - Dude you'll use any excuse. Why

don't you just admit you like one of Van's friends and at least be honest with yourself? You've been crushing on Holland forever. Are you ever going to just admit it?"

Brayden rolls his eyes as he lets out an exasperated sigh. "Dude. I know. But she just broke up with John. I'm giving her some space—for now."

"Just make sure you don't wait too long, or she'll be moving on with someone—and it won't be you," Ryan advises in a way that lets us all know he's only looking out for Brayden.

"Speaking of moving on—have y'all seen that hot redhead behind the bar? I think I'm finally gonna ask her out tonight," Derek boasts in a way that tells me he may have started the party a bit earlier than the rest of us. His eyes are slightly glossy, and he haphazardly throws his arm up in her direction. "I mean... have you seen her? She's beautiful and can make one hell of a drink. What else would I need?"

My eyes wander to where the bartender's standing talking with a customer. I see Derek's point. Her red hair is pulled back in a ponytail and still flows past her shoulders. Her black t-shirt and dark-denim skinny jeans fit her perfect body like a glove. Whatever the girl she's waiting on says, makes her laugh —and it's a beautiful sight to see. Her head's thrown back in full abandon as she holds her belly. It's not often you see people let loose like that, especially in public.

"Dude!" Brayden shouts, pulling my attention to him. "You don't stand a chance with Sydney."

Interesting... I wonder why. Derek never has trouble getting girls. He's not a player—per se, but he's definitely developing a reputation with us for being a ladies' man. The problem is—the girls don't seem to get that he's not ready for a serious commitment—so when they want something more serious—he usually ends it.

Pretending to be defensive, I see amusement in Derek's eyes as he plays along with a devious smirk. "And why is that?"

Instead of Brayden explaining, I'm surprised when Ryan interjects, "Oh, go ahead. We'll just be right here eating popcorn, because I'm sure we're about to get one hell of a show."

As I look between my friends, there's obviously something I'm missing. Ryan and Brayden clearly know something Derek and I aren't privy to. As they just stare at one another in challenge, I break the silence between us. "I don't know about you—but I'm here to have a drink. Anyone care to join me?" I look around for a waitress and see there are none to be found. May as well just go up to the bar and order one for myself.

"I'll go," Derek offers with ease, and I do my best not to snicker. "Besides, your first drink is on me."

Ryan and Brayden each pull out some cash from their wallets and give us their orders. I don't miss the fact that Derek passes the shorter line to approach Sydney. From his determined expression, I can tell he's getting ready to play his A-game.

This should be entertaining, at least.

We wait for a group of girls to grab their orders before Sydney greets us with a smile as she wipes down the counter in front of her. "What can I get for ya?"

If I thought she was a knockout from across the bar, I was seriously mistaken. This woman is downright gorgeous. Her green eyes dance between us as she waits for our response, and I can't help but notice a light sprinkling of freckles across her nose.

"How's your night going, Sydney?" Derek drawls in a tone, as if he's a long-lost friend.

She's not wearing a nametag, so her green eyes darken as her brows pull together, as if she's trying to place him somewhere. In a matter of seconds, it's clear she has no idea who he is. But she pulls out her best customer services skills and pastes on what I'm sure is a fake smile. "Great. What brings you guys in?"

Derek reaches out to pat me on the shoulder. "We're here for my buddy's birthday. What time do you get off? Maybe you can help us celebrate."

Sydney's green eyes dart to mine and looks me over from head to toe. We've never met. But if I'm not mistaken, there's a flicker of recognition from her. We stare at one another for a moment before she returns her attention to Derek. "Thanks for the offer, but I'm closing tonight. What can I get you two to drink?"

Derek orders shots for everyone and a pitcher of beer, then continues his quest for her attention. "Maybe you can join us on one of your breaks?"

Sydney takes in a sharp breath and releases it slowly as if she's trying to regain control of her emotions. I swear, I'm a little afraid for what's about to happen to my dear friend Derek. Her fingers slowly open and close into fists at her sides. In an instant, I can clearly tell she's taking zero of his bullshit, and I have to say, she's sexy as hell when she's pissed—but clearly, I don't want to be on the receiving end of what's to come.

Not wanting this to escalate, I slap my palm on his back. "Hey, man. Let's just get our drinks and get back to the guys. If she wants to join us, that's cool. But if not, let's get out of her hair."

Sydney looks to me pointedly, and her tone turns to ice. "I'll need to see both of your IDs before I can serve you, *birthday boy*."

3

SYDNEY

OF COURSE, I KNOW THEIR IDs WERE CHECKED AT THE DOOR BY one of our bouncers—so I know birthday boy's of legal age. But I want to be a bitch to his friend because he's the fourth asshole who thought he'd have a chance of taking me home for the night. Therefore, I'm not about to back down when it comes to my level of bitchiness for the moment.

But when I look at the birthday boy, I'll admit I lose a little of my steam. His hazel eyes are far more perceptive than they should be. He totally gets that I'm about to lose it on his friend. Instinctually, he defuses the situation without any prompting. This is totally crazy, but I swear, it's as if he knows me already. Maybe I've seen him in one of my classes, but I can't place his name. So being the nosey bitch that I am, I use my authority to my advantage to get his name while I'm at it.

His cocky friend blurts out, "But we showed our ID at the door."

I pay him no attention but continue holding my gaze

with the tall, handsome man before me. In a lighter tone, I still snark, "Well, you can show me again, or there's the door."

I don't miss the corner of this man's lips quirking, nor the crinkle at the corner of his eyes. He doesn't say anything but pulls his wallet from his back pocket, opens it, pulls out his ID, and hands it over.

Vincent Daniel Larson—Date of birth—Today.

I glance to the man in question, grateful to put a name to the beautiful face before me, before I scrutinize the piece of plastic in front of me further.

Damn, even the DMV managed to get a dimple to pop and make him look sexier.

How is that fair?

Six-foot-one—One hundred eighty pounds—all muscle from the looks of it. Broad shoulders, trim waist—Organ Donor.

I can't help but notice he lives on the same side of campus as I do.

When I look up—he's staring at me expectantly with an outstretched palm.

What is he waiting for?

Oh, right. His license.

I quickly hand it back then force myself to look at the cocky asshole next to him. He's irritated. Good—it serves him right. Maybe he will leave me the fuck alone next time. I don't care who he is—if he can't see, I'm clearly working—he could be the cutest guy on the planet—and the answer would still be no. Have some respect already.

I hold my hand out expectantly but don't bother to grace

him with any words. He's resistant at first, but when I glance to the nearest bouncer, he can see I'm not budging.

Grumbling something I don't quite catch, he whips out his wallet and pulls his ID from the front pocket. "Here."

I don't even bother to look at it precisely. I just want to show him who's boss around here. I could truly give two fucks about his name or anything other than his date of birth. Once I see it, I shove the card back in his direction then turn to make the drinks he has ordered.

As soon as I'm finished, I look Vincent directly in the eye. "Hope you have a great birthday, Vincent."

Vincent brings a finger to the bridge of his nose and ducks his head for a moment, as if he wants to say something. Then he dips closer so I can hear. "It's Vince. No one calls me Vincent unless my family thinks I'm in trouble."

Oh, he's trouble all right.

I'm sure I'm smirking when "Well, we wouldn't want that now, would we," rolls off my lips.

This earns me a gorgeous grin. The DMV photo captured nothing compared to this man in person.

"I can't say that I do," Vince says as he holds my gaze a moment longer than necessary.

His rude friend interrupts as he grabs two shots and the pitcher of beer. "Dude, are we drinking, or what?"

Vince rolls his eyes and sighs. "Yeah, man. I'll grab the pitcher if you want to take a third shot with you back to our table."

Wanting to make sure I haven't been a total bitch this evening, I soften my tone and add, "Seriously, Vince. Happy Birthday!"

In return, I get a beautiful chuckle and a smile that could melt my panties. "Thanks. Have a great evening, Sydney."

With that, he turns and walks back to his friends. Of course, I notice the view from the back is nearly as good as the front.

Damn, he can fill out a pair of jeans.

I don't get to appreciate the view for long because my next customer steps up to the bar and places a big order. I absentmindedly go through the process of making their drinks and then ones for the steady line that typically picks up at this time of night on the weekend.

Vince doesn't come back to the bar for the rest of the evening. When his table needs a refill, one of his friends comes up with the pitcher instead. I know this because I can't keep my eyes from drifting in his direction throughout the evening.

One thing's for sure, Vince is not a typical twenty-one-year-old out for the night on the town. He and his friends are relaxed and in a steady flow of conversation. They don't head out to the dance floor and other than his friend hitting on me, they pretty much keep to themselves. They must be good friends because often I'll hear laughter from their direction when the music slows.

When a patron has to get my attention by waving a hand in front of my face, I scold myself.

I'm not even sure why I'm paying attention to Vince. I'm on a man diet. I've had my share of assholes, and I've sworn to take a break. I force myself to look away and not turn back in their direction while I serve the next rush of people.

When I slip up and glance in that direction again—he's gone.

Glancing around the bar, I see two of the guys from their table on the dance floor. But he and the tall guy he was sitting next to are nowhere to be found. Maybe they're in the bathroom? I busy myself by cleaning and restocking my area. I wait on a few more customers, but for some reason, my eyes scan the room. After a while, I accept the fact that they've gone home.

The rest of the night seems to go slower than a sloth at the DMV. We have a steady stream of customers, but the clock barely moves. By the time we announce last call, I'm eager to get out of here. I quickly go through my closing duties and have never been more thankful when Asher, our head bouncer, asks if I'm ready to walk out with him. Eagerly, I accept. Thank God, this night is over.

As I'm walking across campus to my last class of the day, I'm craving Swedish Fish. I pop into the convenience store on campus and grab a small bag to snack on during my next class. The line's much longer than I expect, so by the time I'm done, I'm forced to powerwalk to be on time for my next class.

Just as I reach the door of the building, a man's hand darts in front of me to reach for the handle. Absentmindedly, I mutter a thanks and wait for him to pull it open. But his hand doesn't move. I glance up to make eye contact with the moron who's holding me up, and I'm startled to find Vince's hazel eyes staring back at me. Though this time, instead of looking at his tousled brown hair, it's covered in a baseball cap, and he's wearing dark-rimmed glasses. He still looks handsome as ever, but I wouldn't necessarily recognize him like I did at the bar Friday night.

"I knew I recognized you," I mutter more to myself than to him.

"It appears you do." Vince slowly smirks as he opens the door. "What class are you heading to?" he asks with genuine interest.

"Financial management."

Vince's eyes widen, and his jaw drops. "How have we *not* met before?"

I shrug. Because what can I say?

When we get to our destination, he opens the door once again for me. "Thank you," I say sheepishly as I make my way into the lecture hall. There are close to one hundred people in this class, as it's only offered spring semester. But I still can't get over the fact we're just now meeting.

Instead of making our departure awkward, I cut right and take a seat in my typical area of the lecture hall. When I turn to take off my backpack, I'm surprised to find Vince following me down the aisle.

He raises his hand in innocence. "I'm not a stalker or anything. But it felt like our conversation wasn't quite over, and I didn't want to make things awkward, either."

"It's no problem at all," I assure him as I take my seat. "There's plenty of room." I gesture to the few vacancies around me.

Vince doesn't say anything but takes his time to plop himself in the seat next to me and gather the things he'll need for taking notes. By the time we're both settled, neither one of us get the chance to say anything because the professor walks up to the podium to begin class.

Of course, there's no way *not* to notice Vince sitting next to me. He flips up the built-in table and makes himself comfortable. His large frame takes up the space, and his legs stretch out and cross naturally in front of him.

But that's not what captures my attention and never lets go. No—that would be his musky cologne that almost has the effect of catnip to a kitten. Even though I'd *never* act upon it, I feel my nerve endings zing with hypersensitivity to his closeness. With each and every move he makes, electric currents zip through my body. Like a magnetic force I can't seem to grab control of, the electric pulses involuntarily roll up and down my spine and rumble into my belly.

When the person to my right drops her pen on the floor, I'm brought back to reality.

What the fuck am I doing?

I don't react to guys like this.

I'm not some dumb teenager experiencing her first crush.

But as I rack my brain trying to figure out what makes this man different from the others, I come up empty-handed. I've never had such a visceral reaction to anyone.

Maybe I'm just being hormonal?

It has been awhile since my date with 'Fucking Brad,' but I quickly squash that thought like a bug on the windshield.

That's no excuse.

I refuse to let that douche-canoe have the power to shape my future. He was just another bad experience in a long line of horrible dates. I don't have the time or the patience to put forth the effort it takes to be in a lasting relationship. I'm perfectly fine on my own and don't need a guy to make me happy.

Besides—that's what I've paid good money on my trusty vibrator for.

Smirking at the thought, I'm interrupted by the movement from the people around me. They're shoving their notebooks into their backpacks and exiting the lecture hall.

Holy shit. Did I daydream through this entire class?

When I look to Vince, he's packed but looking at me expectantly. "You okay?"

Shaking the rest of the cobwebs from my brain, I rush out, "Yeah. Sure. Sorry—got lost thinking about something the professor was saying."

Vince's lips tip at the end, almost as if he's holding back a smile. "Really? What's that?"

Not wanting to completely lie, I spit out, "It's not that big of a deal. I was just thinking about the assigned reading from last night and how applicable it would be to real life."

Vince's eyebrows lift past the rim of his glasses, but he doesn't say anything.

Needing to fill the awkward silence, I quickly change the subject. "Are you done with classes for the day? Or do you have another one after this?"

Vince stands and lets the person I didn't know was waiting on my other side, pass by us. "I'm done for the day, you?"

"I've been going since nine and thankfully, this is my last class," I reply, following Vince out of the hall.

Vince glances at his watch. "It's nearly five. Just how many classes are you taking?"

"Oh, just eighteen credits. I've loaded Tuesdays and Thursdays so I can sleep in after working my late shifts. I only have one class on Mondays and Wednesdays—so that's a win in my book."

God. Sydney. Shut up. Why are you telling him your whole life's story?

Not knowing what to do, I look anywhere but at Vince. When I finally allow myself to meet his eyes, I'm relieved to find he isn't looking at me as if I've just over-shared. No, he's nodding in agreement. "Working at a bar must mean late nights; that's a smart plan."

Huh. Not what I expected.

"I must be a glutton for punishment because with back-to-back classes and only time to go home, grab some dinner, and change, I keep going until we close." I shrug as if it's just a fact of my life, trying like hell to stop making things awkward.

Vince lets out a low whistle. "Wow. That's a packed day. I thought I had long days—but my days end by five—even when I have to work."

Wow—being off by five. That must be nice. "You work on campus?"

Vince holds the door as we exit the building. "Yeah. I got an internship in the university's marketing department my sophomore year, and I've been working part-time ever since."

"Wow, that's great. I started as a waitress, but bartending makes more."

Vince nods in agreement. "I can see how it would, even in a college town."

I sigh heavily as I admit, "I don't have to work as many

hours to make ends meet now. When I do get the extra hours, I can put it aside and save it for a rainy day."

"That's great," he says as we get to the bottom of the steps outside the building. "Which way are you heading?"

Pointing in the direction of my apartment, I thumb over my shoulder. "This way, you?"

Smiling, Vince shakes his head. "Seriously—I have no idea how we've made it this long without running into one another. Mind if I walk with you?"

Instantly, I recall his address being near mine—but a few blocks further. He must live in one of the houses up the road, so I nod in agreement. "Sounds good."

We turn and walk casually across campus. Neither of us say anything for a few moments—but thankfully, nothing is awkward either.

Eventually, Vince breaks the silence, "So... you're taking financial management. I take it you're a business major?"

"Marketing, actually. I want to be in public relations with an emphasis on developing the brand or products. What about you?" I ask, keeping the conversation safe. After the way my thoughts drifted in class, I certainly don't need to make things difficult.

"I'm double-majoring in marketing and international business," he tells me as we wait for a car to pass before crossing the street. "If all goes to plan, I'll be done next spring."

"Same here. Wait... Have you been at CRU the whole time?" It's really odd this is the first time we've met if he's been here all three years. CRU isn't that big of a campus. But maybe he's a transfer.

"Yeah." He shrugs. "I started as a freshman. My family has a house here in town, so I've never lived in the dorms."

"Wow. That must've been nice. I couldn't wait to get out of the dorms. Thankfully, I met my roommates Abby and Chloe and only lived in one freshman year. Do you live with your parents?"

Something dark flickers across Vince's features, and I suddenly feel as if I've asked the wrong question. His jovial expression is gone as he shakes his head and practically whispers, "No. I don't live with my parents," on an exhale.

Crap. What do I say now? Clearly he's in a bad place with his parents, and I need to change the subject before I put my foot in my mouth further. Think. Think… Got it. I pop off the first question that comes to mind that he seemed to be okay with talking about. "So… what is it you do for the university? You mentioned your internship led into a job on campus?"

"I help market and recruit potential students. It's really grunt work, like getting mailings set up. I put a lot of labels on mailers and send out pamphlets. But sometimes I get to design and create a campaign we want to run. It's not much, but it pays well—so I'm not complaining."

"That's great work experience, too!" I thought about trying to do something in my field, but I just can't give up the money I make now.

"I hear ya. You gotta do—what you gotta do. We'll have plenty of time to work in our fields later, but you've gotta get that degree first before anyone will hire you."

When we get to the entrance of my apartment complex, I contemplate walking further because I don't want my time with Vince to end. But knowing I have limited time until my shift at the bar, I stick with honesty. "Well…" I point to the complex on our right. "This is me. It was great talking with you, Vince. I'll see you around."

"Sounds good. Save me a seat for next class. Maybe we can do this again," Vince offers, and my mind races into a tailspin.

Thousands of thoughts flicker through my brain, starting with—he wants to see me again—to—I'm so screwed if I have another day like today. I can't make rhyme or reason of them as they flow like a strobe light through my brain.

Somehow, among all my internal ramblings, I manage a coherent reply, "Sure, sounds good."

I'm rewarded with a beautiful smile that renders me speechless. "Until then…" he trails off then turns and keeps walking down the street, while I'm left to admire his backside. Thankfully, he doesn't look back—because I'm rooted in place.

Fuck. I am so screwed.

4

VINCE

*U*NTIL THEN... *REALLY?* M*AN*, I'*VE GOT ZERO GAME*.

I'm still thinking about that ridiculous comment hours later, after I've gotten Julia through her nighttime routine and read her a bedtime story. I'm sitting at the kitchen table, trying to study, but all I can think of is the fiery redhead from this afternoon.

Not that I have time to date as I'm typically helping Van and Julia. Van picked up an evening shift to cover for someone calling in sick. This is a typical Tuesday for us. Not that I'm complaining.

I will do anything to help Van not become a teenage statistic. Dad drilled it into both of our heads that less than two percent of teen moms graduate from college before age thirty. Mom and Dad were planning to help Van through school, but after their accident, I became hellbent on ensuring she graduates from college on time. Besides—Julia's one of the best kids in the world—so it's no hardship spending time with her.

Van hates not being here for bedtime—but occasionally when someone needs a shift covered, she knows I'm here to help. For the most part, she can handle everything on her own, but one of us has to be home with Jules for bedtime. That's non-negotiable. So, when I can lighten her load, I always try.

Van goes above and beyond to be there for Julia. She's at the diner by six every morning and arranges her class and work schedule to be done before the on-campus daycare closes. She's a freaking rockstar, and I couldn't be prouder of her if I tried. It's a crazy life, but I wouldn't have it any other way. I love my mornings with Julia before dropping her off at daycare on my way to work or class by eight.

When I've realized I've read the same paragraph for the third time, I know it's time to give up on studying for the night. It's already after nine, and Van should be home any minute. I clear my things from the kitchen table and stash them in my room before checking on Julia one last time. Usually she'll chatter a million miles a minute, but the second her head hits the pillow, we barely get through a couple pages of a bedtime story, and she's out like a light.

When I peek into her room, I notice she's already got one leg out and a hand is draped over her head. She's out for the count, and I doubt we'll hear from her before morning. Now that she's growing out of the toddler stage, waking up in the middle of the night is rare.

Not that I typically get up with her, but that doesn't mean I haven't taken my turn, to let Vanessa get some sleep before her early shifts. I swear, it takes a village to raise a kid. I have no idea how Van would do this entirely on her own. I know she's more than capable, but why should she need to be? That's what I'm here for.

Just as I settle onto the couch and pull up NCIS from the DVR, I hear the garage door open. I pause because I know she'll watch it with me if I let her take a quick shower and change first. Thank God, she's not a shower lingerer. I know we'll be watching the show within twenty minutes or so.

Standing to greet her I stretch my arms almost to the ceiling, as she walks into the living room. "Hey, how was work?"

Vanessa shrugs as she tosses her purse on the table next to her favorite over-sized chair. "The usual. Hopefully, Tara will be better by tomorrow. She's called in a few days now—apparently, she's finally able to eat solid food again. I spoke with her on the phone and from what she says, I'm more than happy she stays away until this sickness is long gone. No, thank you—We certainly don't need the flu in our house."

"No," I reiterate the sentiment. "We definitely don't need that. Are you hungry? I was gonna make a snack and watch NCIS. Care to join me?"

"Sure. I grabbed something on my last break, but if you want to get me some iced tea, I'd gladly drink it. I'll be out in a few."

When she turns toward her bedroom, I make my way into the kitchen and make a plate of nachos for myself. I stack on a few more chips than necessary, knowing these are something Van can never refuse.

By the time I've got drinks and nachos ready, I hear the water shut off in the bathroom. While I wait, I scroll through my favorite social media site on my phone. When I see an ad with a cute redhead, I can't help but wish I knew Sydney's last name. Not that I'd be stalking her—but I am curious to learn more about her.

Thankfully, I don't have time to dwell on this because Van appears dressed in her pajamas, brushing her long, wet hair. Typically, it's a lot blonder than mine, but when it's wet, it's much darker. "So, how was Jules tonight? Did she go down easy?"

"I know how to wear her out." I chuckle. "We went for a bike ride… well, I walked, and she rode. I think she's about ready to ditch her training wheels. When she turns corners, one side completely lifts. Do you mind if I take them off and teach her next time we go out?"

"Really? You think she's ready?" Vanessa asks in disbelief.

I nod, and Vanessa shakes her head. Clearly, she thinks Jules is growing up way too fast.

"Can I be there to record it?" she asks but quickly tacks on, "Please promise me you won't let go unless she's good and ready?"

I give her a *what do you take me for* look, which earns me an eye roll.

God, I love my sister.

Chuckling, I ask, pretending to sound exasperated, "Are we ready to watch this show, or what?"

"Okay, Vinny. Let's watch the show. I'm opening in the morning."

I don't bother responding, as I already knew this. I settle into the couch by lying back and propping my feet up on the coffee table.

I nearly choke on a nacho when I realize Van's got nothing on the feisty girl I've been thinking about all day.

"You okay, Vin?" my sister asks with concern.

"Yep. Just fine." I manage when I get my first breath of clear air. There's no way I'm telling Van about a girl I've just met. I'll never hear the end of it.

But as I watch the show—one thing's for certain—I won't be forgetting about Sydney anytime soon.

I don't run into Sydney until Thursday before class. *Though is it really running into her if I purposely lurk outside, pretending to scroll through my phone while I wait for her?* I haven't been able to get her out of my freaking mind, and I want to see if I've built her up in my imagination—or if this weird connection we have really exists. Not that I'll do anything about it. But I've had this nagging feeling that I just can't walk away from.

When I finally spot her, I plan my approach so we reach the door at the same time from different directions. Like last time, I reach for the door to open it for her, but instead of being surprised, I'm greeted with the most beautiful smile. Her green eyes light up with delight as a chortle escapes. "So—is this gonna be a thing?" she asks, her voice laced with sarcasm.

I shrug nonchalantly. "Only if you want it to be."

With a beautiful smirk, she shrugs. "I'm not complaining. Want to sit together again?"

"I'm game if you are," I tease. The way her green eyes dance, I want to banter with this woman till the sun goes down. And I'm not so sure I'd want to stop—even then.

She walks into the lecture hall and takes the same seat as before. I promptly sit beside her and get comfortable. Pulling out my notebook and pen, I prepare to take notes. Sydney must have a great auditory memory, as she didn't take a single note last time. I wish to be so lucky.

To keep her attention, I throw out the first question that comes to mind, "Do you close again tonight?"

"Yeah," she sighs. "Since it's two-dollar wells night, we're usually packed 'til closing. Thank God, I'm free until my evening shift tomorrow. I've got a paper to write and desperately need to catch up on laundry—after sleeping in of course. I so need a date with my pillow. It's been a long week. What about you? Now that you're finally legal, will you be hitting the town?"

Her teasing tone causes a smile involuntarily to stretch across my face. "Nope. My shift starts at eight, and I need my beauty rest," I tease—though Jules hardly ever sleeps past six.

Sydney looks me over with care. I feel her gaze as it takes stock of what she sees. "We wouldn't want you to miss out on your beauty rest. Clearly, you've been lacking lately."

I know without a doubt her perusal of my body is a clear excuse for her to check me out, so I just smirk and roll with it. "Yep. I'm crabby without sleep."

"Somehow, I doubt it. But thanks for the warning. I'll be sure never to disturb your slumber, princess."

I feel my lips involuntarily turn up as I shake my head. "Princess, is it? All because I enjoy my sleep?"

A belly laugh rips out of Sydney, and I quickly join in, causing stares to erupt around us. When she regains her composure, she swats at my arm. "Princess… we all enjoy sleep. But thinking you need beauty rest is absurd."

Cocking my head to the side, I smirk. "Really? Why's that?"

She pats my thigh complacently, and the heat from her hand lingers. "I'm sure you hardly need rest to be beautiful." Suddenly, her freckled cheeks pinken, and she gasps. "Shit. That came out wrong…"

"You callin' me ugly?" I tease, and her cheeks darken a hue more. Damn, she's gorgeous. I'll make fun of myself every day if she reacts like this.

Her hand flies to cover her mouth. "Oh, no… that's not what I meant. Quite the opposite… honest."

Raising an eyebrow, I stare for further clarification.

Her hand comes down on my thigh, and it takes everything in my power not to reach out and hold it there. Then she pins me with her emerald-green eyes to make sure there's no miscommunication. "Vince. You're a great looking guy. Let's leave it at that and let me stop digging myself into a bigger hole."

"Thanks," I whisper, holding her gaze for as long as she'll let me. I swear I feel static electricity floating in the air as if it's about to zap me. Of course, the professor chooses this moment to start class, and Sydney's attention is quickly averted to him.

Her hand immediately pulls back, and she takes notes furiously as he launches into a lengthy explanation of what's on our exam next week. I diligently jot down notes of my own to distract myself from the intriguing woman next to me.

By the time class is over, my hand hurts, my head is spinning from what I'll need to remember, and yet I'm hopeful to walk Sydney home again. After opening and closing my fist a few times, the feeling in my hand returns to normal. While packing my things, I finally break the silence between us. "Are you heading home?"

Sydney sighs as she stands and hoists her backpack over her shoulder. "Yeah. I've got to be on shift in a few hours. Wanna walk together?"

I'm fairly certain my grin is verging on creepy, but I could give two shits. Sydney wants to spend time with me. But before I look like a total freak, I force myself to calm the fuck down and remain casual. "Sure thing."

Once outside, Sydney's unusually quiet for the first few minutes. Knowing the best way to glean as much information about her as I can is to ask a question. I start with the easiest. "So, where are you from?"

She rolls her eyes as a light laugh escapes. "I'm from a small town in Eastern Washington you've probably never even heard of."

"Try me," I challenge to keep her talking.

She juts out her chin and cocks a brow in my direction as if to raise the ante, "Pomeroy."

I pretend to think it over. But this causes Sydney to stop in her tracks and face me as she waits for my response. After a few moments of being captured by her beautiful green eyes, I cave and finally admit, "Nope—Not a clue. Where the hell is that?"

Her eyes bug out at my unexpected response. Then she immediately bursts out laughing at my pathetic attempt at being competitive geographically. Boy. I'm a real charmer, I'm sure.

When she captures her breath, she draws out, "Well... it's

about twenty-five miles from Pullman and about fifteen from Clarkston."

"I know where Pullman is. But I can't even say I've heard of Clarkston," I admit. "I've lived on the west side my entire life and if we went to Eastern Washington, it was usually to Spokane on my way to my relative's house in Montana."

Sydney swats her hand in the air dismissively. "It's okay. I don't know the difference between any city between Olympia and Seattle, as they all seem the same to me. But being from the middle of nowhere in most people's eyes, I've just gotten used to saying I live in the southeast corner about thirty miles from Idaho… and even then, their eyes gloss over. So yeah… I didn't expect you to know where Pomeroy is." Her teasing tone keeps a smile on my face.

"Well, we're even…" I start slowly. Then smirk as I add, "Because I'm from one of those cities you'd know nothing about along the I-5 corridor." As expected, I earn another eye roll. If I thought she was beautiful before, she's fucking gorgeous, filled with sass and attitude.

Well—let's be real. In the short time I've known her, I've clearly learned she's gorgeous anytime—laughing, serious, and I've quickly found that when she throws that sass around… well, that's the real her. I'm fairly certain. Her quick wit rolls off her tongue as natural as she breathes.

I've gotta stay on my toes around this one.

"Okay, then…" she trails off for a few heartbeats as she starts walking again. "Hey, Vince." Her tone changes to hesitant, and instantly I'm on alert—But she says nothing.

"Yes, Sydney," I prompt in the same tone, hoping she'll just spill whatever's on her mind.

"Are you a fan of the band Riser?"

"Who isn't?" Why would liking a band make her look—wait—is that nervous?

"I have an extra ticket for their concert in Portland Sunday night. Would you want to join me?"

Even knowing it will make for a rough Monday, I don't hesitate at the chance of spending more time with her. "I'd love to. Let me know how much the ticket is, and I'll cover my cost. What time's the concert?"

"The opening band is at seven, so it should start by eight or so. I'm so glad you can go. My roommate was supposed to go, but since her boyfriend is in town for a rare weekend before March Madness starts, she's ditched me for him—not that I blame her."

This piques my interest as I'm a huge fan of basketball. "I take it he plays on the team?"

"Yeah. Drew's fantastic, and I'm so happy for him and Abby. But she claims—if she goes to his basketball game later this week, she can't go to the concert." Before I can say anything, Sydney quickly explains, "She's extremely focused on med school—well, both of them are. She's already applied but doesn't want to ruin her chances by not getting her top grades. Besides, she's not that big of a Riser fan. My other roommate Chloe is out of town for her great-grandmother's ninety-fifth birthday."

"Wow. That's amazing. I can't imagine being ninety-five. I can see why she can't go to the concert with you."

"Yeah, it really is," Sydney agrees. "I hope I'm still living on my own at that age and able to care for myself the way her grandma does."

By now, we've arrived at her apartment complex. Knowing we likely won't see each other before the concert, and I need to pick up Julia soon, I quickly reach my hand out as I offer, "Give me your phone. I'll put my number in it, and you can call me when you get a chance. I know you're working tonight, so anytime between now and Sunday is fine."

She digs her phone from her pocket and enters her passcode. Then hands it over.

I quickly enter my digits, then type a quick message to myself, and press send.

Sydney: Next time you can pick the place.

I wait for the text to go through, then hand it back.

I grin, knowing I'll have her number as well.

She quickly thanks me.

Then she looks at the message.

Her perfectly sculpted eyebrows reach to her hairline as her eyes widen. "You're that confident you're getting a second date?"

I shrug with way more confidence than I should. "Well, it's only fair. You picked the first one."

She opens her mouth to say what I'm sure would be a great one liner but quickly snaps it shut. Then she levels me with a stare, making me hope I didn't blow our first date before it's even begun.

She slowly pulls in a long breath and releases it. Then she calmly states, "Okay—Vincent Daniel Larson. You'd better be worth it."

Inside, I'm fist pumping the air because I'm sure she just agreed to a second date before completing the first. But even if she didn't, I'll take what I can get. I may not take the time to date much, but something tells me I'll want more than one with her.

On the outside, I manage to keep my cool. "Ohhh—pulling out the big guns I see." My phone buzzes in my pocket, reminding me I have less than thirty minutes to pick up Jules. Shit. I've got to run, or I won't get there on time. Thankfully, she notices when I glance at my phone, so I attempt to play it off the best I can. "Unfortunately, I can't stay and chat about your three-name usage. But don't worry, Syd, I won't give you any cause to pull it out Sunday. I'm looking forward to planning our next date. Call me when you can."

With that, I turn and walk toward home a little less casual than I'd like, as I can't be late for Jules. I have to admit, I might have a bounce in my step—simply because she said yes.

Maybe I'll figure out her last name at some point on this date of ours, too.

5

SYDNEY

"He got me to agree to a second date, and we haven't even been on a first!" I repeat for the fourth time to Chloe while we hang out Friday morning. We've been binge-watching episodes of *The Flash*, as that's Chloe's favorite show and once we start, I'm sucked in right along with her.

"You've mentioned that," she deadpans then adds, "I thought you were on a dating diet from men?"

"I was..." I groan. "But you're visiting family, and Abby bailed on me. And... well, okay... when we almost got back to our apartment, I didn't want my time with Vince to end," I admit.

"I see..." she draws out, likely waiting for me to continue.

"Don't use your psycho-babble on me, Clo..." I warn, knowing she'll make me admit why I asked him out in the first place.

She pushes my shoulder and pretends to be offended. "I'm

not doing that. But you have to admit. There's something about this guy that has *you* of all people, asking him out."

"What? I ask people out."

"Um... no, you don't. You never have to. Guys fawn all over you, and you're usually the one to turn them down."

I balk at her description in a tsk-like noise. "They don't fawn all over me. Sure, I get hit on at the bar when they have their beer-goggles on, but it's not like I get that much attention when I'm out and about."

"Girl... are you believing that line of bullshit you're spewing? You're gorgeous and guys *do* indeed notice you. I think you took this chance on Vince because he didn't throw himself at you. From what you've told me, he seems decent. Just don't let your past cloud your judgement with him."

"I haven't even gone on the date. Why are you saying that?"

"Oh, I don't know – *Ms. Dating Dieter*." She pauses to get my full attention. "You've had yourself a string of shitty dates, and I hope you give poor Vince a chance. I, for one, am dying to meet the guy you're willing to hop off the wagon for."

God, I love her, but she couldn't be more wrong. "I'm not hopping off the wagon. I'm not addicted to dating... or being celibate for that matter. I was just done with dating the wrong guys."

"Okay – we're getting to the good part of this show... so I'll shut up – but you may want to ask yourself, *what makes him so special*?"

What does make him so special? I ask myself a million times and when the episode ends, I have no freaking clue as to how the problem in the show I'd been dying to know about was solved. Shit. I'll have to re-watch this episode another time while Chloe's gone because there's no way in hell I'm admitting my concentration is shit at the moment.

———

As much as I want to talk with Vince, I wait until Saturday afternoon to reach out. I don't know his schedule and I certainly didn't want to appear too eager either.

Me: Are you busy?

Vince: I've got time to talk.

Great. I'm likely interrupting him. But at the same time, my belly flips knowing he's making the time to talk to me. Knowing I want to see him sooner than I'd admit to anyone, I quickly type and hit send before I can over think it.

Me: Would you like to grab dinner before the concert?

Before a response comes through, my phone rings and annoyance sets in because now is not the time for interruptions. But when I notice it's him, all is forgiven.

"Hi." His rough voice comes through the receiver and the flutter in my belly from before picks up the pace. "Thought it would be easier to just call. I've never been a big texter, when you can pick up the phone just as easy."

"No problem." His honesty is endearing.

"Do you want to grab dinner near campus, or in town – closer to the venue?"

"Let's grab it near the venue—that way we won't have to worry about traffic or anything. Even though Sunday should be good."

"I can drive—unless you'd rather," he offers and for some reason, it matters that he's letting me choose.

"You can drive. I live in apartment 3B. It's the first building on your right as you enter the complex. Upstairs and to the left."

"Sounds good. Are you working tonight?"

Why does that mundane question make my heart race?

"Yeah. I try to work most Friday and Saturday nights when I can. They're the busiest, and I hate when it's slow. It makes the time drag on, ya know?"

"I can imagine." There's a loud noise in the background, and Vince muffles the phone the best he can. He must be some place public because I swear it sounds like a gaggle of kids ran by. "Hey, Syd? I'm sorry to cut this short, but I've gotta go. It's hard to hear around here."

Before I can respond, the noise is back, and it makes me laugh. Where the hell is he? "No problem. Pick me up around four, and we'll get to town in plenty of time before the concert."

"Sounds good," he says. "I'll be there."

With that, he ends the call, making me wish this day would pass a little faster.

Unfortunately, it doesn't.

Even though I got called into work early, and we're busy tonight, I can't help but scan the crowd for Vince. It's nearly eleven, and the way he'd asked me if I was working made it sound as if he might be stopping by.

Maybe he was just making casual conversation, and I'm putting something into it that wasn't there?

But truth be told—every time I see someone who resembles him—my heart picks up a beat—and then my hopes are smashed when it's not him.

Jesus, Syd. Get over it. He's not coming, and you have shit to do. I chastise myself and force my thoughts back to reality, just in time for a long line of people from the other side of the bar. I spend the next hour filling drinks and keeping the line to a minimum.

When I notice the tall friend that came in with Vince on his birthday, I take a moment to scan the bar, hoping to see Vince. No such luck. My gut sinks when I realize the tall guy's here with a date and no one else.

Maybe after tomorrow, I should resume my dating diet if I've resorted to being a pre-teen waiting to see her first crush. I'm not cut out for shit like this, and I should probably stick with my original plan. Hopefully, tomorrow night will be a dud, and I can get him out of my mind once and for all.

Crap. Why did I agree to a second date?

Even though I came home and crashed shortly after three, I find myself tossing and turning early the next morning. Sundays are meant for sleeping in. There's no reason I should know there's two seven o'clocks in a day. Especially when my head just landed on the pillow mere hours before.

I roll over for what feels like the millionth time, in a vain attempt for comfort.

Fuck. It's not working.

Groaning, I toss back my covers and crawl out of bed. I pad to my bathroom and shower for the day. I may as well be productive if I can't sleep. Within twenty minutes, I'm out in the kitchen, making breakfast. Well—a bagel and cream cheese anyway. Then I head out to the living room, where I'm surprised by Abby studying on the couch.

"What are you doing here?" I ask as I sit in the chair beside her.

"Drew's asleep in my room, so I came out here to finish a paper. Then I can spend a guilt-free afternoon with him later. Sorry I can't make it to the concert. Did you find someone to go with you?"

"Don't worry about it," I say as I swat the air, shaking my head. "If today was Drew's only night off before heading on the road for the tournament, I'd want to spend it with him as well."

Abby puts down the pen she's been fiddling with and gives me her full attention. "You did find someone, right?" A pang of guilt flashes in her eyes.

I put her out of her misery with ease. "Yeah, I got a friend from class to go with me." I have no idea why I don't tell her about Vince. But with waiting to see where she and Drew get into med school, and him heading into the tournament, she's got enough on her plate. Besides, she likes Riser, but she's been to their concerts before when they were just an up-and-coming band. Tonight's concert is their final one of their tour, and the place will be packed. Abby will go to an arena to watch Drew play, now that she's a fan—but big crowds aren't really her thing.

"That's great. I felt so guilty leaving you high and dry. I know it'll be a great concert."

"Yeah. You know I'd go to the concert solo if necessary, right? I won't miss the chance to see Nick perform in person. I love his voice and could listen to it all night long," I tease, even though I'm sure Vince beats him in the looks department. "I'll be blessed with eye candy all night."

Abby smirks. "I'm sure that will be such a hardship."

She has no idea.

"Yep," I agree. When I finish my bagel, I stand to return my plate to the kitchen. "Well, I'll let you finish your paper. I'm off to beat the crowds and get groceries. Need anything?"

"I'm good. Thanks," Abby says, but I can tell she's already getting back to her paper. She's tenacious about her studies.

By the time I return from the store, Abby and Drew are nowhere to be found, so I have the apartment to myself. It isn't even ten, and there's way too much time before Vince will arrive. Having spent the better part of yesterday studying, I contemplate my choices to occupy my time.

Binge-watch TV or bake?

Yeah, that isn't even an option. Pulling out the ingredients for cinnamon rolls and no-bake cookies, I set into baking.

Eventually, I decide it's finally acceptable to get ready. Looking around my now-clean kitchen, it's obvious I've been stressing out. I've made way more than I intended. Not only have I made a double batch of cinnamon rolls, but I've also made no-bake cookies and a loaf of banana bread. My roommates will love the fruits from my nervous energy. And if all else fails, I know Drew and his roommates will enjoy them as well. His poor roommate Grey says he'll take my day-old rolls any chance I'll make them. The guy can't cook for beans, but he knows how to eat.

Knowing I have plenty of time, I make the effort to straighten my hair, apply just the perfect amount of makeup to make my green eyes pop, and change my outfit at least three times. God only knows why I'm suddenly nervous. I haven't put this much effort into a date since going to my first formal as a freshman in high school. Usually, I just go with the 'come as you are' attitude, and they get what they get.

I've settled on a pair of dark skinny jeans, my favorite ballet slippers, and a loose emerald-green sweater that falls off to one side of my shoulders. I have my jacket and purse waiting on the couch. When I'm sure he must be arriving soon, I finally allow myself to look at the clock.

Shit. It's only a quarter after three.

My apartment's spotless, it smells like Betty Crocker invaded, and I'm ready to go. What the hell do I do now?

Should I make Vince a plate of baked goods?

Or will that make me look too much like a housewife from the 1950s? No, I'll never be Miss Suzy Homemaker. I've got the baking part down pat, but the thought of relying on someone else gives me hives.

I have no idea how long I stand in the kitchen internally debating with myself, but knowing most can't resist my yummy treats, I eventually break down, pull out a container, and load one up for Vince. Just finished, there's a knock on my door.

I quickly wipe my hands with the nearest towel, then find myself rushing to answer. The sight of Vince leaves me breathless. His hair's perfectly tousled, the rich aroma of his sexy cologne replaces my hours of baking, and his hazel eyes taking me in make him even more attractive. When a slow smile spreads across his perfect lips, it's an automatic response to mirror him.

When I finally remember my manners, I attempt to play off my blatant ogling. "Hey, Vince. Come on in."

"Wow, it smells amazing in here. What are you baking?"

I shrug in an attempt to play it off. "I was done studying, and my roommates are gone, so I've got cinnamon rolls and no-bake cookies, if you're interested."

"Are you kidding? I'd give my left kidney for something that smells this delicious." Just then, his stomach rumbles, and we both burst out laughing.

"Well, I've made you a container, but as you're obviously going to die on the spot if you don't get one now—let me dish you up a plate."

He follows me to the kitchen and when he spots my efforts of today, his eyes widen. "You made all this... today?" The way his hand sweeps the counter in a grand gesture is almost comical.

Tucking my chin, so I don't have to look him in the eye, I play off, "Yep. When I'm bored, I bake."

"For the record, I'll gladly consume your boredom anytime you're willing to share. This is unbelievable, may I?" He gestures to a no-bake cookie still on the waxed paper as they weren't quite done hardening yet.

"Go right ahead. But be warned, they're likely to fall apart."

He carefully picks up the breaking cookie and brings it to his mouth. The groan he lets out as the chocolate hits his mouth sends shivers throughout my entire body.

How the hell can watching a guy eat a cookie be a turn-on? Clearly—I'm losing my mind.

When he finishes, and I get myself under control, I offer, "There's a container with your name on it, if you'd like to take some to go."

"Are you kidding? These are freaking fantastic. I haven't had these since I was a kid." He's quiet for a moment as he stares at the counter, but just when I'm about to ask him about it, he shakes his head and pushes the rest of the cookie into his mouth. When his eyes meet mine, I'm sure I just imagined the entire thing. Weird.

"Are you ready?" he asks as he turns to wash his hands and dry them off with the towel I'd left on the sink.

"Yeah, just let me grab my coat and purse." As I head out of the kitchen to grab my things from my room, I stop at the entry. "The blue container is yours. If you return it, I might be persuaded to refill it for you."

Seriously? I just offered to bake more for him?

Before he can answer, I leave the room and walk away from my humiliation. Why in the hell did I make it sound so suggestive? I'm supposed to keep it to one date, not offering up more. Geez, Syd, get it together.

By the time I return, Vince waits in the living room with his baked goods in hand and a genuine smile on his face. His hazel eyes drink me in, and I'll admit, my heart rate spikes in his obvious approval.

Grabbing the door for us, he asks, "Shall we?"

Once outside, Vince leads me to a newer model black Jeep. I'm thankful I wore jeans as it is slightly lifted and may have proven difficult to enter in a skirt. I'm thankful when I notice a bar to step on, so I won't have to look like a beached whale as I attempt to get in the thing. Of course, Vince is right there and even with one hand, making sure I get in okay.

As he walks to the driver's side of the Jeep, I notice that Vince is either a neat freak, or he's cleaned it up for tonight. Either way, I'm nervous for him to see my car; it needs to be dusted and vacuumed desperately. I make a mental note to drive my car through a car wash this week.

When the engine roars to life, Vince turns to ask, "So, have you decided on where you want to grab dinner?"

"Not really. Why don't we see if something stands out along the way? I'm game for anything."

"Sounds good to me."

6

VINCE

From the moment I've picked up Sydney, I've been enamored by her. Not only can she bake, but the more I learn about her, the more I like. She's smart, funny, and full of life. Even when she's telling me about drunken patrons, she's so vibrant in the way she describes them. I can't help but wish I'd seen it in person for myself.

When Sydney suggests getting off the freeway a few exits before the venue, I know just where to take her. "Are you interested in Thai?"

"Sure. Sounds great," she replies eagerly.

I quickly parallel park in a spot on the same block as the restaurant. As soon as I know it's clear, I hop out of the car and rush to her side just as she opens the door for herself. Damn. I need to be quicker.

I do manage to hold my hand out to hers to assist her down. The moment our skin touches, electricity crackles all around us. The air is charged as I close the door behind her.

Not wanting to let go just yet, I keep a hold of her hand as we walk down the block toward the restaurant. The way our fingers naturally intertwine, it's as if we've been doing this for years, rather than for our first date.

Sydney's quiet as we wait to be seated. I can see the wheels turning in her head, and I'd give almost anything to know what she's thinking. When she rolls her bottom lip into her mouth to chew on it, I can't take it any longer. Leaning in, I whisper, "Penny for your thoughts?"

When her eyes meet mine, they're dancing with mischief. "Quarter for your underwear?" rolls off her tongue with ease.

What?

Did she really just say that?

She rolls her beautiful green eyes as she giggles. "Ohmigod, Vince. I'm kidding. You should've seen the look on your face. Seriously. I was just trying to break the ice—obviously, it was stupid. I'm so sorry." She shakes her head then shrugs. "I'm sometimes a smartass when I get nervous, and I didn't mean to make things weird."

I replay her explanation in my head to make sure I heard it right. The minute she started talking about underwear, my mind went right into the gutter. But what hits home is that she's nervous. From all my interactions with her—I didn't think she had a nervous bone in her body. Hmmm—she's always so confident. So, I gotta know. "What's making you nervous?"

"You are."

"Me? What have I done to make you nervous?" I rack my brain thinking about my actions. But I come up blank.

She bites her bottom lip as she looks to the floor. But I wait her out and eventually, the strong woman I've been attracted to from the beginning looks me boldly in the eye as she shrugs. "I have no idea. I just got nervous for some reason."

"Well..." I draw out slowly, wondering how to go back to the comfortable and carefree girl from before. My eyes go to our locked hands, and my thoughts are said aloud, "Does holding my hand make you nervous?" I start pulling away, but she tightens her grip.

"No—it's not that. I'm just being stupid. Trust me. I like holding your hand. Please... forget I said anything." The hostess tells us our table is ready, and Sydney refuses to let go of my hand as we follow her to our table. Unfortunately, I have to let go to pull out her chair, then go around to my side of the table.

Without saying anything, she reaches her hand across the table. When I return the gesture by placing mine in hers, she squeezes reassuringly. "Sorry, Vince. I'm having a great time. Please don't let me being a smartass ruin our evening."

Wanting to put things at ease as well as to speak from the heart, I find myself saying, "I love that you say what's on your mind. Please—never hold back. I'd rather know what you're thinking—even if it *is* about my underwear."

This has its desired effect.

She blushes the most beautiful shade of red, and her freckles stand out against her skin in contrast. "I'll have you know I'm a boxer-brief guy... if that makes it easier."

What the actual fuck? Why did I just say that?

"Good to know." She lets go of my hand to pick up a menu. "Have you been here before?"

"Only once, but I remember the peanut sauce being the best I've ever had. So, it'll definitely be part of my order."

"Ohhhh… that sounds great. I'll do the same."

Okay, let's hope this awkwardness is behind us.

Though now that she's mentioned underwear, I'm curious as to what she's wearing under her perfectly fitting jeans.

Thankfully, Sydney's nerves disperse, and the rest of dinner goes off without a hitch. By the time we get to the concert, there's plenty of time to walk around. Knowing things will be sold out later, she opts to buy a vintage-looking t-shirt of the band Riser, and I pick up a different version for myself to remember the occasion. Normally, I don't buy anything at concerts, but rumor has it this might be the last time they're on tour for a while. Even though they're a local band, it's been said the lead singer wants to take some time off to be with his family. I can't say I blame him. Family is everything.

When Sydney leads us to our seats, I'm shocked. "Wow! How did you score these seats?" I ask as we make our way down the middle of the third row back from the stage.

"Oh, I won them from a contest on campus. So, don't worry about repaying me."

"Seriously? That's pretty cool. It must've been one hell of a competition."

Sydney shrugs. "A drawing, really. Never thought I had a chance, but as luck would have it, here we are. I don't think I've ever won anything in my life. These are some freaking amazing seats."

"They sure are," I say, sitting beside her. Though, being this close to the stage, I'm fairly certain we'll stand the entire concert. "I don't think I've ever been this close to a stage in my life."

"Me neither, unless you count being in a small bar or something, and the dance floor is close to the stage. But never in a venue this large. I've been pumped since I got them."

"No kidding—I'm surprised your friends didn't want to come."

"They've seen Riser before. Besides, Chloe's priorities should be her grandma… and well, if you ever meet Abby, you'll see that she doesn't mess around when it comes to school. She's managed to graduate a year early and be accepted to a few med schools. She's still holding out for her top choice, but with her focus, I'm sure everything will work out."

Before I can respond, the opening lights dim, and the fans across the stadium shriek in welcoming the opening act. Instantly, Sydney and I are on our feet.

From the corner of my eye, I see her place her thumb and forefinger in her mouth. She lets out a whistle like no other I've heard before, then she screams to show her excitement. One thing I'm quickly learning about Sydney—with her around, it will never be boring.

As the opening chords of an electric guitar ring out, Sydney jumps in excitement. Energy fills the stadium, and everyone wants the show to begin. I'll admit, the band may be good, but I get more satisfaction in watching Sydney enjoy the show than focusing on their performance. Every dip and sway as she bops to the beat makes me need to join her. Before long, I give into my urge. When she leans into me and flashes her beaming smile, I could give two fucks about being the guy who normally doesn't dance in public. I'm here with a beautiful woman, and every fiber in my being tells me to hold on tight and enjoy the ride.

By the time the opening act ends, Sydney and I breathlessly take our seats and reach for the drinks we've set aside. Gulping down the soda, I use my forearm to push away the sweat from my brow. I can't help but notice Sydney's flushed cheeks or the way her eyes dance with excitement.

God. She's beautiful.

"What?" she asks defensively when she catches me staring a moment longer than necessary.

I go with honesty. "You're beautiful."

Her cheeks darken, and she rolls her eyes, trying to pass off my compliment. "Okay..." she draws out.

I reach out to brush a loose strand of hair behind her ear and wait until I have her attention and slowly admit, "Seriously. I'm not feeding you a line."

Sydney's eyes flit from one side to the other as if she's gauging my expression, but she doesn't say anything. Instead, she reaches out and cups my cheek, making me lean into her warm and inviting hand. I'm so focused on determining the exact shade of her green eyes, I miss her cue.

When her eyes close, and her soft lips brush against mine, I'm taken off guard and freeze—but only for a second before my body catches up. She pulls back, but I instinctually reach out and cup her face, holding it in place.

Then I kiss her back for all I'm worth.

Her lips part in a gasp, and I take this moment to invade her mouth with my tongue. I run my tongue along her lower lip, and she tastes of Pepsi and something uniquely her. When her tongue meets mine, I linger on her taste and let it consume me. We may be in a room filled with thousands of people, but in this moment, all I care about is Sydney.

Unfortunately, when a male voice introduces his band, and fans fanatically scream, I'm brought back to reality. Forcing myself to pull away, I can't help but smile at the fact we're both breathless and have lost track of where we are. A beautifully shy grin forms on her swollen lips as she stares up at me. I quickly lean in to kiss her quickly once more before resting my forehead on hers. When the first song plays, I spin her around to hold her from behind. There's no way I'm letting her go in this moment. When the first song ends, I lean in and whisper in her ear, "In case I forget to mention it, I'm having a really great time tonight."

She nods her head in return but keeps her focus on the band. When they begin their most recent number one hit, she jumps up and down, and excitement rolls off her in waves. I've heard Riser on the radio a million times over, but watching Sydney enjoy this concert is something I'll never soon forget. The way she sings nearly every lyric, dances without a care in the world, and screams when her favorite songs end will never let me hear these songs again and not relive this moment. Time ceases to exist, and I'll admit I'm shocked when they announce they're playing their final song. Of course, it's their greatest hit of all time, and even I'll admit I scream right along with Sydney as the opening progression hits its famous notes. Riser is freaking amazing in concert, and these seats force you to get lost in the experience.

My ears are still ringing as I merge my way into traffic from the parking garage. This is the only time I wish my Jeep were an automatic because having to shift in traffic forces me to let go of Sydney's hand. After a few blocks of stop and go, to let others merge into the flow of traffic with us, I've never been more relieved than to shift into overdrive and be able to reach for Sydney's hand.

She intertwines our fingers and traces my knuckles with her other hand, sending electric pulses throughout my body.

What the fuck is she doing to me?

I've never reacted to anyone like this, and I'm completely in uncharted territory. Sure, I've dated—but why do I feel as if whatever is going on with her could be so much more than the casual dates I've been on before? This is only our first date for crying out loud.

Shaking my head, I must catch Sydney's attention because she asks, "Everything okay?"

There's no way I'm jumping into this rabbit hole this early in a relationship.

Fuck... did I just say relationship? Date. We're on a date, dummy. Not making commitments or anything.

Though she did agree to a second date...

"I... Uh... am just thinking about what type of date could top this?"

Well, it's not technically a lie. I am thinking about taking her out again... I'm sure neither of us are ready to talk about what crossed my mind... stick just with safe subjects, Vince.

"This is one hell of a first date, and it will definitely be hard to top," she admits. "I honestly don't think I've ever experienced anything quite like this."

I pretend to let out a breath of air I'd been holding. "Good thing I don't have to worry about a first date again then, so the pressure is off."

When her tinkling laughter fills the car, it hits straight at my heart. Damn, I love seeing her happy.

"Whew… pressure's off," she says dramatically as she pretends to wipe her brow with her free hand. "But it does have me thinking…"

"That sounds dangerous," I tease.

"Well…" She looks up to the darkened ceiling of the car as she draws out the word. "Since you've already gotten me to agree to a second date, I *am* curious as to where you'll take me. I mean… the bar *is* set pretty high…"

"That's no pressure or anything," rolls off my tongue in the casual banter I'm learning to enjoy with her.

She doesn't disappoint. "Well… now there's these expectations…" she teases.

Trying to figure out what we could do to top this, I rack my brain for possibilities.

Unfortunately, she mistakes my silence as being offended. "You know, Vince, I really don't care what we do. I'm a pretty low-maintenance girl and don't need a lot of fanfare or to spend a lot of money to have a good time."

I squeeze her hand and quickly smile in her direction before returning my focus to the road. "I'll keep that in mind. If you must know, I was trying to find something to top this. This is by far one of the best dates I've been on and knowing I want to spend more time with you, I didn't want you to grow bored of me."

"I'm totally a just hang out and watch a movie girl, as well. So, please don't think you have to do something extravagant to impress me." I see her cringe and shake her head before she continues, "Honestly, I've been on a string of shitty dates lately. You'd just have to not be a prick, and it would already top the rest."

It sounds like there's a story but not wanting to ruin our evening, I keep it simple. "Good to know. But you can go ahead and set that bar a little higher because I have no intention of being a prick. Sometimes, I can be a dumbass because... well... I'm a guy. But I'll never intentionally be a prick. I can promise you that."

7

SYDNEY

OHMIGOD, WHY AM I TRYING TO SABOTAGE THIS PERFECT DATE? This date tops all others, and I'm sure it has nothing to do with the concert and everything to do with the guy in the driver's seat. Hell, I don't even want this night to end.

Why the hell did I tell him I basically have no standards and that he just has to *not* be a prick to make the date better than my previous ones?

Because it's true?

Shit... I have to rectify this.

"So, I have a rare Saturday night off next weekend, would you want to do something then?"

A sexy grin pulls at Vince's lips. "I think that can be arranged. Mind if we do something during the day? I should be free after one."

"That works. I work the night before and sleeping in is always welcomed."

Vince shakes his head and grunts. "I wish I could sleep in. I'll be lucky if I sleep past six tomorrow."

"Wow. That's rough." But I'm not letting him off the hook this easy. "Any idea what we'll be doing? So... I'll know how to dress—not to put any pressure on you," I tack on to clarify.

God, I probably just made things worse. Shut up already, Sydney!

"Knowing I won't be able to top third row concert tickets... what do you say we grab some lunch? But before I make any further suggestions, I need to know... are you adverse to being outdoors?"

"I'd be up to an outdoor adventure."

"I'll have to check the weather and get back to you for sure. Do you mind waiting 'til Thursday to finalize plans? Either way—just dress casually, and we'll figure something out."

He pulls into my apartment complex and finds a place to park.

Knowing I likely sound like an uptight, pretentious brat, I nod my head in agreement then try to take some pressure off him. "I'm sure we'll have fun in whatever you decide."

He turns off the engine and looks to see me better. His grin is infectious when he admits, "I *am* open to suggestions if you think of something you'd like to do. I really am a go-with-the-flow type of guy. I don't plan out every moment. So never feel like I'm putting pressure on you, okay?"

His hazel eyes are dark in this lighting, but I can make out his dimple on his cheek. His smile is sexy as hell and has me wanting to kiss him again. "I'll keep that in mind," slowly comes out as he reaches out to brush a strand of hair behind my ear.

Holy hell—I consciously have to force myself to breathe normally under his seductive gaze.

His thumb brushes my cheek, and his hand rests at the base of my neck.

I'm not sure who initiates it, but the next thing I know, the gap between us is closed, and I'm kissing him once again.

The moment our lips touch, a fire sets off inside me. Heat explodes in my body like bursts of fireworks dancing across the sky, and I just can't get enough of him. Reaching out to pull him closer, I run my fingers through his amazingly soft hair as he controls our heated kiss by guiding me from the base of my neck. Being with Vince is the perfect combination of push and pull, give and take, and each and every movement he makes has me wanting more.

But when the cabin of the car is suddenly fully lit up by an oncoming car, we pull apart, panting for our next breath of air and sadly remembering we're not really alone.

Vince runs a palm down his face as he rests his arms on the steering wheel. "I... uh... had better get you inside. It's late and while some of us may get to sleep in, I have an early day tomorrow."

The expression on his face clearly doesn't match his words, but he's right. As he gets out of the Jeep and walks slowly around the back to help me out, I gather my things from the floorboard. Taking a few deep breaths, I settle myself, so I'm prepared to meet his handsome face when he opens the door for me.

Damn, Vince is gorgeous.

Instead of reaching for my hand, Vince surprises me by stepping between my legs with his intentions clear. "I'm not done kissing you yet," he growls as he takes possession of my mouth in the most delicious way. You'd think I'd be desensitized by now, but his sexy cologne puts my senses into overdrive, and it takes every ounce of conscious effort not to wrap my legs around his body and climb him like a tree.

Damn, Vince Larson can kiss.

When another car enters the drive, I can tell it's an effort for him to stop.

When he pulls back, a sly grin fills his face as he holds out his hand. "Why don't I actually walk you to your door now. It's late and getting cold out here."

I think I could be standing in a blizzard but if this man were kissing me, I'd still be nuclear hot. But I manage to form words and agree. "Sounds good. Besides, you can kiss me again at the door." Waggling my eyebrows, I bounce down from the Jeep. Thankfully, Vince is there to steady me because my equilibrium is off-kilter, and I'm fairly certain I'm completely drunk from his kisses.

When we get to the door, it's not an awkward goodbye. When I turn to face him, he asks, "Do you mind if I call you tomorrow? I'm not sure I can wait to see you Tuesday in class." The sincerity in his tone has my heartstrings tightening.

I play it off the best I can—though I can't control my grin when I say, "I think I'd like that."

"Sounds like a plan." Vince leans in and gives me a much more controlled kiss goodbye. Before I can lose my mind completely, he manages to pull away and kiss me on the forehead. "Thanks for a wonderful evening."

"I had a great time, too."

Just then, a burst of wind picks up, causing me to finally feel the cool spring air, and I shiver involuntarily.

"Let's get you inside. I'll wait until you lock up before I leave."

I can't even remember the last time—if any has anyone cared about my safety.

Pluck, pluck, pluck—My heartstrings get pulled tighter.

Gah. What is it about this man?

With that, I step up onto my tiptoes to close the gap once more, and I kiss him briefly once more. "Thanks for an amazing evening, Vince. I'll talk to you tomorrow."

Knowing I won't want to stop if he continues to look at me the way he is, I turn and walk inside before he can say another word. I quickly turn the lock and lean my head against the door.

There's no way I'll stay on my dating diet after a night like this.

***

The next day, I'm still grinning when I think about my amazing night with Vince. As far as first dates are concerned, it was the best experience—ever. Maybe it was getting caught up with the music but the more I think about it, the more I know it had everything to do with Vince himself.

I don't even notice Abby until she sits with her bowl of cereal beside me at our kitchen table and says, "So, how was the concert?"

Where do I even begin?

"The smile plastered on your face this early in the morning

tells me you had a great time. You never did tell me, who ended up going with you?"

Not wanting her to read more into it than it is, I downplay my time with Vince. "Oh, I asked a guy from class to go. Riser was amazing, I think this was their best performance yet. They played all my favorite songs and even a few that will be on their next album. And the seats—they were freaking incredible. I've never been so close to the stage. Of course, that meant we had to stand the entire time, but it was so insane, Abby. I had the best time, though I'm sorry you weren't able to make it."

Abby sighs, shaking her head, and shrugs apologetically. "I'm sorry, too. But I'm still not sure I'm ready for this test today, and I have a ten-page paper due this afternoon, too. I'm so glad you were able to find someone to take my place."

"I get it. And not to make you jealous. But I had the best time ever last night. So, stop worrying about me having to find someone else."

"So… this guy you went with, does he have a name?" Abby teases.

"Vince."

Abby raises an eyebrow and eyes me speculatively. But I can play poker like a champ, so my feelings are clearly locked into a vault, and I'm not about to let her in… yet. Besides— things are new. When I'm ready to share more, I will.

So, she'll end her inquisition before it starts, I offer, "We went to dinner and then the concert. Unlike my recent dates, I actually had a lot of fun. But let's not make anything of it. So, how is Drew handling being in the championship tournament?"

"Apparently, he's acting as if it's just another game in the season," Abby admits. "If it were me, there's no way I'd be able to handle our workload and play ball at the same time. I'm sure I'm more nervous for him than he is."

"Somehow, I'm sure he's used to this. At least he has two weeks before the pressure's on. CRU's having an incredible season. I hope like hell they can bring home another championship!"

"You and me both." Abby laughs as her phone buzzes on the table. "That's Drew. He just finished at the gym and will be here any minute." Abby shovels what's left of her food into her mouth and quickly stands to rinse off her dish in the sink.

"The dishwasher's clean," I remind her. "Just leave it in the sink, and I'll get to it when I finish up here."

"You sure?" she asks.

"I've got class later, but I've got plenty of time. Take some cookies to Drew. There's also some cinnamon rolls in the cupboard behind you to share with him as well."

Abby's face completely falls to the point it's almost pitiful. "You mean to tell me I could've had cinnamon rolls instead of cereal? Just what kind of friend are you?"

Shrugging my apology. "I thought you'd see them. Sorry. I was out of it when you came in."

Abby scoffs, and I can't help but smile at her dramatics. "You can say that again. Next time, let me know *before* I eat cereal. You know these are my favorite. Someday, you'll admit you used to work at Cinnabon, right? I mean, who the hell can bake those even better."

Seriously, she'd be disappointed to know I baked from the time I was able to reach the stove, and I *am* using Grams' recipe. When baking's the only thing to keep your sanity, you learn to get good at it. But instead of going with the truth, I tease, "I'll never tell. Now scoot—you can't be late for the all-mighty Drew. Make sure he takes some to his poor roommate Grey. The man needs to eat something besides takeout."

Abby laughs as she calls out from the hallway. "That's what he has Drew for. It's his turn to cook tonight, so I'll likely see you tomorrow. Thanks again for the yummy goodness."

When Abby returns to the kitchen a few minutes later, she opens the snack cabinet and is relieved to see the cinnamon rolls already packed for her. "You are amazing, Syd. Love you."

When there's a knock at the door, I shoo her out of the kitchen. "Love you, too, Abs. Now get out of here."

I laugh as she juggles the containers I've packed with her to the door. Leave it to Abby to go nuts for my baking. I'm so glad I met her freshman year. She and Chloe have easily become my best friends, and I'd be lost without them.

I spend the rest of the morning studying and let's face it—trying not to daydream about Vince. I manage to finish a paper and catch up on my assigned reading for class. I breeze through my class and decide I need to work off some excess energy this afternoon, or I'll go crazy waiting to hear from Vince today.

Sure, I could call him. But I don't want to seem too eager or desperate. Besides. It'd be best to see if he's the type of guy who follows through with his word. I've had too many I've hung my hopes on—to always be the one to make the first move.

Since I have the afternoon free, instead of going to the gym, I feel the need to run on open road. I rush home, change, and zip out the door before I have the chance to dwell on wondering when Vince may call. Knowing he has work and class nearly every day during the week, I know I shouldn't expect anything until later this evening.

Just as I'm about to reach mile three of my run, I see a little girl on training wheels rounding the corner on her bike. Not seeing anyone around her, I turn off my music to check out the situation further. Within seconds, I hear, "Jules. You're supposed to stop at the corner."

She obediently stops and waits for what I assume is her parent.

Relieved she's not venturing out on her own, I stop at the corner and jog in place while I wait for the car coming up the road to pass. The girl was never in danger, but it still made me worry. She can't be more than four years old—the bike is tiny, but she seems to hardly need her training wheels as she corners on only one side of her supporting wheels. From the corner of my eye, I see her dad running up the block to catch up with her.

"Great job waiting, Jules!" her dad hollers, and I freeze.

I know that voice.

Slowly, I turn in the direction of her dad. Sure, I've been thinking of Vince all day—so I must be imagining him jogging up the road toward me. When he spots me, his grin widens, and there's no way I've conjured him in this moment. My memories aren't this crystal clear, and the full force of his grin makes my knees go weak as I'm frozen in place.

"Hey, Syd. I never expected to see you out here today."

I can't speak. I'm still shocked. I look from Vince to the girl beside us now. Then back again. Her matching eyes stare back at me expectantly. There's no doubt. This beautiful girl is definitely all Vince. She even smirks as she teases exactly like him. "I told you I'd win. I'm the fastest!" She pumps an adorable fist in the air. "I won! I won!"

Vince fist bumps her and says, "You win, squirt. Though I think it's time to get your trainers off. You're getting way too good at riding to keep these baby wheels on. You're gonna be riding like a big girl by next week, if I have anything to say about it."

When Jules realizes I'm still staring between them, she says, "Hi! I'm Julia. I'm almost four, and I'm gonna ride a big-girl bike."

I bend down to her level and wave. "Hi. I'm Sydney."

Vince looks to me apologetically. "Sorry, I was gonna call after I took her for a ride. I never expected to meet you here of all places."

Standing, I shake my head, then look back to Julia. "It's fine. Bike rides are way more important. You seem to have your hands full with this speed racer."

This makes the cutest giggle fall from Julia's lips. "Yep. I always beat him. He's *way* too slow for me."

Seeing the feign look of hurt on Vince's face as his hands cross his heart, and he pouts, "You wound me, squirt. I thought I was your favorite."

She gives him a look that clearly says *duh,* as she rolls her perfectly matched eyes to him. "Who else will teach me to ride a big-girl bike?"

I can't help but snicker at her cuteness, though I do my best to cover it with a cough. She must look a lot like her mom as she has lighter hair and complexion. It's clear she gets her playful attitude and eyes from Vince. Like him, she's beautiful.

Vince gets my attention by reaching out and squeezing my hand. Just like last night, my nerve endings zing to life and react to his presence. "Will you be around later?"

Not expecting his question, I just stare.

Julia interrupts by asking, "Can I ride to the next driveway?"

Vince nods and says, "Be sure to stop," as I continue staring at their interaction.

Then he focuses his beautiful eyes on me, and I'm still at a loss for words.

"Syd? Everything okay?"

Shaking my head and remembering I need to answer him in words, I say, "Yeah. I'll be around."

He points in the direction of his tiny tot trekking away. "I'd better catch up with her. I'll give you a call later tonight."

He leans in and kisses my cheek before running off in the direction of Julia.

All I can do is stare in their direction. I watch them until I can't see them any longer as one thought runs through my mind on repeat.

Holy shit. Vince is a father.

8

SYDNEY

"Vince is a father," I repeat to Chloe for the millionth time as I pace across our living room.

"So it seems," Chloe calmly states as if she's trying to pacify me or talk me off the ledge. I'm still not sure what her true agenda is. Frankly, I don't care.

"Holy fucking shit. How could he not tell me he has a kid?"

"Syd, you've been on one date with the guy. Yeah—from what you've told me, it was pretty epic. But it wasn't exactly conducive to spilling his whole life's story. Besides, a lot of single parents don't share the fact they have kids on the first date. Most just want you to get to know them before they introduce you to their family. He's young, and if she's nearly four, he's probably not had that much experience finding someone who wouldn't run screaming in the opposite direction when she found out he had a kid."

"Why do you have to make sense?" I whine. But he still

could've told me. "This is a pretty big bomb he dropped on the street corner. And with her being there, it's not like I could confront him or anything. Besides, what would I say? So—you have a kid? Okay, Captain Obvious. What the fuck do I do now?"

"You *could* hear him out," Chloe suggests in her annoyingly sensible tone. "He's likely still getting her dinner and getting her ready for bed, and you'll hear from him later."

Thank God, Chloe had been walking in the door when I got home; I'd be pacing a hole in the carpet or baking myself to death if she hadn't been here to talk me through this.

"Speaking of dinner," she adds. "Do you want to grab something to eat? I'm starving and haven't eaten since breakfast. Let's go to that diner on the other side of town that Abby always talks about. We can talk away from the college crowd and hopefully, by the time we're through eating, he'll call, or you'll have a plan of action, so you can get out of your head and go on with your night. I know you, Syd. You're not gonna let this go—until you get to the bottom of it."

"I'd call him. But I know he needs to be with his daughter right now, not dealing with my freak-out over the fact he has a fucking kid."

I pace to the other side of the room and turn before returning to where Chloe sits patiently on the couch. "Hell, Chloe, I don't even know if I like kids." I had a shit father growing up and haven't even given any thoughts to having kids. I've been so hell bent on getting out of my situation, I'd never thought that far ahead.

But why am I contemplating having kids? I've been on *one*

date with this guy. It's not like I'm gonna marry him or anything. Hell, at this rate, I doubt we'll even make it to a second date.

Chloe interrupts with, "Are you really being fair to him, Syd? It's not like he planned to meet you and hit off. One date without telling you his entire life's story—is hardly the epitome of evil. He's young and from the sounds of it, still a great guy—who happens to have a kid. Maybe he hasn't found the right girl yet?"

When I shoot daggers in her direction, she defensively puts her hands up and surrenders. "Hey, all I'm saying is give the guy a chance. In the meantime, let's get something to eat. I'm starving. I'll even buy."

I'm so rattled, I'm sure I'll hardly be able to eat, but knowing I'll go crazy if left on my own, I agree. I quickly change out of my running clothes into a pair of leggings and a sweatshirt, throw my hair into a messy bun, and meet her in the living room within minutes.

When we walk into the diner, the smell of delicious food makes me hungrier than I'd realized. I manage to go through the motions of ordering, but I can't get my mind off the situation with Vince.

In an attempt to distract myself, I ask Chloe how her weekend with her family went. Thankfully, this tactic works because she tells me about how her Uncle Marvin, who happens to be her grandma's older brother wouldn't stop pouring them wine. I actually find myself laughing.

"I'm not kidding, Syd. My glass never emptied and the next thing I knew, I had the biggest buzz going. I was dumbfounded and seriously had no idea how it happened. It was the first time I've ever been drunk around my family, and I felt guilty. Of course, I pretended as if I wasn't three sheets to the wind and got philosophical. My cousin got it on video and showed me the next day—then said he felt guilty for not warning me about Marvin's heavy hand with the bottles of wine. Apparently, it's a rite of passage, and everyone waits until he has his next unsuspecting youth in front of him to see how far he can take things."

Holy shit—remind me to never drink with her family. I don't even know what to say with that one. Thankfully, I don't have to respond because she quickly continues, "Can you believe my freaking family actually took bets for the type of things I would do? They're jackasses—the whole lot of them. Good God!" she says, shaking her head. "At least I have some self-control and cut myself off and was only drinking wine. Can you imagine if it had been margaritas or something like that? You know what tequila does to me."

Yes. Yes, I do. I attempt to hide my smile by placing a hand over my mouth, but Chloe sees right through me.

"It was one time," she protests. "You know I love old country music, and I was just following lyrics in the music. Tequila *does not* make my clothes come off..." she practically shouts and draws the attention of the crowd around us.

As Chloe turns beet red, she sinks further into the booth we're sitting at then whisper shouts, "Do you think anyone heard me?"

I take a moment to examine the diner and unfortunately have to nod. "Yeah, I think they did. But don't worry. It's not like we frequent here or anything," I tease—but in reality, maybe it's only the younger couple next to us.

Just as I'm certain she's in the clear, I have the strangest sensation roll through my spine, and the hairs on the back of my neck stand on end. Before I can put any thought to it, the door jingles and Julia comes running into the diner.

I'm frozen in place, and Chloe instantly is on alert. "What? Did I really make that big of a scene?"

I just stare as Julia prances right up to our waitress and throws herself at her. "Momma, I missed you!"

Our waitress bends down to scoop her into her arms. "I've missed you, too, Jules. How was your day?" She looks around the restaurant, I'm sure looking for Vince—but he has yet to show his face.

"Holy shit," I mumble.

"What?" Chloe cues into the fact that my attention is on the scene playing out in front of me. "What am I missing?"

"Uh... that's Julia." I nod in their direction, trying not to be obvious.

Thankfully, Chloe has the sense to not make a scene. But before I can process anything further, Vince makes his appearance.

He walks right up to Julia and her mother and greets our waitress with a huge smile. "How's it going, Van? You'd better not pick up an extra shift tomorrow because I promised Jules we'd take off her training wheels. You're not gonna want to miss it."

Van's eyes widen in surprise, but she ruffles her daughter's hair. "Seriously? Where's the pause button when you need it?"

Then she tickles her daughter who is still in her arms. "You need to stop growing up so quick, little miss."

This causes Julia to giggle. "Silly, Momma. I'm a big girl now. I need to ride without baby wheels."

"Yeah, Van. She's a big girl now," Vince singsongs. "We've gotta let her grow up sometime."

Watching their family's interaction rips me to shreds.

A thousand emotions flood my senses all at once, and it's all I can do not to bolt from the room. Chloe captures my attention by placing a hand on mine to hold me in place.

"Things aren't always what they seem," she whispers.

"I… I gotta get out of here. They clearly *are* a family, and I feel like shit for getting involved with him in the first place. But what's worse is he's just the typical ass who's also a cheater. God, I think I'm gonna be sick."

"Syd," Chloe calls after me as I bolt from the booth. Rushing past Vince and his family to the door, I burst through it gasping for fresh air. I haven't even eaten yet, but I feel like I'm about to lose whatever is left in my stomach.

Running across the parking lot, I spot bushes that could hide my evidence. I may be having a shit day, but no need to ruin someone else's evening.

Thankfully, by the time I get to said bushes, all I need to do is catch my breath. Placing my hands on my knees, I bend over and gulp in air as fast as my body will let me.

When I hear footsteps behind me, I swat my hand in the air to let Chloe know I'm okay and just need space. "I'm fine, Clo. Just go and enjoy your meal. I'll come back in a minute. Or better yet, I'll just walk home. I need some time to think."

"What do you need time to think about?" comes from the

sexy voice I've thought about all day—but didn't do him justice at all. Even from those few words, I can tell they're laced with concern.

Why the fuck is he concerned about me?

Turning on my heels, I glare at the culprit for all my mixed-up emotions.

"What are you doing here?" I seethe.

9

VINCE

THE MOMENT I SPOT SYDNEY RUSHING OUT OF THE RESTAURANT like a bat out of hell, I know something's wrong. Without giving Vanessa any explanation, I quickly mutter, "Can you get Jules settled? I need to go check on something."

Of course, my sister's gonna grill me for all I'm worth when I return, but I'll deal with that later. Something's wrong with Sydney, and I need to make sure she's okay.

I watch her sprint across the parking lot and stop in front of the hedge along the fence. She's bending over as if she's about to be sick, and I know with every fiber of my being that I need to be there for her.

When she mistakes me as her friend Chloe, I'm almost amused. Clearly, she has no idea I've followed her out. Maybe she didn't even see me in her haste to leave. But when she says she needs time to think, I'm utterly confused.

Especially when she spins around and glares at me as if I've just murdered her favorite puppy.

Holding my hands up in defense, I do my best to defuse the situation. "Whoa… What's going on?"

She's pissed.

Her eyes narrow as she takes in a deep breath.

Her fists ball up, like they did at my buddy Derek. But this time, I'm fairly certain she's gonna let me have it.

Holy shit. What the hell did I do?

When she points an index finger, she nearly pokes me in the chest as she enunciates each and every word in my direction. "What are *you* doing out here with me? *You* should be inside with your family."

Without thinking, I blurt out, "Why would I be in there with them when you're clearly upset?"

"I'm not *that* type of girl, Vincent Daniel Larson."

Okay… she's using my full name. I have no fucking clue where her rage is coming from. Clearly, she thinks I've wronged her, and I'm getting to the bottom of this.

"Exactly what kind of girl am I supposed to think you are?"

"I don't break up families." She practically spits in my direction.

"Uh… I never thought you would," I clarify.

"Then what's going on in there?" She points to the diner where I see her friend getting a front row seat of this spectacle from the window.

"Van had to work an unexpected shift, so I brought Julia here for dinner?" I ask, trying to see what this fuss is about.

She takes a long, slow breath as if she's trying to keep from telling me how she really feels. "So, Van's still pretty much in the picture then, I take it?"

"Uh… of course. She's Julia's mom. But what does that have to do with you and me?"

Sydney blanches as if I've just slapped her across the face. *Which for the record, I'd never do—even if I do think she's off her rocker at the moment.*

Before I can contemplate her mental stability, she launches another question at me, "So… do you like co-parent with her?"

"I guess you could say that. I transferred schools to help her out, and we do live together, so yeah—we co-parent."

"Let me get this straight." Sydney takes a long breath to steady herself as she's clearly getting worked up. "You. Live. With. Her?" comes out on each breath as if it physically pains her to complete her thought.

Wait—Why would it matter if I live with her?

"Oh." Oh, shit. No—she couldn't think that.

But the venom in her voice and the death stare that could kill me on the spot says otherwise.

Oh, fuck. Talk about misconceptions.

I can't help the smirk that forms as the last piece of this crazy-ass puzzle falls into place. "Do you think I'm dating Vanessa?"

Something I've said must give her pause. Because her expression morphs from being irate to complete confusion. "Aren't you?"

Oh, shit. She thinks Julia's my daughter. It takes every ounce of effort I have not to let my lips form a smile.

But I can't let her get off that easy. "No. That would be weird."

"Weird? I've seen it for myself. Julia has your eyes, and she called Vanessa Momma? Are you just co-parenting?"

"Yes—we are co-parenting. But I think there might be another important question you might wanna ask me first?"

Her tone turns defensive as she punches her fists into her hips. "Really? What's that?"

Damn, this woman when she's angry. Now that I know I'm not at fault, I appreciate her beauty. Her green eyes are darkened with fury, and her skin is flushed from her frustration. She'd clearly rip off my balls and feed them to me if she thought I'd cheat on her.

"Well—for starters—maybe I'd start with *What's your relationship to Julia?*"

I wait for that to sink in.

She loses some of her fight, but I can still see her holding onto the fury she's worked up about. "But you live with Vanessa? You just told me that."

"You still haven't asked the important question," I point out.

Oh, Sydney, you have no idea how stubborn I can be. Two can play this game.

She huffs out a breath of air, "Fine. What is your relationship to Julia?"

"Finally, we're getting somewhere. I'm so glad you asked, Sydney. You've already met my niece. But if we go back inside," as I point to the diner where we have quite a crowd watching —well, at least Chloe, Vanessa, and Julia are prying at the window, "I'll introduce you to my *twin sister* Vanessa."

She opens her mouth to speak, then immediately clamps it shut. Then opens it again—but no words come out. Now that I'm removed from the anger and defense, I find it downright comical, and I can't control the laughter that bubbles from deep inside me.

When I get myself back in control, I pin Sydney on the spot—so there are no more misconceptions. "For the record, I'm not into incest, and I've never cheated on anyone. And—the only type of green I enjoy seeing from you is in the form of your beautiful eyes. What do you say, Syd? Can you put your claws away and come meet my sister?"

Staring at the pavement below us, she shakes her head. "I think it might be best if I just walk home now."

"Now why would you go and do a thing like that?" She lives miles from here, and I'm sure she has a meal waiting on her to finish.

She crosses her arms and kicks a rock from under her feet.

So, I wait.

And wait.

When I realize this stubborn woman is attempting to outwait me, I step closer. I hear her take a deep breath in—but still nothing.

With a finger, I reach out and touch her chin and wait for her eyes to meet mine. Finally, when I have her full attention, I ask, "Why do you feel like you need to walk home?"

Her eyes drift to our audience and then back to mine. "Because I've clearly read the situation wrong and made a fool of myself."

"Naw... you haven't made a fool of yourself. Sure, you read the situation wrong, but I'm at fault for not taking the time to properly introduce you to Julia this afternoon."

Eating crow does not look good on Sydney, but she's

already been forgiven. Besides, Vanessa's going to die when she hears this.

"How can you be so calm and reasonable? I just completely freaked out on you, made assumptions that clearly made me an ass, and accused you of being a cheater." By the end, her voice is barely above a whisper, and her lower lip is trembling.

Fuck, I can't handle her being upset like this. Reaching for her hand, I pull her close and wrap my arms around her in a hug. Her head leans against my chest and her messy bun tickles my chin. So, I readjust us and hug her fiercely. "It's okay, Syd. You have nothing to be embarrassed over."

"But..." she starts but I cut her off.

"Syd. All this did was prove that even though we've only known each other a short time, I somehow matter to you. If you just thought I was some prick, you clearly wouldn't have given two shits about the fact that I'd potentially been a cheater. I'm sure you would've told me off or just never spoke to me again. You also wouldn't have been this upset over the fact that you ran into me."

"I didn't want to like you..." she whispers.

I chuckle. I can't help it—besides—what can I say to that?

"Well, that's good to know—but I'm pretty sure you've just proven otherwise," I tease.

Sydney pulls back from our hug, rolling her eyes. "You're never gonna let me live this down, are you?"

"Probably not," I admit.

Leaving one arm around her, I turn and look toward the diner. "Would you mind having dinner with me and a very entertaining three-year-old? Or, if that's too much pressure, I can sit awkwardly across the diner and watch you from across the room—wait—that sounds stalkerish. Scratch that. I can just pretend to ignore you from afar."

"Okay, wise ass." And the spunk is back. "I think I can handle dinner with a three-year-old. Though fair warning. I'm an only child and know nothing about kids."

"Just remember—she can sense fear—and most certainly will take advantage," I tease as we walk to the diner.

When we enter, I see Vanessa's brows raise into her hairline with a clear message of *Everything okay*? Even without being her twin, I'm sure anyone who's watching could make out that thought.

Taking Sydney's hand, I walk to where Julia and Vanessa are standing. "Hey, Jules, do you mind if we eat at my friend Sydney's booth tonight?"

She slowly looks Sydney over with care. "Sure, Unks. She's pretty. She has hair the color of Merida, but her hair isn't curly. Can I still get mac n' cheese with bwroccoli?"

Glancing at Sydney, I smile when her eyes widen. But I direct my focus to my sister. "Hey, Van, this is Sydney. Sydney, *this* is my *sister* Vanessa."

Vanessa doesn't miss a beat. She reaches out her hand to shake Sydney's. "It's nice to meet you. I'll be right back with place settings for these two if they're joining you."

"That would be great." Sydney smiles and turns her attention to Julia. "My friend Chloe's sitting right over there. Want to join us?"

Chloe's waving to Julia, welcoming us all.

Since Sydney's food is already on the other side of the booth from her, Chloe scoots further into the booth and asks,

"Hey, Julia, wanna sit with me. I'd love to have someone draw with me." Chloe reaches for the cup of crayons near the window and turns over her placemat.

"Can I use blue? It's my faborite," she says in the cutest tone ever. Her Vs and Rs are difficult to say, but she tries to sound so grown up. Yeah. I'm biased, I know, but Jules is adorable when she puts on the charm.

As Sydney scoots into the booth, I take a seat beside her, mentally wanting to hug Chloe for taking charge of this situation. "Thanks for letting us crash your evening," I offer.

"No problem at all," Chloe says as she draws alongside Julia. "I'm just glad the two of you seemed to sort things out."

Sydney shakes her head as she fidgets with her hands under the table. To put her at ease, I reach over and grab her hand to hold it on her lap. She squeezes it once to reassure that she's okay. "It was a big misunderstanding with a lot of assumption on my part. But I think it's been sorted."

"Let's hope so," I interject before anyone can say anything. "Though when you think about it, it's kind of funny. Van's going to get a kick out of it when I tell her later." Sydney's eyes dart to me and widen in shock as her cheeks darken, making her freckles stand out. Immediately, I backpedal. "What? Too soon?"

Her grimace is freaking adorable, and I don't even attempt hiding my smile.

"Maybe for the moment," she mutters. "Gah... I so jumped to conclusions."

"It's over. Let's move on," I remind her then turn my attention to Chloe. "You two should eat before your dinner gets cold. I called ahead for our order, so we shouldn't have to wait much longer."

"Yeah. Momma works here and always gets our food, fast," Julia pipes in.

"That must be nice." Chloe smiles. "Do either of you want some of my fries while we wait?"

I know she's offered it to both of us, but I'm sure it's more for Julia's sake than mine. Julia doesn't disappoint as she eagerly bobs her head and says, "Yeah."

"Yes, please?" I remind her.

"Yes, pwease." She sighs in my direction, then gives a megawatt smile to Chloe. I'm sure it has everything to do with the fry in her hand. I clearly see where Unks rates in this situation with her new best friend.

Moments later, Vanessa brings out my French dip sandwich with fries and Julia's mac n' cheese with a heaping side of broccoli. "Anything else I can get you all?"

The girls each mutter a version of I'm good, and I shake my head in my answer. Then I ask, "Are you still getting off soon?"

"Yeah, that's the plan. If you want, I'll take Jules when she's finished. I should be done in about fifteen minutes. Then we'll meet you at home."

"Have you eaten?" Sydney asks. "You're welcome to join us."

"Oh, I ate on my break about an hour ago. But thanks for asking." Another customer waves down her attention. "It was great meeting you. I'll be back in a few, Jules. Make sure you eat up and not talk the ears off Unks' friends."

"Momma..." Jules rolls her eyes, clearly meaning *duh*. God

help us when she's a teenager. Van's gonna have her hands full with this one.

With the four of us digging into our food, there isn't much time for conversation. Sure, Julia chatters from time to time about random things the way three year olds do, but neither Sydney nor Chloe are bothered by it.

As if she'd been watching from afar, Vanessa shows up to get Julia just as she finishes. "You ready to go, squirt?"

"But I'm having fun with Cw-oie. Can't we stay a bit longer?" she pleads with Van.

"It's okay, Julia. I've actually got to get going, too. I'll even walk out with you." Then she turns to me. "Vince, do you mind taking Sydney home? You have a car, right?"

"Yes, I have a car," I draw out as I look to take a direction from Sydney.

When she shrugs, I take it as a cue she's fine with this plan. I'm sure there's still a few things we should talk about to make sure we've cleared the air, but I don't like the idea of forcing myself on her either.

The minute everyone leaves, Sydney mutters, "Well, that wasn't planned."

"Did you want to leave with her?" Shit. Did I read her wrong?

She shakes her head. "I swear they orchestrated this. It just felt too convenient that everyone leaves at once—leaving us alone." Then she gazes at me to read my expression as she quickly tacks on, "Not that I'm complaining."

I feel the smile pull up at my lips as I try to remain stoic. "Well, at least we got one thing out of the way tonight."

She cocks a beautifully shaped eyebrow up at me. "You mean the fact that I no longer think you're married with a kid?"

"You did not think I was married," I accuse with a scoff.

"Well... it wasn't out of the realm of possibilities. I mean we've just met and barely know one another. I also read a lot of romantic suspense—so my imagination can run wild when it wants to."

"Thanks for the warning," I deadpan—which earns a giggle from her.

"But seriously, Syd, let's make a deal. If you have questions —you come to me. You don't let them rattle around in that beautiful brain of yours and jump to unnecessary conclusions. I'm not one to hide things from people. Though truth be told —there's a lot more to my backstory that you're going to need time to shake out. I can't have all the skeletons coming out of my closet at once. A man's gotta have some things to reveal later—or what'd be the fun of gettin' to know one another?"

"I think I can handle that," Sydney says with a smirk. "Though fair warning—I've got plenty of secrets of my own."

This earns her a deep belly laugh from me.

Damn. It'll be fun unravelling her. With her sass, I'm sure she'll keep me on my toes.

"So, does this mean we're past our first fight?" I ask, leaning closer to her.

She responds with a tinkling laugh. "I guess it does."

"Good. Then let's get out of here, so we can go make up."

"Really?" She smirks. "And what exactly does that entail?"

"I'm fairly new to this—but I'm pretty certain it'll involve a bit of kissing."

With that, I stand, drop enough bills to cover our meal, and reach for her hand. "Are you ready to kiss and make up?"

The look on her face is one I don't think I'll ever forget.

10

SYDNEY

HOLY SHIT. THE MOMENT VINCE GETS ME AWAY FROM THE crowded diner and in the privacy of his Jeep, he kisses me for all I'm worth. My toes curl, and my ovaries practically explode from my body with the passion of this kiss alone. He could've had a million different responses to my overreacting, but no—he kept me on my toes and handled me better than anyone I know.

Most guys don't see the ticking time bomb before I ignite, but Vince saw it coming from a mile away and defused the situation by respectfully putting me in my place. Sure, he let me rant and get what I needed off my chest, but he also didn't make me feel like an ass for being such a total bitch and jumping to conclusions either.

Then he played it off, like he got some satisfaction of wanting to kiss and make up. If this is how he handles things, I might have to provoke him more often.

Not really—but damn, the man can kiss.

When he finally pulls back, the grin on his face is infectious. "FYI—for the future, I'm not so keen on the pissing you off part, but I have no problems with making up."

He runs his palm down his face and turns to start the engine—while I'm left utterly speechless.

Is he some kind of mind reader, too?

Neither of us say a word as Vince pulls out of the parking lot and heads toward campus. My mind spins a million miles a minute, and I'm having the hardest time latching on to a thought long enough to voice it aloud.

After a few blocks, Vince breaks the silence with, "Do you need to be home right away?"

I shake my head but realize since he's driving, he needs to hear the words. "No."

"Mind if we go for a drive? I'm a little amped up and would love a quick trip up the gorge."

Not wanting our time together to end just yet, I easily agree, "Sure. Sounds good."

He drives us out of town along the Columbia River to an unknown destination. The road is intermittently lined with trees and every now and then, I catch a beautiful glimpse of the river as the sun sets behind us. As Vince expertly maneuvers us through the twists and turns of the road, he must be at a point where he no longer needs to shift, because he reaches over and places a hand on my thigh. Liking the way it feels, I instinctually put my hand over his to keep it in place.

"You know, Syd, I do feel bad that you were upset by something I could've easily avoided."

"Everyone has a past, Vince. I can't expect to know everything all at once," I remind him.

"True." He's quiet for an unusual amount of time. When he finally breaks the silence, his tone is rougher than I expect and laced with emotion. "So, you won't get the wrong idea about me, there's a lot of things that are hard for me to talk about. But please just ask, rather than jump to conclusions, okay?"

"Of course," I whisper loud enough for him to hear as I squeeze his hand. "Please know I typically don't fly off the handle. But there are a few non-negotiables for me. Cheating and deadbeat dads are two things I just can't handle."

Vince clears his throat as he removes his hand from my leg to downshift around a sharp corner. Once we're back up to speed, his hand returns to my thigh, and I resume holding it. "Well, those are two things you can be certain I'll never be. I've watched firsthand what's happened to Vanessa and Julia—in the deadbeat dad scenario—though that's a story for another day. I also don't believe in cheating. If you're contemplating it —there's no point in staying with that person. Your relationship is already doomed. So, you may as well cut bait."

"Wow—so women are like fish to you? Do you think they go bad after three dates or something?" I have no idea where that came from once it's out. My free hand flies to my mouth to keep from saying something more.

What the hell is wrong with me?

Thankfully, my sass only makes Vince fill the cabin with a low chuckle. "I've never heard the saying go quite like that… but something tells me after three dates, I likely won't tire of you."

Great—now we're planning our third date. *What the hell happened to my dating diet?* But the thought of *not* getting to know Vince better also feels wrong. My stomach literally drops at the thought and suddenly feels as if it's filled with lead. No—as long as Vince is around, I'm pretty certain I won't be sticking to that diet.

Of course, I can't let him know that. He already thinks I'm a nutcase and extremely reactionary. "What makes you think we'll be going on that third date? You haven't even made it to our second."

He tilts his head and agrees with a nod. "True. But if you consider dinner and hanging out a date—we technically *are* in the middle of our second—but maybe it's just technically me crashing your plans."

"I'd hardly say you crashed my plans," I deadpan.

"Hold that thought," Vince says as he exits the road unexpectedly, stopping at a convenience store. Of course, this forces me to grip the oh-shit handle as we hit a few potholes I'm sure my Honda would be sunk into.

When he brings the Jeep to a stop, he looks over with a shit-eating grin. "Quick, what's your favorite flavor of ice cream?"

"What?" I ask, not having a fucking clue why he suddenly plummeted into the parking lot.

With pleading eyes, he's determined. "Give me your top two if you can't decide."

"Uh, butter pecan or caramel caribou," I mutter, shaking my head.

"Great. Be right back. I'll keep the Jeep running—so lock it when I leave."

"Okay..." I draw out. But before I can say another word, Vince bolts out of the vehicle and darts into the store. I see him walk to the back of the store and return to the counter to pay for his purchase.

He returns with a bag and a beaming grin. He doesn't say anything but puts his seat belt on and pulls back onto the highway. Just when I can't take in any longer, he pulls into a scenic view of the gorge. He puts the Jeep in gear and sets the emergency brake to ensure we're in park, then hops out.

What the hell is he doing now?

When the back of the Jeep opens, I hear him ask, "You getting out?"

"It's practically dark out here. Where exactly are we going?"

"Trust me," he says as he slams the back door.

Are those the famous last words heard by every serial killer's victim?

I glance around the empty parking lot and see that we're alone, and there's only a few minutes left of daylight. When he opens my door and reaches over me to get the bag from the store, of course, all I can do is stare at him as my wheels spin trying to figure out his plan.

"Where's your sense of adventure, Syd?"

Now that I look him over, I see he's holding a blanket in one hand and the bag in the other. "Where's your shovel?"

He looks to his blanket and bag in his hand. "Haha. There's no light pollution here and if you get out, you'd see there's a million stars showing at the moment. We can sit on the hood of my Jeep and lean against the windshield. I even brought dessert…" He waggles his eyebrows as he holds up the bag. "And… I'll let you choose."

"Okay… you've got me. What do I get to choose?" I'm the

worst at being kept in the dark. I hop out of the Jeep, and somehow Vince catches me when I wobble on the uneven ground, even with his hands full.

As soon as I'm steady on my feet, he hands me the bag with a warning. "Hold this for just a sec. Once we get settled, you can see your surprise."

Even though it's almost dark, I see his eyes dance with mischief. He expertly unzips the blanket in a bag he's holding and spreads it across the hood. Of course, the hood of his Jeep is nearly up to my shoulders, so I ask, "Exactly how do you expect me to get up there? The beached-whale look isn't good on me, I promise."

Without a word, Vince takes the bag from my hands and sets it in the middle of the blanket. Then his hands quickly land on my waist as he lifts me like I don't weigh nearly one hundred and forty pounds. With my ass firmly on the hood of his Jeep, he says, "Get comfortable. I'll come up from the other side."

Instead of lying against the windshield with my legs in front of me, I pull them in, sitting crisscross, and face the view of the river below and an infinite number of stars above me. The sky's a dark shade of purple, and you can see boats low below us on the water. With the sun setting behind us, the stars are more vibrant in this direction.

Vince effortlessly hoists himself onto the hood of his Jeep, as if he's been doing this for years and even though it's cool, my body heats the closer he gets. Like a kid on Christmas morning, he eagerly digs into the bag he's brought us.

"I managed to find caramel caribou and praline pecan. Which do you prefer?" He pulls out two pints of ice cream and two spoons wrapped in plastic. "I'm sure this would be better in the summer, but we'll improvise. If you get too cold, we can hop back in the Jeep. But it's a rare clear night, so I thought we could make this an official date—by having dessert. I have an extra jacket in the back if you need it, too."

I've got a long-sleeved shirt under this hoodie. "I should be good for a while. I'll take the caramel," I say as I reach out my hand for the pint he's holding out for me.

Setting the container on the blanket beside me, I work to take off the lid. Taking a heaping dollop, I moan in pleasure of the caramel goodness.

"That good, huh?" Vince asks as he takes a bite of his own treat.

"Ice cream is my weakness. I'll never refuse it. Especially if caramel's involved."

"Good to know. So... are we considering this a second date now?" Vince teases after scooping some for himself.

I look around us, pretending to contemplate my response. "I suppose so. Though if we're ever asked, we're saying it started from here. No need to mention my mental episode."

"Stop." Vince's tone is stern, catching me off guard. Immediately, I'm frozen in place as my eyes lock onto his. Once he's sure he has my attention, he continues, "If the shoe was on the other foot, I would've jumped to the same conclusions. Let's put it behind us and focus on something else." He looks up to the sky for a moment before asking, "Tell me... what was it like living in Eastern Washington growing up? Were you able to see the stars better than this?"

"Well, I grew up in a town where I actually remember when the first traffic light went in—if that tells you something." Honestly, I couldn't wait to leave– but it had more to do with my family than the town itself. But instead of going down that rabbit hole, I get back to his question at hand. "Let's see... If you went ten minutes out of town, you could see the stars for what felt like a million miles in every direction. One thing I miss about living there was experiencing all four seasons each year. That's something you don't get here at CRU. Summers are hot and winters are cold—but it's dry—so it doesn't seem as extreme."

Vince nods in the darkness. "That makes sense. What was it like growing up as an only child?"

He remembered that small tidbit. Hmmm... "I don't really know any other way. Mom had to work a lot to make ends meet—so I stayed with my grams. Since I was her only grandchild, we spent our time in the kitchen—that's where I learned to bake."

"That had to be amazing. My grandparents lived on the East Coast, so we only got to see them occasionally growing up before they passed. Speaking of baking..." he trails off then lowers his voice conspiratorially, "though I probably shouldn't admit this, I completely devoured those cookies today. Your efforts paid off. Your grandma must've been phenomenal in the kitchen because I would gain about a hundred pounds if I had you baking for me like that every day."

"Oh, I don't bake every day... trust me. Usually it's just when I'm stressed or bored." I shrug in response.

"Okay—so baking's more therapeutic. I'll keep that in mind. Though I certainly hope it's for boredom than stress. Either way, if you're looking for someone to consume said treats, I volunteer as tribute."

"Okay—be honest. Did you read the book or just watch the movie?"

Vince's hand flies to his chest, and his eyes widen in shock. "You wound me. Of course, I read the books. My parents wouldn't let us watch any movie that had been made from a book, without reading them first. And truth be told—books are always better."

Exactly! "A man after my own heart. I have yet to watch a movie that was better than the book—even if I've loved the movies."

"No kidding. I loved Woody Harrelson in the *Hunger Games* though. I've always been a fan but was shocked by his performance."

"I completely agree. Tell me, what was it like growing up as a twin?"

"Like you, I wouldn't know it any other way. Vanessa managed to beat me into the world by a whole seven minutes. A fact she never has let me forget, even though I've always been bigger than her. We were always there for one another— kinda like built-in best friends. Even when we would fight which, trust me, we did as kids, we've always been there for one another. She's still my best friend."

"That's amazing. I always wished for a sibling, but I wanted them to be older, so, of course, that never was possible. But when I got older, I was glad to be on my own, life would've been crazy with more kids for my mom."

"Are you close with your mom?" Vince asks with interest.

"Well... we get along, but when I left to attend CRU, she took the opportunity to enjoy her newfound freedom. She's currently traveling with her new boyfriend around the country, so I haven't actually seen her much."

Vince stares at me for a long moment but doesn't say anything.

To keep things from becoming awkward or to have him feel sorry for me, I quickly tack on, "Don't worry, we weren't all that close to begin with. I was an unexpected surprise for her, so I feel like I owe her this sense of freedom. I love my mom, but when this opportunity came knocking, I encouraged her to take it. With Grams passing away before I left for college, she had nothing keeping her in our small town. She's traveling with her boyfriend who's an in-demand consultant for a tech security firm. She works part time as his assistant, which is how they met. They travel along the Eastern Seaboard as often as their jobs require it."

Vince's tone is thick and filled with emotion as he whispers, "I'm sorry for your loss. It's hard to lose someone you love."

"I miss Grams every day, but she's in a better place. Cancer overtook the last year of her life. It was brutal. Unfortunately, she was stubborn and waited too long before seeing a doctor. By the time she was diagnosed, it had already progressed too far. I was with her until the very end. I know without a doubt she's looking down with a smile on her face. I'm reaching the goals she helped me set, and I'm in a better place because of her efforts."

Vince takes a long, steadying breath as his gaze drifts to the water below us. With the light fading by the second, it's hard to read his expression. When he remains silent longer than what I can handle, panic sets in.

God, I suck at dating.

Vince is the first guy I've actually liked and have been willing to let know the real me. I hadn't meant to get onto such a heavy topic, but for some reason, Vince has me opening like a sunflower on a warm summer day.

What is it about him that's so different?

When I can't take the berating in my head any longer, I place a hand on his shoulder and ask, "You okay?"

Shaking his head as if to clear his thoughts, he returns his focus to me. "Yeah. Sorry. I guess I got lost in my head for a bit."

"It's okay," I assure him. "Please know I'm doing much better now, and this isn't a sad subject for me."

Vince's dark eyes pin me in place. "I *am* sorry about your loss. But as you're clearly okay with it, let's focus on happier things—since this is our second date after all."

He says it with a straight face, but his tone clearly turns playful at the end, and I can't help but match his newfound mood. "Sure. Let's save the heavy stuff for later."

"Deal," he agrees as he takes another bite of ice cream.

11

SYDNEY

TRUE TO HIS WORD, VINCE AND I ENJOYED THE REST OF OUR date last night. As I walk to our shared class, my thoughts run over our conversation. Though I'd never admit it, I'm eager to see him again. I love how easily our conversation flowed after we agreed to keep things light. We chatted about anything and everything under the sun. I learned that he used to play in a garage band in high school, though he claims he wasn't any good, but it was his lame attempt to meet girls—of course, this had me laughing in disbelief.

Knowing what he looks like now, I can't imagine how any girl wouldn't have been into him just a few years ago. Vince has this charismatic charm and sexy swagger about him. He has to know the effect he has on women, right? I could just picture him playing his guitar. Unfortunately, he refused to sing for me last night, so the jury's still out on whether or not he has any talent.

When my eyes land on his beautiful form, the bounce in

my steps accelerate to close the gap between us. I can tell the moment he spots me because his face morphs to a beautiful smile in greeting.

Damn. He is hot.

"Hey, Syd." He leans in and kisses me on the cheek. "How's your day?"

Better now that you're here. "It's been a typical Tuesday. Thankfully, my professors haven't given too much additional homework, and the time flew by."

"That's always a good day. Jules was up before five thirty this morning, so it's been long for me. I hope I didn't keep you out too late last night."

Shaking my head as we make our way to our seats. "Naw. I'm used to living off five or six hours of sleep. I enjoyed our impromptu date last night—so you won't hear me complaining. But I didn't have to be up at the ass-crack of dawn. So—I'm sorry for your lack of sleep."

"I'd much rather spend time with you than sleep." He shrugs as if he didn't just say the sweetest thing ever. "Have you given any thought as to where you'd like to go on date three?"

"Honestly, I'm good with whatever. I've gotta go to the playoff game with Abby this week, but other than that I'm free."

"I think I can work around that. Vanessa's working this weekend. There's always a crowd when we have home games, so unfortunately, I'll be watching the game from my couch with Jules. It's too noisy to take her to a place like that."

"No kidding. But, man, you're missing out. I hope we win the next two games, so we can be in the championship.

Wouldn't it be something if we can pull off another record-breaking season?"

Vince smirks in my direction. "I take it you're a big fan?"

"Hell yeah. I haven't missed a home game since arriving at CRU. I love basketball. I used to play in high school, but I was never good enough to try out for a D-1 school like this. I'm here on an academic scholarship I couldn't pass up, or I'd likely still be playing at a smaller university."

"What position did you play?" Vince asks as he eyes me up and down. Knowing I'm a good head shorter than him, I'm sure my lack of height has him wondering.

"I played point. Don't let my average legs fool you, I still have an amazing vertical jump and can likely outscore you from the back court."

He slowly peruses my legging-clad limbs. "Syd, there's nothing average about you. But I'll make a mental note to never challenge you in HORSE, or I'll likely get my ass kicked." His chuckle has butterflies dancing in my belly.

"Oh, you can count on that. I'm as competitive as they come."

The professor starts class, but I swear I hear Vince mutter, "I have no doubt you are." Leaving a goofy grin on my face, I do my best to listen to today's lecture.

Thankfully, our class goes by in a blur of taking notes and class discussion. As distracting as Vince can be, I am able to fully focus and answer the question I am called upon by our professor when the time comes. Now if he'd asked me a question five minutes earlier, I would have probably mentioned something about sexy-corded forearms, because good God, Vince has to have the sexiest arms on the planet.

I've never been more relieved to be paying attention in my life when I am called upon.

By the time it's over, I'm eager to continue our conversation from last night. I'm dying to know more about him. Don't even get me started on thinking about his scorching kisses. Though the thought alone will get me through a busy night at work. Unfortunately, I already know he won't be stopping in because he takes care of Julia each morning, but at least I won't be disappointed. Knowing my time with him is limited, I'm eager to get out of class and enjoy our walk home together.

When we get outside, Vince casually asks, "Do you have plans for dinner?"

"Uh… I have to be at the bar by seven, but I'm free until then. Why?"

"Vanessa's home tonight and selfishly, I'd like to spend more time with you. But if you're busy, I completely understand."

He can be as selfish as he wants. Hell yes, I want to spend more time with him. "What do you have in mind?" I ask, trying not to sound too eager.

"Well… we can either grab something quickly in town, or I can cook for you?" He shrugs in the most adorable way, as if he's unsure of himself.

"There's no need to go out. I've got everything to make tacos at my place. Chloe might be home, but Abby has to work. Do you mind eating in?"

Reaching for my hand, he links his fingers through mine. It feels as if it's the most natural thing in the world, but my body zings to life when he runs his thumb along mine. "I think I can handle that. But so we're clear—I wasn't trying to skate out of cooking. We can cook together, and I'll be sure to leave in plenty of time for you to get ready for work."

"All I have to do to get ready is put on a t-shirt with the bar's logo, throw on a pair of jeans, and change my shoes. I'm sure I can handle that." I can't help the sarcasm at the end—I don't really primp before work. It's just not worth it. By the end of the night, I'm usually sweaty. My goal is to make money, not draw attention to myself. Besides, I don't want him to think I'm that high maintenance.

"Okay—but just kick me out when it's time for you to leave. I don't want to make you late or anything."

"Don't worry, I'm a stickler for punctuality, so it won't be a problem," comes out more wryly than I anticipate, but I'm met with a glorious smile, so I don't think he took any offense.

As soon as we enter my apartment, I'm relieved we have it to ourselves. Vince drops his backpack by the door and follows me to the kitchen. On the whiteboard next to the fridge, I see a note from Chloe telling us she has a late study group, so eat without her. Turning to Vince, I waggle my eyebrows playfully. "Guess what this means?"

"Uh… we're eating alone?"

"Yep." I grin, stepping closer to snake my arms around his neck. "It also means I can finally do this…" I don't even have to tug him in my direction. As he's already meeting me halfway when I rise to the tip of my toes.

I may start our kiss, but Vince quickly takes control. His hand reaches the nape of my neck in an instant, guiding me just how he wants me. It's the perfect combination of pressure and pleasure. When his tongue slides across my lip, I eagerly invite him in to play. My body ignites, and I can't get enough of his taste, his touch, or his scent. I instantly crave more. It drives me wild and makes me wish I didn't have to work tonight.

Eventually, all good things must come to an end.

When Vince breaks our kiss, we pull apart panting, but the triumphant smile on his face tells me I'm not the only one feeling this way. Though his words don't quite match his expression. "So... dinner?"

His expression is so torn, obviously he wants more, but he's trying to do the right thing. I can't help but laugh. "Sure. It will only take a few minutes to throw this together, then I'm sure we'll have enough time for a few more kisses like that," I tease suggestively.

"Good, because I've been dying to do that all day," he admits with a grin that he tries to rub off his face with his palm.

"On that, we can agree." I turn to the fridge as a distraction so I can refrain from wrapping my arms around him and never letting go. I have no idea what's gotten into me, but Vince pushes my buttons like he's built for me—and me alone.

As I set into frying the meat, Vince makes use of the cutting board and gets the lettuce, tomatoes, and cheese grated. I chose not to include onions because I plan on kissing him more, and there's no way I want either of us smelling of them.

Within twenty minutes, dinner is ready, and we're both sitting at the table digging into our meal. Vince is an expert at rolling the soft flour shells into burritos, and I have to admit I'm a bit in awe of his talents. Finally, when he has his second one loaded and rolled like a pro, I finally ask, "So, are you a professional burrito maker or something?"

"Something like that." He smirks then shakes his head. "My first job was working fast food at a local Mexican restaurant. I had to learn how to roll them quick, or hear the wrath of my boss. I only worked there for a few months, but it'll forever be engrained in my memory the need to be efficient."

"I was never allowed to cook," I admit. "It's not that I can't cook, but I've always been much faster at serving food than making it, unless it came to drinks. As you can see, I'm quite efficient there."

"With the way you bake, I'm sure your efforts are better spent there—you can't rush perfection. I still can't believe how quickly I devoured that container you sent home," he says with a laugh. "You're more than welcome to bake for me anytime."

"I'll keep that in mind," I tease. "Do you have anything in particular that's your favorite?"

Vince shakes his head adamantly. "No. I'm sure anything you bake will be better than I could ask for."

"Wow... no pressure or anything..." I deadpan, but something tells me I think he'd like a few of my special recipes. Maybe someday, when I get the time, I'll show him. The thought alone has me smiling. It's been so long since I actually tried to impress anyone with my skills. What I did the other day was just out of habit—nothing special.

Vince and I carry a casual conversation throughout dinner and into cleaning up. He's not the type of guy who sits back and lets me do all the work. He's right alongside me throughout the entire process, which is refreshing. Just as I'm wiping down the last of the counters and table, I feel two strong arms snake around me from behind when I stand to my full height.

"Mmmmm…" he moans as he brushes my hair aside to reach the nape of my neck. "You smell so good." When his lips trail along my neck to that spot just behind my ear, my knees go weak—literally. If I weren't able to lean against the table, I'd likely be a puddle on the floor. It takes all the energy I have to turn around and loop my arms around his neck.

"I could get used to this," I admit in almost a moan as his lips go from that spot again behind my ear along my jawline to my lips. Once his mouth meets mine, I return his kiss with every ounce of effort I have left.

Damn. Vince can kiss. Don't get me wrong. I've kissed my share of guys—plenty of toads in the pond, too, but he's the first person to kiss me where I feel it in every square inch of my body.

What the hell is he doing to me?

My toes curl, and my need to be closer to him is all I can think about. Needing to feel his skin, I trace one hand under the hem of his shirt and run it along his toned back.

How the hell can just touching his back be so sexy?

I'm like a moth to a flame as I run my fingers along his spine. The more I touch, the more I need him closer. When I drag my fingers to feel his tight stomach and along his rib cage, he murmurs, "Two can play that game."

Oh my God! His fingers feel amazing as they skirt under my shirt and roam their way along my body. My nipples tighten, and my breasts feel heavy, eager for his touch. When he finally cups my breasts and plays with my sensitive nipples, I encourage him to take what he needs. "Oh… right there…" I place my hand over his and apply more pressure.

Vince quickly picks up on my cue, and I'm rewarded with the most amazing gift. My body turns to liquid as Vince forces me to step back so I'm leaning against the kitchen table. He places a leg between my thighs to hold me up for support as he kisses along my neck to my collarbone. Knowing he's just where I want him, I quickly reach for the hem of his shirt and tug.

A low chuckle escapes as he breaks our kiss momentarily to pull his shirt over his head with one hand while giving me the sexiest of smiles. As I slowly peruse his exposed chest, my mouth goes dry. When I meet the hunger in his dark hazel eyes, I swear I feel my clit thrum.

Is it possible to come from just a look alone?

Knowing my roommates are gone for the evening, I make a hasty decision for us by ripping my shirt off as well, so I can feel his skin on mine.

I feel each—and every—inch of Vince's perusal as the heat from his eyes burn into my skin. My nipples stand erect and practically pop out of my satin bra. I swear, if he keeps looking at me like that, there will be a wet spot on his jeans as my leggings are nothing in the form of a barrier to protect my arousal between us. Fuck… he shifts his legs and hits my clit in the perfect spot. That feels so good.

Reaching to his neck, I pull him closer so I can kiss that sexy grin right off his face. Vince doesn't disappoint. His expert hand unclasps my bra from the front, and my boobs spring free from their confinement as he trails kisses along my neck. I squirm in anticipation against his leg, and the pressure builds more and more.

God, I need him now.

He cups one breast, while running his thumb back and forth around my hard as steel nipple as he lowers his head to run his tongue along the other side. I feel the cool wood against my back as I slide back onto the tabletop, causing my clit to press firmly against his leg between my thighs.

"Holy fucking shit..." I pant when he pinches one nipple and sucks hard on the other. My hips buck and are met with the continued pressure from his leg.

"You like that?" he asks around the nipple he's lavishly sucking, as if he didn't already know I'm on the edge of no return.

"Yes, Vince... right there," I encourage as I buck against him again shamelessly.

Sensing I need the pressure, his thigh rubs my clit in the best way possible. Reaching out, I run my fingers through his hair and encourage his efforts.

His tongue runs around the point of my peak, then his teeth take a quick nip, just as he pinches the other.

Stars.

All I see are stars as my orgasm rips through me like never before. To keep the glorious pressure, I grind down on his thigh like I'm chasing the best orgasm of my life. Because let's face it—it is.

I've never come from nipple play like this. As he licks, sucks, and pinches my nipples through each and every quake and quiver, I'm left writhing on my kitchen table and clenching onto his thigh like my life depends on it.

When my breath calms, I open my eyes to see the sexiest man grinning down at me. "You okay?" he asks with equal parts of amusement and concern written clearly across his face.

"Vince..." I draw out, trying to find words. I need words to express what I'm feeling. "I'm more than okay. If I were any better, I'd melt into a puddle of goo."

"Okay then," he teases as he leans in with a satisfied smile to kiss me once more. When he pulls back, he asks, "Do you think you can stand, or did I break you?"

Rolling my eyes, I peel myself from the table and force myself to a standing position. "I think I can manage."

"Good because, unfortunately, you have to go to work, and I need to leave so you can get there on time."

Wondering how he can stand there so calmly, I glance down to see if I'm the only one who's had this reaction.

Nope—there it is, clear as day. I swear just as I make eye contact with his impressive erection, it jumps to get my attention.

"Uh, Sydney?" Vince's voice is almost a plea. "You're not helping matters..." he draws out as he purposely adjusts himself.

"I can help you with that," I tease, licking my lips in appreciation.

"Not helping, Syd," he chastises, but I can see amusement and desire in his eyes as well. "You have to be at work in thirty minutes. We can take care of this another time."

"If you insist," I singsong as I press my entire body against him to kiss him once more. Holy hell. The man is packing. I can't wait to see him up close and in person.

"You're the devil." He grins. "But seriously. Just give me a minute, and it will go away."

"Maybe I don't want it to?" I tease.

Shaking his head, he pulls away. "The devil... I tell you," he mutters. But in a firmer voice, he demands, "Go get ready for work. As soon as I get decent enough to walk down the street without being cited for public indecency, I will be on my way. But this raging boner won't be going away on its own if you're all naked and on top of me."

"I'm just sayin'," I playfully suggest.

"Go... or you'll never be getting to work tonight. I'm trying to do the right thing here, Syd. Don't make it any more *difficult* than it is."

"Okay, Mr. Responsible. I'm going. But don't blame me for your *hard* predicament. I'm more than willing to do something about it."

"Go!" He points in the direction of my room as he rolls his eyes. As I turn to gather my shirt and readjust the clasp on my bra, I swear I hear him mutter, "She's gonna be the death of me."

I can't hide the smile on my face as I walk away and regretfully do what he asks.

VINCE

WALKING AWAY FROM SYDNEY YESTERDAY IS THE HARDEST THING I've ever done. No pun intended. I was so hard that I thought my dick would break if I didn't get some relief soon. It took everything in my power to get that beast under control. I was so relieved she'd given me enough time to calm down before returning to the living room to kiss me goodbye.

Yeah, I walked home with a partial stiffy that didn't go away until I took a shower. A very cold shower and even then, I had to take matters into my own hand to get things under control. God, I've never been more turned on in my life.

Shut the fuck up and stop thinking about it! I scold myself. Being in class with a hard-on is not how today should go either.

I'm picking up Julia after my last class, and she's finally going to learn how to ride with no training wheels. Vanessa's last class gets out after mine, so I told the two of them I'd pick Jules up early so we can go to the park to ride.

As I'm walking across campus to pick up Jules, I hear the sexiest voice call my name. Turning in surprise, I smile in greeting as I wait for her to approach.

"Fancy meeting you here," she teases.

"What are you up to?"

"I just finished writing a paper at the library, and I'm done for the day."

"I'm on my way to pick up Jules from daycare, then we're meeting Vanessa at home to go to the park. Today's the day! She's gonna ride her bike without training wheels," I say eagerly. I know Jules is ready, and they're just holding her back.

"Sounds fun. Mind if I walk with you for a bit?"

"I actually drove to campus. But if you're not doing anything this afternoon, you're welcome to join us."

Sydney takes a moment to let what I've just said sink in. Then for the first time ever, I see a smidgen of self-doubt. "Are you sure? I'd hate to intrude."

"Syd, one thing you've got to learn is I never say what I don't mean. If I don't want you there, I won't invite you."

Her confident smile returns and has me reaching out to pull her in for a chaste kiss. Knowing we're in public, I can't let myself get carried away. God knows what she does to me, and I've got to keep some boundaries firmly in place.

When I pull back, she wipes a bit of her minty Chapstick from my lips. "Sorry. I just reapplied. Wasn't expecting to share it."

"You won't hear me complaining." I grin as I spread what's left of it around further by rubbing my lips together.

Laughing at my antics, Sydney rolls her eyes. "No, I'm sure

I won't. Where are you parked? I'm sure Julia's dying to learn how to ride."

Julia's shocked expression when she sees Sydney in my Jeep is priceless. "Unks? Is this my surprise?" She looks from Sydney to me as if I've just brought her a new puppy.

Trust me, kid. I feel the same way.

The more I get to know Sydney, the more I want to keep her for myself.

When Jules tugs on my arm once more, I'm brought out of my revelry.

"No—you don't get to keep her, squirt. But we're meeting your mom at the house, so we can drive to the park together. Then I can teach you how to ride with no training wheels. What do you say?"

"Yay!" she squeals adorably. "Sydney comes, too, right?" she asks once she's calmed down enough to remember we have company.

"Of course. I wouldn't want to miss your big day," Sydney beams, and my heart melts a little.

Taking a minute to ensure Julia's straps are tight on her five-point harness, I help Sydney get settled into the seat in front of her. Once they're both settled, I walk around the Jeep to drive. Jules is busy chatting Sydney's ear off when I open the door to climb in. Sydney must have asked about her day because Jules is talking about what she did in class and how much she loves to paint.

I don't even get a word in the entire ride home because Sydney's like the shiny new toy Jules has become obsessed with. The two of them are practically old friends by the looks of it when I pull into our driveway and park in the garage.

I help Sydney out of the Jeep then pop her seat forward to let Jules out. Julia jumps down from the vehicle independently because she wants to show how big she is. Once inside the house, she practically drags poor Sydney to show off her bedroom.

I follow them to intervene if necessary, but Sydney is a trooper and manages to hold her own. Just when Jules is done showing Sydney her new dollhouse she got for Christmas, Vanessa hollers through the house. "Anyone home? I thought we were going to the park today?"

Sydney's long forgotten as Julia bolts down the hall to greet her mom. Before we follow, I quickly kiss Sydney on the lips as I say, "I know she can be a lot to handle, but she seems to like you."

"She's adorable. I can't wait to see her ride."

Reaching for her hand, I lead her down the hallway. "Let's go, or she'll be back. Trust me."

Walking to the living room, Sydney casually mentions, "This house is way nicer than any college student's house."

"Instead of renting, we decided to buy. Once we're done with school, Vanessa and I will sell it and split the profits. Or if one of us should choose to stay, we'll buy the other out," I tell her, knowing it made the most fiscal sense.

Sydney stops in her tracks to stare at me. "Seriously?"

Shit. I don't want to get into this now, so I skate around the topic the best I can with a shrug. "Yeah. It just made the most sense at the time." There's no way I'm ready to tell her about what brought me to living in this house. I don't want her pity and with Julia expecting to ride her bike, there's not enough time to explain things properly.

"I guess I can understand that." She looks anywhere but at me. Clearly, she's at a loss for what to say—and I just make it awkward. Fuck, I can't win for losing in this situation, but thankfully, she quickly changes the subject. "So..." She pulls in a deep breath. "What park are we going to?"

God, I swear, I'll tell her everything. I just need to be ready. I don't want the look on her beautiful face to change when she sees me. I need her to know the me I am now, before I unload my past on her.

Thankfully, Julia and Vanessa are great buffers. As soon as we enter the living room, Julia announces, "Momma, Guess what? Unks' friend is comin to watch me ride like a big girl."

Vanessa's eyes immediately jump to us as we enter the room and put Sydney at ease, like a pro. "Hi, Sydney. Glad you could join in the fun."

"Hey. I wouldn't miss it. I can't wait to see the big girl in action," Sydney says enthusiastically as Vanessa's eyes land on our linked hands. Her knowing smile says it all. She's happy for me, and I couldn't agree with her more, even though at the moment, I feel like an ass for holding back.

But how do you drop a bomb like that?

To get my mind off my parents, I focus on the present. "Hey, squirt, are you ready to go ride like a big girl?"

Julia jumps up and down with excitement before grabbing Vanessa's hand and dragging her to the door. "Let's go!"

"Let me just put her bike in the back of my Jeep, and we can take that," I offer Vanessa. Sure, she has an SUV of her own, but I'd prefer to drive my Jeep any chance I can.

"Are you sure?" Van looks between Sydney and me, obviously wanting to know if we need privacy.

"Momma, we have to ride with Unks. Or we'll miss riding with my new friend."

"Yeah, Van. We can't have that," I tease, though grateful for the distraction.

Looking to Sydney, she just smiles with delight.

"Okay—but go potty first," Vanessa says to Julia. Then she turns to us with an apologetic smile. "Sorry. It's a force of habit. The mom in me never turns off."

This earns a beautiful laugh from Sydney. "I can't imagine it ever does. But if you don't mind, I'll use your restroom, too, before we leave."

"You can use mine," I suggest, as our main bathroom is occupied with Julia and Vanessa, who's followed her to help."

I lead her to the master bedroom, which thankfully I remembered to make my bed and pick up this morning. "The bathroom's just inside there." I point to the door on the opposite side of the room. Sydney stares at my California-king bed and shakes her head.

God, what I'd give to know what's going on in that mind of hers.

Wanting to give her some privacy, I offer, "I'll meet you in the living room. I'll load her bike so we can leave as soon as everyone's ready."

I don't give her a chance to respond before walking out of the room. Thank goodness, Julia's bike is small, or I'd have to put the bike rack in place of the tow hitch, which will take much longer.

By the time we arrive at the park, everyone's just as excited as Julia. Vanessa's camera is ready to roll as Sydney stands beside her, cheering Julia on. Taking the time to show Julia how it's easier to start with one pedal up in the air, she catches on like a pro. I fasten her helmet and adjust to make sure it's on properly before holding the seat to steady her.

"Remember, Jules, you need to ride with your chin over the handlebar and keep pedaling. I'll get you steady, but when you're ready to take off, I'll let go. If you think you're gonna fall, remember—the grass is your friend."

Julia sighs exasperatedly. "Unks, I know. You told me already. Let's do this."

Damn. She's fearless.

She positions her pedal, and then she pushes off with one foot as she expertly settles onto the seat. It doesn't take long before she's pedaling her little heart out, and I'm jogging beside her, keeping her steady.

She wobbles a little but steadies it before I have to use all my force to keep her in place. "Remember where your chin goes, Jules." And she juts her chin over the handlebar. Instantly, she steadies and is ready to take off on her own. Not wanting to let her fall, I pick up my pace of jogging beside her and let go.

Holy shit—she's doing it.

When both Vanessa and Sydney holler in encouragement, Julia's attention falters, and she wobbles a bit. Shit. She's about to crash. Reaching out my hand to steady her, I'm surprised when she manages to correct herself before I can give her any assistance. We go a few more feet before she makes a sharp turn at the corner and tumbles away from me into the grass.

Of course, I've trained myself not to panic when she falls over the years, but my heart plummets as I await her response.

Please don't let her be hurt.

Thank God, she jumps up with a smile on her face. "I did

it! I did it, Unks." Then she turns to where her mom is filming her. "Did you see, Momma? I rode all by myself."

"You sure did, honey," Vanessa beams as she and Sydney close the distance between us. Sure, she'd only gone about thirty yards, but it was impressive for her first try.

"Let's do it again, Unks. It's fun riding so fast."

I give Vanessa an 'oh, shit, here we go' look, and she rolls her eyes. She and I both know she's just like her mom when it comes to determination. Julia's gonna keep us on our toes, that's for sure. Please let her make good choices in life, because there will be no changing her mind once it's made up.

I mouth so Julia won't hear as I point to Vanessa. "That's all you."

Van just rolls her eyes and sighs. She can't argue, so there's no use in trying.

With a determined look on her face, Julia gets her pedal where she needs it. She glances at me as if to ask, *Are you ready?* Nodding my head, I grip the seat to steady it, and we start this adventure over again.

The first few pumps look like she's a weeble-wobble, but as soon as I remind her to put her chin over the handlebar and pump harder, she's off like a rocket. I'm able to let go much faster than before, and we make it almost the length of the soccer field the bike path circles. She hasn't quite figured out how to turn, but since she catches herself by standing up before the bike falls, we're off and riding again before Vanessa even has a chance to catch up.

I guide her verbally through the next turn and have to run a little harder to keep up with her. The next thing I know, she's made it around the third corner, and we're almost back to Vanessa and Sydney, who cheer her on from a distance.

By the time we round the corner to the home stretch to return to Vanessa, Julia's giggling so hard with excitement. Her riding becomes less steady, and she wobbles a bit. Thankfully, she's more confident now. She easily corrects herself and makes her way back to Vanessa with ease. When she wants to stop, she even applies the brake. She slows down enough to bail off the bike into her mom's waiting arms.

"I'm so proud of you, Jules," Vanessa gushes. "You're a rock star on that bike. I can't believe you just bailed off it like that. Are you sure you and Unks haven't been practicing without me?"

"No, Momma," Julia says in a firm tone. "He just took my trainers off today. This was my first time, really."

Vanessa looks from Julia to me, to see if we've been conspiring against her, but I hold my hands up in defense.

"Seriously, Van, she's not trying to fool you. This was her first time!"

"I'm impressed," Sydney pitches in, earning a grin from Julia. "I still have scars from when I learned how to ride my bike. I didn't have anyone like your uncle Vince to run beside me, and I was so determined to do it on my own. Are you sure you're only three? I didn't learn until I was almost six."

Julia rolls her eyes and giggles. "My birfday is April twenty-fird. Right, Momma?"

"That's true," Vanessa admits. "She's growin' up faster than she should. I can't believe you're riding your bike all by yourself."

"I'm pretty sure that balance bike we got her for Christmas

helped a lot," I offer the crowd. "She seemed to master that in days. Remember?"

"How could I forget. She could barely stand next to the thing. It was so tall, but she was determined like today to ride it on her own."

Sydney holds out her hand for a high-five. "I'm still impressed, Jules. You're my hero."

Julia's smile beams with pride as she shouts, "Again, Unks! Again." And off we ride around the loop nearly the entire way before she bails off again when we get close to her mom.

By the time Vanessa suggests going home for dinner, I'm exhausted. I've jogged around this loop more times than I can count, not wanting to let her ride solo quite yet. When Julia begs, "One more time, this time on my own," I know she's more than ready. We watch her on bated breath as she starts entirely on her own and maneuvers her way around each and every turn in the path. There are a few close encounters with other people walking along the path, but they give her a wide berth, and Julia just keeps pedaling.

When she makes it back to us without a scratch, I can hear Vanessa's sigh of relief. "Way to go, Jules. Let's ride to Unks' Jeep, so we can get some dinner."

"I'll race ya," Julia beams, and we all chase after her with grins plastered across our faces.

13

SYDNEY

Somehow, by the time Saturday rolls round, Vince and I manage to steal some time together every day. Through texts, talking on the phone, and the short time before, I've enjoyed every moment of it. The only night we didn't see each other was last night, when I went to the basketball game with Abby which thankfully CRU pulled off a win, so they're in the next round of playoffs.

Somehow, I've managed to keep up with my homework, but to keep from a heavy load this weekend, I've spent the morning working on a paper due next week.

Usually, Saturdays are meant for sleeping in, but knowing Vince and I will spend the afternoon together, I work hard to free up more time with him. Just as I'm going through a final read through, my phone buzzes with an incoming text.

Vince: Vanessa just got home. Mind if I pick you up early?

Me: You still haven't told me what we're doing…

Vince: Just dress casually, wear sneakers and bring a sweatshirt. It's been chilly, even though it's March.

Me: You still haven't told me.

Vince: Can't it be a surprise?

Me: Fair warning - I suck at surprises.

I laugh at my response as I await his reply. It's true I suck at waiting, but I'm sure he'll make me do it anyway.

Vince: I'll be at your place in ten minutes. I'm loading my Jeep now.

Loading up his Jeep? Where the hell is he taking me?
Knowing I need to be a good sport, I quickly tap out my reply.

Me: I'll be ready. But I can't promise I'll be patient.

Vince: Relax. It'll be fun. Promise.

Instead of replying, I use this time to quickly make use of the bathroom, run a brush through my hair, and brush my teeth. I'm just grabbing a sweatshirt from my dresser when I hear a knock at the door.

Knowing Abby's studying, I rush to the door so I won't disturb her. I call out, "I got it," as I rush to Vince.

It seems that no matter how many times I see Vince, he still manages to take my breath away. Avoiding the Spanish Inquisition with Abby, I quickly grab my purse that I've left beside the door and step out onto the porch. "I'm ready."

He leans in and kisses me until I'm breathless.

When he pulls back, his expression's almost shy. "I know it's only been two days, but is it weird to say I've missed you?"

I stare at him, wondering if he's able to read my mind. "Not at all," I agree, as if he has taken the words right out of my mouth. He reaches for my hand and leads me toward his Jeep. "Still won't tell me where we're going?" I ask in a vain attempt to get him to crack.

"Nope. Patience—young grasshopper. Good things await you."

Okay—I'll admit it. I'm completely impatient. As Vince drives us off campus, I mull over a million places where we could go in this direction. When he takes the highway leading out to the gorge again, I look him over quizzically.

The man's a freaking vault and gives nothing away. He simply pats my leg and winks. Gah... I hate surprises. Hopefully, he'll learn this soon, so I'm not tortured like this often.

After about ten minutes, Vince takes me by surprise when he turns off a side road I've never been down. I swear he's taking me out to the boonies as we follow this winding road. Instead of speaking my mind, I force myself to bite my tongue. Of course, this also means I can't bring myself to talk about anything casual either. Let's face it, I don't trust myself to not ask the impending questions that will flow from my mouth when I let it go.

Eventually, Vince pulls off the road and parks. Then he reaches in front of me, opening the glove compartment, and places a pass on the rearview mirror. Only then does his gaze meet mine, and the sexiest smile forms on his face. "You're not too mad that I haven't told you, are you?"

"No, but I totally deserve a medal for *not* asking about it," I snark. "I've literally been biting my tongue to stop myself. This isn't fair."

Looking around the heavily forested area, I don't see any other cars around. Without a word, he gets out of the Jeep. Instantly, I hear a river running close by. Before he walks away, his eyes pin mine. "I promise, I have good things planned." Then a flash of something resembling doubt crosses his beautiful face before sincerity becomes the dominant feature. His voice is low when he says, "Thanks for being a good sport and going along for the ride. Give me a second to grab my backpack, and I'll help you out."

It takes him no time at all to open the back of the Jeep and sling a backpack onto his shoulder. From the size of it, it's hard to tell what's in it. It could be hiking gear or something else but either way, it warms my heart that he's gone to great efforts to plan this date. I should give him some slack. Maybe it's the planner in me, but I don't like feeling out of control.

When an apprehensive Vince opens my door, I consciously make the effort to relax and go with the flow. I *can* be flexible and shouldn't let my fear of the unknown ruin my time with him. Honestly, I can't remember the last time someone has gone to such efforts. The fact that he's doing this *might* actually make the unknown worth the while… though the jury's still out.

Greeting him with a smile, I put him at ease. "In case I forget to tell you, thank you for doing this." He still looks a little unsure, so I call myself out on my bullshit. "Yeah—I suck at surprises, but the fact that you went to such efforts is incredible. I can't remember the last time anyone has ever done something like this for me."

"You need a better dating pool," he deadpans then panics. "Scratch that. I'd rather not think of you dating other guys. This can just be our thing, yeah?"

He knows how to go for the jugular. Gah… all the feels with this man. But I can't let him think I'm starting to fall for him. "I think we can manage that," I tease, keeping my tone light.

His outstretched hand steadies me as I hop down from the Jeep. "I thought I'd take you to one of my favorite places for lunch."

"Okay, I'm trying not to ask, but can you at least tell me where we're going?" I finally admit.

"I found some waterfalls just over that hill. It's crazy busy here on hot days, but it's perfect for days like this, especially if you want to get away and think."

Something in the way he says that makes me think there's a story there, but if he wants to share it with me, I'll let him tell me in his own time. I know all about self-preservation and needing to get away from it all. Who am I to judge someone for wanting to find peace? However, the thought of it being his special place makes me feel a bit closer to him, and I'll admit I'm eager to find out more about Vince.

As he takes my hand and leads me down a trail, the sound of running water becomes louder. I'm not sure what I expect but when we round a corner, the view of the river is exquisite. The river's much wider than I expect, and there isn't just one waterfall. Nope—multiple waterfalls from all directions swiftly flow over the smooth rock cliffs. Beneath each fall is a pool perfect for swimming—if it were warmer.

"Wow, this place is incredible," I say in awe. "How did you find this place?"

Instead of answering my question, Vince pulls me to a flat spot and says, "I thought we could picnic here by the falls. I hope you don't mind, but I brought a couple of different sandwiches you can choose from since I don't know your favorite. I brought a few other things to snack on—if you don't like sandwiches at all." He suddenly looks unexpectedly shy. "I guess I should have asked, but I wanted to surprise you."

Aww… can he get any sweeter?

"I'm really not a picky eater, as long as it doesn't have sauerkraut or some pickled beets in it. I'm down with trying anything once."

Confusion fills his features, and he blanches in disgust. "That's… an odd combination? Is this dislike… from experience?"

"Oh, hell no. I was just making up a nasty combination—I hope no one *ever* puts *that* between two slices of bread to prove a point. I mean—that'd be disgusting!"

Vince's laugh echoes off the rocks around us. "Yes, that

would be." He digs into his bag, retrieves a blanket, and spreads it with ease. It appears he's thought of everything as he empties the remaining contents in his backpack. Not only are there a variety of sandwiches, but he's thought of drinks and even a few different flavors of chips in individual packaging.

"Wow..." I say in amusement. "You've really gone all out."

I swear I see his cheeks darken as he mutters, "Well... I like I said. I didn't know what you'd like."

To ease his tension, I swipe the bag of Fritos with a smile. "These are my favorite. But for the record, I would've eaten anything. It looks delicious."

This does the trick as his shoulders visibly relax, and a lazy grin replaces apprehension. "There's chocolate in the side pocket for dessert."

"I may be persuaded to have some of that, too. Especially if it's milk chocolate."

"Well, I'll have to fight you for it because I bought dark chocolate, too, but only to give it as an option... Personally, I can't get over the bitterness, but I wasn't sure your preference."

Rolling my eyes, I chuckle. This guy... "Vince, you didn't have to go to such trouble. I would've eaten it, though maybe not asked for seconds... to be polite, you know..."

"Syd, don't ever do anything to placate me. If you don't like something... tell me."

He doesn't get it... "Oh, I'll never placate you... trust me. But I was brought up to take a bite of everything... including the pickled beets and sauerkraut. As an adult, there are just some things I draw the line on. I don't care how many times Grams forced me to eat those... I hated them each and every time."

This earns me a beautiful laugh from Vince. It's the kind of laugh I can't help but join. It's so infectious. "I totally get it. For the record... I don't eat anchovies on pizza or any type of wilted lettuce or cabbage-type substance. You can be as cute as ever or even beg me... I will still flat-out refuse."

"I'll keep that in mind," I tease. Though when I think about it, he has a point... because... Yuck. Those are both disgusting, too. Instead of responding though, I attempt a subject change. "So... What did you and Julia do this morning?"

"Well..." He pretends to contemplate in this overexaggerated, ridiculous way which only makes me smile even harder.

Is it possible for your cheeks to fall off from smiling too much?

Seriously... His finger taps his chin while he looks to the sky and sucks in a deep breath. He's fucking adorable. "Let's see... we got up at the ass-crack of dawn to eat breakfast and watch cartoons. Julia loves cold cereal for her first meal of the day—so at least I didn't have to make an elaborate breakfast at that hour. When it finally got light enough to be a decent hour, she begged me to take her for a bike ride, and then we spent the rest of the morning doing chores around the house." He ends with a shrug, as if his morning weren't already packed.

"Sounds like a lot busier morning than mine," I admit. "I almost feel lazy. I just got up and worked on my paper that's due next week."

"I typically do homework between classes or after Jules is asleep for the night. She's an amazing kid, but if it's just the two of us, she's my sidekick. Thankfully, she loves to do her 'schoolwork' which consists of coloring or working on a workbook when Van or I are forced to study during the day to fit it all in." The way he used air quotes around her schoolwork tells me there's more to this story.

"She sounds adorable. I can just picture her trying to work by your side."

"Yep. She insists I bring my work to the kitchen table where we can do our work together if her mom picks up an evening shift or something. Vanessa typically has a few breaks during the day, so she completes her work on campus somehow."

"Being a single parent must be hard," I assume.

Knowing my mom was a single parent and the struggles she went through with me, I can't imagine trying to go to college with a kid in tow. I'm in awe of Vanessa for all she's doing.

"It's not easy, that's for sure," Vince admits as he holds out two sandwiches. Lifting his right hand, he says, "Roast beef or turkey? They each have tomatoes, cheese, and I brought some mayo in a small container if you want to add that. We were out of lettuce." He ends with a shrug. "Sorry."

"You won't hear me complain," I interject as my stomach rumbles quietly in appreciation of his thoughtfulness. I swear he's thought of everything. "I haven't had a turkey sandwich in forever. I'll take that."

"Good. Eat up. I don't want you starving to death. Have you eaten today?"

Well, apparently, it wasn't that quiet.

How embarrassing.

Trying to play it off, I scoff, "Yes. But it's been a few hours. I promise not to eat your arm off as you hand it to me," I say, reaching for the sandwich.

"You're cute when you're embarrassed," comes out as an assessment rather than an accusation. I shake my head because he never wants to see me hangry. I won't be cute at all. Grams used to make sure I ate in regular intervals, so I wouldn't *bite the hand that feeds me*, as she reminded me often. *Apparently, me being hangry was the worst temperament she'd ever seen.*

God, I miss her.

Vince picks up on my mood change. Suddenly, his carefree face fills with worry. "Did I say something to offend you?"

Sighing, I reply, "No... I was just thinking about Grams... and how she used to warn me about getting hangry. She used to tease me about it all the time, claiming I'd bite her hands off if I weren't fed fast enough. She swore up and down I was the worst when my hanger struck. She even kept snacks in the glove compartment and in her purse if we were going out for a while."

Vince's eyebrows shoot to his hairline as he draws out, "O... kay... I'll keep that in mind. I'd rather not experience *that* type of hanger..."

Swatting at his arm playfully, I shake my head in complete denial. "That was when I was just a little older than Julia. I'll have you know I'm a lot more controlled with my hanger issues now."

"I don't know... I've seen your feistiness in action the night we met at the bar..." he reminds me, though his tone is light and harmless. He's right. He did see me put his friend in his place—and for some reason, he still comes around.

"I told you, I don't take shit from dipshits who think I have nothing better to do than go home with them at the end of my shift," I defend more than my intent.

"I get it. I wouldn't want people hitting on me either like Derek. But seriously, I don't think he meant any harm by it—but let's face it, if you hadn't turned him down, we wouldn't be here today."

Well... damn... he has a point.

Before I can respond, Vince continues, "I guess I can be thankful he took that chance to talk to you..."

Confused, I ask, "Why is that?"

"If he hadn't pissed you off so much, I seriously doubt you would've carded us. Therefore, you wouldn't have taken the time to notice me."

Oh, I would've noticed him—eventually.

But I keep that thought to myself.

Instead, I just scoff defensively.

"Oh... come on, Syd. You already knew we'd been carded at the door."

We stare at one another for a long moment as he waits for me to admit what he already knows.

I will neither confirm nor deny his accusation.

Clearing my throat, I promptly change the subject, "So, how did you find this place?"

This earns me a smug smile that makes my belly flop in a way that has nothing to do with hunger.

"I go for drives when I need space or time to think. Freshman year..." The way his voice trails off makes the hairs on the back of my arm rise.

Something's happened to Vince. The far-off look in his

eyes as he focuses on the water running below us makes me wonder if he'll ever tell me.

Reaching out, I pat his thigh beside me. "You don't have to tell me," comes out barely above a whisper, but I know he's heard me.

Vince sucks in a deep breath and slowly releases it, making my heart clench. The hallow look in his eyes tells me more than his words ever will.

But before I can give it more thought, he quickly shakes it off and quietly continues, "No…" though I'm unsure if his words are for me or himself.

He's quiet for a few more breaths before he sucks in another deep breath and continues, "No… Freshman year… let's just say… it was a rough one. I was finding my ground and adapting to my new normal. With Jules and Vanessa always around, the only time I got to myself was if I went for a drive."

Going away to school is hard on everyone. It was hard as hell for me to walk away from the only home I'd ever known, knowing that once I left, I'd never be back. Grams was gone, and I have nothing left to return to. At least Vince had his family to support him. "I can understand that…" I prompt, hoping he'll continue.

But he doesn't continue with that mournful tone.

Nope, he forces a smile as he continues in a much lighter tone. "Well… I was driving one day in the early spring and saw the road lined with cars. It was unusually hot, so the top and doors were off my Jeep. When I slowed down, I could hear water running and decided to return when it was less crowded. The next week, I went for an early morning drive and found myself here. I got out and followed the sound of the water. No one was here as it was barely light outside and still chilly from the night air. When I made my way to just about where we're sitting now, I sat and just enjoyed the beauty of the sun coming over that hill. There were a few clouds high in the sky that morning, so the colors were vibrant—full of reds and oranges. I'd never quite seen anything like it. As I watched the nature around me, I finally relaxed."

"It must've been beautiful," I whisper, picturing his description and staring at the hills around us.

"It was. The best part about it was how my stress faded away in that moment. It's weird, but I swear I knew I could handle anything the world threw at me." Shaking his head, Vince turns to look me in the eye. "Sorry... that probably doesn't make any sense. It's just... you asked how I found this place and well... that's how it became my go-to place when I needed to think. Especially early in the morning."

Thinking back on all I've overcome since the loss of Gram, I get where he's coming from. Not knowing what exactly Vince went through, the brief look of despair in his eyes tells me it was catastrophic. *If* he shares it with me—it will be on his terms, and I'll do my best not to push him. If he *never* tells me, I'm okay with that, too. We all have our own demons, and I'm not about to ruin this perfect date by bringing up the past— for either of us.

"Well... thank you for sharing this with me. I don't think I've ever had anyone go to this much trouble for a date." Leaning in, I kiss him on the cheek. "For that, I thank you." Pulling back, I take a large bite of sandwich to keep from saying more.

As if he understands my attempt at keeping things light,

Vince once again relaxes his shoulders and eats his sandwich. Glancing over at me, he grins, and my insides melt just a little more.

What is it about him that turns me into goo with just a simple look?

We eat in silence for a while before a large eagle swoops down from upstream and pulls up a big fish. I jump at its unexpected appearance. As I restart my heart, I stare at the impressive strength of his talons.

"Did you see that?" Vince whispers in awe as the bird flies into a tree up the hill from the other side of the riverbank.

"I'm not gonna lie. It kinda scared the shit out of me." I chuckle at my embarrassment but continue, "Then when it picked up that fish, I couldn't do anything but stare in awe."

"You don't see that every day... but it proves my point earlier. This place is special."

"You're right about that. I don't think I'll ever forget that."

"And here I thought you'd remember this for my expert sandwich-making skills... you wound me, woman..." He pretends to pout, and it's adorable.

"Well, we wouldn't want to damage that precious ego of yours." Of course, I'll remember the effort he's put forth on this date. I wasn't kidding when I said no one has gone to such troubles.

When I shove at his arm playfully, he lunges at me. The next thing I know, I'm lying flat on my back as his upper body hovers over me. He carefully takes what's left of my sandwich out of my hand and sets it on the blanket beside us.

As soon as that task is finished, his attention is solely focused on me. His breath is uneven, and his eyes continue to search mine. Then he melts the firm walls I've placed around my heart when he says, "I have a new reason to like this place…"

"Oh, really, why's that?" I attempt to be flippant, but I'm sure it comes out as breathless.

"I have the most beautiful sight in the world under me."

My belly flops and flits, then a shiver runs up my spine.

Slowly, he leans in to kiss me. His lips are tender against mine, and the entire world around me disappears. The river could rise, and I wouldn't even notice as long as I stayed in his arms.

When he pulls back to end our kiss, I grip the back of his neck, holding him in place. There's no way I'm finished kissing him just yet.

I don't care that I just ate something.

I don't care that I'm lying on a hard rock.

And I certainly don't care that I'm in public.

All I care about is being in his arms and experiencing this fucking amazing kiss.

The forest could go up in flames from the fire burning inside me, and I'd be none the wiser. All I know is I want this man to keep his magnificent lips on mine, and I need to taste more of him.

Unfortunately—we *are* in public.

I hear kids yelling before I see them, and Vince bolts upright, pulling me along with him. His wide eyes search for the incoming family that's fast approaching. He runs a hand down his face and reaches out to adjust my sweatshirt. A sheepish expression forms as he shakes his head at me. "I'm pretty sure you're nothin' but trouble."

Raising an eyebrow, I replay his words in my mind.

Just how does he expect me to take that?

Before my defensive thoughts fly out of my mouth, he leans in to peck me chastely to keep my mouth occupied.

When the family reaches the opening to the trail head, he pulls back and winks. "Simmer down, Syd. I meant that in the best way possible."

14

VINCE

Sydney's a firecracker. That's one thing I'm certain of. But the flame that runs through her burns hot in my soul. I'd only meant to be playful, but she turned my innocent kiss into an inferno in a hot minute.

Thank God, I'm used to listening for Julia, or that poor family would've gotten their eyes full. As my hands roamed Sydney's body under her bulky sweatshirt, all I wanted was more. Her soft skin drives me wild, and the way she knows what she wants... well, I don't think any woman has turned me on more.

Thankfully, we were finished eating for the most part because the family with four kids had the same idea for a picnic. Not that I mind them being here. I tend to lose my mind around Sydney and thankfully, they brought me back to reality.

I discreetly adjust myself as Sydney focuses on the kids

now picking up rocks to skip by the water. Julia would love it here, but for some reason, I've kept this place to myself. I'm not even sure why I brought Sydney other than the fact I wanted to take her to a place that had meaning to me. Our first official date was pretty epic, and I wanted something that could top it —and let's face it, I wanted to be alone with her.

As we watch the family from afar, Sydney picks up her forgotten sandwich and finishes it. I let her eat in silence as I contemplate just what it means to share my sacred spot with her.

When she's finished, I ask, "Would you like anything else to eat?"

She takes a drink of the soda I brought and re-screws the cap.

"Not really." She shrugs, then her eyes light up with a new thought. "I do believe you mentioned chocolate…"

Digging into my bag, I can't help but grin. She reminds me of Julia and dessert. Syd leans forward, reaching out her hands eagerly in my direction.

"Are you sure my hands are safe?" I raise an eyebrow as I hold the bag of truffles just out of reach.

Her beautiful green eyes dance mischievously, and her sass shines through. "Only if you *don't* hold out on me. You should know better than to come between a girl and her chocolate, Vince."

"Oh, trust me… I know…" I draw out as I pull out a piece of candy from the bag to hand her.

"Good. Now that we've got that straight, we can stay friends."

"So, now I've been kicked to the friend zone." I shake my head, feigning being butt hurt. "Wow... Here's the bag... have all you want."

Shaking her head, she grabs the bag faster than I could finish my thought. "Oh, Vince... I think it's safe to say, the last thing I would ever want from you... is to just be your friend."

Doing my best to school my features, I state, "So, you just want me for my body... I see..."

This earns me a playful smack against my arm. "You're body's nice, Vince. But I'm pretty much of a whole package kind of girl." Then her face morphs from playful to fear. "Wait... that came out wrong."

Shaking my head to calm her fears, I laugh. "I think I get it, Syd. No worries."

Practically under her breath, I barely hear, "Ohmigod, please don't think I only came to school for my MRS. degree. I only meant... that I think of you as both a friend and more. Of course... I like your body... I mean, look at you... but please don't think that's *all* I want you for..." By the end, she's buried her face in her hands.

She's freaking adorable.

"Syd..."

She refuses to look me in the eyes.

This just won't do.

"Sydney," I say more forcefully to get her attention. When she doesn't move her hands, I reach over to give them a gentle tug.

When her green eyes finally meet mine, I feel it deep in my soul. Her vulnerability is there. God, she has nothing to fear from me. "Syd… I was joking. I didn't mean to get you so riled up. I think we can both agree that friendship is a must—to move forward. But that's clearly not all either of us want. I certainly don't kiss people who are *just my friends* the way I kissed you. Do you?"

Her eyes flit to the blanket below her. Taking my forefinger, I place it under her chin to encourage her continued eye contact. When she finally does meet mine, I'm met with the most beautiful eye roll of my life as she shakes her head in denial. "No… I don't kiss just anyone like that."

"Good. Now that we've got that settled. Let's get out of here, so I can find a place to kiss you like that again."

A beautiful blush creeps up her neck and thankfully, her apprehension disappears in an instant. "I think that can be arranged."

As I walk through the gates of the arena with Ryan for the championship game, thoughts of my date last weekend with Sydney run through my mind. Somehow, over the past few weeks, she's become a predominant feature in my life. She's the first person I text each morning and one of the last people I talk to each night. Even if we don't talk because she's working, I always wake up to a text from her, telling me she made it home.

Drew managed to get her a ticket to tonight's game to sit with Abby. According to her latest text, she's practically on the court watching the game, so I can't blame her for not wanting to sit in the student section with me and the guys.

"Hey, man, our seats are over here," Ryan points out, pulling me out of my head. When we take our seats, he pins me with a knowing look. "So, what's up with you, man? Are you not interested in the game?"

What? Why would he think that?

"No?" comes out as a question and before I can respond, he interrupts.

"You've been stuck in your head since I picked you up. Is everything okay with Vanessa and Julia? You get this way when you're preoccupied with them."

"Naw... they're good. Sorry. I've been dying for this game." And more importantly—for my potential date after the game.

Sydney's been busy all day because Drew proposed to Abby this morning at the diner. I not only heard about this from Sydney in great detail, but apparently it was a proposal worth writing home about from Vanessa—as she texted me the details practically after they happened. I'll admit, the guy has game on and off the court, though I don't think I would ever propose like he did. He went to great lengths to pull off his surprise—according to Sydney.

Since Sydney was in charge of bringing Abby's parents to the diner, I have yet to see her today. As if my eyes have a mind of their own, they roam the crowd to where I think she's sitting, if the vantage point from her last text is correct.

As soon as my eyes land on her, it's as if she senses me. Our eyes lock, and a smile forms big enough to see across the arena. She gives me a small wave, and I wave back.

"Oh, I get it..." Ryan finally breaks my attention. "So things are still going on with you and Sydney."

I haven't filled him in on much, but Ryan's not an idiot. "Yeah, they're still happening," I admit.

"Are things serious? Man, that's great. I've never seen you date other than when we've forced you out in a group with us." He speaks that last part almost to himself. "I know you have your reasons for staying single... and I get it... but that smile I just witnessed on your face was worth waiting for."

Ryan and I never talk about relationships, especially not in public, so I'm a little shocked to see he's broached the subject.

"Okay..." I draw out, having no idea how to respond to that even if I tried.

Ryan cocks his head to the side and grins. "Dude. Don't worry. I'm happy to see you happy—and paying attention to yourself—for once."

I nod in agreement. Yeah, it's abnormal for me to date, but I'm not complaining by any means. Thankfully, I don't have to say anything because the lights dim, and the crowd cheers as players are announced.

I couldn't have planned this spot better if I tried. As the game goes on, I'm not sure which I enjoy watching more. Sydney cheering her ass off, or the players taking control throughout the game. Sure, there are times when the score evens up, but by halftime, we're back in the lead. But watching Sydney's enthusiasm just might hold out for the top spot tonight.

I'm sure Ryan's caught me grinning like a loon from time to time, but I could honestly give two shits. She's like a magnet. My eyes instinctively search her out.

When she gets upset by a bad call from the ref or when we're leading in points again, I've quickly learned she's extremely vocal. And, boy, is it entertaining. Sure, I can't hear her exact words from across the arena, but I easily read her body language and get the gist of the message. Her spitfire personality shines in true form. Honestly, I can't remember ever enjoying a game more.

The only thing that could top watching her is when we take the lead in the final quarter. I wish more than anything I was there to be the one she chooses to high-five and hug. I'm not jealous of Abby, but it'd be nice to share this moment with Sydney, too. I make a mental note to take her to a sporting event in the future; her enthusiasm beats sitting next to any other fan in the stadium.

When the final buzzer blasts, Ryan and I high-five or fist bump the fans around us. I'm pumped with energy and can't wait to share my enthusiasm about CRU's win with Sydney.

As Ryan and I make our way out of the stands, I feel my phone buzz in my pocket.

Knowing it's likely Sydney, I quickly dig it out.

Sydney: Can I crash your plans tonight?

Me: You can crash them anytime.

Sydney: I'll keep that in mind. I rode with Abby's family. Do you have room for me to ride home with you?

I look to Ryan since he drove us tonight. "Do you mind if Sydney joins us?"

The knowing grin he's been shooting my way all night forms again. "Sure. No problem. I've gotta work early in the morning. Do you mind if I just drop the two of you off at your place to get your Jeep?"

"It might be easier to just drop us off at Sydney's. It's only a few blocks from my place. I can walk home. We can see what she thinks though. Traffic in town is gonna be crazy after a game like this."

"Sounds good." I hear as I type.

Me: Meet us at the North Entrance. I'll wait just outside the doors for you.

Sydney: Sounds good. See you then.

She must have already been able to see me because the next thing I know, someone's jumping on my back and climbing me like a spider monkey. Just as I'm about to pitch a fit, her delicious scent and boisterous cheer puts me at ease.

"I can't believe we pulled it off for two years in a row. Today has been the best day… ever!" she shouts in my ear and squeezes me tight. Before Ryan and I can say anything, she continues to shout, "I've watched my best friend get engaged, and we've won the national championship! The best part is… Now I get to spend time with you!" I feel her release her hold on my neck to kiss my cheek from behind.

Once we're outside, I continue carrying her on my back. I've got her legs hoisted under my arms, and she's not going anywhere soon if I can help it. As we get a bit further from the noise of the crowd, I look over to Ryan who's as happy as we are. "Ryan, you remember Sydney, right?"

Ryan's chuckle can be heard over the crowd around us. "Yeah. Of course. Nice to see you again, Sydney."

"Hi, Ryan," Sydney says with a wave from my back. She's locked her legs around my waist and has settled in for a ride to our vehicle apparently. I've never seen this carefree side of Sydney, but once again, I'm not complaining. Her energy is like a live wire coursing through me and in this moment, I'm just as amped up as she is.

By the time we walk the few blocks to Ryan's SUV, we've chatted about the best plays of the game. Sydney could be a sports commentator for as well versed she is in the basketball plays. I have to admit I'm really impressed. I thought I was an avid fan, but after watching her tonight, I'm fairly certain she has me beat—hands down.

After Ryan drops us at Sydney's apartment, she takes my hand and leads me up the stairs. Her excitement over the events of today shows in every bounce in her step. She's freaking adorable when she's excited, and I can't help but show my enthusiasm with her.

Once inside her apartment, it's unusually quiet for someone with roommates. "Where is everyone?" I ask in curiosity.

"Oh... Abby and Chloe are celebrating with Drew and his friends."

Knowing she's such an avid fan, I have to ask, "Why didn't you join them?"

Sydney cocks her head to the side as if I should know the answer, but her voice comes out as a singsong. "Oh... You know... there's this guy... and I kinda had plans with him..."

Reaching for her hips, I pull her close to me. "I don't want to get in the way of you celebrating with your friends. Today's been pretty eventful for them."

"I know... but we've celebrated all day, and I'm kinda ready to be away from the crowd. And besides... how often do we both get an entire night where we don't have to be anywhere the next day?" Her tone turns suggestive, and my cock stirs to attention as she snakes her arms around my neck.

What the fuck... she's barely touching and has this effect on me?

Slow the fuck down, Vince... slow it down...

Somehow... I manage to find words. "True. Julia's sleeping over at a friend's house, and I would much rather find a way to celebrate with you."

I kiss her once, letting my tongue slide in to tangle with hers. Damn. She tastes of fresh mint and all that is Sydney. I swear her taste could be syphoned as a drug, and I'd be an addict in an instant. Instead of letting myself get lost in her, I pull back to continue our conversation. I need to make sure she knows this is not all I came over for.

"Soo..." I draw out as I kiss her once more before asking, "how was the rest of your day?"

This little distraction does the trick, and my body gets a much-needed reprieve from overstimulation. I discreetly adjust her lingering effects so I can better focus on her actual response, rather than my constant need for her.

"Drew was just perfect," Sydney gushes. "Abby had no idea we were all in on it. I met her parents at their hotel early this morning and drove them to the diner. We waited around the corner to get the text that the parking lot was clear. He arranged with Vanessa to seat them so she couldn't see us enter. Chloe actually sneezed right as we entered... and I swear Abby almost caught us, but Drew was perfect with his distraction." Sydney lets out a huge sigh of relief, and I can clearly picture how grave the situation was in my mind.

Shaking her head at the thought of his plans being ruined, she continues, "Once we were settled, we held our menus to keep our faces hidden in case she looked our way. Chloe and I managed to get the entire experience on video. I can't wait to share it with Abby later. She had absolutely no idea what was in store for her... but obviously you know what her answer was."

"Yeah." I nod in agreement. "Vanessa told me about it when she came home this afternoon. Apparently, Drew's set the bar really high in terms of proposals. I'm not sure if any guy will ever live up to it... well, at least according to Van. She's pretty picky, so I kinda pity the guy who tries to win her heart."

"Vincent Daniel Larson. You shouldn't be so hard on your sister," Sydney scolds me, and I can't help it. I laugh.

Waving my hands like a white flag for truce, I quickly explain, "Seriously, Syd. Vanessa's had the worst luck with guys... well, one guy in particular..." I trail off as I try to figure out how to explain things without going into too much detail. Though I guess raising Jules as a single mom has taken her attention in recent years... so maybe it's explanation enough. "The guy who got her pregnant was a piece of work. Thank God, my parents intervened to keep him out of the picture."

"That had to be rough..." Sydney drops the end of her thought. "My dad was never around, and I've seen it close up what it's like to be a single mom—well, at least from the kid's perspective. If it hadn't been for Grams, I'm not sure what type of person I would've become."

"There's a lot to Vanessa's story I'd rather not get into now... All I can say is that I'm thankful I'm here to support her and help Jules every way I can. But know... Van's pretty guarded, and it will take one hell of a man to come in and sweep her off her feet. I'm sure she'll put him through the wringer before he makes the cut."

"And you won't be the least bit protective... I'm sure," she teases.

"Oh, of course, but I don't think I'll have to. Van's walls are pretty high, and it'll take only the right type of guy to get into that fortress she's built. My poor buddy Ryan has had a crush on her since freshman year, and he's a decent guy, but Van has blinders on when it comes to relationships."

"That's kinda sad," Sydney sighs. "No offense, but your sister's a knockout and just because she has a kid, doesn't mean she's dead—as a woman."

"I'd prefer not to think of my sister as a woman... thank you very much." I chuckle at my automatic response. Then her point hits home. "But I get your point. We're still young. I'm sure if the right one comes along, she'll give him a chance."

"I don't know Van's entire story, but I totally can relate. After my recent dating streak with complete tools, you're lucky I've even given you the time of day..." Her brows crease at some unpleasant thought—and I'm not letting her go there—at least not tonight. Today is for celebrating.

I clear my throat to gain her attention. "I'm perfectly content not knowing about those tools, Syd. I'm not a jealous guy... but why waste your breath on something that clearly made you unhappy? Just promise me one thing..."

"Oh, yeah... what's that?" she asks playfully.

"You tell me *when* I'm being a tool. Like Van, I haven't had a lot of experience with dating in recent years."

Cocking a beautifully sculpted eyebrow in my direction, she punches her hip with a fist. "You say this like you expect it to happen..."

All I can do is shrug.

"I'm a guy. I'm bound to piss you off at some point," I point out the given, but quickly add, "All I'm asking is that you tell me when it happens... I can't stand it when things get blown out of proportion due to lack of communication. We've been through this..." I trail off, reminding her of her poor assumption of me earlier.

Of course, this earns me a beautiful eye roll.

Why the hell is her sass so sexy?

15

SYDNEY

His lips descend on mine in a nanosecond.

I barely have a chance to respond before I'm consumed by all things Vince. His strong hands take hold of my face, pinning me in place, while his fervent kisses light me from the inside out.

I want more.

I need more.

My hands scrape along the hemline of his shirt, searching for his warm skin. When I find what I need, I run the tips of my fingers up and down his spine. A low guttural groan escapes his lips between kisses. "Syd... press harder or stop. This isn't the time to make me ticklish," he demands by the end.

Press harder it is then.

His hand leaves my face to find the hem of my shirt as well.

Remembering all too well the effects he has on me, I manage to moan, "Bedroom..." between kisses to keep this just between us should my roommates return home. "Want..." kiss... "Privacy..." Kiss.

God, the way he makes me feel is incredible.

Vince breaks our kiss and pants, "Which way," as he grabs my hand.

We make it to my bedroom in record time. The minute the door clicks shut behind us, his mouth is back on mine in the most delicious way. I reach for the bottom of his shirt, and he breaks our contact only long enough to rip it over his head.

Seeing his sexiness in action makes me quickly discard mine, too. The hunger in Vince's eyes matches mine as his eyes roam the top half of my body. I'd purposely chosen a black demi-cup bra and matching boy shorts, hoping our night would end this way.

I swear, the heat in his gaze leaves a trail of goose bumps along their path. From his look alone, and I know in this instant, I need to make him mine. Reaching out, I trail my finger along his corded forearms, up to his sculpted shoulder. I'm not sure what he does to have such well-defined muscles, but I like it. A lot. He's not overtly bulky, more just physically fit, but each muscle along my perusal makes me want to lick each and every square inch of him. I've never felt such an attraction before.

When my eyes finally reach his face, I see his tongue slowly trace his lower lip as if he's contemplating which part of me he wants to kiss first. Taking the two necessary steps toward him, I reach out and splay my fingers across his chest. I push him backward, just forcefully enough to let him know I want him to lie on the bed.

At first, I think he'll comply, but his smirk and the shake of his head tells me otherwise. Instantly, he flips our positions and the next thing I know, I'm being tossed lightly into the middle of my bed. I've never been more thankful for my queen-sized bed than I am at this moment.

Vince presses a knee into the mattress and slowly climbs up my body. He's not touching me yet, but the anticipation drives me wild. "You in a hurry or somethin'?"

"I can be patient… if I must." I pretend to pout by sticking out my lower lip.

To my surprise, he leans in and nips at my lower lip. "I don't think you're gonna have anything to pout about, Syd. Besides, when you stick out that lower lip, all it makes me wanna do is bite it."

The tease that I am does it again.

To my utter delight, he pulls it gently with his teeth and growls playfully. His hands slide up past my hips, and he full-on begins a tickle war.

I squeal as I attempt to squirm away.

Two can play at this game.

Knowing his ribs are his kryptonite, I go for them with every ounce of energy I have—and it works. Score!!!

The loud laughter erupting from both of us seems to spur us on further. I can't remember when I've had this much fun in a tickle match.

Finally, he gasps, "Enough… Enough… You win…" as he pulls away and flops back on the bed.

Though I'm entirely breathless, I climb over and straddle him to claim my prize. "I declare victory." I pretend to boast. "I'm the champion of all tickle fights. Bow down to the victor…" I raise my hand and fist bump the air. Then I turn my focus back to him with a playful waggle of my brows, "Hmmm... what will be my prize tonight?"

"I'm sure you'll think of something," he deadpans, and I lose it with laughter all over again.

He pulls his body upright and leans his back against my headboard. "I don't know about you... but I'm pretty sure you're not supposed to keep score in bed."

"True," I agree as another thought hits me, and I pretend to be as serious as possible. "Whatever will we do if we aren't having a tickle fight in bed?"

"Well... we could sleep..." he playfully suggests as he pretends to stretch and be tired all of a sudden. But his heated gaze tells me he clearly has better things on his mind than sleep. "Or... We could play a board game?" He shrugs innocently.

"Yeah, right." I roll my eyes. "Why do I have the feeling you'd rather be playing strip Monopoly?"

Vince's eyebrows raise. "Just how many times have you played that?" Then he cringes adorably. "Wait... do I want to know the answer to that?"

Picking up a pillow from the side of the bed, I smack him with it. "No—for your information—I've never played. But if you keep staring at me like that, I just might make an exception with you."

He taps a finger to his chin as a smile forms on his beautiful lips. "I'll keep that in mind for future possibilities."

"You do that," I say as I reach out and trace the shape of his lips with the pad of my thumb. "But for now, I think I have a better idea."

Without another word, I lean forward and kiss him. Vince

doesn't hold back, returning my kiss with a sizzling force of his own. His hand glides to the nape of my neck and he tangles his fingers in my hair. He keeps the pace steady and slow as if he's in no hurry to rush things along.

His other hand slides up my back to the clasp of my bra. In an expert move, he has the clasp undone, and my bra falls free between us. His mouth leaves mine, only to feather kiss along my jaw and down the column of my neck. When he reaches my collarbone, I moan in appreciation as I throw my head back and enjoy the moment.

Our hips grind in a slow rhythm through our clothes, and I feel the effects of this kiss in every inch of my body. My nipples peak and harden as I anticipate him kissing them. Before he makes it there, he abruptly flips us so I'm on my back, and he can trail hot kisses everywhere.

Holy shit!

This is even better.

"Oh. My. God." What is he doing to me? Heat spreads through my body, and I find myself moaning uncontrollably in white-hot pleasure.

When his tongue lashes at my nipple, I writhe beneath him, needing pressure at my core. His leg slips between mine, and I find the force I crave against his thigh. He nips and sucks at one nipple as he gently rolls the other between his fingers.

"More," I urge as I guide his head by fisting his hair. "I need more."

"I've got you, Syd. Just have patience."

Slowly, he makes his way down my rib cage and across the top of my hips that poke out from my jeans.

"Haven't you learned I'm not patient," I groan in frustration as he kisses along my navel, leaving a torture trail of hot kisses along his way.

When he chuckles, his breath tickles my tummy.

"Vince," I groan in utter frustration.

"What do you want, Syd? Tell me… and it's yours."

"Need to come…" I practically beg as I push my hips toward his frame.

Apparently, I've reached the point of begging, but I have no shame when it comes to this man. I'm so fucking turned on, if he stops, I may just have to kill him. I have no idea how he gets me so close with so little effort, but the man has magic hands or something.

He chuckles again as he unbuttons my jeans. "I think I can help you with that."

I wiggle as I help him push my jeans and boy shorts over my hips, and he peels them off with ease. As soon as they are out of the way, he returns his attention to me.

"Tell me how you like it?" he asks with interest.

Lifting my head, I stare as if I didn't hear him correctly.

"What gets you off the hardest?" he asks, leaving no doubt this time.

"I just need you," I say as I reach up to pull his face closer to mine so I can kiss him. "Though I do like it when you nip at my nipples and apply pressure on my clit."

"I think I can handle that," he says on a lazy grin as he makes his way down my body. His deft fingers find my clit with ease as he pays ample attention to my breast.

Suddenly, I feel a slow build deep within my body.

"Holy shit… how do you do that so fast?"

And he stops… he fucking stops…

"Do what so fast?" he asks with great interest.

"Ugh… I was just about to come so hard…" I practically whine.

"Don't worry, Syd, I've got all night."

"You don't understand… I never have multiples… or come this fast… I'm afraid I just lost it…"

He looks as if he didn't just burst my favorite balloon.

"I told you, Syd, I've got all night. I'm not gonna leave you hanging."

Like before, Vince shows he's in no rush to take things further. He takes his time getting to know each of my breasts intimately as he perfectly strums my clit as if he's been given the key that can unlock my body in an instant. Warmth fans throughout my limbs, and my nerve endings crackle.

The only way I can describe this intense feeling as it flows into every pore of my essence in such a slow burn is that it's euphoric beyond description. It flows down my spine and into my extremities. My face literally numbs as I focus on the energy coursing through me. It spreads out in waves and has yet to actually spark.

God only knows how Vince keeps me on the precipice for what feels like an eternity. I swear he hits a pause button on reality because time ceases to exist. It's just me and him. I want more… I need more, but I'm conflicted because I'm not sure whether to chase this ecstasy further. I'm just not ready for it to end.

I hover on the edge.

The brink of no return.

Just when I think I'm ready to fall over, he changes up his pace and brings me to a whole new level of high. When he inserts his fingers and starts to scissor as he strums my clit with his thumb, I'm sure I've started speaking in tongues.

"What the fuck are you doing to me?" I ask in awe as he manages to keep my orgasm at bay and excite me further.

My thoughts are so incoherent that if he says something in return, I simply don't hear it.

All I hear is the blood rushing throughout every inch of my body as it chases the orgasm of a lifetime, as he kisses down my body.

Then he flicks my clit with his tongue. The world could stop turning in this instant, and I wouldn't even care. I've been to Nirvana, and there's no need in returning to reality.

My body tenses stiff as a board as I come over and over again. He manages to prolong my orgasm for longer than I could ever imagine.

When my muscles unclench and relax, I can't even open my eyes. It's just too much effort. Vince crawls up my body, pulling me into his arms like the rag doll I've become. I feel his warm breath on my neck as he kisses me softly from behind as we morph into the big spoon.

I can feel his erection—but I'm so wrecked, I can't even turn to face him.

"Owe you..." is my last coherent thought as I drift off to sleep.

When my eyes drift open, light creeps through my window as if it's barely dawn.

What the hell happened to me?

I look to where I thought Vince was supposed to be sleeping, but the bed is empty. Not that I expected him to stay over, but despair washes over me.

Before I can contemplate a pity party, I feel the covers lift and the bed dip. Soft kisses feather up my leg to the apex of my thighs. He wasn't in a rush before, but he is now as his hands splay me open, and his tongue flicks across my clit.

"Well, this is quite the wakeup call," I tease.

"Can't talk now... busy..." he mumbles between fervent kisses.

How the hell can he take me back to where I was last night in such a short time?

VINCE

I CAN'T HELP THE TRIUMPHANT GRIN THAT'S LIKELY TO BE permanently etched across my face when Sydney comes down from another intense orgasm. I mean... I did that... and I'm damn proud of my efforts. Last night, her orgasm went on and on and this morning, I had every intent of replicating it.

When the last of her quakes finish, I crawl up her body to hold her once again. I've never actually stayed the night with a woman before. Sure... it took me forever to actually sleep, due to the raging case of blue balls, but hands down, it is worth every ounce of pain to wake up with her like this today.

As I pull her fully sated body against mine, I wrap my arms around her like she's meant just for me. Nuzzling my chin into the crook of her neck, I whisper, "Good morning."

I feel her laugh before I hear it. "If that's your idea of a wakeup call, I volunteer as tribute for repeats."

"I'm sure that can be arranged." I shrug it off as if she didn't just rock my world, too. "Though truth be told. You're the first person I've ever stayed the night with." I have no idea why the truth spills out. But I guess if I think about it, I'd rather she knows the truth.

Her tone is playful as she sighs, "Ahhh… so you're a love 'em and leave him guy, are ya?"

"Nope… can't say that I am," I admit with another truth.

Sydney doesn't say anything, she just flips over to face me and leans against my bare chest. Her leg intertwines with mine as she takes a moment to find comfort.

Not trusting myself, I slept in my jeans last night, so I'm sure the denim's scratchy on her delicate skin. But as she worms her way closer to my side, I'm not certain she cares.

"You okay, Syd?" I ask when she stills and doesn't say anything for an unusual amount of time.

"Just enjoying this moment," she whispers, then sucks in a deep breath and moans on an exhale. "You smell so good…"

Really? I haven't showered since before the game, and I slept in my clothes.

"Okay…" I laugh lightly, still in shock at her words. "If you say so…"

"I do. I can't get enough of you. I want to take your scent and turn it into a candle for when you're not here." Suddenly, her body tenses, and she mutters, "Wait… forget I said that…" She burrows her head into my chest so I can't see her expression.

"Syd?" I ask, trying to gain her attention.

When she finally peeks my way, her beautiful freckles nearly disappear with the heat that rushes to her face. Before I can question her further, her words gush out. "It must be the sex-induced coma you put me into last night.... I blame that for sounding creepy."

"You were pretty comatose last night," I tease. "But I think I get it. I couldn't get enough of your taste last night... I mean... look at how I couldn't keep my hands off you this morning."

"Vince... you will *never* hear a complaint from me with a wakeup call like that. You're way better than any alarm I've ever had."

"I'll be sure to remember that," I tease as I draw lazy circles up and down her back.

God, she feels amazing, and I can't stop myself from touching her.

A few minutes later, I hear her stomach rumble with hunger and when I look at the clock, I realize it's later than I thought. "What do you say to breakfast out today?"

"What?" She feigns shock and adds, "You don't cook?"

"I'll have you know... I cook nearly every morning... so I'd like a day off... thank you very much. My only request—as good as it is, we avoid the diner. I love my sister more than anything, but I'd rather keep you to myself than share you just yet."

"I get it. If I got up and cooked you breakfast here, I'd potentially have to share you with my roommates. Can we just stay in our bubble for a while longer?"

I nod in agreement as I push back the covers. "I think I know just the place."

We end up at a small mom and pop restaurant just outside of town along an old country road. The place is busy, but thankfully, we're able to score a booth before the crowd sets in.

We've placed our orders, and Sydney's sipping on a fresh cup of coffee while we wait.

"You mentioned Julia was with a friend last night. How did you manage that?"

"One of her friends from daycare also happens to have a parent who's a close friend of Vanessa. She and her husband offered to watch her when they found out CRU was going for another championship title. Julia's only stayed the night one other time, but it was amazing for them to offer."

I laugh at the memory of that experience. "Van was a wreck the entire time because Julia's only stayed with family. We were prepared for her to come home in the middle of the night or something, so we slept with our ringers on full blast just in case. But nope. That's not Jules. She basically waved us off from the moment she left the car and begged to stay the night again as soon as possible when we picked her up."

Sydney smiles wide as she shakes her head. "She's independent, that's for sure."

My head shakes in approval as laughter spills from my lips. "You have no idea. We're gonna have our hands full with her later. She already acts like a mini-adult. I just freaking hope she chooses the right path in life because there will be no swaying her once her mind is set."

"I might've resembled that as a kid." Sydney shrugs guiltily. "I don't think I've turned out that bad."

"No... you certainly haven't," I agree. "Though I can just imagine you filled with spitfire and sass as a teenager. Your mom must've had her hands full."

"Not really. I mellowed out," she sighs. "Though, I'm sure it had more to do with the fact I was more the parent growing up than Mom." Shaking her head as she looks to the sky, she lets out a loud sigh. "I should probably thank Grams for that. I'm only at CRU because she insisted I apply for my scholarship. It also helped that she left me just enough money in her will to cover my expenses for the first two years. Since last year, I've been on my own. But with the hours I pick up at the bar, I should be able to graduate without being in too much debt."

Damn. Another thing we have in common. Though I shouldn't be shocked; she's a hard worker. I've seen her in action, and nothing she's told me is out of character for her so far.

When I'm quiet for longer than necessary, Sydney changes the conversation with ease and after taking another long pull from her coffee mug, she asks, "Does Vanessa work tomorrow morning?"

I swear I see a flash of disappointment cross her face so quickly that if I hadn't been paying such close attention, I would've missed it.

"Yeah. She grabs as many hours as possible when there's a big event in town. The alumni always tip well, and it practically triples her paycheck."

"Wow. I usually work after big events on campus, too. But there's no way I'd miss the championship game. I requested last night off before we qualified for the championships. I just had this feeling, ya know…"

CRU had another amazing season, that's for sure. "Do you like to watch other sports when basketball's not in season?"

"I'm a huge football fan as well."

"Okay—we can't be friends if your team's not the Rainier Renegades," I deadpan, hoping I'm not wrong about her choice in teams. But let's face it, she could like my most hated team, and I doubt it would have any effect on my feelings toward her.

Her seriousness is almost comical as her posture turns rigid, and her expression is stone cold. "Uh… Luke Leighton has brought so much to the team since taking over as head coach. How could I not?"

When she breaks her hardened stare, we both laugh.

Shaking her head at her adorable antics, she sighs. "Though truth be told—Grams loved the Renegades, and I really wasn't allowed to like anything else. She and her friends always threw football parties at the local VFW. I can't remember a weekend without watching the game if I was with her."

"Your grams sounds like she was pretty cool," I surmise. I would've loved being close to my grandparents.

"She was the best," Syd says wistfully as our waitress interrupts with our food.

Neither of us speak while we dig into the feast before us. I'm ravenous and from the way Syd devours her biscuits and gravy, I'd say she worked up quite the appetite last night.

We eat in comfortable silence as we both consume most of our meal. I'm not sure what about Sydney puts me at ease, but I know one thing's for certain. I like it—a lot. Probably way more than I should, but I'm not sure I have much choice in the matter.

Sometimes, Syd's like a whirling hurricane on the outside, yet at the same time, when you cut to the core of her issues, she's completely calm at the same time. I've never seen anything like it. She's quite the anomaly and as I study her, I'm not sure what to make of it.

"What?" she asks, breaking my concentration.

Apparently, subtlety is not one of my virtues this morning as she's caught me blatantly staring at her.

Shaking my head to clear my thoughts, I mumble, "It's nothing."

Cocking an eyebrow, she stares in disbelief. Her bullshit meter is strong, and there's no pulling anything past her.

I take a moment to finish chewing before I put her at ease. "Seriously, Syd. It's nothing. I just got lost in thought. Sorry for staring."

Well... that isn't a total lie, but it's the safest response—for now anyway. I'm not sure I want to lay all my cards on the table, when I barely know what game I'm playing. Not that I'm playing a game—because that's not the case—but rather I'm in uncharted territory, and I'm uncertain what my next move should be.

"What were you concentrating so hard on?"

"I have no idea." I shrug off, hoping she'll let it go. It's not that I have anything to hide, but I don't want to explain my thoughts about her just yet either.

"You know you can tell me anything, right?" she assures me as she finishes another bite of biscuit.

"Yep," I agree because she's right.

Shaking her head, she digs into another bite.

The subject forgotten—for now.

After eating a bit more, Sydney brings up an assignment from our mutual class due this week. We prattle on with ease about how to complete it. I'm a little further with it than she is, so I give her some pointers about where to start with her research as I hit a few dead ends with a few of the sources that were given.

As we leave the restaurant, I'm brought back to reality by my phone buzzing in my pocket. Quickly, I pull it out to find it's a call from Vanessa.

Never missing a call from her, I answer immediately, "Hey, Van."

"Hey, Vince. Are you home?" I can hear the cringe in her voice and shake my head. Clearly, she'd rather not be calling.

"No," I draw out. "What's up?" I ask, wanting to cut to the chase.

She lets out a heavy sigh. "I'm still at work, and we're slammed. Julia's supposed to be picked up by noon, so they can go out of town for the day." She's quiet for a moment, and I can tell she's likely chewing on her bottom lip, as her tell for being nervous. I have no idea why she's acting so strange. Her request isn't unusual—it happens when a big event is in town.

"Want me to pick up Jules?" I offer. But as the words leave my mouth, I realize that means I'm cutting my time short with Sydney.

"I... uh... didn't want to interrupt your plans, but I feel bad for leaving here at the same time. I swear everyone within a fifty-mile radius has come in for brunch today."

Looking to Sydney, she nods in understanding, and my unease disappears.

"It's no problem. I'll have to run home to get my Jeep to have the car seat, but I should be able to make it there with plenty of time to spare."

"Thanks, Vin. You're a lifesaver. I love you more than chocolate."

Shaking my head at the lie, I laugh. "No, you don't, but I love you anyway," I tease with our running joke. I learned at a young age not to come between my twin and chocolate, but I also know outside of Julia, I'm her favorite person in the world. "I'll see you when you get home. I've got Jules covered, so just do your thing."

"Thanks, Vinnie," she says as she pulls out the nickname she only uses when she gets her way. "I love you, but please know I *am* sorry for interrupting your plans for today."

Not wanting to get into it in front of Sydney, I keep the conversation short. I'm sure Vanessa will grill me later on the details about Sydney. Not that she'll learn much, but she's my sister, so I know she'll try. "Don't worry about it. Love you, Vanny. See you at home."

With that, I hang up the phone. Then turn to Sydney with a cringe. "I... uh, gotta go pick up Jules."

Shrugging, she shakes her head. "I heard. Really, Vince. It's not a big deal."

I'm not ready for our time together to end.

"I'm sure you have other more exciting plans for the afternoon, but if you're free, you're welcome to hang with me and Jules. We throw down a mean dance party, and there's bound to be an art project or twenty to throw into the mix."

"A dance party, you say... that I might just have to see. But be warned... if there's a competition, you're going down."

Her serious expression makes me erupt with laughter. Damn. This girl.

She's competitive through and through.

I'm sure I've just met my match with her.

17

SYDNEY

The last thing I expected when I woke up this morning was to spend the entire day with Vince's family. But they welcome me with ease. Julia's easy to like and as I soon find out, so is her mom.

Julia hadn't wanted to leave her friend's house when we got there, and I could tell from the car she was giving Vince a hard time. I couldn't hear her words, but her reluctance to leave was almost comical. She smiled and waved goodbye to her friend but as soon as it was the two of them, her body drooped, and she walked defeatedly to the car.

Her foul mood changed the minute she spotted me in the car.

Instantly, her face morphed from sad to excited in a nanosecond. I would've laughed aloud if I didn't know better.

She practically ran to the Jeep squealing with delight. You would've thought Vince brought her a new puppy, she was so excited. I'm not that exciting—trust me. But to a kid, who am I to complain.

Vince handles Julia like a pro. He cooks us lunch with ease—though I am still stuffed from breakfast, I can barely eat anything. Then we play card games until she asks to draw.

Apparently, Vince's hidden talent is drawing carton caricatures. He can whip them out and tell stories on the fly like no other I've seen before. He claims he's just fooling around, but it feels like there's more story there than he's willing to admit with Julia in the room.

After we finish drawing, Julia jumps up like popcorn in a kettle on high. "Unks, let's go for a ride."

"On your bike?" Vince asks for clarification.

Julia rolls her eyes and shakes her head. Duh... isn't heard, but I swear if she were a bit older, it would accompany her expression as she juts out her chin adorably. "You know I can't drive a car... I just learned to ride my bike... and I'm still in a car seat."

"Okay, Miss Priss. Let's ask Sydney if she even wants to go before you just demand a bike ride. She can ride your mom's bike if she's interested, but we're not going to pressure her either. So, you'll have to accept her decision—and no arguments. Got it?"

"Yes, Unks." She lowers her head then looks to me expectantly.

I can tell she's trying not to pressure me, but I'm not about to let her down either. "Sounds good... if you're sure your mom won't mind."

I look to Vanessa who arrived not too long ago for

assurance. There's no way I'm taking her limited time away from spending it with Julia.

"I'd love nothing more than to take a shower and work on a paper I have due this week. You're more than welcome to use my helmet and bike." Then conspiratorially, she whispers, "Thanks a million, Vinnie. I owe you big time," as she hugs him briefly.

"No problem, Van. It's what I'm here for." Vince shrugs it off as he focuses his attention on Julia. "Get ready to go, squirt. Syd and I'll be out in the garage in a minute."

Julia rushes down the hall as if she's trying to qualify for the Olympics, and we all laugh at her antics.

"Seriously, Sydney. Thanks. You're like her new best friend. I hope you don't mind spending the day with her."

Spending the day with Julia means spending the day with Vince in his element. It's a no brainer. But there's no way I'm admitting that. "It's no problem, really. She's adorable, and I've enjoyed my time with her."

"Feel free to go for a *long* ride. I'm *really* behind on my paper, and I could use the kid-free distraction for a bit. I should've gotten more done yesterday, and I'm regretting the me time I took while she was away last night. I watched an adult movie and everything." The way she tries to play it off makes me realize just what I take for granted as a single co-ed. I can't imagine being a single parent, while trying to go to school.

"Let's go, or she'll leave without us." Vince's tone is teasing, but I'm sure there's some hidden truth as well. Julia's quite independent.

We end up on a paved walking path that leads to a local park. There's a lap around a soccer field Julia rides with ease for the better part of an hour. After making countless circles around the soccer field, Vince and I take a break on a bench and watch her zoom round and round several more times. The girl's like the Energizer bunny when it comes to riding that bike.

Now that I've spent time with his family, I finally have the courage to ask, "So, what happened to Julia's father?"

Vince's expression goes from carefree to a grimace in an instant, and I instantly regret my question.

Shit. That's what I get for being nosey.

Vince's tone remains indifferent when he speaks, "The short version is that he didn't want anything to do with being a dad. I know he was in high school, but it's totally his loss. Julia's one of the most amazing people I know. The even shorter version to this complicated story is Dad ensured he signed his rights away so he can't change his mind about things either. In doing so, Vanessa's on her own when it comes to being responsible for Julia. But she's never been alone. We've supported her from day one, and Julia's been the biggest blessing."

He watches her wistfully for a few minutes in silence, and my walls crack open for him even further. He loves her without a doubt. He and Vanessa have a bond only twins share. I love that he considers Julia a blessing for himself as well; it makes my heart squeeze with a rush of emotion.

Gah... all the feels with knowing this man.

When he reaches for my hand to intertwine his fingers in

mine, I squeeze his hand once, afraid to let my emotion rush out. I have no idea why, but the way he said that makes me think of Grams… but in a happy way. It's weird, I know—grief hits at the strangest of times.

By the time I get home later that night, I'm still in awe of how well Vince and his sister handle having a child in their lives. I guess for them it's become second nature, but not having been around kids growing up, it makes me take stock of things. I feel like such a slacker only having to balance work and school. I can't imagine what life would be like to be a teenage mom as well.

But that's reason one million, nine hundred eighty-eight thousand I have an IUD. I love sex—and I'm not ashamed to admit it, but I'm not ready to be a mom anytime soon.

Abby finds me sitting at the kitchen table staring off into space, while the glass of juice I've poured sits untouched.

"Everything okay?" she interrupts as she walks into the kitchen to get herself some water.

"Yeah…" I sigh. "Just thinking…"

"About?" she probes.

Where do I start?

Letting out a long breath, Grams' words come to mind. *Just start from the beginning, and it's usually not as bad as you think.*

Not that this is bad, I just don't know what it means that Vince has consumed my thoughts.

Instead of telling her what's on my mind, I deflect.

"So, how is that sexy fiancé of yours?"

This does the trick. Abby's eyes turn starry as a grin becomes the predominant feature on her face. "He's wonderful. I still can't believe you helped him pull off that surprise before the game. I seriously thought he was just nervous for the game. I had no idea he would propose."

I know… I was there, but I won't steal this moment from her.

"Have you thought about when you're going to move in together?" I don't know if I can swing her portion of the rent and finding a roommate this close to the end of the school year would be nearly impossible. But I won't worry her with those thoughts. She deserves to be happy, and if Drew makes her happy, I'm happy for her.

"Don't worry… you're not getting rid of me that easily. With only a few months until we graduate, we're waiting until Baltimore to get a place of our own."

"It's not like you don't already spend nearly every night together," I tease. "Now that the season's over, I'm sure you'll actually get to enjoy what time you have left here. I'm going to miss you so much. I'm so happy you're graduating early, but what the hell are Chloe and I gonna do without you as a roommate?"

"Let's do a girls' weekend soon! I know I've been preoccupied lately. But I love you both like sisters and will miss you like crazy when I'm on the other side of the country. Holy shit… I'm gonna be married and living on the other side of the country. How did this happen?"

"Uh… you got into the school of your dreams and fell in love?" I deadpan.

"I'm actually surprised to see you here today. I thought you'd be celebrating with Drew all weekend."

"With his apartment being run over with family and

friends of his roommates, I came home to do some laundry and grab a few things I'll need for the week. Drew's getting ready to have dinner with his parents before they leave. They'll be here any minute to pick me up."

Standing, I reach out and pull her into a hug. "I'm so happy for you, Abs. You deserve everything that's happening to you. Just don't forget us little people when you become a hotshot doctor."

She releases me with a smirk. "You're way too hard to forget, Syd. Besides, I'm only a phone call away if you ever need me."

I know. But it won't be the same as having her right next door, like she's been since my freshman year. I'm so freaking happy for her, but it doesn't mean I won't miss her.

"So where did you jet off to after the game? I thought you'd celebrate with us."

It's my turn to smile. "I... uh... had plans..." I draw out.

"Do these plans have anything to do with that guy you took to the concert a few weeks ago? You've been pretty tight-lipped about him. Usually we hear about your dates with duds loud and clear."

Her teasing tone does the trick. I laugh and admit the truth, "No... he's definitely not a dud. It's still pretty new, but Vince is a great guy."

"Ah... he has a name... Wait... You're not gonna friend-zone this great guy, are you? The last time you found a *great guy*, the poor sap followed you around like an eager puppy vying for your attention."

"Oh... he's got my attention. I'm just not sure what to do with it," I admit. "I honestly thought I would date him and get him out of my system, so I could move past him… you know me. But Vince's not the kind of guy I'm easily able to walk away from."

"Uh-oh," she says in warning.

"What?"

"Nothing…" She shakes her head, and the brat that she is refuses to insert her opinion by saying anything more. So typical of Abby.

I harden my stare to get her to break, but all she does is shrug.

Damn her. Her silence could mean a million things, but I know she won't budge either.

When she realizes I'm just as stubborn, she just shrugs. "It's nothing… honest. I'm happy you finally have found someone that makes you think twice about them."

Once. Twice. A million times… not that I'll admit that. She totally has me there.

Since I don't say anything, she breaks our silence with, "When you finally decide if he's worthy of introducing us, I'd love to meet the man who's got you tied in knots."

"I'm not in knots," comes out defensive, even to my stubborn ears.

Her phone buzzes, and I'd bet my last paycheck that it's Drew. Only he has this effect on her.

Sheepishly, she shrugs. "I gotta go. Please don't overthink things. Just enjoy the moment and let your walls down, Syd."

"Go be with Loverboy," I tease as I push her in the direction of the door. "Tell him congratulations and that he rocked the court last night."

She gathers her purse on the counter. "Will do. Take care you. Love you."

"Love you, too!" I holler as she reaches the door.

When she leaves, it doesn't even take an entire breath, and my mind's back on Vince.

What am I going to do with him?

18

VINCE

I HATE BEING LATE, BUT AT LEAST I'VE GOT A GOOD EXCUSE. Sydney's meeting me at my place for dinner. And of course, today of all days, my professor asks me to stay after to discuss my mid-term project. At first, I am nervous. But my mood seriously changes the moment he tells me that he wants to put the plan I outlined in my mid-term into action. I thought the project was simply for a grade, but unbeknownst to me, it's actually for a marketing campaign with a local company. Therefore, I can't begrudge him the extra time. It's a huge accomplishment to have my design chosen. The best part is there's a potential side job for me, if I want to take it on as well. It's something I can do from the ease of my home, and the pay is good, too.

Despite the fact that this impromptu meeting cuts into my limited time with Sydney, my steps are light as I make my way across campus. How often do you stay for a meeting and come out with a potential job? Not only will it be a great resume builder, but it might give me a lead on something that could turn permanent.

When I finally make it home, I hear Jules and Van in the kitchen busy with dinner. Instead of joining them, I bee-line it to my bedroom for a moment to decompress as I put away my things from school. Knowing I need to respond to the email my professor forwarded me, I pull out my laptop and get to it. After carefully constructing my email, I look it over carefully before feeling confident to hit send.

Glancing at the clock, I realize it's much later than I thought, and Sydney's still not here. Hopefully, something hasn't come up. I don't think I can wait much longer to share my good news.

Knowing it's unlike her to text if she's late, I glance to my phone.

Nope. Nothing. No call or text.

Where is she?

My sister interrupts my thoughts by calling my name throughout the house. "Vin. Dinner's ready."

"Coming!" I holler, stashing my phone in my pocket.

Sydney's a big girl. She'll call if something's wrong. I remind myself.

When I step into the hall, laughter fills the air. And instantly, I know it's not just my family. Sydney's familiar tone makes my pace quicken to greet her.

Walking into the kitchen, I see everyone's already seated at the table.

"Hey, you." Sydney beams at my arrival.

"When did you get here?" I chuckle, realizing I must've

been into that email I was writing to not hear her knock on the door.

"Oh, I ran into your sister on campus. We've been hanging out for the last few hours."

Well, that's unexpected.

Slowly, I look between Syd and my sister to see if they're conspiring against me or something.

I'm not sure what expression I reveal because Van rolls her eyes as she swats the air. "Really, Vin?"

"What?" comes out defensively. "I didn't say anything."

"You don't have to," Sydney interjects with a light laugh.

"Your sister's a riot. She's been dishing all the dirt on you." Syd points a finger and waves it playfully. "You should be very worried, Vincent..." She looks suspiciously to Van, and the little shit just smirks knowingly in my direction.

"Vincent... eh?" I pretend to glare. If Julia wasn't watching the entire exchange on bated breath, I might have reacted like I was fifteen and let my petulance shine. "Just what do I owe the honor of being full named?"

Surprisingly, Sydney breaks.

She almost looks bashful as words flow from her beautiful lips. "Ohmigod, Vince, you are *too* funny. Though I happen to like your sister, have no fear. She hasn't revealed your deep-held secrets or anything that isn't too embarrassing."

Sydney looks so adorable with her backpedaling, I almost kiss her. But Julia stops me in my tracks.

"Really, Unks. We haven't told any of your secrets... like how you stash the last of your favorite cookies up behind the pasta... or anything." Then she gasps and covers her mouth as if she realizes what she's just revealed.

She's so adorable, I can't even be mad.

"So… you're a sweet hoarder?" Sydney's playful voice makes me grin.

"Only when it comes to your baked goods," I admit. "I wasn't that good at sharing."

Sydney turns to Julia. "Did he share *any* of them?"

Julia nods. "He gave me *one* after I finished my dinner. But I saw him hide the rest."

Guilty.

I shrug, adding, "You did make them for me," as I shrug my selfishness off.

"Well, there's an easy way to remedy that. I'll just have to make some for everyone next time." She looks pointedly at me, reminding me of how Mom used to calmly get her point across when she wanted something.

"I will never complain to more of your baked goodness."

With that, I join them at the table. Reaching under the table, I squeeze Sydney's thigh to let her know I appreciate her being here. Then we dig into the delicious meal Vanessa has cooked for us.

Glancing to Sydney as she laughs at another of Julia's antics, I realize just how right this feels. Oddly enough, having Sydney at the table with us feels as natural as breathing. The conversation ebbs and flows easily as we eat. It's obvious Sydney and Vanessa are becoming fast friends; they even have some inside jokes I'm not privy to.

I can't say that it bothers me though; I don't think I could date anyone my sister doesn't like. It's not that I need her approval. It's more that I don't have time for anyone who doesn't accept our situation.

I get squeals of delight when I reveal my news from before. Even though we're sitting at the table with my sister, Sydney congratulates me with a quick hug and peck to the cheek. If I'd known this is how she'd react, I might have waited until we're alone to mention it.

Eventually, the conversation turns to their experiences with being a waitress and bartender, and they find they have even more in common. They both joke and commiserate about their experiences with annoying patrons.

"The worst is when a guy thinks *you're* on the menu..." Vanessa throws out there as if this is a daily occurrence.

What. The. Fuck? The hairs on the back of my neck rise as this is the first I've heard this complaint.

"Seriously. I can't tell you how many times I've told someone where to go—and how to get there. Though they're usually harmless and only have their drunken courage to thank for their boldness... it's annoying as ever."

"No one should *ever* think either of you are on the menu," I insert a little too forcefully. "That's... just..." I stumble over my words as anger replaces my playful mood.

"Relax, Vin. It happens all the time," Vanessa assures me. "Usually they're just trying to show off and flirt in front of their friends. Sometimes, it's welcomed—other times, I just shut it down."

"Exactly," Sydney chimes in. "You've seen firsthand what I've experienced at the bar the night we met."

True. Derek did make an ass of himself.

"But the worst is when they don't take no for an answer. I've had to get my boss to politely remind them of their manners a few times."

My jaw drops as my eyes swing to Vanessa. "Why is this the first I'm hearing of this?"

She points in my direction and swirls a finger at my face. "That. Right there. I handled it, and it wasn't a problem after."

"Thank God, we have bouncers for that reason. When someone gets out of control, I just cut them off, and one of the guys stacked with muscles escorts them off the premises. I usually don't have to worry about it then." Sydney shakes her head for some reason, and her expression drastically changes to irritation. "Though there have been times they stay pissed and take it out on me the next time they come in."

"That's bu…" I glance to Julia and quickly change my word choice, "…malarkey."

Sydney grins at my impromptu choice of cursing.

I glance to Julia, and she nods in approval. "It is malarkey. But that's why we have bouncers, so bartenders only have to worry about slinging drinks."

"I still don't like it," I grumble.

"None of us do," Van sighs. Then she pats my forearm across the table to placate me. "Don't worry, little brother. The instances are few and far between, so there's no need to get your panties in a twist."

"Okay, shorty," I concede only because there's no point in causing a scene—especially over something I have no control over. "You'd better not keep it from me next time," I leave hanging in the air as a warning.

Don't think for a second I missed the eye roll exchange between my sister and Sydney. Traitors—the whole lot of them, I tell ya. How the hell can I help them if I'm left in the dark?

My thoughts are interrupted when Julia tips her cup, and milk spills across the table between the two of us. On instinct, I throw my napkin over the spill and reach for the extras we always keep on the table for this reason. "Whoa, squirt. Slow down," I warn as she tries to bolt out of her seat to help clean her mess. "I've got this."

Within seconds, I have it under control, and we're back to eating our meal—business as usual. When Sydney squeezes my thigh under the table in appreciation of my quick reflexes, I realize this might be so normal for her.

After dinner, Sydney asks if we have the ingredients for no-bake cookies and to Julia's delight, we do. As I clean up the kitchen, she and Julia set in to making dessert. Jules is right up to the counter with her on her trusty stool, helping her measure the ingredients to add to the pan.

Since it's essentially boiling the ingredients, Julia waits patiently as Sydney stirs the gooey concoction to perfection. The smell alone could put someone into a sugar-induced coma—but my mouth salivates in anticipation for finally getting to taste their efforts.

They've prepared the counter with waxed paper, and Sydney's as patient as ever as she lets Jules use two spoons to drop dollops of the melted goodness out to harden. When I think I won't get caught, I reach over and snag a warm cookie to taste test. But of course, Jules notices and swats me away.

"Get out of here, Unks. Can't you see we're cookin' here?"

"But it tastes so good!!!" I draw out, feigning my impending doom if I don't get a taste right this instant.

"If you don't scat," Sydney warns playfully, "there will be no cookies for you."

Jutting out my lower lip, I pretend to pout. "But you said Jules gets to lick the bowl. Aren't I essentially doing that?"

"Not. The. Same. Unks. Go do something." She shoos me like a pesky fly then points to the living room. "Go watch a show with Momma or something."

"Okay, sassy pants. I can take the hint." But I glance at Syd, ensuring she's okay with Jules if I do what she asks.

Syd looks apologetic, but there's a hint of a smile to let me know she's okay with this. I can take the hint. So, without another word, I go into the living room to hang with Vanessa, until I'm allowed back into the kitchen.

"She kicked you out, eh?" Vanessa giggles quiet enough for just me to hear.

"Yep. Apparently, tasting as we bake is *not* an option."

"Sounds rough. Are you sure Sydney's okay with her in there? I would've stayed, but I took that phone call, then just found myself sitting on this couch and can't get the motivation to get back up."

"I'm pretty sure Sydney is just fine," I say, patting her on the shoulder as I pass to the couch. But I really take a closer look at Van as I sprawl across the couch. "You need to take time for yourself, Van. You've been burning the candle at both ends lately, and you don't need to."

Van sighs hard enough to blow the few strands of blond hair away from her face. "I know... I've just been helping out when they're short staffed."

"That's not always your responsibility," I remind her. "We don't need the extra money. We're fine with your regular shifts."

We were each left a trust fund, but we can't draw on it until we're twenty-five. We had college funds available to us, which cover almost everything—but no one expected us having to factor medical insurance into our monthly bills, so that takes up the rest of our monthly allotments. We made the choice to sell our family home because it was just too painful to think of returning without Mom and Dad. Besides, it allowed us to purchase this home free and clear—with money left over for unexpected expenses. We don't have to work—but we choose to.

"Yeah, but you know me… if someone needs help, and I can, I always offer. It's not that bad. Now that the tournament is over, it should slow down a bit." She stifles a yawn, and a grimace forms on my face. She's exhausted and needs a break.

"Why don't you get your things done for tomorrow, and I'll handle bedtime with Jules? I highly doubt you'll make it past her bedtime if you don't." I stare at her pointedly until she realizes I'm not budging.

She yawns heavily, but still asks, "Are you sure?"

"Van, you look like you're gonna pass out at any moment," I point out but then tell her what she needs to hear. "I'll have Jules come say good night before bed. But if you're sleeping, we'll blow a kiss from the door."

Slowly, she rises from the couch and comes to hug me. "Thanks, Vinnie. I love you."

"Love you, too, Van." When I pull away, I point to her room. "Go get some rest. I've got things covered tonight."

"I know… I know…" Another yawn comes, and she doesn't even attempt to hide it. God, she must be exhausted. "Night."

"Night, Vanny."

Watching her walk in almost a zombie-like state to the

hall, I do my best to chuckle. *What is it with the stubborn women in my life?*

Flipping on the TV, I settle into the couch. Nothing holds my interest as I'd rather be in the kitchen with the sexy redhead and my niece. But since I've been exiled, I do my best to find something to pass the time.

Eventually, I settle on an episode of *Cash Cab*, as I love trivia games, and it won't matter if I get interrupted. Dad always liked trivia games, and it wore off onto me. As I quietly answer the questions as they're displayed, I realize just how much I've missed this show. After Dad died, I steered clear of shows like these, but lately I find myself able to enjoy them. This must be a rerun, as the series was cancelled, but I still love it all the same.

When the host, Ben Bailey, asks, "Do any parks in New York City come close to the size of Central Park—when referring to acreage?"

Before I can even think of the answer, I hear, "Pellham Bay's Park in the Bronx."

"What?" I turn to look at Sydney who just grins like the Cheshire cat as we await the answer. Of course, the couple in the cab is choosing to phone a friend. "I've never heard of that park," I say in disbelief.

"There are a few others. But that's the biggest," she states matter-of-factly, which causes me to chuckle.

"I guess the better question is *why* do you know that?"

Her green eyes twinkle, and her perfect lips smirk. "I had to do a report on New York City in middle school, and I became obsessed with everything about New York." She shakes her head then sighs, "I've never been there but have always wanted to go. It's definitely on my bucket list."

"I went my junior year in high school with my parents and Van. We did all the touristy things. I would love to go back sometime."

"Someday I'll get there. I've read so many books about New York City, and I can't wait to see it in person."

Julia inserts herself into the conversation. "Can we go there someday, Unks?"

"Maybe when you're a little older, squirt. We'll have to plan it."

Julia beams then turns to Sydney. "Maybe we can all go together?"

Sydney's smart and stays non-committal. "We'll see…"

Wanting to change the subject before Sydney's forced to make promises, I waggle my eyes playfully, "Are the cookies ready yet?"

"Unks, we have to let them get hard." She waves a finger at me in warning. "And Sydney says if you eat too much, you'll get a tummy ache."

"I'll keep that in mind," I promise.

Sydney sucks in a deep breath. "I hate to say it, but I have to head out. I've got an exam tomorrow and a long day."

Glancing out the window, I realize it's dark, and she didn't bring her car. Standing, I offer, "Want a ride home? Jules and I will happily drop you off."

"I won't turn one down. I can't wait until the days get a bit longer." Sydney smiles, and a tingle flows through my spine with excitement to prolong our time together—even if it is chaperoned.

Turning to Julia, I suggest, "Hey, Jules, run and get your shoes and coat from your room."

She eagerly bolts down the hall.

Knowing my time to be alone with Sydney is limited, I make the most of it. Closing the distance between us, my eyes focus on her beautiful lips. "Thanks again for coming to dinner."

"Thanks for having me; it was fun." She reaches up on her toes as her arms snake around my neck.

I pull her in for a goodnight kiss.

Heat sizzles between us, but we don't get carried away.

When the patter of tiny feet can be heard in the distance, I break our kiss all too soon. I brush my thumb along her lips to wipe off any trace just as Julia arrives. "Sorry," I mutter for my haste. "Van's heading to bed early as she was almost asleep on the couch when I came in. I told her I would take care of Jules for the night."

"It's not a problem, Vince."

Kissing her quickly once more, I whisper, "Thanks." Just in time before Julia rounds the corner from the hall.

"Ready to go?" she eagerly asks the room as she loves going for rides.

"Sure, squirt. Let's go. When we get back, it's bath time for you," I warn.

"Okay..." she drags out. She loves the bath but doesn't always like that bedtime follows.

19

SYDNEY

As I drive to work the next day, I can't scrub the smile from my face as I replay my afternoon. Even though we have hectic schedules, Vince and I make this work. My heart soars when I remember how naturally he just grabs my hand to walk to my apartment to pick up my car after class today, after asking me to dinner. It makes my heart race in the best of ways. I have to say—I love our new routine. Not only is Vince a great cook, but oddly enough, I find I want to spend as much time with him as possible.

Unfortunately, reality strikes, and I have to leave for work all too soon for my liking. But his taste lingers on my lips as I drive away. Julia had been playing in her room with Vanessa, so we may have gotten a little carried away after cleaning up from dinner.

Pressing a finger to my swollen lips, I relive the memory and how Vince is wrecking me for kissing all other men. He barely has to do anything, and I'm on the brink of no return when it comes to the sizzling chemistry between us. I have no idea how he does it—but I certainly don't want it to stop anytime soon. If he can get me this worked up with our clothes on, I can only imagine what it will be like when we finally remove them completely.

When I arrive at the bar, I park in the overflow parking lot reserved for employees. I flow through my pre-shift routine on auto-pilot. I greet my co-workers but do little in terms of carrying a lengthy conversation. No—my mind's too preoccupied with Vince.

We're down one bartender tonight, so when the crowd picks up, I have zero time to contemplate anything but the next drink my customer needs. That's why I don't see him in line…

Fucking Brad.

The douche has the nerve to step up to my bar and expect me to wait on him.

"Hey, Sydney… long time no see."

Trying to remain professional, I coldly ask, "What can I get for you?"

"How about another date? This time, I'll even pay."

Remembering what a cheapskate he was, I shudder in disbelief. The guy split the hors d'oeuvres by percentage of how many I ate—and don't get me started at what a deadbeat dad he is. "Uh… no, thanks," rolls from my lips before I give myself permission to speak my thoughts.

"Ah… come on, Syd. Seriously, I think you've got the wrong impression of me."

"No… I'm sure I saw the real you," I snark. "What do you want to drink?"

"But, Syd…" he starts, but I cut him off.

"Either order or move along. The line is long, and I don't have time to talk to you at the moment."

"Fine…" he grumbles. "I'll have a Sam Adams."

"Are you sure you want to afford that?" I grumble under my breath as I turn to fill his order. He has some nerve talking to me again. I thought I made it clear I wanted nothing to do with him when I left him high and dry abruptly.

Shoving his drink at him, I ask what's required of me, "Anything else I can get you?"

"Only another chance with you."

Seriously? What the fuck is he thinking? He'd have a better chance of a snowball surviving in the depths of hell before I'd consider breathing the same air as him—on purpose.

His eyes feign remorse, but I'm not buying it. This guy is in a class all to his own when it comes to his douchery. Yeah, I made that word up, but you get the point. There's no fucking way I'd ever consider it—even if Vince weren't in the picture.

"Uh… No… thanks," I tack on when I see my boss step up next to us.

"Everything okay, Syd?" he asks more for Fucking Brad's sake than mine. This is what happens when he realizes someone is giving his bartenders a hard time or they are unwelcome.

"No problem at all," Brad mutters like the fucking douche-canoe he is as he grabs his beer from the bar.

"That's what I thought." Asher stands a bit taller and glares in Brad's direction as he hastily retreats and disappears into the crowded bar.

Then his attention is on me. "Are you sure you're okay, Syd?"

"Nothing I can't handle," I assure him with a confident smile.

"Good. I'm here if you need anything," he reminds me as he walks to help another customer at the end of the bar.

My next patron steps up to the bar and within minutes, Brad is out of sight and out of mind. The rest of the night goes by in a blur and the next thing I know, we're making 'last call,' and my shift is almost over.

As Asher walks me to my car at the end of night, I see Brad getting into his. He doesn't see me, but the thought of him being here this late after the bar closes gives me the creeps.

As soon as I shut my car door, I instantly push the locks and crank the engine. Asher waves and mouths his goodbye as I put my car in reverse and flee the parking lot. I know nothing happened, and I can totally handle myself when it comes to Brad, but him being here gives me the heebie-jeebies for some unexplained reason.

The next day, I work on a project and study for an exam rather than join Vince and his family for dinner. Though I'm disappointed I'm unable to spend the evening with him, I can't afford to get behind in my studies either.

Just as I'm about to call it quits for the night, I get my nightly text from Vince.

Vince: How was your day?

Me: I got a lot done.

Vince: Call?

Instead of typing my reply, I hit the dial button on my phone, and the thought of hearing his sexy voice has a smile tugging at my lips.

"Hey, you," his gruff sleepy voice greets me.

"Hey, you," I parrot—lost in the way his voice sends butterflies swarming through my veins.

"How was your day?" he asks with curiosity.

"Not bad. I got my project done, and I'm ready for our test tomorrow."

"I'm ready, too. In fact, I just finished studying and wanted to reach out before crashing. Jules was up at four thirty this morning. Though Van had to get up with her, I heard them, and I couldn't get back to sleep."

"Man, that's rough. I didn't get to bed until nearly three, so I'd be dead on my feet if I were you."

"Damn, I have no idea how you keep that schedule."

"Easy." I smile. "I get to sleep in and have no responsibilities until the afternoon, remember?"

"Speaking of work, you never told me earlier how last night went."

"Uh… it was fine…" And then I cringe, remembering Brad's brief appearance.

"That doesn't sound fine…" he draws out, picking up on my sudden discomfort.

Shaking it off, I downplay it for what it was. "It's really

nothing. A guy I went out on one disastrous date with showed up and wanted me to give him another chance."

"Okay…" The way Vince stretches the single word, I know without a doubt he's expecting me to answer his unasked questions.

Knowing he needs further explanation but not wanting to get into it too much, I force a laugh. "Don't worry, Vince… You have nothing to worry about. I told him no. And that was the end of it." Basically.

"I'm not worried." Vince sounds a tad defensive, but I'm not entirely sure if that's the correct word to describe his tone.

"Seriously, Vince. If it were something, I'd tell you." Because let's face it. Nothing did happen, and I'm not about to make a mountain out of a mole hill.

"I know you have to work tomorrow night, but you're welcome to drop by before your shift for dinner. I know it's selfish—but I'll admit that it sucked not seeing you today."

This guy. My heartstrings pull, and my smile returns.

"Of course. I'd love to. I'm caught up with schoolwork."

We're both quiet for a long moment until Vince clears his throat.

"Listen. I'm sorry to cut this short, but I need to crash. God forbid, Jules doesn't sleep again tonight. I think I might pass out in class if that's the case. Today I was draggin' ass big time, and I can't do it again tomorrow."

"No problem. I'll see you in class."

"Night, Syd." His rich timbre makes my body melt into the couch. God, I really like this guy.

"Night, Vince," I force out then end the call.

After hanging up, I find myself clutching my phone to my chest, savoring this feeling as long as I can. Though, eventually, I force myself to get off the couch and get on with my night.

Just as we're all sitting down to dinner the next night, Vanessa's phone rings.

"Wonder what the daycare is calling me for at this time of day?" she voices aloud.

Vince looks warily to his sister, and our conversation from before abruptly ends while we wait to see what happens.

"Oh my...." Her expression morphs from shock to contemplation as she mutters, "Okay... we'll make that work... Let me know when it's back on... thanks for calling.... I will."

As she turns to Vince, her face fills with worry. "That was the center. Apparently, a water main broke and parts of the daycare flooded. They don't expect water to be running at the daycare until tomorrow afternoon, so Julia doesn't have a place to be tomorrow."

Before either of us can respond, Vanessa practically shouts in frustration. "Shoot. I have two exams tomorrow and can't miss class."

"I've got one, too," Vince sighs. "We'll figure something out," he says as if he's trying to calm her.

"I've got an idea..." I toss out to the room.

With all eyes on me, Vince asks me to explain when I freeze. "And what's that..."

"Well, I'm not sure how you'd feel about this... but as I don't have classes tomorrow, I could watch her."

"But you work until nearly three in the morning. I have to leave a little after seven to make it to my first class across campus. Would you want to be up at that time?"

"I've survived on less." I shrug in an attempt to not make it a big deal. "As long as I get to bed at a decent time tomorrow night, I'll be fine."

"Are you sure?" Vanessa asks apprehensively.

"If you'd rather find someone else, I'm okay with that, too," I offer, trying to let her off the hook if she'd prefer I not watch Julia.

Julia interrupts the conversation, "Will I really get to spend the day with Sydney?"

Her eagerness makes every minute of lost sleep entirely worth it.

Vanessa emphatically shakes her head. "No... I'd love it if you watched her. I have the early shift at the diner and like Vince said, he has to be at class early. Would you mind coming over before he leaves? It's likely easier to hang out here for the day—with all of Julia's things here."

"No problem at all." I smile, and it's set. I'm officially Julia's babysitter tomorrow.

VINCE

Just as I'm getting into bed the next night, my phone vibrates with an incoming text notification.

Knowing there's only one person who'd text at this hour, a smile automatically forms on my lips.

Swiping open the screen, I'm delighted to find she's sent a beautiful selfie—not that she's ever not beautiful. All it shows is her face, but her smile is infectious, and my mood lifts higher.

Sydney: I'm on break and just wanted to say good night. Ready for your exam tomorrow? Or still studying?

Me: I'm ready. How was your night?

Sydney: Ugg... Brad showed up again, and he hasn't left.

Instantly, I'm on alert. Carefully, I consider how to construct my next message to keep from sounding like an ass.

Me: Has he been bothering you again?

Sydney: Yes and no. He tried to get me to talk with him earlier, but he's not bothering me anymore.

Me: You okay?

Immediately, the dots appear.

Sydney: Yeah… he's just a nuisance.

Me: You sure?

Sydney: Gotta get back on shift. We just got a rush. Night.

Well, that didn't answer my question.
I flop back into bed and attempt finding comfort.
Yeah. That's not happening.
Contemplating my options, I stare at the ceiling.
Instinctually, I flop back the covers and pull on a pair of jeans. There's no way I'm letting her be harassed by some douchebag if I can help it.
I slip on my shirt from earlier as I exit my room. Unfortunately, my venture won't go unnoticed because I run into Vanessa in the kitchen. She jumps at my unexpected rush into the room.

"Where are you off to?" Confusion is evident in her voice.

"I need to check on something," I mumble, slipping on my shoes.

Concern immediately replaces her confusion. "Everything okay?"

"I think so…" But I need to see for myself, to be sure. There's no way in hell I'll be able to sleep if she has to work the rest of her shift before I hear from her. "I'll be back in a bit. Just lock up… and I'll tell you more in the morning."

Vanessa's expression clearly says she wants to say more, but she just nods in understanding. "Tell Sydney I said hello."

Somehow, she always knows.

Shaking my head at her intuition, I mutter, "I will."

Without another word, I rush to the garage and jump into my Jeep. It revs to life in an instant. Irritation flows through me as I wait for the slower as shit door to give me enough clearance.

Thankfully, the streets are empty as I make my way to the bar, but for a school night, the parking lot is packed. Sydney mentioned something about a drink special that drives the crazy co-eds in, but since I don't really frequent bars, I don't understand the hype.

Thankfully, there isn't a line and when I flash the bouncer my ID, I'm let in with ease.

Immediately, I spot Sydney behind the bar, and relief washes over me. Damn, she's beautiful. Her long, red hair is pulled back into a high ponytail, and she's pouring drinks like a woman on a top-speed mission. Her beauty and grace make it difficult not to stop and stare. There's only one other bartender helping with this crowd, and he's on the opposite side, busy with his own customers. The line behind the person she waits on is about five people deep.

As if she senses me, her eyes dart to mine and widen like saucers—but she doesn't miss a beat with the drink she's mixing.

Shit.

She doesn't exactly look happy to see me.

I make my way to her line through the crowd to wait my turn. Her eyes dart to mine every few seconds, making me doubt my reasoning for being here in the first place. I have no fucking clue what to make of her expression. Sometimes, she looks happy to see me, yet I swear that's not necessarily the case.

When I finally step up to the bar to place my order, her tone is cold and nowhere near her usual self. "What can I get for you?"

Shit. This isn't good. "Uh... a Coke?"

Syd's eyebrows raise to her hairline. "You came all this way to get a Coke... at midnight?" Yeah... she's clearly not buying it.

Trying to sound playful, I smirk, "I was thirsty."

"And you thought coming here would quench your thirst?"

Oh, that sass is in full force.

Having only ever seen her use this tone with my buddy Derek, I can't say I'm thrilled with this kind of shade thrown at me.

In for a penny, in for a pound. "You do make the best drinks in town."

"Hey, buddy? Are you ordering more or what?" a guy from behind me interrupts.

"Wait over there," she demands, pointing to an empty

barstool as she hands me a glass of Coke. "I'll deal with you in a minute."

Deal with me… shit, this really isn't good.

"Okay." I nod in agreement and take a seat.

At least I have an excuse to sit at the bar and watch her while the line behind me remains steady. There's no telling if she'll actually get to talk to me before closing time and as I watch, I'm not sure what reaction I'll receive when she finally does get back to me. Sometimes, I'd swear she's happy to see me, but the minute that thought crosses my mind, I'm gifted with an annoyed glare. Eventually, she ignores me altogether but then again, she's slammed with customers.

I guess only time will tell.

To pass the time, I alternate from watching the dance floor as well as Sydney, so I don't look like a total creeper. Sydney focuses her attention on the patrons in front of her. Occasionally, I'll catch her eye, but she immediately pulls away —almost as if she doesn't allow herself to look in the first place.

When a girl slides up to me and tries to make conversation, I barely get to respond before Sydney's right there asking, "Is there anything else I can get for you?"

Smiling, I use this opportunity to let the stranger realize I'm not interested. "I'm good, Syd. Just waiting for you."

Immediately, the girl stiffens then turns abruptly on a dime in the other direction. It's almost comical to watch her slither back to where she came from.

When she's lost in the crowd, I turn my attention to Syd, and it's all I can do not to laugh at her shocked innocence expression. Coyly, she grins. "Was it something I said?"

"No idea. But I'm glad she figured out the only one I'm interested in here is you."

"Flattery will get you nowhere, Vincent Daniel Larson. I've still got a bone to pick with you—even if you are completely adorable when you act like a Neanderthal."

"Neanderthal? Really?"

Pointedly, she puts me in my place. "Yes. Really. But since it's only about thirty minutes to closing, you'll have to wait until then so we can talk."

Shit. Is it really that late? Glancing at my phone, I realize she's right.

I'm so gonna hate my alarm in a few hours.

But if she can survive on such little sleep, I suppose I can, too.

"I guess I'll wait for your wrath then," I tease, trying to lighten the mood.

Her lower lip quirks, but her mouth remains closed as she turns to finish restocking the bar. The other guy behind the bar hollers, "Last call," and the remaining crowd gets their last drink for the night.

I have no idea how Sydney keeps up the way she does with orders being shouted at her over the music, but her customers are satisfied and walk away happy.

When the DJ turns off the music, only a few people remain. The lights get brighter, and the crowd disperses quickly when this happens. A bouncer approaches me but before he can ask me to leave, Sydney says, "It's okay. He's with me."

Shrugging as an apology for reading it wrong, he nods

once in my direction and disappears into a back room off to the side of the bar.

The longer I sit, the more I feel like an ass for coming in the first place. No one approached her other than to get a drink they ordered. I wonder who this "Fucking Brad" is. Did he leave before I got here? Or had she already handled the situation?

Pulling out my phone, I reread the texts.

No—I wasn't wrong in coming here. Clearly, he'd been bothering her. Don't even get me started on how she left things... what else was I supposed to do?

But now she thinks I'm a Neanderthal.

My thoughts are interrupted with a tight, "Are you ready?"

Clearly, she's back to being upset.

She doesn't reach for my hand or show any emotion for that matter. She simply walks without another word to the door.

Okay, Larson... how are you getting out of this one?

She's silent as she walks out the door and into the parking lot. Seeing her car across the street, she heads in that direction.

But right before she stops to cross the street, she spins to face me with a finger poking in my direction.

"I don't do jealous." Holy Hell... she's pissed.

"Whoa... that's not what's going on..." I attempt to defuse but no luck.

Her head instantly cocks to the side as she punches her hip with her other hand. "Really? Because that's not what it looks like. I mention a guy I went out on ONE date with... one... and don't get me started on how it was the date from hell... but you come rushing down here to stake your claim?"

Ahhh... fuck... I can see how she could think that... but damn... that's not the case. How do I explain this—and not come off more like an ass?

Of course, I don't get a word in because she's obviously been bottling up her emotions, and her pent-up anger is about to spew like a volcano. Her cheeks darken, and her green eyes turn to slits as she scowls in my direction.

"I can handle myself. I don't need you," she continues to poke the air with her finger. If we were one step closer, I'm sure she'd be poking my chest. "...Or anyone else swooping in to save the day. There are four fucking bouncers who could've stepped in if necessary. But no—you jump out of bed and rush down here to do what? Drink Coke at the bar all night? How the hell are you going to be up at the ass crack of dawn to be ready for your test if you're stalking my ass all night?"

"Well... I wouldn't say stalking," I manage to get in, but it lands on deaf ears, and apparently, it was a rhetorical question.

Great.

"I don't need a knight in shining armor."

"Good—because from what I hear, that's heavy shit to walk around in," I say, attempting to defuse the situation, and I swear I see her lips quirk but remain locked in the scowl directed at me.

She's more than capable of handling herself. "I..." I start, but reality bitch slaps me as I fully take in her perception of how things went down. She's wrong... but... shit... she has a point.

Maybe I am a bit of a Neanderthal.

Her eyes narrow perceptively as she must be able to see my

freaking epiphany and surprisingly, she doesn't say anything, but her face clearly says, *this had better be good.*

"Okay..." I draw out, buying myself some time.

Out of nowhere, I hear my mom's favorite truths loud and clear. *Honest simplicity will go much further than lengthy explanations.*

"First, I'm fully aware that you're more than capable of handling yourself. But if you were in my shoes, would you be able to sleep after our brief text exchange? I'm not one to sit idly by and stew on things when I can confront the situation head on."

"But still..." A bit of steam releases as her rigid posture droops.

"Seriously, Syd. What did you expect me to do? Toss and turn all night wondering if you're okay, when I know it will be after closing before you can respond? I don't think so."

"You still didn't have to stay all night." She juts out her chin in my direction as one fist punches her hip, holding firm to her beliefs that I've overreacted, I'm sure.

I run a finger down my nose as I work through my words carefully. "Uh... If I remember correctly, *you're* the one to tell me to take a seat—that you'd *deal* with me later."

She opens her mouth to say something, then shuts it.

I have her here... she can't argue about me staying all night, and she knows it.

Instead of letting her stew for long, or come up with another excuse for why she's mad at me, I forge ahead with my point. "I will never sit by when the people I care about are in need."

Sydney sucks in a deep breath and releases it slowly as she

looks to her watch. "Look... it's late. Even though you *clearly* overreacted, I *do* appreciate your reasons. I..." She looks to the sky as she releases another deep breath. "I... I guess I can see your logic. But so we're clear... if I need your help. I'll ask for it. You don't need to come barging down here like a bat out of hell otherwise."

"Duly noted... but so we're clear, if I think you're ever in danger... all bets are off."

"Total Neanderthal..." she mutters more to herself than me as she rolls her eyes to the sky.

The thought of her truly being upset with me is unsettling at best, so I ask for reassurance, "Are we good?"

Slowly, her eyes rise to meet mine, but her expression is unreadable.

I'm not sure when her answer became so crucial, but in this moment, it feels like the most important thing in the world. My breath hitches as I wait for her to fully assess me. Her eyes slowly close, leaving me any window of opportunity to decipher her mood.

Slowly, she nods, and my breathing returns to normal.

"We're good." She nods in agreement, and relief washes through me.

I close the distance between us in an instant. My hand lands on her hip, and I pull her to me. Reading my intentions, her head naturally tilts to the side as my lips slant over hers.

When I press my lips to hers, I feel the tension I'd been holding onto slip away. Her body melts into mine as she runs her fingers through my hair. God, this woman can kiss. Knowing that she's no longer upset adds fuel to my fire, but I force myself to remember we're in public. In all too short of time, I break the kiss and simply pull her in for a hug.

"I'm sorry I upset you," I whisper as I kiss the top of her head. Even after working all night, she still smells like vanilla and spice and hints of her apple shampoo.

"I'm sorry I worried you," comes out as muffled words against my chest.

She squeezes me tight before pulling back to look me in the eye. "You have an early morning. You didn't need to come down here."

I will always be here if I think she's in need. Though instead of arguing this point, I deflect, "I'm not the one spending the day with a three-year-old," I remind her. "I'm used to her energy, *you're not*. Let's get you home so we can both get some sleep."

Sighing heavily, she releases her arms on me completely and turns to cross the street. "I suppose you're right," she practically pouts, and I can't help but smile at how adorable she is. Clearly, she doesn't want our time together to end, and that thought alone makes my heart soar.

Reaching for her hand, I lead her across the street to her car. "I'll follow you home and make sure you get inside okay, since it's on the way. Then I'll see you bright and early in the morning."

She unlocks her door and turns to face me. "You don't have to do that."

"I know," I admit. "But I'm going to all the same."

Her beautiful lips spread wide as a giggle escapes. "I'm beginning to see that." She reaches up on her toes to close the distance between us. She kisses me quickly then whispers, "Thank you, Vince."

"Anytime, Syd. Anytime." I squeeze her in a hug once more then turn to open her door. "If you're lucky, she'll nap tomorrow. Though those are rare. But if you take her for a bike ride and wear her out, you just may get some rest yourself tomorrow afternoon."

"I've survived on less sleep. I'm sure I can handle Julia tomorrow. You don't have to worry."

"I'm sure you can handle anything, Syd," I say as I kiss her chastely once more before shutting the door. "Now let's get you home." I shut the door and jog over to my Jeep, so she won't have to wait for me.

It takes us no time to get to her apartment as the streets are empty. I patiently wait for her to park and walk up the stairs. She waves and blows me a kiss as she turns to go into her apartment. Her playfulness makes me laugh aloud. Damn. I love how full of life she is. Even though I clearly upset her, I'm still glad I got to spend this stolen time with her.

SYDNEY

"Wait up, Julia!" I holler as she rounds the corner on the bike path at the park. I decided I'd go for a run and kill two birds with one stone before heading back to Vince's house for lunch. But the girl is faster than I realized. I kick it into high gear and catch up within a matter of seconds.

Julia's giggle can be heard as soon as she spots me. "I'm right here, Sydney. I won't go too far. Grownups worry a lot. I was riding like a rocket and couldn't slow down."

"You sure are fast. Are you sure you don't have a superpower I'm not aware of?" I tease as she starts riding again.

"Nope... it's just me. I can go fast."

Julia's freaking adorable as those eyes that remind me so much of Vince twinkle in delight. We continue along the path as she chatters about how she's so much faster without training wheels. But that doesn't hold her attention long because she suddenly talks about where she and Vince usually ride when he runs.

Knowing the path she's talking about, I let her take the lead, and we chat about everything a three-year-old can imagine along the way. Sometimes, I have to stop running because she has me bent over in stitches as she explains the world through her eyes. One thing is certain through all of this—the Larson family is easy to like.

When we get back to their house, it's time for lunch. Julia asks for a grilled cheese sandwich and tomato soup. As I make it for her, I'm reminded of my time with Grams.

"You know, Jules, when I was your age, my grandma used to make this for me all the time. It was my favorite," I say as I let her stir the soup on the stove. She insists her mom and Vince let her do it, and since I'm right here with her, and the handle is long, I allow it. God, how do parents let their kids do things like this? It makes me nervous as hell just thinking of all the possibilities of how they can get hurt.

"Really?" she beams. "It's mine, too. Do you see her?"

"Grandma?" Well, I didn't expect this. How do you talk about death to a three-year-old? I go with the truth. "Unfortunately, no. She passed away right before I came to college." God, I hope she understands that much. I don't want to have to explain much further.

To my utter shock, she nods in understanding and matter-of-factly states, "So did mine."

Really? She must be mistaken. Vince hasn't said anything about his mother dying. Hmmmm... maybe she doesn't understand what I was saying after all. But God, what if that's the reason he was looking for a place to think when he first arrived at CRU? Even though my mom and I've never been close, I can't imagine losing her so early in life.

Julia says something, but I don't quite hear it, and I'm pulled back to reality.

Shit. What did she say?

"… Is the sandwich ready?"

This isn't a conversation we should be having, so I quickly flip the grilled cheese sandwich I have frying in another pan onto a plate for her. Eager to change the subject, I ask, "So, which way do you like your sandwiches cut—in the middle or diagonal?" I motion with my fingers to show her what I mean, and she smiles eagerly.

"Momma cuts them diagonal," she beams. "We need spoons."

As we sit at the table to eat, Julia wrinkles her nose.

"What is it?" I ask while mentally listing off the things I could have forgotten.

"Your shirt is all sweaty like Unks when he runs. You forgot to shower."

Looking down, I see sweat stains around my collar and under my armpits. I sniff and thankfully, my deodorant hasn't expired… but she's right. I do need a shower. "I'll get one later." I shrug, not knowing how I'll get a shower in and babysit her at the same time.

"You can shower, and I watch a show?" she states, but it comes out more like a question.

"What do your mom and Vince do?"

She rolls her eyes as if I just asked the stupidest question on the planet. "Uh…if they stink, they shower. I watch my show on Unks' bed, and I promise not to leave the room when he's in the tub."

I can do that. I brought a change of clothes... and a shower sounds much better.

"What's your favorite show?" I ask as she takes a big bite of her sandwich, then turn to grab the soup I'd set on the counter.

With her mouth full of food, she answers anyway, "*The Descendants*. I want purple hair like Mal when I grow up." When she finishes chewing, she adds, "Will you watch it with me?"

"Well, let's hurry up and eat so we can."

She may not get a nap in, but I'm sure after the ride we took, she could use the rest.

Of course, a three-year-old knows how to work the TV better than I do—which I find completely comical. She gets the show started and settles into Vince's bed with ease. Then in an almost mom-like voice, she says, "Go take your shower. You're starting to get smelly."

"Gee, thanks," I grumble. I'll never have to guess what's on Julia's mind, that's for sure.

As I walk into Vince's bathroom, it smells of him. On instinct, I take in a deep breath and revel in the scent as it pulls me into my favorite memories of being close to him. Knowing I don't have a lot of time, I don't let myself dwell on those delicious thoughts but get to work on the business at hand.

Though as I step into his large walk-in shower and begin to wash, I find myself lifting the lid of his shampoo and body wash to figure out which one he smells like most.

Damn, they both smell good, but my favorite is definitely his body wash.

Lathering my hair with his shampoo, I quickly go through a shower routine.

I'm not gonna lie.

I totally fantasize about sharing this shower with him—but I can't let myself linger on those thoughts because Julia's waiting on the other side of the door. After getting out and toweling off, I realize I brought my other bra but didn't bring any clean underwear.

Shit.

There's no way in hell I'm putting dirty underwear back on, so I guess I'm going commando under my black leggings. I can't say I've ever done this before, but I'm sure it won't kill me. Besides—who's gonna know?

Grabbing my brush from my bag, I enter Vince's bedroom and am relieved to see Julia's relaxed and completely consumed with her show.

When she finally does notice me, she pats the bed beside her. "Wanna watch with me?" Her pleading expression makes it difficult to resist.

"Sure. Hand me that pillow, Jules. There's no way I'm letting you hog them all."

She takes the top pillow from under the two she's been lounging on and hands it over. Propping myself up against his wooden headboard, I slouch into the pillow to make myself more comfortable.

Damn. Even his pillow smells like him.

"Lie down like me, Syd," Julia encourages, and I happily oblige as I take in a deep breath. His bed is huge—a California king. It's the perfect combination of firm and cozy. It feels like I'm floating on a cloud.

Julia yawns as she settles into her pillow further. Maybe if we lie here long enough, she'll take that nap Vince teased about.

"You want a blanket?" I ask, barely above a whisper.

"Naw… I'll just crawl in the covers." Within seconds, she's pushed the down comforter past her hips and squirms her way under the blankets. "You getting in, too?" she asks in a sleepy voice.

Should I? Will it make her fall asleep faster?

"I think I'll just stay here," I say as I roll on my side and adjust my position to see the television clearly. "I'm pretty cozy."

"Unks' bed is the best. It's *so* big."

"Yeah, it is," I agree as I take another deep breath.

"This is my faborite part!" she squeals. It's absolutely adorable how she can't pronounce her v's in favorite. "You gotta see this."

We watch the movie in silence. The characters dance in the street to a catchy tune in the musical. I can see why she likes it. The song is powerful, and the choreography is addictive to watch. Even I'm sucked in.

When the song ends, I notice Julia's breathing is long and steady. Her eyes droop and if I'm not mistaken, she's about to conk out at any moment. My heart melts when she reaches out to hold my hand.

As she loses her fight with sleep, I stay as still as possible, so I won't wake her. Before I know it, her eyes are completely shut, and I think she's asleep. I attempt to untangle our fingers, but when her eyes jolt open, I think better of it. Instead, I close my eyes and pretend I'm falling asleep, too. I feel her body relax further, and her breaths get deeper with each intake.

Eventually, she lets go of my hand and rolls away from me, sound asleep.

Not wanting to risk the chance of waking her, I let myself get lost in the movie. Eventually, I must succumb to the comforts of Vince's bed, because I, too, lose the battle with my heavy eyelids and drift to sleep.

The next thing I know, I hear Vince's deep, sexy voice in a dream. But when I pop my eyes open, all I see is his beautiful face staring back at me.

VINCE

I'M DRAGGING ASS TODAY. I HAVE NO FREAKING CLUE HOW Sydney works these hours and still functions throughout the day. Thank fuck, I studied as well as I did; the exam in my first class is handled with ease. The rest of my day slugs on, and I can't wait until I can see Sydney again.

For the most part, I know Julia's pretty easy to handle, but I hope she's on her best behavior for Sydney. Like any three-year-old, she's unpredictable at times, but if Sydney can handle drunk frat boys, I'm sure she can handle Jules.

When my last class finally ends, I rush home. The thought of seeing Sydney has my drowsiness disappearing. I drove to campus today so I could get home quicker. I'm sure she would've texted if there was a problem, but still... I worry.

When I enter through the garage door, the house is unusually quiet. I call out, but there's no answer. From the living room, I can hear the sound of a television faintly from my bedroom. Knowing that's Julia's favorite place to watch a movie, I smile as I shorten the distance between us.

Wondering if Julia's sleeping, I peek around the corner.

My heart melts when I see not only Julia is fast asleep, but Sydney as well. Julia's done one of her sleep-ninja moves. She's lying with her feet intertwined with Sydney as one arm flops over Syd's belly. I almost feel sorry for Syd; sleeping with Julia's like sleeping next to a category-three hurricane. The covers are tossed over Sydney, so if I had to guess, I'd say she started with no covers on her. Otherwise, they'd likely be pooled on the floor.

Syd's long, red hair sprawls out behind her across my pillow.

Is her hair wet?

Glancing at my bathroom, I see her bag and clothes piled on top from what looks like a run. No wonder they're sleeping.

She must sense me staring, because her lids flutter open, and her green eyes find me at the doorway in an instant.

"Hey, you," I whisper.

Wordlessly, she smiles at me, then takes in the situation with Julia entangled with her and looks to me helplessly.

I cover my mouth to stifle a laugh. They're such a tangled mess, I have no idea how she'll get out of there if left on her own.

Holding up my finger to stop her movement, I walk to Julia's side of the bed. In a well-practiced move, I expertly untangle her legs from Syd's without any disruption. I can't even count how many times I've had to untangle Julia from Vanessa to let her get some well-needed sleep. I swear from the moment she was born, this girl's like an octopus and grows extra limbs in the night.

As soon as she's extricated, I'm blessed with the most beautiful smile as Sydney mouths, "Thank you."

She slips off the other side of the bed with cat-like reflexes.

As soon as she's standing, I motion for her to follow me out of the room.

Reaching for her hand, I close the door behind us. As soon as we're out of earshot in the living room, I stop and face Sydney, and I can't help the smile that plays on my lips.

"How was your day?" I ask, barely above a whisper.

"Good." Then she shakes her head as if another thought has struck her. "I can't believe I fell asleep, though. Sorry. When she insisted I lie down, that was my demise."

"Jules is persuasive," I admit. "Besides, you must've needed it. Van and I often fall asleep with her if she'll actually lie down. You're a miracle worker just getting her to rest in the first place. How did you manage to wear her out?"

Syd pulls in a deep breath and slowly releases it. "Let's see…" She ticks things off on her fingers. "We made pancakes for breakfast."

"Seriously? She ate cereal before you got here."

Sydney shrugs. "She said she was hungry. Then we played with Legos, did a few puzzles, and when it was warm enough, she rode her bike, and I ran beside her for about four miles if I had to guess. She said it was a route you often take with her, so I went with it. When we got back, I made her some soup and sandwiches."

"Wow, that's a lot."

"I hope you don't mind. I used your shower after she, in so many words, said I stink."

Ohmigod… Julia didn't.

Sydney's wrinkled nose says I couldn't be so lucky. "I'm so sorry…" I start.

But Sydney cuts me off with a shake of her head, "No… she wasn't wrong. I was a hot mess and in desperate need of a shower. No offense was taken—trust me."

Okay… how do I respond to that?

Seeing this subject is a slippery slope, I quickly change it. "You may be sick of us, but would you want to stay for dinner tonight?"

"I could be persuaded…" she singsongs.

Before I can respond, I hear Julia call out from my room, "Sydney?"

"I'm here," Sydney calls out and immediately, we hear the pattering sounds of tiny feet rushing through the house.

"Unks! You're home," she gushes as she runs into my arms for a hug.

"Hey, squirt. Did you have fun today with Sydney?" I ask as I set her back on the floor.

"Yes!" she boasts. "I had the best day *ever!*"

"Whoa, whoa, whoa…" I protest. "I thought your best days were reserved for me."

"But she made pancakes and grilled cheese in one day, Unks! And we got to watch my favorite movie."

"I see how it is." I pretend to pout.

"Oh, Unks…" she says on a huff. "What are we gonna do with you?" Just like her mother would say.

When I look to Sydney for help, she's caught red-handed trying to stifle a laugh.

"I see how it is!" I roar as I tickle Julia. "Syd's your shiny new toy, and I'm just your old boring Unks. Traitor! You're a traitor, I tell you."

Julia giggles between gasps of air and protests, "No… No… you're not boring, Unks." Big gasp. "Really…" gasp. "Not…" giggle, "Boring."

Putting her back on her feet, I smile triumphantly. "*That's* what I thought."

"So besides having sooo much fun, were you good today?"

"Yes, she was," Sydney insists.

"Good to hear," Vanessa chimes in, and I turn in surprise at her voice from the hall.

"Momma!" Jules rushes to greet her. "I had the best day today. Can Sydney babysit me again?"

Vanessa chuckles. "Well, that's up to her." She looks to Sydney and shrugs. "But your daycare called, and you're back to business as usual tomorrow. The pipes are fixed, and they miss you."

"Okay…" she draws out as if she's not quite convinced but isn't about to argue either.

"What are you up to tonight?" Vanessa asks Syd and me as she sets Julia back on the floor.

I look to Sydney who simply shrugs.

"I'm thinking about taking Jules to the movies for a Momma date."

"Really?" Julia squeals. She's been begging for a date with Vanessa for the last week or so, but with the tournament and excess crowds, she hasn't had the time.

"Yep. Go get your shoes on, and we'll head out for dinner first." When Julia rushes off to her bedroom, Vanessa turns to us. "You don't mind, do you?"

"Not at all," flows off my lips with ease.

Having the house to myself with Sydney sounds perfect.

Of course, this only causes Vanessa to laugh in my face. "Don't sound too eager to be rid of us."

Rolling my eyes, I lie through my teeth, "I'm not."

Yeah, my twin sees right through me. "Sure, Vinny. You keep telling yourself that." But then she focuses her attention to Sydney. "Did today really go well?"

"Absolutely." Sydney fills her in on the events of their day just before Julia comes running into the room with her coat and shoes on.

"I'm ready, Momma. Are you?"

We chat for a few more moments before Julia's chomping at the bit to leave, and Vanessa complies to her wish. We walk them to the front door and wave as they drive off together.

The second the door snicks shut, and we're alone, I snake my arms around Sydney's waist and pull her in for a kiss. Her arms drape over my shoulders as her fingers find the strands of hair at the base of my neck. Damn, she feels amazing.

Not wanting any risk of interruption, I break our kiss only long enough to scoop her up into my arms and walk to my bedroom. I have zero expectations—but I know how often Julia will forget something, and we have to return.

Syd laughs as she reads my determined expression. "In a hurry much?"

Rolling my eyes, I explain, "My family *always* forgets

something. I'd rather not have them walk in and see a different kind of show."

The total brat she is waggles her brows suggestively, "Really? You're certain there'd be a show?"

"Oh, I'll give you a show," I say as I dump her on my bed, and she shimmies herself toward the pillow.

Sure, the blankets are a tangled mess, but that is the least of my worries. The sexiest woman in the world is giving me a look that clearly makes her intentions clear—she wants me.

Knowing I must keep my wits about me, I take every ounce of power I have to focus my attention solely on Sydney. As her hair fans out across my pillow, I'm taken by her beauty. Her long lashes flutter, revealing her green eyes which are now a dark-emerald shade as a smile pulls at her lips.

"So, what kind of show are we talking about, Mr. Larson? Are we talking like Magic Mike?"

As if...

Yeah, there might be an eye roll thrown at her, but if she wants to see more of me, that can be arranged.

Ripping off my shirt, she grins wider in appreciation. I'm not stacked with muscles, but I do work out, and I'm proud of my accomplishments. I keep my pants on because the rough barrier is the only thing keeping me from disgracing myself with her.

She's utter perfection, but to keep from showing her just what she does to me, I run through a list of sure-tell things to keep my raging hard-on at bay.

Cold showers.

Smelly gym socks.

Jumping in a frozen lake.

Yeah, the usual list isn't working, but I'm not about to let her down.

Maybe if I keep things playful, I won't lose control.

Reaching for her ankle, I pull her to me as I crawl up her body from the bottom of the bed. She giggles with the unexpected move, and her shirt raises to show her stomach.

"You know... I'm all for equal rights, Syd. If I'm shirtless, you should be, too."

The brazen woman before me doesn't even hesitate. Her shirt is up and over her head in an instant. Her breasts fill the cups of her bra perfectly.

Holy shit. Maybe this isn't such a good idea. If I thought I was on the brink of control before, I'm fucking screwed now.

Ice baths.

Pi is three point one four one five nine...

Thank fuck, that calms me down, and I regain control of myself.

I bring my lips to her rib cage, and she smells like my body soap—but also like her.

I lick, suck, and nip my way up her chest.

I palm her breasts, but Sydney pushes my hand away to rid herself of her bra.

Sydney on full display is a sight to be seen.

Her breasts are round and full and fall naturally apart. Her areolas match her lips perfectly, and freckles lightly scatter across her body, making intricate designs, making me want to run my tongue from spot to spot and explore each and every inch of her.

I run my teeth along her hip bone, and she bucks up in appreciation.

My hands roam to her hips, and her black leggings leave little to the imagination. My need to please her outweighs my own. One hand splays across her ass to pull her closer as the other finds her center, and I apply pressure at her clit.

As she writhes beneath me, a soft moan escapes. "More... Vince. I need more." She wiggles her ass as she pushes at her leggings.

Wanting to give her my full attention, I drag her leggings over her hips, and I'm greeted with the most delicious sight. "Holy shit! You haven't been wearing underwear?"

"I forgot clean ones." She shrugs as if that explains everything.

But she hasn't been wearing underwear.

Why the fuck that's such a turn-on is beyond me. But hell if I can think straight now.

She hasn't been wearing underwear.

"Uh... Earth to Vince..." She waves a hand in front of my face.

Shit. Did she say something and I missed it?

"You're not wearing underwear."

And the award goes to Captain Obvious.

"Uh... I'm wearing a lot less than that." She smirks. "Are you gonna just stare at me, or are you gonna do something about it?"

"Oh, fuck yeah... I'm gonna do something about it." I practically growl as I kiss the ever-loving fuck out of her. My hands roam as I deepen the kiss. When my fingertips stroke up her center and find purchase with her clit, she rewards me greatly with a moan.

Wanting to keep from making a fool of myself, I focus at

making this the best experience possible for her. As I work her core, I kiss my way down her body, giving ample time to each breast before kissing down her rib cage to where I know she wants me most.

Her pants and moans have her practically speaking in tongues by the time I bring my mouth to suck at her clit. I insert a second finger to her core, and I pump them in and out, finding a rhythm to suit her needs. Her hands fist my hair, pressing me harder on her clit when I scissor my fingers as I continue my pattern.

It doesn't take long before her body stiffens, and her screams cry out. God, Sydney's gorgeous when she loses her battle against an impending orgasm. Her body writhes as she pants and moans undecipherable words.

When she releases my hair and relaxes into the mattress, I look up to be greeted with a glorious grin. She's completely sated, and I won't deny my chest puffs out a bit to know I put that look on her face.

"Come here" She gestures.

Of course, I comply—because I'd be a fool not to.

"Give me a sec to recover, and then I'm gonna rock your world."

Oh, she already has. But I continue with our playful banter from before. "Oh, you think so…"

Then reality hits. I don't actually have any condoms. What am I supposed to do now?

"What's wrong?"

And apparently, she can read me like a book.

How the hell do I tell her?

Sticking with honesty. "I… Uh… don't have any condoms."

"There are other things we can do that don't involve condoms," she teases like before.

"Oh, really, and what's that? Are you up for playing a game of Scrabble later?"

"Oh, I'll make your vocabulary grow, but I didn't quite have board games in mind."

With feign innocence, I tease, "Why, Sydney... are you trying to steal my virtue?"

Sydney moves to her hands and knees and kisses my chest. "Is it stealing if it's given freely?"

She has no idea just how true her words could be.

But she kisses my pec and licks down my rib cage. "Hmmm..." I moan but all thoughts of conversation are forgotten as she reaches for my belt and unclasps it.

Holy shit. In an expert move, she has my buckle undone and the fly of my jeans slowly being opened. She kisses along my stomach as she tugs at my jeans to get them as well as my boxers apparently over my hips.

With her intentions clear of rocking my world, I quickly assist her in discarding my clothes. I don't even get a chance to think before she strokes the length of my dick with one hand while cupping my balls in the other.

Holy hell, coherent thought jumps right out the fucking window when her tongue darts out and swirls around my tip.

I'm already on the verge of exploding, and she's done little more than kiss and lick me. Her slow and steady breaths make my sensitivity reach nuclear levels in a nanosecond.

Not wanting to be a one-pump chump, I recite basketball statistics in my head. When that doesn't work, I repeat my lists from before. They have some effects, but Sydney is winning my fight for control. As much as I'd love to lose myself in her completely, I want this experience to last a bit longer as well. Because, let's face it, I never want this to end.

She sucks me from root to tip as she plays with my balls in the best possible rhythm imaginable. But that isn't what does me in. No—that would be when she pushes on that spot right behind my balls as she nearly swallows me that has me convulsing in an instant.

"Syd…" I warn, knowing I don't have much time.

She continues her rhythm, ignoring me.

"Syd," I rush out almost in panic. "I'm gonna…"

The witch that she is hexes me completely when she doubles down on her efforts, and I go off like the Fourth of July. All I see are stars, and I swear my world almost goes black. I've never come this hard in my life.

But I'm not just coming. No, Sydney won't let me do that. She milks me for every cent I'm worth, and there likely isn't a drop to be found in me.

When I stop twitching and sink far into the mattress, she pulls off me with the most devious grin I've ever seen. "You okay, Vince?"

As if she doesn't know…

Fuck… when her grin turns triumphant, I want to kiss that sass right off her.

"I'd say I'm good. Come here, gorgeous," I say, pulling her to me.

Thank God, she doesn't put up a fight because I'm not at all certain I could even walk in the state she's left me in.

Without hesitation, I pull her right up my body and kiss her. She tastes of me, she tastes of her, but most importantly, the way she kisses my mouth brands me like no other before. I feel this kiss from the depths of my soul.

Time ceases to exist beyond the two of us. When we break for air, I pull her in close beside me. Her body melts into mine as if we've been molded together. I know we won't be able to stay like this forever, but for the first time in my life, I know without a doubt, I'd really like to.

SYDNEY

I'M STILL RIDING MY ORGASMIC HIGH AS I MAKE MY WAY THROUGH my morning routine. My mind is on a replay loop of my evening with Vince. Damn. I've never felt the way I do when I'm with him. When I reach the kitchen, I find Chloe already at the table eating her breakfast.

"Good morning, stranger. I haven't seen much of you," she teases as I pour some granola into a bowl and top it with milk.

"I've been around," I rebuke.

"How was your day with Julia?" she asks as she takes another bite.

"It was great. We had a lot of fun."

"I didn't hear you come in last night. Were you out late?"

"I actually fell asleep and didn't come home until early this morning."

"I knew you looked happier," she teases. "You've got that whole blissed out from too much sex thing going on."

I'm sure she's right because my body's as languid as it could be, but it's not actually from sex. Of all people, Chloe would be the one I'd talk to about this; we don't have any secrets. "I think it might be just a Vince thing; we haven't actually done the deed."

"Really? You stayed over *all* night and didn't have sex with the man? I could've sworn you have that *I just had the best sex of my life look* on you. Are you sure you're not holding out on me? Remember, it's been ages for me. Please be kind to the little people and let me live vicariously through you."

This earns her the laugh she was hoping for. "Trust me… I'm riding an orgasmic high, but it's not from actual sex. We've done nearly everything but have sex. But, the thing is, he usually doesn't take it that far. Trust me, there have been plenty of opportunities. I'm not sure what to make of it."

Last night, when he said he didn't have a condom, I didn't think much of it. But now that I'm away from him and in the light of day, I can't help but wonder why we haven't taken things to that next level.

"What's wrong?" Chloe probes.

"It's nothing…" How do I explain these thoughts to her without looking like a selfish ass?

"Do you expect me to believe that line of shit you're spewing?"

God. Leave it to Chloe to say it like it really is. Since freshman year, we've always been close, and she and Abby are about the only people who can see right through me. Abby's usually studying, so Chloe's had more opportunities to probe me when necessary.

"I'm not spewing shit," I protest. "I'm just not sure *why* we haven't actually had sex yet. I mean most guys are more than willing to push things to the next level, especially if I give them all the signs telling them I'm interested. But Vince hasn't even brought it up. In fact, last night was the first time he even mentioned it when he said he didn't have any condoms."

"Oh, man, that's rough. Were you almost in the act when he told you?" Chloe asks in horror.

"No. He of course had just given me the best oral of my life, but he wasn't expecting any reciprocation," I admit. I'm spilling more information than I should. But this is Chloe. We tell each other everything.

"Really? I knew I liked him for you."

"What is that supposed to mean?" I ask, defensive.

"Oh, don't put too much thought into it, but there's just something different about him. I can't really explain it."

Laughing I remind her, "You don't even know him."

"But I know you," she reminds me.

"True..." I admit. "I really do like him..." I trail off, not knowing what else to say.

"Maybe that's why things don't feel forced with him. You can just be you." She shrugs.

"But, Chloe, our chemistry is out of this world. I mean... If he can make me feel like this, and we *haven't* had sex, what will happen when we do?"

"Um... you sit back and enjoy the ride?" She smirks, then quickly adds, "Pun totally intended."

I scoff. "Of course, I'd enjoy the ride." But what about when things end? Will I be able to handle that?

But what if it doesn't end?

"What's going on in that head of yours, Syd? I know you. If you bottle things up and let them fester, you'll only be worse off."

"True," I admit. "I just feel like he's holding something back. Julia said something yesterday, and it's got me thinking."

"What did she say?"

"It may be nothing, but I was talking about Grams and mentioned she had passed away. Julia said her grandma has, too. Maybe she didn't understand what I meant, or it's her great-grandma or something, but now that I think about it, Vince hasn't ever talked about his parents before. Maybe something did happen to his mom?"

"You know the only way to get to the bottom of things is to ask him about it." She shrugs as if she'd rather not be the bearer of bad news.

"What am I supposed to say, Chloe? Hey, Julia mentioned her grandma died, can you tell me about it?"

"Uh... I wouldn't say it like that..." she points out the obvious. "But talk to him. You know... communicate with him so there aren't any misconceptions." She may as well have added duh to the end of her case, as that is clearly her tone.

God, I love her. She always just says it how it is.

When I'm quiet, she adds, "Have you considered googling it? Death certificates are public record."

"I don't even know his mother's name. I'm sure there's a lot of Larsons in the greater Seattle area. Besides... if that really happened, I'm sure he'll tell me in his own time. It's not like we've known each other forever. If it was recent enough for

Julia to remember it, then maybe it's too fresh in his mind to even talk about."

Knowing what I went through after Grams died, I want to give him the space and time he needs. Even though my mom and I aren't exactly close, it would be hard to lose her.

"True. Though it seems you have two major conversations you need to have with him."

"Really? What's the first?"

"Asking him why he won't jump your bones!" she teases. "Though he clearly is satisfying you, you still need to let him know you're a woman with needs."

"Oh, God, Chloe, you're awful."

"But I don't hear you denying it," she singsongs as she rinses her bowl and puts it in the dishwasher.

She's got me there.

***

The next night, as I get off from work, Asher walks me to the car as usual then heads off to his own vehicle. When I get to my car, I lock myself in but take a moment to check the messages waiting to be read before starting my car.

As usual, there's one from Vince.

Vince: Gonna crash. Have a good night. Text me when you get home.

Normally, I'd have a chance to respond during the night, but we were slammed. I swear you'd think more people would stay home to study as the semester continues, but nope—this place is always full.

Turning my key in the ignition, I'm met with a dreaded sound of clicking instead of the engine coming to life. Fuck... this cannot be happening.

I try again and all I get is click... click... click.

The lights are on at full force, so it's likely not a dead battery, but damn. I don't know much about cars.

I glance around the parking lot and see Asher's taillights disappearing in the distance. Fuck. If it weren't so late, I'd just walk home.

With it being this late, it could be hours before I get a tow and be charged a fortune. Fuck... this is the last thing I need.

Pounding my fist on the wheel, I plead to the car gods, "Please... just start..."

In a desperate attempt to deny my reality, I try one last time to start my car, but no luck.

Defeated, I slump into the seat.

Think. Think. Think. Who should I call?

Vince is the first to pop to mind... but it's late.

Abby's likely at Drew's, and Chloe's like waking the dead if I call at this hour.

Before I can talk myself out of it and just walk my ass home, I pull up his number and press the call button.

It only rings twice before I hear a groggy, "Hello?"

Damn, his voice is sexy, but I feel guilty as hell for waking him. "Hey... Um... my car won't start."

"Are you safe?" Of course, that's his first concern. I hear rustling in the background, and I can tell he's on the move.

"Yeah, I'm locked in my car. Asher and I were the last ones here, but I didn't try to start my car until he'd already left."

"He doesn't wait for you?" he accuses.

"Usually he does. I turned my lights on… but he drives a loud truck and must not have realized I didn't start my car."

"Sit tight. I'll be there as soon as I can. Tell me what your car's doing."

"When I went to start it, it just clicked. Like the battery is dead or maybe something is wrong with the starter," I wonder aloud. I know the basics about cars, but beyond that, my knowledge is shit. "But my interior lights are bright, so maybe it's not the battery."

"I'm getting in my Jeep now. Talk to me until I arrive."

God, could Vince be any sweeter?

"I'm sorry to wake you." I shake my head, knowing he's got to be up in a few hours with Julia. Guilt rolls through me in full force. "I guess I could've called an Uber or something."

"Syd, you can call me day or night, and I'll be there. I'd rather you not get into a stranger's car at this hour without anyone knowing where you are."

I sigh, realizing he has a point.

It's not long before I see his Jeep heading up the road in the distance. When he pulls up beside me, I get out to greet him.

He hops down from his Jeep and pulls me into a hug. He quickly kisses me once, then pulls back. "Pop the hood. Try starting it again, and I'll see if you need a jump. I have cables in the back."

I try again, but there's not even a click this time. He fiddles with the battery cables, then asks me to try again.

Nothing.

He hooks up the jumper cables to both vehicles, and we wait patiently for the battery to be charged. When he thinks enough time has passed, he asks me to try again.

I get a few clicks, but the engine doesn't turn over.

"Well, shit. That doesn't sound good. I think you're right about the starter. Do you want me to wait with you to call a tow? Or…" He glances at his watch before adding, "Would you like to deal with this tomorrow?"

My exhaustion from the day hits as I yawn. "I'd rather just get to bed. It will be safe here for tonight, and I'll deal with it later. Besides, you have to be up at the crack of dawn with Jules and work all day. Let's get you home and back to sleep."

"I'll be fine," he insists. "But let's get you home. You've got to be wiped out. That's the third yawn I've witnessed, and I haven't been here that long."

Had I been yawning all this time?

Crap, just the thought makes me yawn yet again. He's right. I'm tired.

He helps me grab my purse and a few things I don't want to leave in my vehicle and lock up. Then the gentleman he is, guides me to his Jeep and kisses me once before helping me in. Then he rounds the front of the vehicle and takes the quickest route home.

He parks right in front of my steps, knowing no one will be bothered by us at this hour. Then he helps me carry my few valuables up the steps and kisses me goodnight.

"Get some sleep, Syd. If you want, I can look at your car further tomorrow."

Knowing this isn't the first time my car has failed me, I

shake my head. "That would be great. Depending on what's wrong, I might have to wait until payday to get it fixed."

The sweet man he is just nods. "Sure. I understand."

He leans in for one last kiss. It's short and sweet but keeps me wanting for more. His face fills with regrets when he mumbles, "I have an early morning. I'll text you when I'm done with class."

"Sounds good. I have to work tomorrow night, I'll see if I can get a ride."

He gives me a look that clearly says, *are you kidding me?* But his words don't have an ounce of sarcasm. "I can drop you off and pick you up, if it comes to that."

"You have better things to do at two a.m. than hang out with me. Besides, don't you have to watch Julia bright and early Saturday morning?"

"I don't mind. But if you'd rather, you could just take my Jeep."

Seriously? He'd just offer his Jeep. "Uh... that's extremely generous. But unfortunately, I've never driven a stick, so it's of no use to me."

Even in the dark, I can see his eyebrows meet his hairline. "We'll have to fix that. You need to be able to drive anything, so you're never stuck anywhere."

I've always wanted to learn. But he doesn't have to teach me. Instead of saying anything, I remain noncommittal. "We'll see."

Vince chuckles. "Why are you nervous all of a sudden? It's not that hard."

"I'm not nervous. I just don't want to put you out or anything," I stammer.

Shaking his head as if he doesn't quite believe me, he offers the sexiest of smiles. "Get some sleep, Syd."

And with that, he leans in to kiss me once more before he turns and runs down the stairs.

I'm not sure what tomorrow will bring, but knowing Vince will be a part of it makes me smile as I head inside and lock up behind me.

SYDNEY

Unfortunately, Vince isn't able to fix my car. Since he has AAA, and it doesn't cost anything out of pocket, he insists on having it towed to his place. When it got to his house, he took out the battery and took it to the parts store to have it tested. It was good, a bad battery and alternator have been eliminated. Knowing it's likely the starter, we also price that.

Holy shit. I'll still be out nearly four hundred dollars if I replace it with what is currently in there—and that's *if* Vince does the work himself.

There's no way I can afford that this week. I'll have to wait until payday to make that kind of purchase. Of course, Vince offers to pay upfront, but when I practically throw a fit, he quickly backs down, knowing how serious I am about handling it myself.

There's no way I'm letting anyone pay my way. If I can't afford something, I'll go without it before borrowing money. Besides, money always muddies the water with relationships, and I never want to be indebted. I learned that lesson the hard way with my mom early in life. I simply can't accept his offer. He's kind enough to do the labor, but there's no way I'll let him foot the bill, even if it is just for a week or so. There's no telling what might happen, and I won't let money come between us.

Knowing I have to work within the hour, he doesn't put up much of an argument. Instead, he offers to drive me to work and pick me up. Then he asks, "Are you busy tomorrow morning?"

"How early are you talking?" After this week, I'm sleeping in.

"Whenever you wake up. Vanessa's off tomorrow, so I thought I'd pick you up tonight and maybe stay at your place. Then we can sleep in, and I'll teach you how to drive a stick."

"You don't have to do that," I offer, knowing he's likely got better things to do than teach me how to drive.

"Uh… it's for completely selfish reasons—trust me." He chuckles at the end.

"Really? Why's that?"

"Well, since you're gonna be without a car for a week or so, there's no way I'll be able to pick you up at closing on the nights you work. I'd rather you have a vehicle so you're not relying on others at that hour. I'll teach you how to drive this, so you can."

I'd rather not rely on rides either, but am I putting him out?

Apparently, he's also a mind reader because he quickly tacks on, "I only use my Jeep when I have plans after my last class. Stop thinking I'll be inconvenienced." Then he goes for my Achille's heel. "I know it's hard to let others help you, but everyone needs to know how to drive a stick. This is a life lesson you'll thank me for. Trust me."

Yeah, I hate asking for help.

But it would be fun to drive this beast.

"And you won't be mad if I mess up your clutch?" I ask, thinking of all the potential problems we could encounter.

"Uh… if you learn how to drive it right, that won't be an issue. Besides, you can't be as bad as Vanessa was when she learned how to drive. It survived then, and I'm sure it'll survive you, too. Besides. I know a guy who can fix it if necessary."

"And would that guy be you?"

He just shrugs and gives me a sexy as fuck grin.

That look alone could get me to do nearly anything.

When I walk out to the parking lot that night, I've never been happier to see Vince waiting in his Jeep for me. He gets out to greet me as Asher watches from the door that I make it to a vehicle safely.

Vince looks sexy as hell, even though he has dark circles under his eyes. He's wearing a pair of dark-gray sweats and a black hoodie. When he greets me with, "Hey, Beautiful," I'll admit I swoon a bit. He pulls me in for a quick kiss before helping me into the Jeep.

Once we're on the road, he's quieter than normal as he reaches for my hand and drives us to my place. He looks exhausted, and I feel a twinge of guilt for keeping him up.

He parks in my spot in my apartment complex, since mine is on the street outside his house at the moment. He grabs a backpack then reaches for my hand as we walk up the stairs to my apartment. Once inside my room, Vince's sleepiness disappears as he kisses me properly now that we have privacy.

When we break apart breathless, he asks about my night.

"It was good, but we're training a new bartender." Shaking my head, I cringe at the memory. "Man, the girl doesn't understand that you don't stand between another person and the bar. To the side, yes... directly behind them, no. I turned around in a hurry to serve the next order and ended up wearing not one but two glasses full. I desperately need a shower."

I pull back my sticky shirt at the reminder. "Don't get too close to me."

"I'm sure a little drink won't hurt me," he says as he leans in to kiss me once more but keeps our bodies from pressing together, per my request. Damn. The man can kiss. He tastes entirely of him, and all I want to do is take him right here and now.

Before I can get too lost in the moment, I force myself to break our kiss then suggest, "Why don't you climb into bed and get comfortable? I'll be right back." I'd love to have him join me, but it'll be much faster with a solo trip.

Nodding, Vince sits on the edge of the bed and toes off his sneakers. "Sounds good. Take your time, I'm not going anywhere."

His sexy grin makes my body light up and my eagerness to return even greater. Rushing to my dresser, I grab a pair of undies, a tank, and some sleep shorts. I zip to the bathroom and turn on my shower to warm it up while I get undressed.

Of course, the thought of Vince waiting on the other side

of my door has my hormones flying into overdrive. I rush through washing my hair, but wanting things to be perfect for us, I take a few extra minutes to shave everywhere necessary. Guys have it so easy as most women won't mind a bit of scruff, but prickly legs might not have the same effect.

By the time I towel off, brush through my hair, and quickly braid it so I won't wake up like Medusa, a lot more time has passed than I realized. Not wanting to skip my nightly routine, I quickly apply some moisturizer and eagerly step into my sleep shorts and pull my tank over my head.

When I pull open the door, the first thing I notice is Vince's sexy chest on full display with the covers gathered at his trim waist. My eyes are pulled to the sexy V that dips below the blankets, and I can't help but wonder what he's wearing.

As I drag my eyes up his sculpted body, I realize I may have taken too long. His arm covers the top part of his face, and his slack jaw indicates he's fast asleep.

Glancing at the clock, I realize it's after three in the morning, and my disappointment disperses. I can't blame him at all. The poor guy's been up since before six, and he must be exhausted. Not wanting to disturb him, I turn on my bedside lamp and turn off the main light.

Crawling into bed, I pull the covers over the two of us. Instinctually, he reaches out to me and pulls me close. Since he's got all the pillows behind him, I use this opportunity to use his chest as a pillow. I find the place on his chest that makes the perfect pillow, and I wrap an arm around his waist as my leg crosses through his.

Reaching over, I turn off the lamp beside us.

"You smell amazing, Syd," he says sleepily as he inhales deeply.

"Shhh… let's sleep," I suggest, not wanting to disturb him.

Wordlessly, he snuggles into me further, and I feel my body relax into him. Yeah, I was hoping for a different outcome tonight, but times like this are just as memorable. Drifting off to sleep, I can't help but hope for more small moments like this.

Vince must really be tired because I actually wake before him. His deep breathing and steady heartbeat keep me relaxed, instead of thinking about the millions of things on my to-do list on a Saturday morning.

It also helps that I don't have to be anywhere until later this evening. God, I love Saturday mornings, but having Vince here makes it even better.

Somehow, I've managed to use him has a pillow all night. With my arm draped over his chest, I can't help but trace the lines of his ribs and along the planes of muscles along his abs.

I must be too focused on my conquests because he startles me when he flattens my hand along his stomach. "Good God, woman, you're relentless. You *do* know I'm ticklish, right?"

Oops.

"Sorry," I cringe. "I didn't mean to wake you."

"You can wake me with your hands all over me *anytime*. But for the love of God, can you *please* stop with the tickling."

I try pulling my hand away, but he won't have it. "Don't get me wrong, I love having you touch me." He presses my hand further into his now rock-hard abs, as they are flexed and prepared for battle. Then he pulls my hand so that my body follows, and I'm straddling him.

Time ceases to exist as I stare into his beautiful hazel eyes. Today, they look more blue than green around the rim, and the sexiest grin plays at his perfectly kissable lips. Instinctually, I reach out to run my finger along his jaw to feel for myself the perfect amount of stubble that's not rough or prickly. His large hand rests at my hip, keeping me in place, while the other one reaches out to brush a strand of hair that's fallen from my braid behind my ear.

"Hey," he whispers, and a shiver runs through my spine. "I think we outta get out on the road if you want to learn how to drive without much traffic. I know just the place to go if we want to keep traffic to a minimum."

Really? He's focused on trying to drive. That's about the last thing I'm interested in doing with Vince at the moment.

Placing a hand behind my neck, he pulls my face closer to his. "Don't worry, Syd. I've got you."

As if he can read my mind, he flips me over, so my back is to the bed, then he kisses me softly. His elbows keep him propped up, the lower part of his hard body slides between my legs.

Every ounce of sexual tension I felt last night, comes racing back in an instant.

How the hell does this man get me from zero to sixty like this?

I don't just want him. I fucking need him.

He expertly applies pressure to our kiss that has me practically begging for this to go further. My body tingles, and a pulse pounds at my core. As if he's been given the secret code to make me needy in a nanosecond, I buck beneath him.

His large hand brushes from my knee to my core, reading

the map to my body perfectly. My sleep shorts leave nothing in terms of a barrier between us and in an instant, his fingers brush my panties to the side.

His finger slides along my slit, finding my clit with ease to apply just the right amount of pressure. As he kisses his way down my neck, my back bows into my pillow. He somehow manages to pull down my tank and sucks on my exposed nipple. Nipping, sucking. Just as he goes to pull my hardened nipple into his mouth to suck, he repositions his hand at my core, and his finger enters me as his thumb continues to strum my clit. When he presses against my inner wall with a come-hither motion—I am gone.

Heat explodes up my spinal cord, and electric pulses zip from my toes to the top of my head. Not wanting to wake my roommates, I stifle my scream by biting into his shoulder.

Vince doesn't falter or change his pace. He stays right there with me as I enjoy each and every pulse that flows through me. Holy hell, he's wrecking me completely.

When I come down from my orgasmic high, his grin is triumphant. "Now that's a wakeup call, don't ya think?"

God. This man.

All I can do is smile and nod.

I seriously can't even string coherent words because all I manage is an approving moan as a sound effect.

Vince kisses me quickly once more, then jumps to his feet. "I'm gonna jump in the shower. I'll be out in a few minutes. Then we'd better hit the road."

As he turns to walk to my bathroom, the evidence of his arousal is clear by the tent that's pitched in his sweats. "You know you could let me do something about that."

Pointing at his obvious discomfort, I shrug like it's no big deal.

But I've had an up close and personal encounter with him. I know better. Vince is a big deal.

"Your witching powers won't work on me, Syd. If we start that, we may never leave the bed. Now get up and get dressed. I'll only be a few minutes."

"Won't it take you longer than a few minutes?" I reply innocently.

"Not with the images you just created in my mind," he teases then shrugs. "Or a lot of cold water. If you keep looking at me like that, I may need both."

I don't get another word, but I do get the view of his glorious backside as he drops his sweats on the floor at the last second, and his perfect ass walks away from me.

VINCE

"WHEN YOU HEAR THE ENGINE REV, LET OUT ON THE CLUTCH. There's a sweet spot where the gear grips, and you'll move forward," I say as I explain to Sydney how to drive a stick. I've already shown her how to listen to the engine to know when to shift, but I want to make sure she knows how to start out in first gear.

"I can hear the difference. Does it feel that way under the pedals?"

"Yeah. I'll let you get the hang of it in the parking lot, then we'll go out to some hills. If you can consistently start on a hill, you can drive this anywhere."

"Why is it such a big deal to start on hills?"

"If you're on a hill, and you take your foot off the brake with the clutch in, you roll back."

Sydney's confidence waffles a fraction, and I see from the corner of my eye, her hard swallow.

"Don't worry, I know the perfect spot to teach you, and you won't have to worry about rolling into anything. I won't let you fail."

After a few more pointers, I pull over and hop out. "The only way you'll learn is by doing it. So, you're up, Syd."

I expect her to hop out of the Jeep and meet me halfway but to my surprise, she remains seated in the passenger seat. When I reach her door, I open it as I ask, "What's wrong?"

She's biting on her lower lip, staring out the windshield. Eventually, she admits, "I just don't want to ruin your Jeep."

"If you only knew how bad Vanessa was at first, you wouldn't even hesitate. My parents would only buy us a vehicle if we learned how to drive a manual transmission first. Then we could choose. Of course, we put this Jeep through the wringer, but if it survived the two of us, then I'm sure it can take your abuse with ease."

Sydney huffs defensively, "I'm not gonna abuse the Jeep on purpose."

"Since when do you back down from a challenge?" I hedge.

Immediately, her shoulders stiffen, and she glares in my direction. "Since never."

That's what I thought. "So... what are you waiting for?" I shrug, knowing this will go one of two ways. She'll rise to the challenge, or turn her efforts onto me and get pissed.

"Okay," she huffs. "Let's get this show over with," she grumbles as she hops down from her seat.

I grab her wrist as she tries to stomp by me and turn her to face me. "Hey, I'm on your side... always. No need to be upset."

The tension she's been holding onto releases with her exhale. "I know. I just don't like looking like a fool. I may suck at this." She bites on her lower lip as if she's contemplating all the things that can go wrong.

"I don't see any fools here… so stop. There's always a learning curve, and not everything comes natural to people. It takes time and effort. We've got the time, are you ready to try?"

"Yeah… let's get this over with." Her grimace returns when she thinks I can't see her.

She looks sexy as hell when she hops into my Jeep and takes charge of the vehicle. After adjusting the seat and mirrors, she pushes in the clutch with her other foot on the brake and starts the engine. Since I left it in gear, she eases her foot off the brake and tries for the gas. The engine revs. "Slowly release the clutch," I remind her as she presses the accelerator.

Like a pro, she finds the sweet spot with ease, and we creep forward. As we get up to speed, the RPMs climb on the tachometer gauge. She hears when it's time to shift, so she uses the clutch to switch into second gear. It's a little jumpy as she releases the clutch a bit early, but overall, she's getting the hang of it.

When we reach the end of the parking lot, she slows down too fast before reengaging the clutch, causing the Jeep to sputter and stall.

"Shoot." Sydney panics and hits the brakes harder than necessary, causing us to rock forward in our seat belts.

"Don't worry. This happens," I encourage. "Just put it in gear and start over as we turn the corner."

She gets the Jeep going again and when it's time to slow down, this time, she downshifts with ease, making the next turn. Granted, we never make it out of third gear, but she's able to easily toggle between the gears. After a few more trips around the parking lot, she's ready for the road.

"Let's pull out of the lot and hang a right."

"You want me to drive this on the road?" Her panic is faint, but I can still hear it. The fact she's gripping the wheel as if her life depends on it is another tell, but I don't let her know I'm sensing her stress.

"We'll stick to flat streets for now. Promise. Worst-case scenario, I'll hop out and drive if you get uncomfortable."

"Okay…" she draws out with uncertainty but complies.

We make it to a stretch of road where she's actually able to get into fifth gear or as I tell her, overdrive. When she's finally able to cruise, she admits, "Okay, I can do this. It's not so bad."

"I knew you could do it. You think you're ready to tackle some hills?"

"Might as well. I'd freak out if I were on my own, and it kept rolling backward."

"It still happens to me from time to time, but on the steep hills, you can always use the e-brake as an assist. Seriously though, once you get the hang of it, it won't be so bad. Trust me."

Sucking in a deep breath, she's adorable as she says on an exhale, "You haven't steered me wrong so far."

"I love that your confidence in me is so unyielding." My words roll sarcastically off my lips and to my surprise, I'm gifted with her laughter. Maybe she's finally relaxing.

I direct her through a neighborhood that has a few hills with stop signs.

When we get to the first stop, she rolls back a good six feet. Knowing there isn't a car behind us, I'm not too worried.

Though Sydney grips the wheel tighter and lets out an uncomfortable squeak.

"Remember, you have to use that sweet spot on the clutch to your advantage. It will keep you from going back and forward. Give it more gas and ease off the clutch until you find it." The engine revs, but we only rock a foot or two then it catches, and we propel forward through the intersection.

"I did it!" Syd exclaims. Her joyful expression's infectious.

When we get to the next sign, she tackles the hill with ease, and I fist pump the air with a "Whoop," in encouragement.

This earns me a beautiful eye roll.

Yeah, Syd's getting back to herself, and I couldn't be happier.

"What do you say to the highway? I think you're ready to get into some traffic."

"Are you sure?" she asks with a raised eyebrow in my direction.

Shit. Her apprehension's back, but hopefully it won't stay for long.

"It's the only way you're going to get through your fear," I remind her. "But honestly, Syd, you're ready."

Once we're on the highway, I encourage her to follow it up the gorge. Yeah, it has twists and turns, but it won't require a lot of shifting. It's a beautiful afternoon, and we might enjoy the beauty of a drive.

"So, how did you learn to drive a stick so well?" she asks as she puts it in overdrive and finally relaxes into the seat.

"My dad took me out long before I could ever legally drive on the road."

"Really? Just how old were you?"

Shit. How old was I? "Um, around thirteen if I had to guess. I might've been younger. His friend had a farm in the country, and I drove the farm truck when I helped hay the fields that summer."

"Let me guess, you were a natural."

"Not at all. The clutch on that truck was touchy as hell. I can't even tell you how many times I stalled it. But since it was just Dad and his friend, they were patient and kept reminding me I had to learn somehow..." God, that was an amazing day. I'll never forget how proud Dad was of me when I finally got the hang of it.

Though the memory is a good one, and my heart aches with how much I miss him, I can see his smile perfectly, and I revel in the memory for as long as I can. It's weird how you forget the little things when they're gone. I've learned to hold on to the good memories for as long as I can. Someday, I might not be able to remember his laugh, and I'll hate when that day comes.

"You okay, Vince?" Sydney's voice breaks me from my revelry.

Clearing the lump that's formed in my throat, I swallow before whispering, "Yeah... I just miss him."

"Who?" Sydney's confusion is clear.

Fuck. Had I said that last part aloud?

I'm not prepared for this conversation. But when she reaches out to squeeze my hand, I know I'll tell her all the same. I just didn't want to dampen our great day together.

"My dad," I admit on an exhale.

Fuck, this is gonna be harder than I thought.

As if she can sense there's a story there, she probes, "What do you mean?"

Where do I even start?

Even though I've told this story before, I cringe at the thought of her seeing me differently. I don't want to be that guy —you know the one who's gone through shit and you never see as the same once you know his backstory. It's been so nice not having to unload my baggage on her. Staring out at the trees zooming by, I muster up the courage to find the words needed to explain everything. To explain that it's all my fault.

Sure, logically, I know it wasn't. Everyone I know has told me repeatedly. I've been through counseling and logically, I accept the truth. But in times like this, when I miss them more than words can explain, the guilt eats at me.

"There was an accident right after graduation," I start, cold and clinical. I've told this story enough to know if I stick to the facts, I can get through it without letting emotions take over.

"Okay..." she draws out as if she's hesitating for what to say next. God, I don't want her to see me differently. I love that I've been able to be happy and carefree with her. She doesn't need to walk on eggshells around me due to my past and unexpected emotions.

Clearing my throat, I find the strength to lay out the facts, so there's no wonder or hesitation from her.

"It was the night of graduation actually. I'd gone to the all-night party our school threw, and they were chaperones. Vanessa had stayed for a while, but she got permission to leave early so she could be home to feed Julia. Since she was breastfeeding, and everyone wanted her to be included as much as she could, no one hesitated with her request. Our parents were signed up the four a.m. to eight a.m. shift as chaperones."

When Sydney reaches out for my hand to squeeze it, I realize she's stopped driving, and we're parked on the entrance to an abandoned driveway. When I meet her eyes, my voice catches, and I'm unable to remain clinical.

Fuck. Why is this so hard?

It's not like I haven't had years to process this. But grief is a bastard when it comes to creeping in on you. And fuck, I'm fairly certain no amount of time will make telling this story any easier.

"It's okay, Vince. If you're not ready to tell me, you don't have to." The fact she knows me well enough to offer me an out makes my broken heart stretch tighter. Knowing she's here for me brings about the sense of peace I need to get through this. Forcing myself to continue, I pull in a deep breath and begin.

I'd rather she know the whole story and not draw her own conclusions.

"They wouldn't have even volunteered if I hadn't been there. They were supposed to do the earlier shift, but since they watched Julia until Van came home, they volunteered for the later shift. They just wanted us to experience everything... ya know. They were the best parents I could ever ask for."

"I'm sure they were. You and Vanessa are two of the most amazing people I know," Sydney whispers as I squeeze her hand harder.

I will get through this. But damn, it's hard to look at her face full of empathy. She hasn't heard the worst of it, but I'm sure she can tell what's coming.

Just stick to the facts. You can get through this, I remind myself before pulling in another fortifying breath and force myself to say the words.

"Our class had chosen to do our Grad Night at a ski lodge. It was the start of summer, so the snow was gone. But we rented out the hotel for the night. We weren't allowed to go into any rooms, but we had access to a huge ballroom, basketball courts, a swimming pool, and a few game rooms. Our graduating class raised money and even rented charter buses so we could ride to the resort in style."

"That sounds like a lot more fun than my school," Sydney adds, and I ease up on the tension in my hand. No need for her to lose the feeling in her fingers. Instead, I take both her hands in mine as she sits crisscross in the driver's seat, facing me.

"It was one of the last great memories I had of just being a *normal* kid."

"Oh, Vince," she sighs breathless as unshed tears fill her eyes but remain tucked behind her dark lashes.

Exhaling hard, I steady my thoughts and my breathing to continue.

"I didn't find out until I got home to Vanessa. Thank God, I'd been with her when we heard the news. I would've hated myself forever if she'd gone through it alone."

I hear Sydney take in a deep breath, but I can't look at her to see what I'm sure is agony on her face. Instead, I retell the story as if it were yesterday.

"Apparently, on their way to chaperone, my parents were run off the road by a drunk driver in a hit and run. Their car was stuck in a ravine for hours, but from what I'm told, there's no way they didn't die instantly from the force of the impact."

Sydney gasps quietly but remains silent.

"I got home, and Vanessa was playing in the yard with Jules on a blanket. It was a beautiful June morning. We hung out, and I filled her in on what she'd missed. We laughed about our friends and the typical drama of high school. But every ounce of playfulness stopped the instant the patrol car entered our driveway.

"I remember knowing something was wrong in an instant. And it was like the world just went into slow motion," I try to explain.

"The officers wore the most unreadable expressions, and, in that instant, I knew something was wrong. Vanessa must've sensed it, too, because she reached for Julia, trying to protect her from whatever news they were there to deliver. Of course, I reached for the two of them to shield them from what I could. But it was useless."

I know I have to get through the worst of this. But, God, I still feel guilty, even now. My chest feels like a vise grip tightening with each second that ticks by.

"There I was, having the time of my life, and my parents were dead, and I didn't even know it. I'd fallen asleep on the bus ride home, so I didn't even know there had been an accident. I'd wondered why I hadn't seen my parents but just figured they were giving me my space at the party. They were fucking dead in a ditch, taking their last breath."

When I glance to Sydney, her unshed tears from before are streaking down her face. "I'm so sorry, Vince."

Not wanting to be distracted, I force myself to continue as clinically as I can manage. But damn, even after all these years, it's so fucking hard to tell this story.

"When they asked us to confirm our names and who our parents were, they suggested we go inside to discuss the matter further. I'm not even sure we knew how we got inside, but the next thing I knew, we were in our family room sitting on the couch beside each other, and the officers had pulled chairs up to face us as they explained the events of the evening. Apparently, they guy who'd run them off the road ran off the road himself a few miles away and was twice the legal limit with his blood-alcohol levels. He managed to survive but didn't remember hitting my parents at all. We later found that this wasn't his first brush with alcohol, and he's still in jail to this day, paying the price of that evening."

"Ohmigod." Sydney sniffles.

"Those months that followed were the hardest of my fucking life. If I didn't have Vanessa and Jules to keep me sane, I'm not sure I would've made it. Well, Jules is probably what saved us both. We were determined to let her have a normal life, so we've done what we could to pick up the pieces and keep her stable world intact."

"You mentioned before that you transferred to CRU, but I never understood why until now."

"Yeah, I was supposed to go to school on the East Coast, but thank God, my parents made me apply here as well. After we told the dean of admission our story, I transferred here with ease."

"That's incredible of you," Sydney says as she wipes the tears from her eyes.

"I don't know if I'd call it incredible. I'm here for selfish reasons as well. After losing my parents, I wasn't ready to leave my twin or niece. They're literally the only family I have left.

I'll move heaven and earth to make sure they have all they need."

"Oh, Vince," Sydney says, seeped in admiration.

"It was one hell of a summer. Van and I realized we couldn't live in our family home without our parents. It was too fucking hard. Everywhere we turned, we felt like it was a time warp, and we couldn't move forward... ya know?"

God, I hope she understands. Explaining this is way harder than I ever imagined.

When Sydney nods, I continue, "Thankfully, Dad was a planner. We have college funds to pay our expenses now and trust funds with their inheritance when we turn twenty-five, but selling the house made it so we wouldn't have to have many monthly expenses, especially since we live together, and our home is paid off."

"That has to make things easier," Sydney says as she brushes my hair from my face.

That simple act alone makes me fall even harder for her.

Well, that and the fact she isn't looking at me with pity. I can't even describe the expression on her face, but it's more with revelry, or respect, than remorse. My chest loosens, and I relax now that she knows my truth.

"It does. We still work because our college and trust funds didn't cover health care. But overall, I can't complain. We're giving Jules the best life she can have. I think we've done a decent job so far."

"I'd say more than decent," Sydney admonishes. "That girl is fucking incredible, and you'd never know there had been hardships in her life from the looks of her."

I sigh heavily when I think of Julia. "She's already had so

many things happen that she just accepts as normal. A sperm donor that wanted nothing to do with her, the loss of her grandparents and only babysitters she'd ever known. Van and I are just doing the best we can to put her needs first, to make sure she knows she's loved and has stability."

"Uh... you do so much more than that. I'm in awe of you and your sister. When I lost Grams, I was a fucking mess, and I'd had a chance to prepare for the loss for months before it happened. You and Vanessa had your lives ripped from you, and you've done an incredible job of overcoming your adversity, if I say so."

Shrugging, I admit another truth, "Failure isn't an option. My dad drilled it into me that Vanessa needed to follow her dreams. So when he died, I felt it was my place to take over his wishes for her. Do you know that less than fifty percent of teen moms even graduate from high school—and only two percent of them graduate from college before they're thirty?"

"Holy shit..." Sydney's nose scrunches in disbelief. "I knew the odds were low, but that's crazy."

"Yeah. But I'm not gonna let that happen," I say with determination. "There's no way in hell we're gonna come this far—to only get this far. I have zero doubts Vanessa will graduate next year. We've only got four more years until our trust fund kicks in, and we'll both be debt free and college graduates, too."

"I have no doubt about that." Sydney's smile makes my stomach flip with her sheer confidence in me.

We stare at each other for a wordless moment. I take this time to brush away the last of the wetness under her eyes. The tenderness and compassion I feel in this moment is the balm I never knew I needed. Now that she knows my truth, the burden I'd been holding by harboring this part of my life is lightened.

I know without a doubt, I can trust her with just about anything. I just hope she'll accept my reality and not let this get in the way of any future we may have together.

26

SYDNEY

HEARING VINCE TELL HIS STORY PULLED AT MY HEARTSTRINGS. I knew that he'd been through something, but it's unfathomable to believe he'd lost both of his parents in one day. I'm in awe of both him and Vanessa. What they've done to survive is incredible.

Holy hell, is it possible to fall even harder for him?

I reach for his face and brush my thumb along his cheek. His stubble is thicker from last night but still just as sexy as ever. Wanting to show him just how much he means to me, I guide his face close to mine.

With our lips inches apart, his eyes remain on mine, as if he's testing to see if I'm the one who's okay. I'm not the one who just had to relive a horrific experience. The fact he's concerned about me warms my heart even more.

Leaning in, he slants his lips over mine. Unable to wait, I close the distance between us.

I feel his tension slip away as he kisses me back for all he's worth.

This kiss isn't about sexual tension or the need for more.

No—this kiss is about connecting, being open to one another and showing him how deep my feelings run. This wonderfully unselfish man who's given up his plans to be there for his family. Vince puts other's needs ahead of his own and will move heaven and earth to make all their dreams come true.

He's driven, and I doubt there will ever come a challenge he won't rise to the occasion for. I don't think I've ever met anyone sexier than Vincent Daniel Larson.

Unfortunately, when a car zooms past, causing the Jeep to shake, I'm brought back to reality.

Talk about getting carried away.

With my eyes never leaving Vince, I pull away, drawing in ragged breaths until they steady. His hazel eyes search mine as if they're looking for something, though I'm not entirely certain what it could be.

"What?" I ask before I can stop myself.

His head shakes as if he's clearing his thoughts. "I guess I keep waiting for you to scream and run away when I tell you something you don't want to handle." The fear in his features makes my heart break for him.

Who the hell has he been entrusting his secrets with?

The minute that thought fills my head, I know the answer... no one.

Oh, Vince.

Trying to bring some levity to the situation, I sigh heavily.

"Uh... The only place I'm going is for a drive. What do you say we head out to the falls for a bit?"

His genuine smile makes my heart expand.

Don't worry, Vince. I've got you.

It takes me a minute to resituate myself so I can drive.

I crank over the engine, put the Jeep in gear, and rev the engine to find the sweet spot with the clutch.

The Jeep lurches forward as the engine sputters and stalls.

"Shoot," I mumble as embarrassment flows through me.

So much for being smooth.

My faux pas does the trick though. Glancing at Vince in mortification, I don't miss that he's doing everything he can to hold onto the laugh dying to escape. His hand covers his lips, and his eyes dance with joy.

Even though the joke's on me, it feels so good to see him smile.

Clearing his throat, he reassures me, "It's okay. Just take your time and try finding the sweet spot, again."

Shaking off my nerves, I restart the Jeep.

Putting it in gear, I switch my foot from the brake to the gas.

I find the sweet spot and release the clutch.

Too fast...

Again.

We jump forward, and my foot instinctually slams on the brake, making me nearly miss my forehead against the steering wheel.

When I regain control of the vehicle, Vince's holding on to the *oh shit* handle with white knuckles. But I've got to give him credit. His face remains free of emotion until he makes the mistake of meeting my eyes.

A light laugh escapes as he shakes his head. "Okay. Let's try this again. Enough with the herky-jerky."

"Ohmigod..." I gasp with the laughter bubbling inside me. "Herky-jerky? Where the hell did that come from? Are you seventy?"

"No... but we may be that old before we get on the road if you don't start paying attention to what I've taught you."

I huff. But I've got nothing...

"Okay... let's do this again."

Patiently, he walks me through the steps once again. On my next attempt, he lets out a "Whoop" when I effortlessly make it to the pavement and drive up the highway.

"Okay, smartass," I pretend to grumble. "You're the navigator. Where are we going?"

Later that night, I drive with ease to my apartment. Thank God, I didn't have to close, and I'm home at a decent time— well, decent in the sense that it's before midnight. To my surprise, Chloe and Abby are up and watching a movie, and Drew is nowhere to be found.

"Are you two having a girls' night without me?" I tease when I see Chloe sprawled out on the couch and Abby with her feet up on the coffee table. There are bowls of half-eaten ice cream in their hands, and each are mid-bite.

"Not intentionally. Drew's hanging out with his roommates to celebrate their win. Apparently, it's tradition that there be a *girls-free* night where they just hang and roast one another after a team dinner." She shakes her head as if she's confused. "I didn't get it, but it's their way of keeping things low-key and the public spotlight off them. It's at his coach's house and more or less mandated."

I nod, understanding completely. "No, Coach B has had this tradition for years. I've heard a few players talking about it this week at the bar. You've got nothing to worry about, Abby. It really is on the up and up."

Abby rolls her eyes. "I'm not worried. It gave me an opportunity to hang with Chole and now you. I'm surprised you're already home. We'd planned on waiting up for you."

Chloe laughs. "Well, at least trying. I might crash on this couch if I don't get up and move a bit." With that, she sits up and offers the other end of the couch to me.

"Give me a minute to shower and change." A girls' night in sounds just about perfect.

As I exit the room, I hear the TV return to the movie they're watching. We'll likely not watch the end of it as we always end up chatting through most of it anyway. I quickly rush through a shower and put on my pajamas before returning to the living room.

Since I haven't had the chance to catch up with either of them in what feels like forever, I ask the room, "So, what have I missed?"

"Uh, not much." Abby shrugs. "I'm just pestering Chloe to give up the deets on her night with DeShawn. She's been tightlipped—and we all know Chloe. She always has something to say about her dates."

Chloe blinks and shakes her head in denial. "Nothing to say... what can I tell you?"

Yeah, she's lying. When she gives her tell by pulling on her ear, I call her out on it. "You're telling me that you went out with DeShawn and all you did was eat ice cream?"

"I'm a sucker for this stuff... you know that," she admonishes and scrapes what's left of the ice cream in her bowl as if that's proof.

"Seriously, Chloe, you don't have to say anything, but know... I've got an active imagination, and your silence only makes my mind wander," Abby practically singsongs. Unable to keep a straight face, I bust out laughing.

"Yeah, Chloe, now that she's engaged, I'm sure she's got a vivid imagination to compare things to. Before long, she's going to imagine that you were whisked off to Vegas for a quickie wedding or that you at least had some hot, sweaty monkey sex with that beast of a man," I tease, knowing full well she hasn't done any of these things, but maybe if I downplay the situation, she'll fess up.

"DeShawn, is hot," Abby agrees.

"Hey, don't you have your own *hot* fiancé to lust after," Chloe reminds her.

"Chloe—I may be engaged, but I'm not dead or blind for that matter. My eyes still work, and I can see you have the hots for him."

"He is hot," I admit but heed a warning at the same time, "Just be careful... he's got a reputation for being a player off the court. I'd hate to see you hurt."

"I can handle myself. *Thank you very much,*" Chloe pouts in mock-defense.

"I know you can," I agree. "That's why I want to know what went down." I try one last time to get her to cave.

"We went to *ice cream*," she enunciates like I'm ninety, needing a hearing aid. "Nothing happened worth mentioning." Chloe's quiet for a second before she turns the table on me, and her expression turns devious.

Oh, shit... what's she up to?

"So... what's up with you and Vince? Have you figured out why he hasn't *rung your bell* yet?"

That little shit. Of course, she'd go here to get the attention off herself.

"Really?" Abby asks with interest.

Turning to face her, I clearly inform her, "Oh, he's rung my bell... multiple times... just not in the way you think."

Abby's knowing smirk says it all. "Really? Do tell..."

Falling back into the couch, I sigh heavily as I think of how to explain Vince in a nutshell. "I swear the man was given the secret code to crack my body. He barely has to do anything, and I'm lighting up like the Fourth of July." I shake my head when I realize just how cliché that sounds. "It's more than that... and it isn't about the sex... or lack thereof. He just seems to get me."

"Uh-oh," Abby whispers, then looks to Chloe wide-eyed.

Apparently, they're having a secret conversation or can suddenly read each other's minds because their expression morphs as they nod in agreement at some unspoken topic.

"What?" I say defensively.

"Oh..." Chloe draws out as she looks to Abby once more, who only nods in return. "We were talking before about how we think you're falling for Vince."

"And this is a secret?" I ask, knowing there must be more, all the while making sure I neither confirm nor deny their assumption. "What else were you talking about?"

"Well…" Abby looks to the ceiling before she finally makes eye contact with me. "We were just saying that if you can find someone you're that compatible with without doing the deed, then he may be the one."

"Doing the deed? Okay, Dorothy, did you really just say that? Are you suddenly one of the Golden Girls?"

"Oh, she's way more like Blanche. Don't ya think?" Chloe interrupts, completely missing the point. "Now that she's getting hot sex regularly, she assumes we all must be getting some."

Chloe's smug expression makes us all bust out laughing.

"Ohmigod, you guys are awful," Abby admonishes as she swats the air in our direction. But under her breath, she mumbles, "Everyone should experience hot sex. Mediocre sex just isn't worth it."

"Preach," Chloe blurts out, which brings more laughter to the room.

"No kidding," I agree.

"To hot sex." Abby fakes a toast to the air, and we follow her lead.

God, these girls. What would I do without them?

But the thought of hot sex…

I can only imagine what it will be like with Vince. Our chemistry could catch the sheets on fire… if only we'd go there.

I don't miss when Chloe pulls in her lower lip and glances my way.

Shit. She's caught me contemplating, and she knows it.

"I still say you should just talk to him," she whispers between us, though Abby clearly hears.

"Syd, I love you. But when have you ever held back your thoughts?" Abby points out.

We all know the answer is *never*.

Instead of answering either of them, I deflect by focusing our attention on Abby. "Have you found out when you're moving to Baltimore?"

"The plan as of today is after graduation, we'll fly out for a week to check out apartments and see what we'll need. Then we'll come back and drive our things across the country. I might end up selling my vehicle, but it's still up in the air."

"Wow, that's a lot of changes in the next month or so."

"Don't worry, I'm still planning on paying the rent through our lease. But I'll likely be gone by the middle of June," Abby assures us. But that's the least of our worries.

"We're so excited for you, Abs, but I'm not gonna lie..." Chloe holds her hand over her heart as she fights back emotions. "We're gonna miss you when you're gone."

Nodding my head in agreement, I remain silent because I know I totally suck at goodbyes.

27

VINCE

SYDNEY AND I'VE BARELY SEEN ONE ANOTHER ALL WEEK, BUT I plan to make up for our lost time this weekend. Van and Julia are off to the beach for their mommy date, and I've invited Syd over for brunch.

With Syd having the entire day free, I'm hoping to spend as much of it with her as possible. Normally, Saturdays are for sleeping when Vanessa's off, but brunch won't cook itself. For the better part of an hour, I've been making Sydney's favorite breakfast: homemade biscuits with sausage gravy. Thank God, I can follow a recipe on Google.

Sure, I could have taken her out to eat, but that means sharing her with the public. I want a quiet day hanging at the house so we can relax. With only weeks left of the semester, we could use the rest before finals.

When the doorbell rings, I set the pan on a different burner and rush to greet her. If I didn't know better, I'd swear I am addicted to all things Sydney.

Opening the door, I'm greeted by her beautiful knowing smile, and her green eyes dance as she steps past me. "Mmmm... it smells delicious. I thought we were cooking together?"

"I was hungry," I admit. "But I've waited for you. Promise."

She reaches up on her toes and kisses my cheek. "You'll never hear me complain if you choose to cook. You can even write that down because I'll never pass up a homecooked meal I don't have to cook."

"You may change your mind after we eat, but I'll hold you to your promise," I tease.

Her expression clearly reads, *oh, shit, what have I gotten myself into*?

It's fucking comical.

"Don't worry, I taste tested it, and it's edible... or we'd be heading to the nearest diner," I finally admit as we reach the kitchen.

I've already set the table, so I motion for her to sit as I grab everything we need. Heading to the fridge, I pull out a fruit salad and orange juice. Then I grab the plate of sausage and biscuits I'd left warming in the oven.

"Wow, Vince, you've really gone all out. Thank you," Syd says as her eyes widen at the mound of food I'm carrying.

"It's not a big deal," I assure her.

Once I've got everything settled, I take a moment to appreciate her beauty. She's wearing a simple black hoodie with her gorgeous red hair piled on top of her head in one of those messy buns girls always wear. Her face is free of makeup, and her dusting of freckles make her absolutely breathtaking.

"What? Do I have something on my face?" she asks as she grabs a napkin and pats at her lips.

"No," I assure her.

"Then what are you staring at?" Her tone is clearly defensive as her green eyes scrutinize my face.

Yeah, I'm not getting out of this one. I've been caught redhanded.

"Uh... Just your gorgeous face," I admit shyly.

Rolling her eyes as if she's unwilling to take the compliment or thinks I'm crazy, she mutters, "Whatever."

She has no fucking clue as to what she does to me.

Before either of us can say a word, she asks, "Did I tell you that Chloe found out she only has one semester left of school?"

No. "What does this mean for you?"

"Well, since she won't be staying all year, she can't sign our lease. So that means I need to either find *two* new roommates, or a new place. I can't afford more than what I'm paying now. But I've got a few months to figure things out. I'm not too worried." She stops for a moment, and her nose crinkles like she's just tasted something bad. "Ugg..." She exhales heavily. "The thought of living with new roommates sucks. Maybe I can find a studio or something."

Never having to deal with living with strangers, I can't say I can relate, but knowing they've lived together for the past few years can't be easy to give up. "I'm sure you'll figure something out," I assure her. "Thankfully, you have until August to settle things."

As soon as we finish eating, she's up and out of her chair to clear her dish. On the way to the sink, she yawns heavily and asks, "After breakfast, what do you say to binge-watching this new show Chloe told me about on Netflix?"

I don't care what we do, as long as she's here is my first thought, though the words, "Sounds good," somehow spill from my lips coherently.

"Would it be too much to ask if we watch it in Jules' favorite place? I promise I won't put up a fight if we nap either. Last night at work was rough, and I'm dragging today."

Snuggling with her will never be a chore. "I think I can manage that." I smirk at where my thoughts go.

Of course, my dick likes that idea, too, as it jumps to attention. Denim is my best friend at the moment.

Dammit, Larson. Get it together. And for the love of God, get your mind out of the fucking gutter.

Thankfully, Sydney remains none the wiser of my trip down Horny Lane.

God. I've got to get things under control, or there's no way I'll be able to concentrate on anything but her—I am not a pubescent perv.

Hand in hand, we walk to my room where my king-sized bed awaits.

God, this is so not helping.

Glancing to the bathroom, I quickly say, "I'll be out in a second," and dart through the door before she can respond.

Turning on the water as cold as possible, I rinse off my hands and run it over my wrists as I watch my frustrated expression through the mirror calm. This works for now. Taking some water, I splash my face to clear my thoughts with the help of its frigidness.

After drying off and making sure there's no evidence of

what I've been up to, I leave the bathroom to find Sydney snuggled under the blankets with the show set to start. Her smile lights me up from the inside out, but not necessarily in a sexual way—though there are plenty of thoughts where that's concerned.

"You ready?" she asks on another long yawn when I hesitate next to the bed.

She pats the space beside her, and I comply. Though I lie on top of the covers.

I've never claimed to be a saint, but I'm not tempting myself to join her just yet either.

I will behave like a gentleman plays on a loop as a constant reminder as I instinctually reach out, pulling her close so her head can rest on my chest.

Keeping my focus on the program, I will myself to calm down. I feel the rest of me relax and soon, I'm able to pay attention to what the show's about.

Feeling Sydney relax fully into me, as her breathing deepens, I'm fairly certain she's asleep, but I'm not willing to risk waking her to find out. She must be exhausted if she's out so quickly.

Somehow, I end up getting sucked into the show. When the episode ends, I find myself letting the next episode cue up. I can't describe the plot but hell, the characters do crazy shit, and I'm sucked in to see what their consequences are. It's not my typical choice, but it's entertaining. With Syd sound asleep, I'm not willing to move anytime soon.

Just as the second episode finishes, Sydney stirs. Her legs stretch long, and the arm she has draped around my chest tightens. Her long lashes flutter, and her sleepy gaze finds mine in an instant.

"Hey, sleepyhead," I whisper. "Get a good nap?"

Looking around the room confused, she asks, "How long was I out?"

Brushing the loose strands of hair from her face, I glance at the television. "I just finished the second episode."

Sydney winces. "Geez. I'm sorry. I guess I'm not the best of company."

"I can't think of any other way to spend the day."

Rolling her eyes, she scoots away. "I'm just going to use your bathroom. I'll be back out in a minute."

Not wanting to watch more of this show, I turn off the TV while I wait for Sydney to return. Leaning back against my headboard, I close my eyes and relax into the pillows behind me. This is just the type of Saturday I needed after the hectic week I've had.

When Sydney returns, her hair is down, and her face looks fresh as if she hadn't been sleeping mere minutes ago next to me. As soon as her eyes meet mine, her smile turns devious, and she pounces onto the bed, pinning me down.

"Humpf…" I'm knocked breathless.

As she straddles my waist, and her hands lock in mine, she pulls them up, placing them on my chest for balance.

Not putting up a fight, I grin at her playfulness.

"So, now that you have me, what are you gonna do with me?" I challenge.

"Oh, I'm sure I can think of something," she singsongs.

Damn, she's adorable when she gets cocky.

Bucking my hips, I slide down the bed, and her eyes widen.

"Hey…" She pretends to pout.

"Not going anywhere," I assure her. "Just moving down a bit."

Liking this new position, she pulls my hands from my chest and places them on each side of my head. "I think I can handle this."

Oh, I'm sure she can.

Sydney's eyes bore into mine, then they move to my lips as she slants her face over mine. Her tongue darts across her lips, leaving them glossy. Slowly, she lowers her mouth to mine but instead of kissing me like I expect, she runs her tongue lightly along the seam of my lip.

Fuck, I feel it everywhere.

Wanting to move things along, I practically growl, "Kiss me, Syd."

When our lips meet, my tongue darts out to dance with hers. Her body shifts against mine, and I'm suddenly hypersensitive.

Fuck… this won't work.

As much as I fucking love letting her be in control. I will lose every ounce of mine if I let her continue. Making an executive decision, I release her hands and quickly flip her so she's on the bottom, as I adjust myself so she's not gonna set me off before things get started.

Her hands run through my hair as the temptress tops me from the bottom. Her hips buck into my thigh, and she pulls me closer.

Nope. Gotta change it up, so she can stop calculating how to turn me on even further. Her force is stronger than a siren call playing only for me.

Ice Baths.

Bengay.

How many MVP players have made it to the Hall of Fame?

Fuck, I can't remember.

Maybe if I just focus on her… I can stop focusing on how fucking good she makes me feel.

Reaching for the hem of her shirt, I run my fingertips from her stomach to her rib cage. When I brush the underside of her bra, I lift it so I can make direct contact with her nipple. Knowing it fucking drives her wild when I alternate between pinching and pulling them, I do just that.

I won't deny my pride soars when she bucks and pants, "Take it off."

Breaking our kiss only long enough to rip her hoodie and t-shirt up and over her head, she leans toward me and almost as if she's a contortionist, maneuvers her hands in an instant to unclasp her bra.

How the fuck she can do it so quick is beyond me, but seeing her full breast on display stops any coherent thought in an instant.

Gravity causes her perfect round globes to separate as they naturally fall apart. Her nipples stand erect as my eyes roam over them.

"Damn, you're beautiful, Syd." My words escape before I can filter myself.

A light blush creeps across her cheeks and onto her chest, causing her light freckles to stand out in contrast to her creamy skin.

When her hand reaches my neck to pull me closer, no words are needed for her intention.

I need to finish what I've started.

Leaning in, I kiss her once more as I palm her breast and pull at her nipples between my fingers. When she moans, I break our kiss to feather her with kisses along her jawline, to that spot she loves just behind her ear.

I'm rewarded with a breathless, "Oh, Vince." So, I continue my quest to pleasure her.

When my tongue darts around her nipple, I'm rewarded with the pull of my hair. She lets this continue before she pushes me further down the bed.

"I'm getting there." I chuckle as I kiss along her ribs to her abdomen.

Reaching for the waistband of her dark leggings, I quickly drag them down her legs. When I return my focus to her, the movement of her breasts quickly draws my attention as she props herself to watch the show that's about to rock her world.

Not being able to help myself, I growl as I lean in and kiss one nipple, as I play with the other. When I pull and suck just the way that drives her mad, she becomes practically feral.

"God, Vince. You're gonna make me come, and you've barely touched me."

"Is this a bad thing?" I tease, knowing I won't let her down.

"I swear your tongue is magic."

"Well, that's a first," I mumble as I kiss my way down her body.

Brushing my fingers along her seam, I draw her wetness up to circle her clit.

Sydney's so fucking responsive. Her back bows as a loud moan escapes, making me grateful we're alone in this giant house.

When I lean in to kiss her breast once more, I circle her areola with my tongue and nip her nipple with my teeth all the while strumming her clit the way I've learned she likes it. I quickly circle, applying pressure while brushing over her clit every few strokes.

"More, Vince..." she cries out. "I need more... so close. I'm so... so close."

Doubling my efforts at her breast, I lightly pull her nipple with my teeth as I circle her clit with greater speed.

Sydney fists my hair and pulls at the strands as her entire body tenses then convulses over and over as a scream rips through her.

Yeah, I'm glad we're alone.

And I'm fairly certain there may be a bald spot.

As she releases my hair and falls back to the pillow beneath her, I can't help but rub the tender spot on my head. I'm shocked to find I somehow still have hair there.

Her beautiful blissed-out expression makes it all entirely worth it.

When I plop down on the pillow next to her, I can't stop myself from touching her. My fingertips trace her rib and abdomen, drawing unknown patterns as I stare at her flushed face.

After her breathing returns to normal, her eyes blink open, and a lazy grin forms at her lips. "Hey, you..."

"Hey, yourself," I say as I lean in to kiss her once more.

Instead of her typical comatose state after making her come, I'm greeted with a kiss that has nearly the amount of passion that started this to begin with. She reaches for the hem of my shirt and whispers, "This needs to go."

Of course, I comply.

Naked as the day she was born, she throws a leg over me and straddles me. I can feel her heat on my stomach, and her breasts dangle beautifully in my face. I don't know what I've done to deserve this incredible sight, but I've never been more thankful.

She leans in to kiss me once more, and her nipples graze my chest. "I need you, Vince," sounds sexy as hell falling from her lips.

The vixen she is presses her ass against my straining dick in my pants.

Shit. I need to keep things under control.

But damn, I don't think I've ever wanted anyone like I want her.

When my jeans become past the point of comfort, I curse out a moan. "Fuck...Syd... You feel so good."

She reaches behind her and cups my cock through my jeans, making her intentions clear.

"Do you have any condoms?"

Why the fuck haven't I bought any condoms?

I've never hated myself more than I do in this moment.

Closing my eyes because I can't bear to look at her as I cringe my answer. "No..." God, she's gonna hate me.

I swear I'll make it up to her though.

When she's quiet for way too long of time, I crack one eye open to peek at her.

She's got one eyebrow cocked and a curious expression on her face. Seeing she has my attention, she whispers, "Why?"

Shit... how do I say this... "I... Uh..." Great, I've got an impeccable vocabulary, and it totally fucking fails me in this moment.

What do I even use as an excuse? It never even crossed my mind.

I'm such a dumb ass! And incredibly moronic, unprepared dumb ass.

Completely misreading my discomfort, she shrugs. "What would you say if I brought some?"

Well, shit…

SYDNEY

VINCE'S MOUTH FORMS A PERFECT O.

Shit, maybe he's not ready for this?

I know I am but dammit, I never considered he's been holding off because he doesn't want us to go there.

"Or maybe not," I backpedal, and I start to climb off him.

But he catches my wrists and clasps our hands together as he holds them against my chest.

"No... it's... not what you're thinking... I'm sure."

Flippantly, I spout, "So, you aren't avoiding having sex with me?"

Damn, I hate my sass in times like this.

I swear my thoughts roll off my tongue without even letting me have a chance of filtering them.

"I'm not avoiding you..." he rushes out but stops and looks to the ceiling as if he's trying to gather his thoughts.

"I just didn't think to buy condoms," he whispers. His deep

voice seems pained or filled with some emotion I can't pinpoint.

"It's okay, Vince," I say, still trying to put some distance between us. "If you're not ready to take things to the next level, I don't want to pressure you." But his grip remains firm.

Staring directly in my eyes, he sighs heavily. "It's not that I'm not ready... I just... fuck... how do I say this without sounding like a complete tool..." He closes his eyes once again as his deep voice trails off.

I wait as he fights for the words he's trying hard to find.

I'm not certain, but I'm sure there's something else he's not telling me.

When his eyes open, they find mine in an instant. "Sorry... it's... uh, hard to have this conversation when you're deliciously naked on top of me."

"Uh, if you'd let me go, I could get off," I point out the obvious as I pull at our hands.

Shaking his head as if I've missed the point, he mumbles, "No... I rather like you as you are..." He sucks in a deep breath, then continues, "Fuck... why is this so hard to say?" Then he looks me up and down and shakes his head as if he's internally scolding himself for ogling me. "I guess what I'm trying to say is that I've never had a need to buy condoms... so I never thought about them."

What the hell is he talking about?

"Need them?"

"Yeah," he sighs heavily, and my entire body shifts with his effort. "I've never bought them before because it was my way of refraining from sex."

"Vince... if you're not ready, I completely understand."

He releases one of his hands and drags it down his face. "Well… there's a long story that goes with it… most you already know… but I've never let myself get close enough with a woman to want her the way I want you."

What is he trying to say? I scrutinize his expression but come up empty-handed. "You're not making any sense."

Rolling his eyes, he looks again to the ceiling. After another long exhale, his eyes find mine. "After we found out about Jules and then the accident…" He trails off.

What the hell is he talking about? Panic sets in. Has something else happened I don't know about?

"Calm down," he says as he brushes my hair from my face. "Nothing bad has happened… It's just… Van getting pregnant in high school… well… it was the ultimate birth control for me. I didn't want to be with anyone in fear of being a teenage parent…" He takes in another breath before continuing, "Then after my parents… well… I knew I already had two people who needed me, I couldn't afford to let someone else in. That is… until you came along…"

I think I'm following him, but I'm not prepared to make assumptions. "What do you mean?"

"First, you're the first girl I've even considered having more with. You're the first one I've let completely in and would even consider changing things for."

I know he said he never dated much… but I'm the first? First what?

"What are you considering?" I push for clarification.

"I'm at a place in my life where I have less than a year until graduation. Van and Jules will only need me for a short period of time and will be fine if I focus my attention on my wants and needs, too."

"Oh, Vince," I sigh. He's so sweet to think of his sister like that. His adoration only makes me fall harder for him.

"So, we're clear, Syd. I want you." He adjusts me so I can feel his intentions.

"But…" Why does he hesitate? And why has he told me all of this? It doesn't make sense.

"I've only hesitated because this is all new to me." He reaches out to place a hand on my cheek. The sincerity in his eyes makes my heart clench harder for him. "I… I'm a virgin, Syd. I want to make sure I meet your needs and expectations, and I…"

I can't take this. "Stop."

"But…" he pleads.

"Just stop, Vince. The fact that you have done nothing but meet my needs is more than enough. What about your needs? Don't you ever think of yourself?"

He grins sexily. "Uh… yeah… why do you think you're here?"

"If you want to wait for sex, I'm more than okay with that," I assure him.

"Uh… no, that's not the point, Syd. I'm ready for sex. Especially with you. I was just the dumbass who didn't think to buy condoms when we finally have the house alone for the day. Did you really bring some? Or were you just tempting me?"

Nodding, I admit, "They're in my purse in the kitchen."

Before I can even finish the thought, he rolls me to the side and bolts off the bed. I hear his feet slap against the hardwood floors and disappear. Within seconds, Vince returns breathless with my purse in hand. "I never dig through a woman's purse," he offers in explanation as he tosses it at me.

Reaching in my purse, I glance to him. "Are you sure you're ready for this? I don't want to pressure you."

Unbuckling his jeans, he drops them to the floor. Then he crawls up the bed wearing only his boxers. "I love you for caring, Syd. But honestly, this thing between us is exactly what I want. What I need," he says as he reaches for my purse and sets it on his bedside table.

Wait? Did he just say he loves me?

I don't get to contemplate his words as he crawls up my body. "You've just gotta tell me what to do... so I don't hurt you or anything," he explains. Then he sheepishly adds, "Or forgive me if I come too soon... or don't satisfy you... I'm a quick study... I'm sure with practice I can learn what you like."

Ohmigod... this man.

His sincerity as he leans in to kiss me completely seals the deal for stealing my heart. "Vince... stop worrying..." I wait for him to look me in the eye before continuing. "You're the only person who seems to have the magic code to cracking my body as quickly as you do. Trust me... you leave me more than satisfied."

"Really?"

Shaking my head at his absurdities, I say, "As if you didn't just wreck me. Would it be easier for you if I were on top?"

"Only if next time, I am." His beautiful hazel eyes dance as he teases me playfully.

I've laid out an entire strip of condoms on the pillow beside me. "Well, I do have these..." I pull him in for a kiss.

After kissing the hell out of Vince for a few minutes, I pull away breathless and pat his leg, suggesting he roll over. Once he's on his back, I grin. "That's better."

Crawling up his body, I kiss him some more before trailing kisses down his jawline and onto his chest. Knowing he's ticklish, I quickly make it to his happy trail that escapes into his boxers. As I kiss down his sculpted V, I remove his underwear.

As soon as they are thrown to the floor, I focus on his bobbing cock that's begging for my attention. Grasping his shaft, I take my thumb and wipe off the precum that's already glistening at his tip. I slide my hand up and down a few times before licking his tip.

Vince groans in appreciation.

Reaching in with my other hand, I cup his balls as I suck him as far as I can down my throat. I swear his cock gets even harder with this move. Loving this reaction, I do it again.

"Uh, Syd," Vince interrupts. "If you plan on doing anything else, you may not want to continue with that…"

Getting his message loud and clear, I reach for the foil packet on the pillow beside him and tear it open. Pinching the tip, I roll the condom over his cock and can't help but grin when Vince adjusts it at the end to make sure it's in place.

Reaching into my purse, I grab the new bottle of lube I'd picked up with the condoms and put a drop or two at his tip, before spreading it around.

Not knowing how losing one's virginity feels for a guy, I straddle his waist once more and kiss him again. When I pull back, I offer him one last out, "Are you sure?"

He nods eagerly with a dopey grin plastered on his face.

"I'm not sure I've ever been *more* ready. God, Syd, you are absolutely gorgeous."

Lifting up as I kiss him once more, I guide his shaft to my center. When I know we're lined up, I press down a bit to let him enter me, then I slowly retract to the tip again. Vince groans hungrily, and I'm encouraged to continue. Trying to let him acclimate, I repeat this process until our pelvic bones meet.

"Fuck... Syd, you feel so good," he pants as he reaches for one breast to kiss it.

Needing to move, I set a slow and steady rhythm that will make me join him if we keep this up. "Oh, God, Vince.... This is incredible..."

As if he can read my mind, he presses a thumb to my clit and circles as I pick up my pace riding his cock. "I'm not sure how long..." he starts, but I interrupt.

"Me, too... Right there. I'm so close..."

All thought goes out the window as I chase this orgasm with him. The moment I start to break, Vince practically roars as he lets go and pulsates right along with me.

His eyes meet mine, and he brushes the hair from my face as he kisses me through the last shivering quakes of my orgasm.

When I'm completely spent and barely have the ability to form coherent thought, I slump to his chest, his cock still twitching inside me with the new movement.

"You okay, Syd?" His voice is filled with concern.

"More than okay," I assure him. "You?"

His chest rumbles with laughter. "Are you kidding me? I don't think I have a drop of cum left in me. You're a fucking goddess who's completely wrecked me. I didn't think it could be like this."

"It typically isn't," I admit. "I haven't had a connection like this with anyone."

Holy. Fucking. Shit.

If this is how sex with Vince will be every time … I am done for.

VINCE

Now that I've had sex with Sydney, I want it all the time. In the shower, on top, on bottom, against the wall, from behind. I'm determined to experience everything with the goddess who's completely wrecked me for all others.

I guess that's why I'm driving home at five a.m. on a Saturday from her house, so I can watch Julia this morning while Van pulls an early shift at the diner. I'd picked up Syd from her shift at the bar, and I'm proud to admit she's just going to bed now.

God, I hope Jules will sleep for a few more hours as I haven't slept since the short nap I took before arriving at the bar. Not wanting to risk the chance of waking Jules with the garage door, I park on the street and enter through our front door.

Seeing the kitchen light on, I wander in to let Vanessa know I'm here and that I'm sorry I'm a few minutes late. She still has about ten minutes before she typically leaves for her shift, but I don't want her to worry.

"Hey," I whisper as I round the corner so that I won't frighten her. "Sorry I'm running late. I forgot my phone charger, or I would've texted to let you know I was on my way."

But my excuse lands on an empty room. Where is she? I start to go check her room when I notice it.

There in the middle of the kitchen floor is a small puddle of blood, and a broken bowl lays next to it. I follow the droplets to the drawer we have towels in and see it, too, has smudges of blood.

Shit. What happened?

Quickly, I rush to her room to make sure she's okay. The lights are on, including in Julia's room, so I holler, "Hey, Van? Where are you?"

I check both bedrooms and the bathroom.

Fuck. Something must be wrong.

Rushing to the garage, I fling the door open, only to find it empty.

Needing to get my charger to make a call, I curse myself for letting it die last night. I should know better.

I'm a fucking wreck as I fumble with my phone to get it to charge.

Zero percent battery.

Fuck, it will take a few minutes until I get enough juice to see if Van's left me any messages.

There are two different hospitals within fifteen minutes of us. I have no idea which one she'd go to as our insurance will cover both.

Trying to get my phone to power up, I frantically press the

button over and over again to no avail. Fuck, if I didn't need it so desperately, I'd chuck it across the room in frustration.

When it finally powers up, I find one voice mail, and I can't cue it up fast enough to find out what's happened.

"Hey, Vin. There's been an accident, and I need to take Jules to the hospital. You're not due here for about thirty minutes, so I assume you're sleeping or something." The sounds of Julia crying get closer, then Vanessa comforts her, "Come on, baby, let's get you in the car. I'll call you when I know more." Click.

She doesn't even tell me which hospital.

What the fuck happened?

Grabbing the portable charger from the kitchen we keep as a spare, I rush back to my room to change into a pair of jeans and grab a hoodie. Connecting my phone on the way out the door.

The moment my phone connects to my Jeep's hands-free device, I dial my sister.

It rings once… twice… three times and no answer. When it connects to voice mail, I leave a message letting Van know I'm on my way and to call me back.

But fuck… Which hospital?

Letting my twin senses guide me, I follow the easiest route to a hospital. I don't see Van's car in the parking lot, but the place is huge and fairly crowded for this early in the morning.

Running through the emergency room doors, I scan the waiting room in hopes that I'll find them. Nothing. The place isn't too full, but that doesn't mean they're not here and already being seen by a doctor.

A kind nurse at the triage desk asks, "Can I help you?"

"Yeah," I pant. "My sister and niece had an accident, and I want to know if they were brought here."

"Why don't you tell me their name, and I can see if I can help?" She taps on her computer before I can even get out their full names.

When she grimaces, my heart sinks.

"I don't have anyone by that name here. Let me check one more place. I just came on shift, and maybe they're being triaged."

Why the fuck didn't I charge my phone last night?

Hell... if I hadn't been having the time of my life, they might not even be here in the first place.

"You're in luck," the person behind the desk says. "I've found them. We'd just called them back. Can I get your name, and I'll tell them you're here?" She points to the lobby. "You can just wait right there until I return."

I'm still on edge, but my anxiety decreases slightly knowing I've come to the right place. Since they'd obviously been waiting for some time before I arrived, maybe the injury isn't as bad as I'm making it out to be.

I can hope, right?

Now isn't the time to let my vivid imagination run wild.

Knowing I have enough energy to pace a hole in the shiny white tile, I force myself to do as the woman behind the desk asks. Walking to the closest chair available, I plop in the seat and wait.

My leg bounces as I mull over the possibilities of what could've happened. If it were life threatening, they would've come by ambulance. Fuck... there are still so many things it could be. The blood wasn't enough to cause catastrophic injuries… but damn, there's quite a mess. I'll have to head home before them to clean up. No sense in making another trip to the ER today.

When the woman from before motions for me to follow her, I jump from my seat to shorten the space between us. When I get close enough to hear, she says, "They're in curtain number four. Just take a left after you get through that door, and you'll find it on your right."

My legs can't carry me fast enough, and I force myself to walk at an acceptable pace, watching the numbers above each designated area. My chest tightens as I get to the right place when I hear Julia cry, "Nooooo."

Pulling back the curtain, my eyes frantically dart to my little niece in the enormous hospital bed. Van's beside her holding her hand while a doctor examines a gnarly cut above her brow.

"Hey, hey, hey," I manage in a much calmer voice than I actually feel, "what's going on?"

"Unks," Jules calls out, clearly forgetting what she's been protesting about seconds ago with her attention now focused on me.

"Hey, Jules," I greet as if she isn't lying in a hospital bed in her blood-soaked pajamas. Sure, head wounds are known for excessive bleeding, but Van must have freaked out if she saw that gash.

"Hey, Vinny." The relief in her voice makes my heart ache. Especially when she reaches out her hand for mine.

Fuck. I should've been here.

Closing the distance, my stress eases a bit when she squeezes my hand in hers. When our eyes lock, I know without a doubt we will get through this—together. I feel her tension release, and her bravery remains strong. She's the best mother apart from our own, and I can't imagine what she's gone through this morning.

The doctor interrupts my thoughts with, "This will definitely require stitches. You were right to bring her in immediately. With your permission, I'd like to call in our facial plastic surgeon. Since Julia's so young, with their help, this laceration will soon become a distant memory, rather than a predominate feature."

No shit.

Of course, we want the scar to be as concealed as possible.

Van and I nod our heads, but she voices her thoughts aloud, "Yes. If you think that's what's best. I'd prefer there to be as little of a scar as possible."

"Sounds like a plan." The doctor nods in agreement. Then he turns his attention to Julia. "I have a daughter just about your age. You don't by any chance like Disney movies, do you?"

Wide-eyed, Julia nods her head enthusiastically. "*Descendants* is my favorite."

"You're in luck. I know we have that one in particular in our on-demand videos here at the hospital. Would you like me to get a nurse in here to help you cue it up?"

Julia nods eagerly.

I could care less that this is likely the millionth time she's watched this show. As long as it works as a distraction from the obvious pain she's been in, I'll watch it a gazillion more.

The doctor leaves, and a nurse immediately replaces him before I can find out how they ended up here in the first place.

"I hear there's a *Descendants* fan in here. I'm personally envious of Evie's fashion. Who's your favorite character?"

Julia rolls her eyes but winces as she says, "Uh... Mal, I want purple hair just like her."

"Oh, boy, here we go again," Van whispers more to herself than the room.

Yeah, she's gonna have her road cut out for her with this one. I'm not sure who will win in the battle of wills. Hopefully, the dye will be temporary.

As the nurse distracts Julia momentarily, I whisper to Van, "So what happened?"

Sucking in a deep breath, she sighs heavily. "I'd just gotten out of the shower when I heard the crash in the kitchen. Apparently..." she side-eyes Julia, "someone couldn't wait for me to get her a bowl for her cereal and climbed on the counter to get one of those bigger ones we keep up high without using her stool. When she went to jump down, she somehow hit her head on a cupboard door or something. From what I can tell, the bowl broke when she dropped it on her way down."

"Did she let you know she was up?"

Vanessa's head shakes defensively. "I had no idea she was up until the screams."

Noticing the nurse leave, I turn my attention to Julia. "What were you doing up on the counter, squirt?" Recalling the scene at the house, another question comes to mind. "And why didn't you just use your stepstool?"

Julia shrugs. "I wanted cereal... and I was hungry."

"We have snacks in your cupboard, Jules," Van reminds her.

"But Froot Loops and milk is better," she explains so

matter-of-factly. "I didn't know I'd bonk my head. Blood was everywhere, Unks. It didn't stop. Momma said I had to come here and fix it."

Looking at the bandage the doctor had used to cover the wound and seeing blood seep through, I heartily agree. "Momma's right. I'm sure you scared her."

"Sorry, Momma," comes out in a whisper as Julia looks to her toes under the blanket.

"Oh, sweetie," Vanessa coos as she reaches in for a hug. "I'm not mad. I just got scared because I didn't know where the blood was coming from. I love you and just want you healthy."

No kidding. Who knew we needed to worry about her climbing the counters? She's never even attempted it before. Maybe if I'd been there, I would have heard her meandering around.

With the opening credits finished, Julia's attention returns to the screen.

I take this moment to check on Van. I'm sure this has rattled her. I can't imagine walking in on that scene. "You okay, Van?" I ask, pulling her in for a side hug and kissing the top of her head.

Exhaling heavily, I feel her body droop into mine as she whispers, "Yeah. I'm good. You wouldn't believe how much a relatively small cut in retrospect can bleed." I'm not sure if she says that last part for my benefit or to herself, as it is nearly inaudible by the end.

Squeezing her tight, I assure her, "It's all gonna be okay. I'm here... and we'll get through this together."

"Thanks, Vinnie. I don't know what I'd do without you."

That's something I hope she'll never have to worry about.

Later that night, when I finally lay my head down to rest, my mind whirls like a tornado. A million different thoughts fly at me, but nothing I can grab hold of. I'm exhausted, yet I'm certain sleep will evade me for hours to come.

I've heard from Sydney today but explained that something came up with my family, and I"ll talk to her tomorrow. She understands, but I don't think she can. How the hell do I explain my guilt and anger? It's not like she's ever been in my shoes.

Here I was off, having the time of my life, and I let my fucking family down.

It's unacceptable.

When they needed me, I wasn't here… and look what happened.

Something could've seriously happened to Julia. Jesus, this accident is just the first of many guaranteed to happen in her lifetime. How the hell are Van and I supposed to protect her if there are so many unknowns?

Van shouldn't have had to go through this alone, either.

Thank God, I'd chosen the correct hospital, so I got there when I did. It was agonizing to watch the doctor stitch Jules up as if it were just another day.

Well, maybe it was for her. It took everything I fucking had not to come undone watching my niece get her stitches like a champ. I've had stitches myself, but I've never had to watch it done firsthand. God, that was gross.

My phone buzzes on my nightstand, but I don't have the energy to answer or even look at the incoming text. I'm sure it's from Syd, but I don't even know what to say.

I haven't said much to her other than Vanessa needed my

help today. I'm sure I owe her an explanation, but where do I even start? Maybe when I wake up tomorrow, I'll know what to do.

Tossing my pillow over to the flipside, so I can feel the cool sheets on my cheek, I roll onto my side in hopes of falling asleep and ending this miserable day.

I've been so fucking selfish.

My final thoughts before I finally drift off to sleep are loud and clear.

I need to get my priorities in check.

VINCE

WHEN I WAKE UP THE NEXT MORNING, I'M STILL OUT OF SORTS. Knowing Van has the day off to spend with Julia, and it's a Sunday, I ensure another accident won't happen by setting out cereal and a bowl on the table. Then I head out to burn off this pent-up energy I can't shake.

After warming up, my feet keep a steady beat on the pavement. Willing my endless thoughts to disappear for just a few fucking minutes, I push myself to eat up the distance between myself and the house. When a clear mind continues to evade me, I push harder.

After several miles, I'm no better off than when I started my journey. My mind is clogged with the realization that I've been a selfish bastard. I've put my own needs first, and the result is Jules got hurt.

Every time I had looked at Julia's bandage yesterday, my stomach clenched, and my heart sank. The plastic surgeon claims her scar will hardly be noticeable... eventually. But for me, it's a constant reminder that I let my eye slip from the prize.

Clearly, my family needs me, and I'm not sure what to do.

God, I love how Sydney makes me feel, like I get to just be me.

She gets me in ways no one ever has.

With her, it's so much more.

We connect on ways I never thought possible.

But is my situation fair to her?

No matter which way I look at it, the stark reality is no.

Syd deserves to be with someone who puts her first. Someone who isn't committed to his family the way I am.

Fuck... My family.

There's nothing I won't do for them.

God, Van and I are so fucking close at reaching our goal. In just one year, we'll both be college graduates before Julia reaches kindergarten. We've overcome such adversity, most didn't think we'd be able to handle. Pride soars through me when I know without a doubt, she'll no longer be at risk for being a statistic because we've worked our asses off to make sure it didn't happen.

Does being with Syd put me at risk of losing this dream of ours?

God knows, Sydney hasn't had it easy. Between her deadbeat dad and immature mom, then losing her only real support system, she deserves to be treated like a queen. She deserves to find someone who puts her first no matter what.

Someone who will never even fucking ask themselves this question.

Fuck, my gut aches at the thought of her being with someone else.

That's my stark reality, though. I should let her go.

I know my physical experience is limited with women, but I've never felt the connection I do with her. I don't think it's just about sex. No. It's a connection on a cellular level. I swear, it's like we're magnets or something. If she moves, I'm instinctually pulled with her.

She's the type of woman my mom used to tell me about.

Fuck… I haven't thought about our conversation in years.

Mom used to say physical attraction only gets you so far. I need to find someone who challenges me, who understands my loyalty and won't take advantage, and someone for whom I will gladly put their needs above my own.

I don't know how I manage, but I smile at the memory like it was yesterday. The last time we'd spoken of this was the night I'd come home after spending the evening with Anna Hastings with a hickey on my neck and my clothes a rumpled mess. We didn't have sex obviously, but we'd done everything but. Yet somehow, Mom just knew.

After blatantly denying what I'd been up to, Mom just gave me a knowing grin and said, "You know, Vin, there are gonna be plenty of women you'll meet along the way that will make you feel good, but I want you to pay close attention to the ones who get you in here." She placed her hand over her heart. "Knowing you, it will be someone who's stubborn, challenges you, and won't let you get away with the crap you're trying to pull right now."

Oh, you can bet she gave me her infamous raised eyebrow.

I thought she was crazy at the time, but now that I've met Sydney, I realize Mom might've been on to something.

I mull over this as I slow my pace back to the house. Once inside, I shower off the sweat from my intense workout. However, I'm still undecided about what to do. I'm torn between being selfish and doing what's right for Sydney. She needs someone who can love her the way she deserves.

Fuck... The thought of someone else taking my place rips me apart.

Why couldn't I've met Sydney a year from now? It would be so much easier if my life were my own, and I didn't have two others who depend on me.

Sighing heavily, I force myself through the motions of getting dressed.

I hear my phone vibrate with an incoming message, but I'm in no mood for company. Exiting my room, I leave my phone on the bed and go in search of food.

"Good run, Unks?" Julia asks as I enter the kitchen.

I startle because in my current funk, I clearly don't see her coloring at the kitchen table, which makes her giggle.

Shaking my head to clear my thoughts, I shrug. "It was okay. But I'm starving. Did you leave me any food in the fridge?"

Looking at the bandage above her eye, it takes everything in me not to cringe. But of course, I stop myself because that's the last thing she needs.

"Oh, you silly, Unks. I can't eat *all* the food in the fridge. My tummy isn't that big."

"Oh, really, I bet if it was all broccoli, you would."

She puts her hand on her chin and looks to the ceiling as she seriously thinks about my suggestion. "Maybe..."

Shaking my head at her antics, I say, "Squirt, I'm not sure your tummy is big enough for an *entire* fridge full of broccoli, unless you have two hollow legs and can store it in your arms."

Jules gives me just what I need. Her light tinkling laugh is infectious, and she has me joining her.

"Oh, Jules. Thank you," I say when I finally pull in a solid breath.

Her lone visible eyebrow shoots to her hairline, causing her to flinch. "Does it hurt too bad?" I ask, pointing at her injury.

Shaking her head, she says, "Only when I do that."

"Well, stop already then," I tease.

God, I hate seeing her hurt.

In an attempt to change the subject, I ask, "What are you coloring, Jules?"

"I'm making Momma a picture of the kitty I want to get. Did you know that my teacher's kitty had babies and they need new homes? Can we get one?"

I'm not stepping on that landmine with a ten-foot pole. I'm only the Unks for a reason. "Oh, squirt." I chuckle, knowing Van's gonna hate me. "That's up to your mom. You'll have to win that battle with her."

Julia's eyes sparkle with delight as she pushes back her chair from the table and runs out of the room like her feet are on fire.

Vanessa's gonna kill me, I'm sure of it.

"Walk!" I holler after her, though I'm sure it lands on deaf ears. The patter of her feet echoes throughout the house, and I can only shake my head as I quickly throw a sandwich together and retreat to my room.

My phone buzzes on my bed, and Sydney's name flashes across the screen.

As much as I want to talk to her, I'm just not ready. But I can't help myself when I pick up the phone to open my text messages.

There are actually several messages, and guilt eats at me as I scroll through the messages from this morning. The first one came through around nine.

Sydney: Good Morning (Smiley face emoji)

The next one came through an hour later.

Sydney: Are we still on for studying this afternoon?

Just now, the message reads:

Sydney: Did miracles happen, and you actually slept in??? Call me when you get this. I'm starting to worry.

Glancing at the clock, I realize it's after eleven. Not wanting to get into things via text, I take the coward's way out and quickly type out a reply.

Me: Still dealing with family things. Need to cancel. Sorry.

Yeah, it's a dick move, but I'm so fucking torn at the moment.

I see the message quickly turn from delivered to read, then the three dots appear immediately.

Sydney: Everything okay?

No, it's not fucking okay. But I'm not ready to deal with this shit now.

The lie flies out of my fingers, and I press send before I can second-guess myself.

Me: Yeah. Just dealing with family stuff.

Syd's reply is instant.

Sydney: I'm here if you need me.

Not knowing what else to say, I quickly reply with a noncommittal text.

Me: Thanks.

Before she can send another text that I'll be forced to reply to, I cut the conversation off abruptly.

Me: Gotta run. Can't talk now.

I'm such a fucking liar. But what else am I supposed to do?

SYDNEY

Vince has been avoiding me since Sunday morning. He's texted but has been completely disconnected. I expected to get to the bottom of things when he came to class today, but to my utter shock, he didn't show.

I've texted to see where he was, thinking something might have happened but get no response. I might as well have skipped class for all the good it does me sitting there. My body is present, but my mind is on the man avoiding me. What the fuck is going on?

The minute class is over, I high-tail it over to Vince's. Whatever's going on, I'm getting to the bottom of it. I just hope he's home when I get there.

Knocking on the door, I'm greeted with a surprised Vanessa. "Hey, Syd. What are you doing here?"

"Hey, Van," I mutter in an attempt to keep my emotions at bay. "Is Vince around?"

Confusion continues to cloud her expression. "Uh… don't the two of you have class today?"

Nodding, I admit, "He wasn't there."

"Hmmm… That's odd." She looks behind her into the house for a second before stating, "He's not here, and I have no idea where he is. Have you tried calling him?"

Nodding, I shrug. "I've tried, but he's not answering."

Vanessa shakes her head and pulls her lower lip into her mouth. "Hmmm…"

Hmmm… What?

Shit. I shouldn't put her in the middle of things. That's not fair to her.

Wanting to let her off the hook, I quickly add, "You know what? Never mind. Just tell him I stopped by."

Sympathy fills her face as she shrugs. "I will. Sorry for my idiot brother."

Idiot is right. If something's wrong, he needs to talk to me. Not avoid me like the plague. I can't help him if he's not honest with me.

As I walk back to my place, I can't help but wonder what the fuck is going on.

Vince isn't in class on Thursday either. His phone has been turned off because it goes straight to voice mail the few times I've called. When I text, my messages remain unread.

Panic and fear that something is wrong has me on edge. I'm half-tempted to reach out to Vanessa, but I'm not that desperate… yet. But I'm close.

Something must've happened between the time I fell asleep early Sunday morning. When he left, I swear things between us had never been better. He'd spent hours devouring my body and letting me happily reciprocate. I just don't get it. What the fuck happened?

It's also not like Vince to ghost me.

Wanting to give him the space he needs, I'm trying to be patient and let's be honest, it totally sucks. He said something is going on with his family, but is there more to it?

Vanessa didn't seem like there was an emergency.

Did I actually give her a chance to speak though? Replaying our conversation, I cringe because if I'd been the least bit patient, I would have a fucking clue as to what's going on.

Knowing I have to work for the next three nights, I'll give him until Sunday to come to his senses... then all bets are off. If I need to pull out full stalker mode to get to the bottom of this, I will. Something had to have happened, and I need to know if I'm to blame for something.

If this were with any other guy, I wouldn't give him the benefit of the doubt. I'd write it off and walk away without a glance. I don't play games, and I certainly don't wait around for someone who doesn't feel the same way as me.

Vince is different. Our connection has been so strong. I know in my gut something has happened to cause him to flip a one-eighty on me. He's loyal to a fault—and if something happened with his family, maybe he's sorting things out. Who the fuck knows? Not me—because he's ghosting the fuck out of me.

I growl in frustration as I go through the motions of getting ready for work.

My reality hits me smack in the face as I stare at my reflection in the mirror. Fuck, there's no way I'm gonna make it until Sunday to confront him. I'm possibly the least patient person on the planet. I miss him like crazy, and there's an ache in my chest that won't go away. I'm also pissed as hell that he won't talk to me.

I confront things head on, and he's not giving me the fucking chance to get things off my chest. It feels like a stack of bricks are piled on my chest, making it almost difficult to breathe. My need to see him and ensure he's okay almost outweighs my frustration with him. Almost. I know something is wrong that he's not telling me. But what could it be?

On autopilot, I drive myself to work and proceed to have the shittiest night possible. When I arrive, my manager mentions that one of my co-workers called in sick so it will just be me and him slinging drinks. On a typical night, that would be rough, but tonight I'm so stuck in my freaking head, I seem to fuck up at every turn.

"You okay, Syd?" Garrett asks when I spill the third drink of the night down my shirt.

Groaning, I admit, "This day can't get over fast enough."

"As soon as we've gotten the line under control, you're welcome to take a break if you need it."

Shit, things must be really bad if he's offering to cover the bar by himself for a while.

Pull it together, Syd.

Focus. Just fucking focus on the task at hand.

"I'll be okay," I mutter as I remake the bachelorette party's drinks I'd spilled.

I manage to work another twenty minutes or so without incident, until the nasally voice of Fucking Brad is brought to my attention. "Hey, beautiful. I'll have a rum and Coke."

Just ignore him and do not engage, I repeat as a mantra as I make his drink.

Sliding his drink across the bar because there's no way I want to risk contact with him, I go through the motions of saying, "That'll be four-seventy-five."

The cheap, cocky bastard he is holds up a five-dollar bill but doesn't hand it to me. Then smirks. "If I let you keep the change, can I get another date with you?"

All the pent-up emotions from the day boils into rage in an instant. Without a second to think through the consequences, I fling the contents of his drink in his face as I practically scream, "Are you fucking kidding me?"

He blinks as if he's actually surprised by my actions and wipes away the brown liquid dripping down his face. He starts to sputter, "You... you..."

He's so fucking lucky there's a bar between us, or it may have been my fist coming at his face. Before he can get another word in, I point my finger in his direction and yell above the music. "You have some fucking nerve even showing your face in here. You think I'd go out on another date with you for a quarter... A FUCKING QUARTER? You... big tipper you... You. Are. An. Arrogant. Asshole," I spit out each word as if it were its own sentence. "You're such a fucking cheapskate... And don't even get me started on the fact that you're the epitome of a deadbeat dad. I feel sorry for the child that has to share your

DNA. Don't you *EVER* ask me out again, or even talk to me for that matter."

Seeing Asher approach and knowing he'll have my back, I continue, "Get the fuck out of this bar, Brad. You're no longer welcome here."

Asher's got a good six inches and about fifty pounds on Brad. Brad sees him coming but shakes his head, letting him know an escort will not be needed. He slinks off toward the door, and I inhale a calming breath.

When I turn, Garrett's eyes are wide, and his hands are raised as if he's either showing he's defenseless, or about to lunge after me, if I try anything on him. "Everything okay, Syd?"

I think it's time I take that break.

I nod slowly as I look around the bar. Quite a few eyes dart quickly away as if they don't want to draw my attention. Guilt crashes over me for causing such a scene. "He uh... expected to go out with me for letting me keep his change as a tip. He thought a quarter was sufficient."

Garrett's mouth drops to almost the floor as his eyes bug out. "And you only threw his drink at him?" He looks in the direction of the door, and I swear the protective guy that he is wants to go after Brad himself.

God, I love having friends like him.

Asher's deep voice is right behind me as his laughter escapes. "Ha... Damn, he didn't even let me kick him out. For the record, Syd, you're worth *way* more than a quarter."

Rolling my eyes at his lame attempt to bring levity to the situation, I mutter, "Gee, thanks."

Garrett chimes in, shaking his head as he looks to Asher, "I don't even think a Benji is worth a date with that douche-canoe. Our girl here is priceless," he says as he pulls me in for a side hug and squeezes me tight.

I hug him back.

God, I needed this. He may be my boss, but we've worked together long enough to consider him a friend as well.

"Thanks," I mutter.

His dark eyes lock with mine and holds my gaze until he finds what he's searching for. "You sure you're okay, Syd?"

Nodding in assurance, I assure, "I'm good. But I think the line that's stacking up, could use some attending to."

Knowing I won't budge in admitting anything could be wrong with me, he rolls his eyes. "Let's get to it then."

VINCE

When I get home from studying on campus Friday evening, Vanessa meets me at the door, her hands on her hips and an accusing expression. "Vinny, what the hell is going on?"

Not sure what she's so upset about, I ask, "What do you mean?"

"Uh... Sydney stopped by on Tuesday saying you hadn't been in class, and if I had to bet, I'd say you've been avoiding her all week."

"Why do you say that?" I deflect. There's no way she knows what I've been up to.

"Oh, I don't know. You've been in a miserable mood all week. You're here in the room, but your mind is elsewhere. I've been watching you mope around all week when you think I'm not looking."

Hell, she's not wrong. "I... Uh..." I stammer as I don't know what to say.

When her hand reaches my shoulder, her frustration disperses. "Vinnie. Talk to me. What's wrong?"

Sighing heavily, I ask, "Where's Jules?"

"Well, if you'd paid any attention this morning at breakfast, you'd know she was staying the night at her friend's again."

Really? How had I missed that?

"What about her stitches?" I ask in concern. Should she be staying over at a friend's when she was just hurt this week?

"Vince. She's fine. If you'd actually been paying attention this week, you'd see the only one who seems to be out of sorts is you."

I open my mouth to say something but close it immediately when I'm at a loss for what to say.

Reaching for my hand, Vanessa pulls me to the couch.

Shrugging off my backpack, I lay it beside us on the floor as I join her.

"Talk to me, Vin. We don't keep secrets, and it's killing me to see you this upset."

I should've known I can't keep this from her. She knows me better than anyone on the planet and keeping secrets is like expecting the sun not to return each day.

Exhaling heavily, I finally admit, "I think I fucked up, Van."

"With Sydney?" she asks for clarification.

"No… I mean… yes… but I fucked up with you and Jules first. I'm so sorry."

Vanessa's hazel eyes fill with confusion. "What do you mean?"

God, where do I even begin?

"I wasn't here for you. If I hadn't been so selfish, Julia might never have been hurt."

"Seriously?" Her head rears back with uncertainty. "What the hell have you been doing to consider yourself selfish?"

"I've been so preoccupied with Sydney, that I haven't been here like I should for you and Jules. You needed me, and I wasn't there."

"Uh... if I remember correctly, you were at the hospital within a half hour of us arriving. You spent the entire day with us, and you've been here every night since."

"But I wasn't home when she got hurt. I always get up with her while you're getting ready, and I was with Syd."

Van's hand flies to her mouth as she inhales sharply. "Ohmigod, Vinnie. Do you somehow blame yourself for Julia's accident?"

Uh, of course I do, but the look on Van's face tells me I shouldn't say it aloud, so I just nod.

"Vince, no one could've predicted she'd climb on the counter and fall off. She's done it a million times. I'm sure she'll do it again. That wasn't your fault." Then she stops for a second and stares into my eyes looking for some unknown answer to a question she has yet to ask. "Wait... why do you consider that selfish? Dumb luck, yes, but selfish? What does Jules' accident have to do with you being selfish?"

Though it's hard to admit, I manage to whisper, "I've been spending so much time with Syd."

"Uh, last I checked, she's your girlfriend. Of course you should spend time with her."

"But that's the point. I'd been off having the time of my life and when your world fell apart, I wasn't there for you."

"Uh..." She looks utterly confused. "When exactly did my

world fall apart, Vin? Last I checked, Jules and I are doing fine. Sure, she has a mark that may be there for a while, but we aren't falling apart. Is that why you've ended things with Sydney?"

Fuck, just the mention of her name makes my gut ache. I miss her so fucking much. Avoiding her has been the worst form of torture. But I need to get past this, if I'm able to do what's best for her in the end.

Closing my eyes, I lean my head back into the couch. "She deserves better than me."

Vanessa's tone changes from concern to annoyance in an instant. "Vincent Daniel Larson—I love you more than life itself, but *you* are an idiot."

What the fuck? "Why?"

"You're so in love with Sydney, it's made you stupid."

I blanch at her unexpected words.

Yes... I am stupid, but do I love her?

Fuck... without a doubt, I do. But that's why I'm trying to let her go. If I can't be the one she needs, then I need to let her go.

"What?" Vanessa points an accusing finger at my face. "What's going on in that thick head of yours?"

"I do love her, Van. But I also love her enough to let her go. I can't be the type of man she deserves. I can't always put her first."

Rubbing at the pain in my chest that never seems to end, I exhale heavily and allow myself to miss her as I stare at the floor beneath us.

Vanessa's quiet for a moment, and when she's been unusually quiet, I risk looking at my sister.

Unshed tears well behind her thick lashes, and her lip quivers.

Fuck, tears are always my undoing. It wrecks me to see her upset.

Vanessa's voice is stronger than I expect after she takes in a slow breath. "I know you've made sacrifices to be here at CRU with Julia and me, but I'd *never* want to stand in the way of your happiness, Vin. You've always put us first. Is that why you don't think you deserve to be with Sydney?"

How do I admit this and not make her feel worse than she does?

But knowing I can't keep anything from her if I tried, I admit, "I don't know. Maybe?"

Reaching out to squeeze my hand, she says, "Vince, you have the biggest heart of anyone I've ever known. I'm certain there's room in there for you to love all three of us."

"But I wasn't there the day you and Julia needed me most," I finally admit the guilt that had been crushing me for the better part of a week.

"God, you're such a doofus. But I will always love you for it, Vin," Vanessa says as she shakes her head in disapproval. "You may not have been here the second the incident happened, but you've been there for me when I've needed you most. Newsflash, Vince… kids have accidents. As much as we'd like to be there to prevent them, we're not. From my understanding, kids can be accident prone as they gain their independence. All we can do is be there for them, to pick up the pieces. Was Mom or Dad there when you broke your arm at wrestling practice in middle school?"

"No, I was just with the team. What's your point?"

Rolling her eyes, she sighs at my apparent idiocy. "I know deep down you know this, but I'll spell it out for you. Accidents are just that... accidents. You can't put us in protective bubble wrap and expect us to gain independence and fly on our own either. Mom and Dad didn't do that for us, and I'm not about to do that to Julia."

Then she cringes at some unknown thought. "You... uh... didn't break up with Sydney, did you?"

Did I? No... but she's likely to dump my ass the next time I see her. My chest tightens, and I rub at it in hopes of relieving the pain. But it's no use. There's a gaping hole where my heart belongs.

"Not technically," I admit as I realize just how much of a dick I've been. "But I've really fucked up."

"You did this after Mom and Dad's accident. You pushed everyone away. God, Vince, please don't do this to Syd. I like her for you."

"I like her for me, too," I admit. "But I haven't spoken to her all week, so it may be too late."

What would I even say anyway?

"Vin, it's never too late to apologize. If she loves you the way I think she does, she'll forgive you. She'll soon learn you can be an idiot sometimes and know when to call you out on it."

Fuck... call me out on it...

I swear Vanessa's channeling Mom when she says, "What are you waiting for, Vinny? You know you love her."

"Yeah, I do," I admit as I pop off the couch and pace across the living room.

Glancing at the clock, I know she's just started her shift at the bar. Maybe if I could just see her, I could apologize.

But will she accept it? That's the bigger question.

Stopping mid-pace, I close the distance between Van and me. "Thanks for everything, Van." Leaning in, I kiss her on the cheek and rumple her hair like I always do. "I love you. But I've gotta go make things right."

I just hope I'm not too late.

SYDNEY

I FEEL VINCE LONG BEFORE I SEE HIM. THE BAR'S CROWDED, BUT I swear I know the moment he's stepped inside. My spine crackles with energy as a sense of warmth sends tingles from my head to my toes.

The moment my eyes meet his, I feel them reach the depths of my soul. His eyes are dark in this lighting, but I can tell from just a single glance, he's spotted me as well.

I'm frozen in place as he closes the distance between us. He's as gorgeous as ever, but as he gets closer, I see he hasn't shaved for the past week, so there's the start of a beard growing. Dark shadows are a predominately new feature under his eyes as if he hasn't slept since Sunday either. His hair looks disheveled more than usual, like he's been pulling on the ends. It practically stands up on its own.

My heart aches at the sight of him.

"Uh... Miss? Are you gonna finish making our drinks?" my

current customer asks as she waves a hand in front of my face, breaking my concentration from Vince.

Coming out of my revelry, I stammer, "I...uh... yeah... sorry."

I focus my attention on making the amaretto sour and rum and Coke for the couple in front of me. Then I collect their money after handing them their drinks.

By the time I finish, Vince is behind them, waiting patiently in line.

We've been relatively slow for a Friday night, but the line remains steady.

When he has my full attention, I hear his husky voice over the live band playing on the stage. "Hey, Syd."

Not knowing what to say, I keep things casual by asking, "What can I get for you?"

Then I get a little irritated. He's had all week to come to me. He chooses the bar as his first point of contact?

Apprehension clouds his face, but he says, "Can we talk?"

"I've been trying to talk to you for the better part of a week," I say harsher than I intend, but my point is made.

Pushing his hands into his pockets, he rocks back on his heels. "I deserve that..."

He stares at his shoes for a moment before drawing his eyes up to meet mine. Damn, he's gorgeous. But he needs to know he's not getting let off the hook that easily. "You've ghosted me for nearly a week, Vin. Then you show up at my place of work and expect to talk?"

"I can explain..." he starts, but I cut him off when another customer stands behind him.

"Look. I'm busy. I'll give you a call when I feel like getting around to it," I respond snarkier than I should. But dammit, I'm hurt. I've shed tears for this man, and he doesn't get to just waltz in here with *hey, can we talk* and get away from it.

Shaking his head, he looks completely defeated when he says, "I guess I deserve that, too. I'll... uh... just be on my way then."

Oh. My. Heart.

I swear the sound of it breaking can be heard over the music that fills the room.

Before I can say another word, he turns on his heels and briskly walks away.

And like the fool I am... I just watch him go.

God, I'm such a bitch...

For the rest of the night, I go through the motions, but my heart just isn't in it. No, it left with the man whose heart is broken nearly as much as mine. For as long as I live, I don't think I'll ever get over his hopeless expression of despair. This is so much worse than not hearing from him for the past week. I'm fairly certain Vince was here to explain his actions.

Fuck... Fuck... Fuck... why am I so stubborn?

Knowing I can't very well try getting out of closing after last night's fiasco, I set my mind to the task at hand to finish out the night as quickly as possible. But of course, time moves like molasses in January.

By the time I leave the bar, it's nearly three o'clock. Everything in my being tells me I should just go straight to his house. If it weren't for the fact that I'd be waking Julia, I'd consider it. I'm that desperate.

When I get inside my apartment, I know there's only one way I'll be able to fall asleep. Reaching into the cabinet we keep the hard alcohol in, I pour three fingers of Maker's Mark and down it quicker than I should. I bought it for a special occasion, but desperate times call for desperate measures. My throat warms as it slides down, and the hints of butterscotch and spice are left behind.

Knowing it won't take long for it to have its desired effects, I head to the bathroom to shower off the grime from the night. By the time I finish my shower, I feel slightly more relaxed. Slipping between my sheets, I make one final wish before I drift off to sleep.

Please let me fix this.

The next morning, I awake to the sound of one of my roommates in the kitchen. I've been tossing and turning for the better part of the last hour, so I toss the covers off and join whoever's in the kitchen.

To my surprise, it's neither Abby nor Chloe in the kitchen, but Drew.

"Good morning, Syd," he says as he pours some coffee from the pot. "Want some?"

"Sure," I reply, reaching for a cup in the cupboard. "Is Abby up?" Maybe she can help me un-fuck this situation I've got myself into. I look in the direction of her room, hoping she'll join us soon.

"Uh... not even close. Is there something I can help you with?" Drew asks as he sits at the table to eat the cinnamon roll I'd baked yesterday morning in my despair.

"I... uh..." How do I even begin to explain the mess I'm in?

With an easy grin, Drew puts down his fork and stares at me for a moment before looking at the sweets I've stashed on the counter. "Don't get me wrong, Syd, I'll never complain about your baked goods, but is something bothering you… you know… since you've turned the kitchen into an upscale bakery this week?"

Sighing heavily, I flop into the chair across from him and soothe myself by holding my warm mug between my hands. "Yeah… I'd guess you could say there was. But it's a long story."

He shrugs. "I've got time and two working ears. DeShawn and Grey say thanks for the treats, by the way. We'll never turn them down, but I'd rather you made them for happier reasons."

"Where do I begin?" I ask more to myself than him. But he answers me anyway.

"My best guess is the beginning," he says patiently before taking another bite of the gooey roll before him.

Knowing I need to get this off my chest or I'll explode, I unload the entire story on him. I start by explaining how things had been perfect last Saturday night and led up to Vince's departure Sunday morning. I don't go into specifics, but he gets the gist of my state of mind when Vince left that morning. Then I explain how he ghosted me all week, and end with Vince showing up last night.

"I still can't believe I sent him away," I practically whine at the end. "I mean, I miss him so much, but my anger got the best of me, and I lashed out at him. I have no freaking clue what pushed him away to begin with, but what if I've missed my only chance to get back together with him?"

Scratching at the back of his neck, Drew hesitates before

saying what's on his mind. "You know, Syd, I don't claim to be an expert on relationships, but are you aware that Abby almost dumped my ass before the championship game?"

"What?" This is news to me.

"Yeah. Apparently... she had it in her mind that we couldn't be together because she'd gotten into the school of my dreams, and I hadn't. She even went so far as to try to push me away. It was fucking agonizing. Trust me... but maybe this is something of the same nature. Maybe he did have a family thing going on. Abby's mentioned he transferred here to be here for his sister. Maybe something came up with them, and he felt conflicted with you. I know what it's like to keep your eye on the prize and not want to lose focus."

"But wouldn't that mean I should steer clear of him and not get in the way?" I ask, not understanding his point. How is this supposed to encourage me?

I rub at my chest and push my cup of coffee away.

"You're missing the point. It wasn't until Abby and I communicated clearly that we got our priorities straight. Go to him... tell him how you feel... then if it doesn't work out, you'll know you've done everything you can."

Hope shines for the first time in this bleak morning.

Popping up from my chair, I take a step closer and surprise Drew with a hug. "You know what, Drew? You're right. I'm gonna head over to his house right now and set things straight. Thank you."

"Anytime, Syd. Anytime." I hear as I rush to my room to change my clothes.

When I get to Vince's house, it's dark. Not a light on or signs of anyone awake.

Knowing it's nearly nine, I'm sure they're awake, so I ring the doorbell and eagerly wait.

For nothing.

I ring it once more... still nothing.

Pulling out my phone, I call him. It goes straight to voice mail.

Maybe they're at the diner?

Hopping in my newly- fixed car, I zip down the street to the diner. Not spotting Vince's Jeep in the parking lot, I don't give up hope. Maybe Vanessa's working, and she'll tell me where he is.

Thankfully, I spot Vanessa as soon as I walk through the doors. Once she's finished with a customer, I get her attention. "Hey, Van, do you happen to know where Vince is?"

"I, uh... thought he was with you? I haven't seen him since last night. Though I did go to bed early to be here by six this morning. Hmmm.... Have you tried calling him?"

Nodding, I sigh, "Yeah. He wasn't at the house either."

"When Vince likes to think, he often goes for a drive."

A drive? God, could it be that easy?

Reaching in, I hug Vanessa for the idea. "Thanks, Van. I think I know where to find him."

"Okay?" She giggles as if she's questioning my sanity at the moment.

Maybe she is, but I've got a good feeling I know exactly where he is.

VINCE

I'M SKIPPING ROCKS INTO THE RIVER WHEN I HEAR THE MOST beautiful voice call my name. It must be a figment of my imagination because why would Sydney be here at this hour? Knowing she usually sleeps in, I've apparently reached a delusional state. Let's face it—I miss her desperately.

I get why she didn't want to talk yesterday. She had every right to send me packing. I've been a complete dumbass and deserved to be kicked to the curb. Who the hell would waste their breath on someone who couldn't bother to reach out for nearly a week?

I never expected last night to be easy, but being completely dismissed stung. I at least thought she'd let me stick around and grovel or something.

"Vince?"

My spine tingles as I turn, hoping like hell my mind isn't playing tricks on me.

Just the mere sight of her makes my breathing easier. Her long, red hair blows in the wind as her pace quickens.

As much as I want to close the distance between us, I'm frozen in place. A mixture of shock and uncertainty war with each other, rendering me speechless. I can't afford to fuck this up. I've been so miserable this week without her, and I hope her being here means she'll listen and forgive me.

"I'm so glad I found you. I've been looking for you everywhere."

Really?

Instead of voicing my shock, I admit, "I've been here since dawn." After tossing for most of the night, I gave up and left so I could avoid Van. I wasn't ready to admit I'd struck out, and misery doesn't always love company when said company can be a know-it-all sister.

"What's going on, Vin?" Sydney asks, wrapping her arms around her torso.

As I look at her beautiful green eyes, I've missed her more than I could grasp before this moment. I clearly see she's had just about as much sleep as me. Dark circles I've never seen before rest on her cheekbones.

Clearly, this past week hasn't been easy on either of us.

Forcing myself to concentrate on her question, I shrug. "Couldn't sleep so I went for a drive."

"I mean… what's really going on? Why the disappearing act?"

How do I even start? Looking to the sky as if it holds all the answers, I suck in a deep breath as I search for the words.

"When I got home Sunday morning, there had been an accident." I still cringe at the memory.

"Ohmigod, Vince, was it serious?"

"It's fine now, but at the time, I had no idea what had happened. There was blood all over the kitchen. What made matters worse was my phone had died, so Van couldn't get a hold of me. I was a complete wreck."

Sydney reaches for my hand and suggests, "Let's find a place to sit."

The moment her hand entwines in mine, the hope I'd been squashing resurfaces. The tightness in my chest loosens as we take a few steps up the riverbank and sit on a large boulder.

"Why didn't you tell me, Vince? I could've been there for you and your family."

"I know that, now. But at the time, I had this overwhelming sense of guilt for not being there when they needed me most. Here I was—off having the time of my life—and Jules got hurt."

Syd retracts her hand immediately. "You blamed me?"

Oh, fuck.

"No..." I cut off that thought in an instant. "Not at all. I blamed myself for being selfish. For allowing myself to have a life. You see... for the past... well, since my parents' accident, I've done everything in my power to put Van and Jules first. Being with you... well... that's the first time I've done something for myself."

"So... you do blame me..." She stares at the water below as my heart thunders in my chest.

"No..." Reaching out, I cup her chin so she can be clear of my intentions. "I didn't blame you in the slightest. And I still don't. This is *all* on me, Syd. You know the night my parents died, I'd been partying with my friends..." Pulling in a deep breath, I admit my embarrassing truth. "Well, somehow through it all, I had this fucked up notion that the only way we'd survive is if I didn't allow myself to truly find happiness."

Syd raises an eyebrow but doesn't say anything. Sensing her obvious confusion, I force myself to continue, "You see... I thought I was happy before I'd met you. Now, I know without a doubt, I was merely content at best. The thing is, Syd, as you and I've gotten closer, you've made me wish for things I'd never dreamed of."

"Really? What's that?" she asks with genuine curiosity.

Looking at the water, I let everything I've been holding onto off my chest. "For the first time *ever*, I fell in love and was happy beyond belief. I allowed myself to hope for what my parents had. To have a partner in life who pushes me to be better. But of course, I'm stupid and pig-headed and threw it all away because I didn't think I deserved it."

When I finally glance in Sydney's direction, her mouth hangs open.

Fuck. That's what I thought. I did throw it all away.

Shaking my head in defeat, I look to the sky to gather the strength I need to get through whatever it is she'll eventually say. I can't even look to confirm my reality because the thought of losing her completely makes my stomach feel as if it's been lined with lead.

Syd's sassy tone doesn't disappoint. "Are you kidding me?"

Still not able to look, I mutter, "Nope."

"Vincent Daniel Larson, if I didn't love you much more than you irritate the fuck out of me in this moment, I'd smack you back to reality."

What?

Slowly, my eyes open, and I force myself to meet hers.

Did she really just say what I think I heard?

Needing confirmation, I sputter, "W... What did you just say?"

Sydney's finger points at my chest, and the fire within her comes to life. "First, you don't get to decide how I react, Vince. You don't deserve to play the martyr, but most importantly, why the hell do you think those things you want aren't obtainable?"

Taking a moment to process her words, I lose my chance to respond.

"You haven't thrown things away... at least not as far as I'm concerned, but if you've changed your mind... well... then I guess you're entitled to."

Her confidence wanes for a split second before she's back in full force. "You know what? You're right, you *are* stupid *if* that's what you choose to do."

My voice is thick as "I don't" slips out.

"Wha...?" she starts, but it's my turn to interrupt.

"I don't want to lose you. I love you more than I could possibly imagine. I'm miserable without you, Syd. I'm so sorry for putting you through everything this past week. Will you please forgive me?"

"Oh, Vince... there's nothing to forgive—because you've done *nothing* wrong. Though, I'd rather you didn't push me away, I understand *why* you felt you needed to. I should've talked to you last night, but I'm sure you've figured it out by now—I'm a bit stubborn, too."

Standing, I pull her to me so that we're chest to chest. "I'll make you a deal, Syd."

Syd's beautiful smirk sends a direct bolt to my heart. "Oh, yeah, what's that?"

God, I love this woman.

"Since neither of us can guarantee we won't be stubborn, let's just agree to call each other out on it. I've always had a strong belief that family sticks together through thick and thin."

Sydney blinks. "But... I'm not... your family."

Shaking my head, I realize she's missed my point, so I spell it out for her. "You may as well be. Besides, if I have anything to say about it, it'll only be a matter of time."

Syd's mouth drops open, and her eyes bug out.

I can't help my smirk that I've rendered this beautiful woman speechless.

"Did you... are you..." she sputters.

"Not yet," I say with confidence. Then I assure her with, "But you'll be the first to know when I do."

Sydney's beautiful smile practically splits her face in two. "I think I can live with that." She pulls me in for the best kiss of my life.

When we pull away breathless, Sydney reaches for my hand. "As much as I love this place, are you ready to get out of here?"

"I could be persuaded to leave," I tease. But God knows, I will follow this woman anywhere.

EPILOGUE

Vince

Seven Years Later...

"You can do this, Syd," I encourage, knowing she's exhausted. "Push..."

Rage flashes across Sydney's beautiful and exhausted face as she squeezes the fuck out of my hand. "You did this to me," she groans as she gives in and does what I ask.

Apparently, my lovely wife has been in labor for the better part of the day but wanted to make it to her baby shower before admitting this was actually happening. Well, the joke's on her, not that I'd ever tell her that. Her water broke just as everyone arrived, and we had to rush to the hospital. Unfortunately, after we arrived, she was told it was time to push—so we're past the point of being eligible for an epidural.

Holy hell, I've always known women are the stronger

species but watching her endure this only proves it. Contractions are coming one after another, and I feel so fucking helpless. I'd give anything to take this pain from her.

"You're doing great, Sydney. Just one more push," the doctor says, and I pray she's right. I just want Syd out of this misery.

My fingers go numb as Sydney bears down, and she gives it all she's got.

It's okay. I didn't really need this hand to begin with.

I guess that's why I've been given two, right?

The next thing I know, the sound of a crying infant fills the room, and relief washes over me. As I watch the doctor bring our child into view, I'm overwhelmed with emotion. My eyes well up with tears as I witness this precious miracle before me.

Hearing the words, "Congratulations, it's a girl," are almost lost on me as I look at this precious miracle we've made.

Leaning in to kiss Sydney, I whisper, "Thank you."

"Don't thank me yet." She smiles through tears as well. "I still have one more opportunity to break the hell out of your fingers."

Chuckling, I shake my head and my hand out to prepare for the next round. "She's got your hair," I state as the doctor hands me my daughter.

"She's beautiful," Sydney sighs.

Leaning in to let Syd get a closer look, I'm startled when Sydney's hit with another contraction.

"It's time, Dad," the doctor says, and a nurse comes to take my baby girl away. "The nurse will clean her up and get this precious girl ready for her brother."

Leaning in, I kiss Syd's forehead. "In case I don't tell you enough, I love you."

"Love you, too," Syd says on a groan as she reaches for my hand to squeeze.

Through Sydney's loud growl, I hear the doctor say, "Let's do this again, Syd. Push."

Apparently, my daughter has paved the way for my son, because after two strong pushes, he's brought into this world with a cry much louder than his sister.

"Wow, he's got a good pair of lungs on him," our doctor acknowledges as she cuts the cord, then hands him off to another nurse in the room. "Let's get him near his sister to see if he might calm down."

Damn. He's pissed.

My ears rattle as he screeches out his anger. Holy hell. How can someone so small make such a loud noise? I'm sure his voice is heard throughout the entire maternity ward.

But sure enough, the second he's near his sister, she calms him.

I can't help but wonder if Van and I were like that for my parents.

My heart constricts, wishing they were here to ask them. I know they're looking down on us and smiling with joy. Even though they didn't like the circumstances that brought Julia, they were the best grandparents possible.

Seeing my parents with Julia was amazing. They only got to experience her for a short time, but from the very beginning, she had us all wrapped around her tiny fingers.

"You okay, Vin?"

My voice is thick when I answer, "Yeah. Just wishing my parents could be here to see this."

"I wish that for you, too. They're still so much a part of you, so our kids will know them," she reminds me.

The doctor takes Sydney's attention for a few minutes to ensure everything is the way it should be after delivering the twins. While the nurses clean and examine our beautiful children, I'm left to stare in awe as she's examined, realizing life as we know it will never be the same.

Once the twins are cleaned, diapered, and swaddled, the nurses bring them over for us to hold.

"Do they have names?" one of the nurses asks, handing my son over for me to cradle in my arms.

Sydney grins proudly as she reaches for our baby girl. "This sweet girl is Emery Ann, and Vince is holding Everett Daniel."

"Oh, how precious! I love that both names start with the same letter," the nurse closest to me gushes.

Grinning, I admit, "Just keeping with tradition. My twin's name is Vanessa. Her kids are named Julia, Jordan, and Jasper. Can't be outdone by them."

"I was an only child until I met Vince," Sydney admits. "But I'm lucky enough to have joined a family that started as small, but we're growing exponentially."

No kidding. Van's family is officially up by one compared to ours, but her extended family has adopted Syd and me into the fold as well. We spend our holidays together, and I'm fairly certain if I were to walk into the waiting room at this moment, there would be a few of them waiting to greet our newest family members.

It warms my heart to see how far Van and I've come since that fateful night after graduation. Determined not to be statistics, we most definitely pulled ourselves up by our bootstraps and made the dreams our parents had put into motion for us come true.

One thing is certain, I wouldn't be where I am without this beautiful, headstrong, challenging woman beside me. From the moment we met, her feistiness wormed its way into my heart, and I'm proud to say I've never let her go.

Looking into my son's eyes, I can't help but notice they almost mirror Sydney's. The rest of his coloring matches mine, but he's definitely his Momma's boy.

"You ready to switch so I can meet my little man?" Sydney asks, kissing the top of Emery's head. "I wanna see for myself which one of these two will be the soccer player of the family."

Wanting quality time with my daughter, I expertly relinquish Everett to Sydney's waiting arms as I maneuver Emery to the crook of my opposite arm. Most dads would be afraid of handling new babies, but after my nieces and nephew, I consider myself an expert. Don't get me wrong, I'm still extremely careful, but Julia broke me of the fear of breaking them.

Leaning in to kiss Sydney once more, I offer, "You ready for me to bring in the cavalry? I'm sure the waiting room is full of family wanting to meet the latest additions."

"With you by my side, Vin, I'm ready for anything."

Stopping at the door, I turn as a thought hits me as I look at our twins. "Ha! I have a feeling we're in for the ride of our lives with these two."

"You and I against the world, Vin. You and I against the

world," Syd says as she rolls her eyes. "Especially when they're teenagers."

"Oh, God... let's not borrow trouble," I grumble.

Walking into the waiting room, I don't think I could love this woman more if I tried. Family is everything, and I can't wait to introduce Emery and Everett to the world.

THE END

Thank you for reading Vince. I would love to know what you think of this story. Please consider leaving a review at your favorite retailer. You can stay up to date with all things Amanda Shelley, by joining my Newsletter: https://geni.us/AmandaShelleyNL

If you want more from this series, be sure to check out Damien: Book Three of the Perfectly Independent Series where Vanessa's story will continue.

Beautiful girls are not hard to find at Columbia River University.

The coeds on campus are great to look at but I was over that scene after graduation three years ago.

These days, outside of being part of the largest civil engineering job on campus, all I'm searching for is a decent meal and some peace and quiet. It's why I'm happy to have found what I consider a hidden gem in the diner I frequent.

All I need to do is finish this job and move on to the next by year's end.

Should be easy enough. Only when Vanessa walks up with a sexy smile and a mouth full of sass, she does more than take my order. She completely takes my breath away.

Next thing I know, I'm here every morning, making every excuse to dine with this intriguing woman. Not only is she smart and sexy, but she's laser focused on reaching the goals she's set for herself.

The more I get to know her, the more I'm convinced she's the one. I just have to find a way to get her to deviate from her perfectly laid plans and take a chance on me.

Or if you haven't read how Abby and Drew got together, be sure to check out Drew: Book One of the Perfectly Independent Series.

Of all people, why him?
He didn't EVEN bother to introduce himself, just assumed I knew him from his fame on the court.
Between his arrogance and the constant interruption from basketball groupies, there's no way I'll survive this semester.
Sure, he's hotter than anyone I've ever laid eyes on in a science lab, but I can't afford to pull someone along to maintain the grade I deserve.
Just when I think my self-control is in check, he does

something to remind me that he isn't the egotistical, self-centered jerk I thought he was.

With one stupid smile he makes my mind melt, my heart race, and my palms sweat.

Will my perfectly laid out plans disappear, if I take a chance on Drew?

https://amandashelley.com/books-by-amanda-shelley-2/

ABOUT THE AUTHOR

Amanda Shelley loves falling into a book to experience new worlds. As an avid reader and writer, sharing worlds of her own creation is a passion that has inspired her to become an author. She writes contemporary romance with characters who are strong and sexy with a touch of sass.

When not writing, Amanda enjoys time with her family, playing chauffeur, chef, and being an enthusiastic fan for her children. Keeping up with them keeps her alert and grounded. She enjoys long car rides, chai lattes, and popping her SUV into four-wheel drive for adventures anywhere.

Amanda loves hearing from readers. Be sure sign up for her newsletter and follow her on social media. Join her reader's group *Amanda's Army of Readers* to stay up to date on her latest information.

Readers group: https://www.facebook.com/groups/Amandas ArmyofReaders/

Goodreads: https://www.goodreads.com/author/show/19713563. Amanda_Shelley

Newsletter: https://geni.us/AmandaShelleyNL

www.amandashelley.com

ALSO BY AMANDA SHELLEY

If you enjoyed this book, you will be happy to discover Amanda Shelley primarily writes in one world. For a complete list of the series reading order as well as a chronological time line, please visit:

https://amandashelley.com/reading-order/

Zander: A Perfectly Independent Series Novella

(Available for free on All Retailers)

Zander's known for being a player both on and off the court. When his name shows up as my next client, my heart stalls, and not in a good way. There's no way I'll survive the semester with him. I just don't have the patience.

However, when I need help, Zander makes a proposal I can't refuse. He'll be my fake date to my best friend's wedding so I don't have to face my ex and his new girlfriend alone.

The weekend goes off without a hitch as we effortlessly pretend to have the time of our lives.

All is perfect... until I realize my feelings for Zander are no longer an act.

What will I do when our arrangement comes to an end?

https://geni.us/AmandaShelleyBooks

Drew: Book One of the Perfectly Independent Series

Of all people, why him?

He didn't EVEN bother to introduce himself, just assumed I knew him from his fame on the court.

Between his arrogance and the constant interruption from basketball groupies, there's no way I'll survive this semester. Sure, he's hotter than anyone I've ever laid eyes on in a science lab, but I can't afford to pull someone along to maintain the grade I deserve.

Just when I think my self-control is in check, he does something to remind me that he isn't the egotistical, self-centered jerk I thought he was.

With one stupid smile he makes my mind melt, my heart race, and my palms sweat.

Will my perfectly laid out plans disappear, if I take a chance on Drew?

https://geni.us/AmandaShelleyBooks

Damien: Book Three of the Perfectly Independent Series

Beautiful girls are not hard to find at Columbia River University.

The coeds on campus are great to look at but I was over that scene after graduation three years ago.

These days, outside of being part of the largest civil engineering job on campus, all I'm searching for is a decent meal and some peace and quiet. It's why I'm happy to have found what I consider a hidden gem in the diner I frequent.

All I need to do is finish this job and move on to the next by year's end.

Should be easy enough. Only when Vanessa walks up with a sexy smile and a mouth full of sass, she does more than take my order. She completely takes my breath away.

Next thing I know, I'm here every morning, making every excuse to dine with this intriguing woman. Not only is she smart and sexy, but she's laser focused on reaching the goals she's set for herself.

The more I get to know her, the more I'm convinced she's the one. I just have to find a way to get her to deviate from her perfectly laid plans and take a chance on me.

https://geni.us/AmandaShelleyBooks

Making The Call

Dani

As a bestselling romance author, most assume my life's glamorous, filled with combustible chemistry, and most of all, romance. Ha! I can only wish. With a deadline looming, I've escaped to my family's cabin on Anderson Island to free myself from distractions. My plan's great, until a man, who could pass as a cover model on one of my books, comes to my rescue. Is there chemistry? Sure. Is he everything I'd look for in a guy? Absolutely. But will my career be at risk if I give into my desire?

Luke

For a player, women line up outside the locker room. For coaches, we're lucky to get in the game. As the youngest NFL coach in the league, I live, eat, breathe, and even sleep football. To gear up for this season, I return to my home on Anderson Island for a much-needed break. When Dani literally crashes into my life, my mind's suddenly on the sexy brunette with a sailors mouth, rather than my team's next play. She has me dusting off another playbook entirely, making me wonder, did I make the right call?

https://geni.us/AmandaShelleyBooks

The Boy Upstairs

I ran into Derek while trying to escape the neighbor from hell.

Instantly, we hit it off. Since he's only here for three months and the microbrewery leaves me little time for commitments, it's the perfect setup for a fling.

He's adventurous, challenges me, and he just gets me from the inside out.

With our expiration date quickly approaching, I'm left to wonder… Will my heart ever be the same without the boy upstairs?

https://geni.us/AmandaShelleyBooks

He Saved My Boy

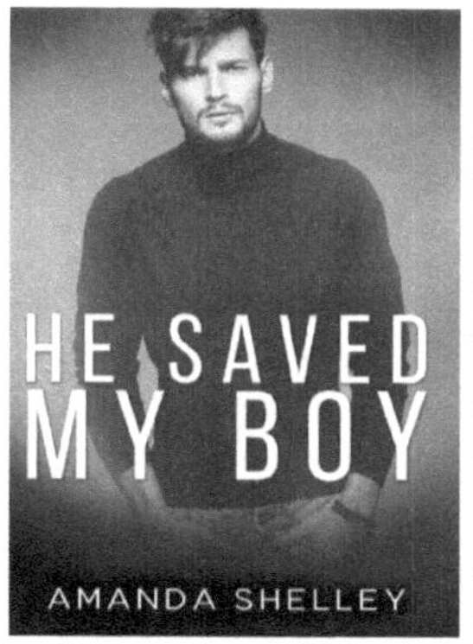

Davis is the first guy to catch my attention since... hell, I don't even know.

Instantly, he makes me think and feel things I've forgotten existed. It has been forever since I put my needs first, so I take the chance and let him light me up from the inside out.

Our night is the kind that will ruin me for all others.

But then I get the dreaded call.

I rush out without a second glance, knowing I'll likely never see him again.

My son will always come first—Always.

Imagine my surprise when Davis walks in, and I find he's the only one who can save my boy.

This cannot be happening—*I guess it's time to pull up my big girl panties and see what happens.*

https://geni.us/AmandaShelleyBooks

The Vegas Pitch

This pitch could make or break my career.

Not only will it set a personal record for the biggest account I've ever landed, but it could set my newfound company three years ahead of schedule for expansion.

Thank god I've got Nate Bellinger on my team.

Even though I had my reservations hiring the sexiest man I've ever laid eyes on – he more than meets my expectations with his hard work and determination. Together, we've formed a solid team and play off each other perfectly.

As we wait for the final verdict, I begrudgingly take Nate up on his offer for a night on the town. After all, this is Vegas and I need to let the chips fall where they may.

Imagine my surprise when I wake up the next morning to find we've not only won the campaign, but I'm apparently married to the man I've only ever let myself fantasize about.

The kicker of it all – he has no intentions of letting me go.

But what will it mean once we leave Vegas?

The Summer Dare

Leave it to Nana to think of everything.

After a grueling semester, I'm ready for a peaceful summer in Seaside with my sisters.

Imagine my surprise, when I'm woken by the screeching sound of a saw coming through my wall, the first official morning of break.

Not only did I come flying out of bed swinging, but I gave Ryan, the unsuspecting carpenter the surprise of his life, when I came wielding my killer coat hanger and all.

Too bad, I was only in a tank and undies and it wasn't nearly as effective as I'd hoped.

Of course, he insists he's only doing his job. Since it's Nana's last request to care for us, I can't refuse.

However, I won't let a tall, pesky, sexy as sin, know-it-all get in my way of my summer plans. I pretend I ignore him – that is until my youngest sister pokes her nose in my business and throws down a dare I can't back down from.

Kiss the next single guy who walks up to the bonfire – or explain to my sisters why I get riled up over the contractor.

When Ryan suddenly appears, I know I'm screwed in more ways than one.

Not only will my sisters learn my secret, but from the determined look on Ryan's face, I'm afraid he's eager to reveal it to the world as well.

What have I gotten myself into?

As I walk toward him, one thing is certain – this summer dare will either make or break me.

https://geni.us/AmandaShelleyBooks

The Summer Ultimatum

Watching my sister fall in love last summer gave me something I hadn't expected—hope. It gave me hope that there might be someone out there for me and hope that I might get past my misguided fears and finally let someone in.

With my help, Ryan's planning the most epic proposal. I just have to get the know-it-all musician I work with to fall in line to make it work.

Jax is wicked smart, extremely talented, and sexy as sin. But he can't see the forest for the trees when it comes to his potential. He'd rather keep playing in dive bars along the coast than take a real shot at success.

When the Seaside festival has a music competition, I present Jax with an ultimatum that will either make or break both our careers.

I've laid it all on the line, but can he?

https://geni.us/AmandaShelleyBooks

The Summer Proposal

My sisters are dropping like flies.

They're falling in love and having the time of their lives.

Don't get me wrong, I'm ecstatic for them. I love seeing them happy.

But I'm not ready for that type of commitment.

I can't even keep a plant alive, let alone find someone worthy of getting past a third date.

As the only sister done with school and single as a pringle, I have to do something fast, or I'll be my matchmaking aunt's next victim.

When Jax's drummer joins him for the summer and needs some help with his image, I make him a deal he can't refuse.

All is perfect—until I realize my summer proposal has one minor flaw.

Our relationship may be a sham, but there's nothing fake about my feelings for Finn.

https://geni.us/AmandaShelleyBooks

The Summer Arrangement

One, two, three—it's all down to me.

As the youngest and only single Lancaster, I'm eager to spend my summer in Seaside, Oregon, with my sisters. It's something I've looked forward to all year, and I'm determined to make every minute count. After all, I've only got one year before I graduate from college and have to adult for real.

However, if I want to graduate debt free, I need to work. I have a lead on the perfect summer job with the nanny agency I've spent the last three summers catering to.

I just have to win over an adorable three-year-old and convince her single dad I'm the right one for the job.

Simple enough, right?

Except when I show up at his door, I'm shocked to find he's the guy I hooked up with a few times last semester.

This cannot be happening.

I need this job. There's too much on the line to walk away. Maybe we can put the past behind us and make some sort of summer arrangement?

https://geni.us/AmandaShelleyBooks

The Summer I Found Home

Being a pilot is all I've ever known.

I served my country and I'm damn proud of my career.

But sacrifices were made, especially when it came to family.

I've missed first steps, first days of school, and first dates to name
a few.

My kids grew up. They're having families of their own.

Was it worth it?

When an opportunity brings me to Seaside, I jump feet first no
questions asked.

It means experiencing all those firsts with my grandkids.

With family as my focus and my guard down, I don't even see Faye
coming.

She's a force to be reckoned with and has me holding on for dear life.

I thought our ship had sailed, but now that I'm home for good—I just
might get more than one second chance.

arrangement?

https://geni.us/AmandaShelleyBooks

Resilience: Book One of Resilience Duet

Resolution: Book Two of Resilience Duet

Samantha never saw Enzo coming.

As the dust settles from her divorce, her life is full. She doesn't have
time for distractions. She's too busy running her own company and

checking off numerous items from her kids' demanding schedule to have a life of her own.

Then he walks into her kitchen with his breathtaking green eyes and a mischievous grin. He's there to surprise his father - her contractor, but his presence makes everything off kilter.

Enzo's perfectly content with his adventurous life as an elite rescue pilot, until a harmless prank turns on him. Instead of surprising his father, he finds his world thrown off course by the beautiful woman with a sexy smile, wicked sass and the mouthwatering ability to keep him on his toes.

With his limited time on leave, is she worth the risk to his heart?

https://geni.us/AmandaShelleyBooks

Collide: A Sweet Romance

Falling head over heels was the last thing I expected.

Literally.

Coffee is everywhere – and more than my ego is bruised.

When the handsome stranger I plowed into calls me by name, mortification sinks in.

He rushes off to class. I run home to change, hoping to forget the whole incident.

If only I could be so lucky.

I quickly find it's a small world and Gavin Wallace is completely unavoidable. Everywhere I turn he's there. In my classes. Hanging with my friends.

I've got his full attention and I have to admit, I like it a lot more than I should.

https://geni.us/AmandaShelleyBooks

www.ingramcontent.com/pod-product-compliance
Lightning Source LLC
Chambersburg PA
CBHW061041190726
48286CB00006B/1554